NOX
FIE
THE VEIL
STONE SONS
MERCHANTS
YN

THE ADVENTURERS GUILD

NIGHT OF DANGERS

THE ADVENTURERS GUILD

NIGHT OF DANGERS

ZACK LORAN CLARK
AND
NICK ELIOPULOS

DISNEY • HYPERION
Los Angeles New York

First Edition, December 2019
1 3 5 7 9 10 8 6 4 2
FAC-020093-19305
Printed in the United States of America

This book is set in FCaslonTwelve/Monotype
Designed by Mary Claire Cruz and Phil Buchanan
Map art by Virginia Allyn

Library of Congress Cataloging-in-Publication Number: 2019947088
ISBN 978-1-4847-8861-5

Reinforced binding
Visit www.DisneyBooks.com

Logo Applies to Text Stock Only

For David—guildmaster, advocate, and friend

—ZLC & NE

Chapter One
Zed

Makiva stood in the crowded market, gazing across a crush of people. She watched with eyes that were not her own. Thin, tawny fingers—Zed's fingers—brushed the scepter that was sheathed at her side.

People.

She had known so many of them in her long lifetime. All sorts. She'd walked the royal courts of both human and elven capitals. She'd seen the dwarves of Dragnacht forge their rune-enchanted blades—a secret no outsider had ever beheld. She'd hunted wolves with the northern orcs and enjoyed a meal of fragrant cheeses in a halfling hillhouse. She'd even witnessed the Day of Dangers firsthand, and the many atrocities that *people* were capable of, after the illusion of civilization had been dispelled from their world.

Makiva had met some of the best and worst people that Terryn had to offer. She'd even taught a few.

She'd despised them all.

How long had she spent among these soft, comfortable cowards, crammed within their walls like maggots inside a—

"Mmmmm, delicious."

Ahead of her, Brock took in an obnoxiously loud sniff of the air, interrupting her thoughts. "I love the scent of the market in the morning," he said. "The freshly baked bread, the crisp sawdust . . . and it's early, so there's only a *hint* of garbage smell." Brock turned to grin at his friend, and Makiva forced Zed's lips into something resembling a smile. There were teeth, at least.

"Indeed," she muttered blandly.

Once Brock had turned back around, the smile coiled into a sneer. Of all the *people* still clinging to this mudball of a world, Makiva especially despised Brock Dunderfel. She could barely get a minute away from the mouthy twerp anymore. No matter how cold she was to him, he seemed determined to repair the boys' fractured friendship.

That, or he'd grown suspicious of Zed, and was keeping an eye on him. Makiva wasn't sure which was more irksome.

"I still think you'd have had better luck at the smithy's," said Liza. "Frond prefers *practical* gifts to . . . whatever it is you're hoping to find here." She frowned at the tailors' stands and the reams of colorful cloth that festooned the market's garment rows.

"Well, you only have yourself to blame for *practically* buying the Smiths Guild out of stock," Brock said. "How many throwing stars can one woman own before the king starts to worry?"

The three apprentices wandered the market with Lotte, so Brock could retrieve a last-minute birthday present for Alabasel Frond. The guildmistress turned a mere fifty years old that day, but the adventurers acted as if she'd climbed into a dragon's maw and lived to gossip about the cavities.

Frond had said no celebration. She'd demanded it, in fact. But apparently it held some significance to the guild that their leader's age was once again divisible by ten. Enough so that Lotte had disobeyed a direct order and planned a surprise party.

Now Lotte glanced down at Makiva. An expression of concern pursed her brow. "Zed, are you sure you don't want a little silver for a gift? Honestly, I wouldn't mind."

Makiva shrugged, glancing away from the quartermaster and back toward the shoppers and merchants who buzzed about the square. "I've already finished my preparations," she said in Zed's high tenor.

It was almost true. Makiva had so many wonderful plans for Freestone: a garden of horrors that was just on the verge of flowering. Some had been years in the making, but Makiva was very patient.

As she watched the adventurers joke and chat, she brushed Zed's fingers against the mythril chain that was wreathed around his neck. For the first time that morning, a true smile graced Zed's lips.

These people had no idea what was coming for them.

*

Zed watched his own back as it moved through the market, ambling unhurriedly behind his friends.

Watching was all he—the real Zed—could do anymore.

On a cool, dark morning shortly after his possession, he'd found himself abruptly ejected from his own body, as if Makiva had shouldered him out. He still remembered the shock of suddenly seeing *himself* rise from bed—the cold horror of his lips smiling and his arms stretching lazily upward, all without him. "Finally, a little elbow room," Makiva had sighed with pleasure. It was the last time she'd acknowledged him.

He followed now as a strange sort of spirit—a smoky, invisible bystander, billowing just a few feet away. Though he moved through the crowd, eyes passed over him without notice. No one could see him.

Though not for lack of trying. Zed had spent the last several weeks trying desperately to break through to his friends. He'd screamed in their ears from morning bell till night, and made horrible, vulgar faces just inches from their noses. He'd tried pleading and cajoling and calling them names. Nothing had worked.

So far.

"Oh, what about these leather bracers?" Liza said, skipping to a nearby tanner's stand. "Frond's last pair were melted by a spitting multipede."

"Not bad, but I've got something a bit . . . frillier in mind." Brock's eyes twinkled mischievously.

"Oh, no," Liza breathed. "Brock, what did you do?"

"I wasn't here," said Lotte, rubbing her temples. "I had no part in this. Frond will be mad enough about the party."

"Brock once bought his dad a silver-plated shoehorn," Zed announced. *"He wrote a note saying he should have 'something nice to wedge his head from his own butt.'"* Zed laughed at the memory. Occasionally it helped just to talk to his friends, to pretend like things were normal.

Though sometimes it made him feel worse. Zed's laughter ebbed. *"I wish you all could hear me,"* he said with a sigh.

He knew the others had no sense that he was there. Maybe he was only torturing himself. But loneliness had been taking its toll.

"Brock, tell me this isn't going to be another silver-plated shoehorn."

Zed's attention snapped to his body, where Makiva was smirking. She flicked *his eyes* to him—the briefest glance—then back toward Brock.

Brock laughed, slapping a hand on the imposter's shoulder. "No prank is worth the punishment I got for that one. Though it was close."

Zed glared as Makiva giggled in his voice, but she didn't spare him another glance.

"*Be careful what you wish for around her. She'll use it against you every time.*"

A second smoky figure stretched lazily into being. Soon a gaunt man with a tired face and pointed ears sat atop one of the booths. Like Zed, this spirit also wore a chain around his neck, but his edges were more frayed. Smoke curled slowly away from the boundaries of his form.

This was Foster Pendleton, also known as the Traitor of Freestone. He was the most famous elf-blooded man in history, and the warlock who had ended the world.

"*Not now, Foster,*" Zed muttered. "*I'm trying to contact my friends. I'm pretty sure I saw Brock's ear twitch in my direction this time.*"

Foster was a victim of Makiva's, too, though he hadn't yet offered up any details about how he'd fallen into the witch's power. Or about his role in the Day of Dangers.

Then again, Zed hadn't asked. It wasn't that he didn't have questions for the warlock—Zed had many of them, history books full—but a part of him was scared of what the answers would be.

The other spirit merely rolled his eyes. "*As much as I admire your demented determination,*" he said, "*they're never going to respond. Only Makiva can see or hear us. Give it a rest. You're exhausting to watch.*"

"*Well,* you're *welcome to leave,*" Zed responded with a glare. "*I'll call you if I need a depressing grump.*"

"If only I could," Foster said. *"But, like you, I'm still tethered to the chain."*

The warlock exploded into a curl of smoke, then twisted through the air, re-forming beside Brock. He peered down at the boy. *"Hey Brock,"* he said. *"Liza's way out of your league and your punch lines are adequate at best."* Then he turned to Zed, shrugging. *"See? If that didn't give him goose bumps, I don't know what will."*

Foster dissolved again, re-forming several feet away atop the stall of an oblivious haberdasher. He pretended to dust off his eternally undusty sleeves. *"Though it* was *kind of fun. Perhaps you're onto something, after all."*

"Please," Zed hissed. Foster glanced up from his cuff, his smile faltering at Zed's expression. *"She's taken everything from me. . . . I have to keep trying."*

The warlock sighed and shook his head. *"Not everything, Zed. Not by a long shot. When this is over, she'll have taken things from you that you didn't even realize you had to lose."* The spirit extended his arms, and that was when Zed realized where they'd arrived.

Surrounding them was the fountain square. The stage where Zed had undertaken his Guildculling loomed nearby, though today it was bare of flags and frippery. The square's fountain stood at the center of the space, the four Champions of Freestone still watching over the city, immortalized as statues.

Foster's gaze moved between the figures, his lips pressed tightly together. Then he settled on the fifth plinth, the empty one that represented Foster himself. His image was forever unwelcome in Freestone.

"*Better not to hope,*" Foster said softly, "*than to have those hopes turned against you.*"

For a moment, the warlock's edges became indistinct as he stared at the plinth. His features swam, the smoke churning. Then, with an irritated grunt, he snapped back into focus.

"Oh, Brock, no . . ." Liza's voice cut through the noise of the crowd. She began to laugh, a high belly laugh that filled Zed simultaneously with delight and despair.

Brock stood before a tailor's stall, holding a lacy white apron on which the words *World's Best Guildmistress* had been sewn in a loopy script. Both *i*'s in *Guildmistress* were dotted with hearts.

Liza nearly fell over, she was laughing so hard. Even Lotte was working to contain a smile. Only Makiva, watching from within Zed's body, seemed immune to the joke. She glanced distractedly around the square. Zed watched his own eyes as they searched through the crowd.

They alighted on something, Makiva's gaze focusing.

"It cost a small fortune to have it made in time," said Brock, "but I think you'll agree that Frond is worth it."

"I don't know whether I want to be there when she sees it," said Lotte, "or if I want to be very far away."

Zed followed Makiva's glance to a tall, thin man who was standing in the center of the square. He was dressed in the distinctive robes of a magus—a ranking member of the Mages

Guild—though his robes were crimson colored, instead of the usual blue. The mage's hood was pulled up so that it concealed most of his head, but his face was clearly visible. He looked dazed, his eyes far away.

"Help," the man said softly. Mildly. "Please help."

No one in the crowd appeared to hear him. Shoppers passed distractedly.

"Help," the man said again. "Please, I . . . seem to have made a terrible mistake. I just wanted—" He tilted, nearly falling into a woman who was carrying a bushel of wheat. She shrieked as she scrambled out of his way.

The cry caught the attention of the others. Zed watched Brock as he glanced toward the man, and saw his friend's eyes brighten with recognition.

"Master . . . Curse?" Brock muttered under his breath.

The mage was stumbling now, tilting back and forth as he moved. His eyes grew vaguer, his pupils rolling slackly. A ropy line of drool fell from his mouth, dribbling onto his robes.

"Oh dear," the man said. "Oh, no. Help. I just wanted . . . I just wished to expand my mind."

A low hum began buzzing in the air, so soft that Zed could barely hear it. All around him, shoppers and merchants placed their hands to their ears. Some rubbed at their temples, their faces screwed up in pain.

Zed glanced to Foster. "*What's happening?*"

The other spirit's face was grave. "*Something very bad.*"

Lotte touched a finger to her face, just under her nose. It came away bloody. "What in the—?"

The mage's hood slipped, falling to his shoulders. Which was when Zed saw the thing that was clinging to his skull.

It was unlike any creature he'd ever encountered, natural or Danger. Thick tentacles coiled around the magus's head, each pulsing with its own serpentine movements, as if they were separate beings. But the limbs connected at a gelatinous mantle, which clutched his skull like the palm of a large fleshy hand.

Two wide, glassy eyes stared out into the crowd from that mantle, bright with unfathomable intelligence.

The magus's mouth lolled open. "Hel—"

The market exploded with noise. The buzzing sound sharpened, filling the air like a scream. Shoppers grabbed their heads, their faces wild with pain. Those unlucky enough to be closest to the magus fell immediately to the cobbles. Their eyes rolled up so that only the whites showed. Blood dribbled from their noses.

Zed glanced back to his friends, who were similarly affected. Brock pulled at his hair, howling, while Lotte thrashed and fell back into a tent tarp.

Liza sank to her knees, screwing her eyes closed. She tried to reach for her sword, but her hand was trembling so badly she couldn't unsheathe it.

"I've seen this before!" Foster called over the hum. *"It's a type of Danger called a mindtooth! It consumes its victims' brains, using them for psychic energy!"*

Zed rushed to Brock's side. His friend's eyes were frantic. All around the square, more people were seizing and collapsing. The very air seemed to vibrate. It was all Zed could do to hear anything through the noise.

"Why isn't it affecting us like them?" Zed shouted to Foster.

"We aren't really here!" Foster called back. "We're *both trapped in the chain!"*

Zed glanced at his body as Makiva also took a knee. The imposter placed "Zed's" hands to his temples, but his mouth was smiling, and his eyes gleamed with stormy satisfaction. Small waxy stoppers had been plugged into his ears. Makiva had . . . protected herself?

"Makiva!" Zed yelled. *"She did this somehow!"*

"Wow, what a bright kid you are! No wonder the Mages Guild wanted you!"

A shadow fell across the cobbles as a single shape rose slowly off the ground. Zed turned to see that Liza had risen unsteadily to her feet. Clutched in her hand was the Solution, the mysterious green sword she'd won that winter from a sect of elven druids.

Liza took a shaky step toward the magus.

Foster arched an eyebrow, still standing by the fountain. *"Your friend has some spunk!"* he called. *"But she'll never make it! The shrill of a mindtooth is overwhelming. Everyone in this square will be dead by the next bell! Except Makiva, of course!"*

Dead by the next bell . . .

Zed surged forward as a cloud of smoke, then re-formed

beside Liza. "*Liza!*" he shouted right in her ear. "*Keep going! You can do it!*"

Liza gritted her teeth. She took another step forward.

Zed glanced to the magus, a good ten feet away. He was still standing, but his body hung limply—a coat dangling from a peg. The mindtooth's grip had expanded; its tentacles now covered most of the man's head. Those awful eyes continued to stare outward, wide and emotionless.

Liza took two more clumsy steps, then nearly pitched over. Zed followed just beside her. He tried to put his hand on her shoulder, to help steady her, but it dissolved on contact, puffing into a brume of vapor. It re-formed only after he'd pulled away.

Liza shrieked. Blood dripped from her nose and veins pulsed in her temples.

"*Liza, don't you dare give up!*" Zed shouted. "*You are the strongest person I know! Take another step! Take it* now*!*"

She did. Her foot lurched forward, and the rest of Liza followed slowly behind.

"*Another!*"

She took another.

"*And another!*"

"I can't!" Liza screamed.

From the hat stand, Foster leaned forward in surprise. "*Wait, did she . . . ?*"

"*You can, Liza, and by Fie you will!*" Zed boomed. "*Take. Another. Step. NOW!*"

With a warrior's bellow Liza surged onward, making three long strides toward the mindtooth and raising her sword.

Zed gasped as the waves of pressure emanating from the Danger appeared to break over the blade, just like ripples of parting water. One more grueling step, and Liza stood within a foot of the creature. She held her sword high, a lantern guiding her through the dark.

"I can't believe it . . ." Foster said with earnest wonder. *"Keep going, muscular little girl! Keep going!"*

The wide eyes of the mindtooth rolled toward Liza, spinning loosely in their sockets. Suddenly a tentacle snapped free from the magus's head, shooting toward her raised blade. It slithered around the sword and tried to pry it from Liza's hand.

The girl held firm, bracing her boots into the cobblestones.

Another tentacle shot out, then a third. They pulled together, nearly tugging Liza off her feet.

"Liza, you've got it!" Zed shouted from beside her. *"Now do what you do best!"*

"I . . . protect . . . my . . . city!" Liza howled and pulled at her blade. The mindtooth's eyes spun wildly as it scrabbled to cling to the mage's head, but too many of its tentacles were wrapped around the sword. She tore the Danger away from the magus with a ferocious scream.

The buzzing noise cut off suddenly, and every person in the square seemed to slump as one, the tension leaving their bodies.

Every person except Liza. The girl raised her sword over her head and brought the mindtooth down hard against the cobbles—once, twice, three times—each with a viscous, wet *plop*.

"*Shining Lux, she did it!*" Foster hooted, billowing just beside Zed. "*Your friend slew a mindtooth! Wow!*"

All around them, people were beginning to cry and scream. Zed saw that many were rising with dazed expressions, but some—too many—stayed collapsed against the stones.

The body of the magus lay limp in the center of the square, totally still.

Zed rushed to find Brock, but his friend was already standing, helping Lotte to her feet. The quartermaster's face was pale as ash.

Only Zed's own face was calm. Serene, even.

Zed watched as Makiva rose and discreetly removed her earplugs. His own brown eyes were sparkling with amusement. She glanced right at Zed—at the real Zed—and winked.

"*That doesn't seem good,*" Foster muttered.

"*No,*" Zed croaked. Dread gripped his throat. It felt just like a burning chain. "*No, I think things are about to get much worse.*"

Chapter Two

Brock

Brock's ears were still ringing when the healers arrived. They flooded urgently into the market, white robes billowing like flags of surrender.

They were too late, though. Brock had counted thirteen dead. No amount of healing would help them.

He'd done what he could in the moments after the attack, following Liza's lead and moving about the square to pull the survivors to their feet. Some of them had been bleeding and dazed, others crying, and Brock had been helpless to comfort them—either because they'd been left momentarily deaf by the attack or because his words were so entirely inadequate.

"Everything's okay," he'd tried. And, "You'll be fine." None of it rang true.

He sat now on the cold cobbled ground, wedged between Zed and Liza, where Lotte had told them to stay put while she scouted the area. He clenched the apron in his hands to keep from fidgeting. Frond's frilly gift, immaculate white a short time ago, was stained red with blood from his nose. Bitterly, he thought how much better it actually suited her now.

"We really *can't* have nice things," he whispered to himself.

He was only dimly aware of the healers as they went about their work, his eyes lingering as one young monk knelt beside Master Curse, confirming the man was dead before draping a shroud over his face.

Brock had met Curse only a few times, and he held a very low opinion of the wizard. Curse had been loathsome—pompous and rude, short-tempered, and utterly without compassion. But all Brock could think of now was the fear in the man's eyes when he'd stumbled into the square, the quaver of his voice as he'd begged for help. Curse had died afraid. *Terrified.*

Nobody deserved that.

"Did you know him?" asked the monk, and Brock startled on realizing the healer was addressing him.

"Uh, no," Brock said, embarrassed to have been caught staring. But the lie came easily enough. *Curse* wasn't even the wizard's real name, but the alias he'd gone by as a member of the Lady Gray's court of Shadows. For a brief time, Brock had been an apprentice in that court. Now it seemed he'd gotten out just in time.

The monk moved on to the next body, and Zed looked at Brock sideways. "Sure you didn't recognize him?" he asked. "You were staring like you expected him to get up and run around."

Brock sighed wearily. "Now that you mention it, in my own personal experience, about nine out of ten dead bodies *do* get up and run around. Thanks for the timely reminder."

Zed barked out a short laugh, slapping Brock on the shoulder. It felt mildly inappropriate, given the circumstances, but Zed's sense of humor had gotten darker lately. At least he was laughing again.

Knights were filing into the square now, two or three at a time. Brock watched them, musing that they were even more useless than the healers. Swords drawn and shields raised, they arrived ready for a fight that was long over.

Liza had wanted to be a knight, Brock remembered. She'd petitioned them for a chance to prove herself. But the so-called Stone Sons hadn't been keen on adding any daughters to their ranks.

Lucky for Brock.

"Hey," he said, pushing his shoulder into hers. "You were amazing just then. You know that?"

"Not good enough," Liza said solemnly, her eyes on the crowd. Brock knew her well enough to understand that she wasn't counting the lives she'd saved, but the lives she hadn't.

"Anyway, I appreciate you helping me out," he said. "I figure you just need to save me once or twice more, and then we'll be even."

She rolled her eyes in an exaggerated show of irritation, but she also grinned at him. "I thought you were supposed to be good at math."

He grinned back.

"By Fie's running rivers of filth," growled a voice from behind them. "I should have known I'd find Frond's apprentices in the thick of this mess."

Liza leaped to her feet, and Brock and Zed rose more slowly, turning to meet the disapproving glare of Ser Brent, guildmaster of the Stone Sons. Brent had never been especially warm toward Brock or his friends, but since the adventurers had flouted the king's authority to help the elves of Llethanyl, he and his men had been markedly colder toward the entire guild. "Well?" he said. "What in Fie happened here, and how do you always manage to be at the epicenter of my very worst bad days?"

"*What in Fie happened* is that we were all almost killed," Lotte chided as she strode toward them. "A Danger was here—inside the walls—and if not for Liza Guerra, everyone in this square would be dead."

Ser Brent's expression softened at the sight of her. "I didn't realize you— Are you okay, Charlotte? Were you hurt?" He stepped forward, looking as if he might embrace her.

"I'm fine," she said, putting up a hand to discourage him from coming any closer. "Considering."

Brock turned toward Zed, his eyes wide with curiosity. *Charlotte?* he mouthed.

Zed smirked and shrugged.

Brent spoke low and soft. "Your mother is going to have a heart attack when she hears about this."

"Still reporting back to my mother, are you?"

Brent flinched a little bit, and Brock was astonished by the sight. The guildmaster of the knights exuded confidence—the sort of bullheaded, ironclad confidence that men of power wore like suits of armor. Brock had seen little evidence of a chink in Ser Brent's, but Lotte clearly knew better.

He remembered Lotte was from a wealthy family, perhaps even a noble one. She hadn't joined the adventurers until adulthood; she would have left behind lifelong friends when she enlisted. Evidently the stodgy commander of the knights numbered among those former friends.

"You don't fool me, Charlotte," said Brent, his voice low enough that Brock had to lean forward to listen in. "No one thought your little tantrum would last this long, but you've made your point. It's time to come home."

"I'm where I need to be," said Lotte. She didn't bother keeping her voice down. "I know that because I can think for myself. Not that you or your tin soldiers would understand what that's like."

Brock whistled low in appreciation. Ser Brent threw an irritated glare his way but said nothing more.

"Here's the thing that did this," Lotte said, all business, and Ser Brent seemed content to focus on the matter at hand. He joined her at the hacked-up remains of the monster that Liza had pulled from Curse's head.

Zed inched forward to remain within earshot, and Brock grinned to see his friend's newfound boldness. He'd been about to do the same thing, and he and Liza crept up behind him.

"It certainly does appear to be a Danger," Brent said. "Which raises all sorts of uncomfortable questions." He looked around furtively, then lowered his voice. "What if this has something to do with Mother Brenner?"

"Brenner?" Lotte echoed. "How could it?"

"It's too big a coincidence not to be connected," Brent answered. "Two hundred years without a breach, and then two within the span of months?"

Brock's stomach twisted. He'd been there when Mother Brenner, beloved mistress of the healers, revealed she'd been infected by a Danger.

She'd "revealed" it by sprouting tentacles and trying to murder Brock and his friends.

Lotte shook her head grimly. "What happened to Brenner was tragic, but it was an accident, and we stopped her before the infection could spread. The mages examined everyone in Freestone—they assured us that the threat had passed."

"Oh, no," Zed said. "The mages . . ."

The adults turned at the sound of his voice. Brent squinted. "What about the mages?"

Zed swallowed, then raised a timid finger to point at Curse's body. "The Danger was attached to that man's head and . . . well, he's dressed like a magus, isn't he?"

Brent crouched beside the body and pulled back the shroud, then muttered a string of curses.

"You recognize him?" Lotte asked.

Brent replaced the shroud and stood. "His name was Phylo. He was a magus, all right, and one of the archmagus's favorites. But he always made my skin crawl, if I'm honest. Who knows *what* he got up to in that tower of theirs?"

Brock's eyes drifted intown. Silverglow Tower was far in the distance, but it was visible from the market. It was visible from all over Freestone, in fact, stretching as it did higher even than the great wall ringing the city. For as common a sight as it was, however, precious few had ever been inside it. Mages were a rare breed, and secretive.

"Phylo," Lotte echoed. "And . . . was Phylo one of the wizards who screened people for infection?"

Brent sighed, a harsh huff of resignation and annoyance. "I need to report to the king. Right now. Don't you or any of your people touch that . . . that thing."

"Hexam will want to—" Lotte began.

"Not until I've cleared it with the king," Brent insisted.

The knight turned to go, but Lotte stopped him, putting a tentative hand on his arm. "Castor," she said. Brock had almost forgotten the knight *had* a first name, so rarely did anybody use it. "Castor, tread carefully here. Don't jump to any conclusions."

"I never do," Brent replied. "Not about a person's guilt." He gave her a grim little smile. "And not about their innocence, either."

✷

Brock hadn't set foot in the merchants' guildhall in weeks.

It was a strange thing to have been away for so long, now that he thought about it. He'd been coming to the hall regularly his entire life, initially because his parents did their work here; his mother was a bookkeeper, and his father, as a high-ranking manager, even kept an office upstairs. Just a year ago, Brock had been a constant presence within the hall, doing his studies and running errands and shadowing his father's assistants in a sort of pre-apprenticeship, all in preparation for a future that wasn't meant to be.

Then, of course, there was the stretch of time he'd been working as a spy for the organization that kept its own headquarters in the gloomy warrens beneath the merchants' grand building. That arrangement had ended rather badly, and Brock had feared the repercussions with the dread of a condemned man waiting for the blade above his head to fall. As time passed with no word from the Lady Gray, however, Brock had begun to think he was truly free of her. For several glorious weeks, all he'd had to fear were the obvious dangers—monsters lurking in the woods, Lotte's ruthless training, the gobs of gummy spit Frond left in her wake.

Brock had been happy, he realized now. Funny how that was easier to recognize in hindsight.

The hall was quiet and cold. Only servants were present, dusting and sweeping, replacing the fruit set in gilded bowls about the room, and tending to the thousand candles that lit the building's interior. The merchants themselves would all be seeing to business elsewhere this time of day. Several of them would have been at the market; some might number among the dead, though Brock hadn't recognized them if so. He shook that depressing thought away, focusing on what was ahead of him.

Brock strode to a particular candle in a particular alcove, pinching out the flame with his finger and thumb. Then, he waited.

He waited an unusually long time, and resorted to tapping his foot. Finally a servant took notice and crossed the room to relight the candle.

"The light offends my eyes," Brock told him.

"Indeed?" said the servant, a man with thin hair the same shade of gray as his uniform. He tipped a lit candle to the dark, smoldering wick. "Perhaps the young messere should return to his own guildhall? I'm certain it's kept quite dim, to suit its occupants."

Brock bristled at the insult.

"Oh, I get it," Brock said. "They changed the password, did they?"

The man appeared utterly uninterested. "I'm sure I don't know—"

"'My eyes offend the light'?" Brock tried. "'Where there's light there's Shadows'? Hmm. 'Freestone rules and Llethanyl duels'?"

The servant ignored him, moving on to his next task. As soon as he'd turned his back, Brock blew out every candle within his reach. *Take that.*

He didn't need to be escorted, anyway. He knew the way to the Lady's subterranean chamber. It was where he'd met Master Curse—or *Phylo.* The magus had been in the Lady's employ, putting his arcane insights to use in the forbidden study of Dangers. Brock had even provided the raw material for his research, smuggling otherworldly plants and animals from outside the wall. Pieces of them, anyway.

The others naturally assumed that an investigation into Phylo began and ended with his duties for the Silverglows. Brock knew better. If anyone had any real knowledge of what Phylo had been up to, it would be the Lady Gray.

Brock hurried through the kitchens, ignoring the protests and pointed looks of the servants and cooks he passed. With a satisfying flourish, he produced his lockpicking tools from within his sleeve without even breaking his stride, the picks appearing in his hands as if by magic.

Brock would take misdirection and sleight of hand over *real* magic any day.

He was good with the tools, and it took him only a brief moment of tinkering before he heard the *click* of the lock giving way. He pulled the door open, ready to bound down the stairs before anyone could stop him.

On the other side of the door, however, was a pantry.

"Young Messere Dunderfel, are you peckish?"

Brock whirled at the sound of the voice, slimy and smug. Standing in the center of the room, dressed immaculately and leaning upon a cane, was Lord Quilby, guildmaster of the merchants. "There's no need to raid my larder," he said, smiling like a cat. "My people would be happy to make you a sandwich."

"Funny, I just lost my appetite," Brock said coldly. He scanned the room for the Lady Gray, who had a talent for sneaking up on him. "Where's your sidekick?"

"Do you mean your father?" Quilby asked. "He *has* become quite indispensable to me of late, it's true—"

"You know who I mean. Where is the Lady Gray?" Brock demanded.

Quilby scowled. "You're no fun anymore, Brock, you know that?" He licked his lips. "Give us the room, please," he said loudly, and without a moment's hesitation the kitchen staff hurried out into the main hall. Quilby spoke again as soon as the last of them had crossed the threshold. "As I understand it, you and the Lady parted ways. With her, you're either in or you're out, Messere Dunderfel, and that's a decision you don't get to revisit."

"A member of her court is dead," Brock said. "The magus." He studied Quilby's face, and he saw surprise there—all the more genuine for how muted it was. Quilby wouldn't like to be caught unaware, but this was apparently news to him. He let the ensuing silence linger.

"How?" Quilby drawled at last.

"A Danger. Some kind of—of parasite, attached to him. He came to the market—to *your* market, and the thing tried to crawl inside all of our heads. It screamed in our brains—twelve other people died before Liza could stop it."

Quilby blinked furiously. "A tragedy, to be sure. The guild will do whatever it can for the families—"

"She had him messing with these things, Quilby. She had him researching Dangers *right under our feet*, and now—"

"I didn't have anything to do with that," Quilby said. He'd gone pale in the face. "I never—" He stopped to compose himself. At length, he continued, "Understand: she does not answer to me. I don't find her, not ever; *she* finds *me*. Whatever she's done, it has nothing to do with me."

Brock scoffed. "You're worried about getting into trouble? That's where your mind goes?" He shook his head. "Quilby, we can worry about blame later. Right now we need to find out what Curse was up to, whether there are any more of those things—where did it even *come* from? I never brought them anything remotely dangerous, certainly not a living Danger. This is exactly what I was worried about when she had me doing her dirty work, and—"

Brock came up short as a horrifying idea dawned on him. He didn't want to believe it, but it made too much sense to ignore.

"Quilby . . . does the Lady Gray have someone else inside the Adventurers Guild?" His voice was flat, his mouth suddenly dry. "Does she have someone who could have brought this thing through the wards for her?"

"I don't know," Quilby said. At Brock's look, he insisted, "I don't! But if she let *you* go . . . if she didn't fight to keep you . . ." He licked his lips again. "Yes. Yes, she almost certainly has someone else."

Brock cursed under his breath. *Someone else* under the Lady's thumb, an adventurer, forced to break the city's most sacrosanct laws at her whims. Someone he knew. And today that person had made a terrible, tragic, *fatal* mistake.

Unless, of course . . . unless they'd done it on purpose.

Chapter Three
Zed

"*She heard me!*" Zed gushed. He was so excited that his whole smoky body churned like a billowing chimney. "*Liza* actually *heard me!*"

In his agitation, Zed lost his substance for a moment, melting into a pillar of vapor. Then he re-formed facing the opposite direction.

Toward Foster.

"*You saw it, didn't you?*" Zed pressed. "*She definitely responded.*"

The warlock shrugged. They'd trailed Liza, Lotte, and the imposter Zed back to the guildhall, where Lotte immediately disappeared inside, barking at any guildmembers milling around to head to the market and assist the knights with crowd control.

Last Zed heard, she was storming away, shouting for Hexam.

News of an attack had already made its way to outtown. During the tense journey back, many townsfolk had rushed past them in the opposite direction, either to help or gawk. Others whispered among themselves, giving the adventurers a wide berth as they moved.

The fact that all three had been stained with blood might have contributed to the commotion.

"It's hard to say," Foster muttered noncommittally. *"She might have heard you, but it's not like she's been thanking you for the emotional support since then."*

In fact, Liza looked miserable. Her usually olive skin was ashen, and her dark eyes were red rimmed. She and the imposter Zed stumbled into the common room, disheveled and bloody, where they interrupted the other apprentices putting the finishing touches on the decorations for Frond's party.

Jayna and Jett rushed to Liza's side, sitting her down in the nearest chair. Micah, seeing the states they were in, hurried to the imposter to check for injuries, but Makiva waved him off with a scowl.

"What is *with* him these days?" Micah grumbled as the false Zed headed off to the barracks to clean up. Rather than follow Makiva, Zed lingered with his friends. As long as he didn't stray too far from the chain, he could move freely around the guildhall.

"What's with him is a hundred-year-old witch," Zed muttered. Micah frowned. He scrunched his nose and turned curiously

toward Zed. Zed perked up . . . until he realized Liza was removing her sweaty boots just behind him.

"Do they know what it was?" Jett asked, once Liza had recounted the attack through gritted teeth. "What kind of Danger, I mean?" The dwarf sat heavily on a bench, drumming his fingers absently along his mythril leg. Magic sigils flared with each touch, before slowly fading away.

Jayna kept the shield spell inside charged with mana, and Jett had gotten quite good at triggering it quickly. In the past few weeks, they'd been spending more time together, planning further applications for the young wizard's enchanting. The Adventurers Guild didn't own a forge, but Jett still had access to his parents' smithy; he and Jayna could disappear there for hours experimenting.

Zed decided to try breaking through again. He billowed to Liza's side, right by her ear, just like in the market. "*A mindtooth!*" he shouted. "*The monster was called a mindtooth!*"

Liza shook her head. "We're not sure," she said hoarsely. "Lotte went to ask Hexam, I think. Where's Frond?"

"Syd, Fife, and Nirav were keeping her busy," Fel answered from her perch on the ladder. She'd been hanging blue and silver streamers from the chandelier for the intended birthday party, but now half of them dangled limp and unfinished, like lank strands of hair.

"They're still outside the wall," she added. "Fife made up a story about seeing a strange Danger in the woods near the city.

He called it a 'sen-twar.' He said it had the upper body of a human, but four legs from a horse." The young night elf gave a baffled smile. "Have you ever heard such a ridiculous lie? So, the horse's head is *half a human*? It doesn't even make sense."

"I'd take Fife's sort of nonsense over that *thing* in the market any day," Liza muttered. Jayna placed her hand on the girl's back, reaching right through Zed's misty torso.

Zed sighed. "*You still can't hear me . . .*" he said. "*But why? Why did it work earlier?*"

Across the room, Foster was floating with his arms crossed. "*You do realize they can't hear your questions, either, correct?*"

"*I was talking to* myself," Zed grumbled.

"*A charming habit for a charming young man.*" Foster cleared his ghostly throat. "*Well . . . listen. I hesitate to tell you this, because I don't want to get you all riled up for no reason. But there is* something *you haven't tried yet. And it could be connected.*"

Zed's eyes goggled, glancing back at the warlock. Seeing he'd gotten Zed's attention, Foster chuckled. "*So much for managing your expectations.*" Then, slowly, his shape softened and melted away. The mist cascaded to the floor and re-formed into a small, smoky animal with burning green eyes. A fox.

"*Recognize me?*"

Zed billowed closer, looking down at the creature. "*It's the fox from my dreams,*" he said. "*I forgot all about that. That was . . . you? You were trying to warn me about Makiva.*"

The fox bared its teeth in a canine grin. "*Exactly,*" Foster said.

"It's easier to connect with a person when their mind is . . . soft. Such as when they're dreaming, or having their psyche shredded by an otherworldly parasite. And by easier, I mean possible at all."

Zed's thoughts whirred. Of course! The answer had been literally staring him in the face all these weeks. Somehow *Foster* had reached him while he was sleeping. What was to stop Zed from doing the same with his friends? He glanced back to the others, all murmuring together. *"I could visit their dreams, too? The way you did for me? Talk to them there?"*

"If it were that easy, believe me, I would have shouted my innocence into my friends' ears every night until they died of old age. Well, all right, I did. They branded me a traitor anyway."

Zed tilted his head. *"But you still tried to warn me. I thought you said it was pointless to hope."*

"You've proved me right, haven't you?" the fox muttered. Though Zed thought he detected a hint of bashfulness in Foster's echoed voice. *"Anyway, it was easier with you. We're connected by the chain. Sometimes it was all I could do to keep out of your frenzied little head."*

Foster surged across the room, landing on the stairway that led up to Frond's quarters. Micah stood nearby, uncharacteristically somber, watching the exit to the barracks with a frown.

Zed just gazed at the fox for a moment. *"I never thanked you,"* he said. *"For trying to warn me."*

The fox lifted its paw and gave it a dignified lick, pluming the mist. *"Oh, don't get mushy on me now, Zed. We'll be spending a lot of time together and I don't want it to be awkward."*

"Still . . . I appreciate it. And I'm sorry your friends never heard you."

"It wasn't their fault," Foster said. *"Nor was it yours. Dreams are bizarre and confusing. It's hard enough to remember them, much less comb them for portents and warnings. Even if you spend all night jabbering at your friends, Zed, only a few flickers might make it through."*

"I've still got to try," Zed declared. *"It's my best chance."* He grinned at Foster the fox. *"One more question, though,"* he said. *"Why a fox? Why didn't you appear to me in your own shape?"*

The warlock caught himself midlick. He paused his grooming, lowered his paw, and slowly retracted his tongue. *"This form is special to me,"* he said defensively. *"But beyond that, it's also smaller and easier to maintain. You've only been Makiva's prisoner for a short time, but these ethereal bodies—such as they are—don't last forever. Without a true body to return to, they eventually . . . well, fade away."*

Zed's smile fell as this news sank in. *"You mean . . . ?"*

"I mean eventually I'm going to disappear. As will you. If whatever Makiva has planned doesn't end us first, of course."

"How do you know this?" Zed asked.

"Because I'm not her first victim. Not by far. Centuries ago, when she trapped me like this, there were two other witches who showed me the ropes, just as I'm doing for you. They weren't nearly as charismatic as I am, lucky you, but they were fine enough people, and comforted me when . . ." The fox exhaled dismally. Then, with an eddy of smoke, Foster himself sat where the fox had been, back in his elf-blooded shape.

"Well, they were fine people," he continued. *"But slowly they began*

to grow quiet and sleepy. They seemed to have trouble holding their shapes together. Then one day they revealed the truth to me; they were leaking away, just as every victim of Makiva's eventually did. We'd hypothesized that these ghostly bodies are actually our mana, or what's left after she's burned through it. That's why she collects us. Give us a seed of power and we'll cultivate it for her, until there's enough that she can harvest."

Zed watched the warlock for a long beat, the grave voices of his friends filling the silence between him and Foster. "*What happened to them?*" he asked finally. "*The two witches.*"

Foster shook his head. "*Eventually, they just disappeared. First Ranella, then Tala. I waited for days, hoping they might find their ways back. Then weeks. Before I knew it, years had passed.*"

For maybe the first time since Makiva had trapped him, Zed considered how long Foster had been alone like this. Perhaps even worse, he'd *had* companions but lost them—had watched them fade to nothing. Zed pitied the warlock.

"*Foster,*" he started. "*I—*"

"Well, *Guildmistress Frond*, here we are!" Fife's voice rang out, cutting through the conversations both real and ghostly. "Back at the guildhall! All of us! With Frond hurryingaheadvery-quickly!" No sooner had he finished than the door to the common room burst open, Frond stomping inside.

She took one look at the space—the half-finished decorations, the battered apprentice and empty hall—and came to an abrupt stop.

"HAPPY BIRTHDAAA—" Fife appeared behind her, his

smile and voice both dropping as he caught sight of the room. Behind him followed Syd, Fife's best friend and a fellow journey-rank adventurer, along with Nirav.

Nirav was an older apprentice. Until several weeks ago, he'd also been a statue that decorated the common room. Formerly a squire of the Knights Guild, he was drafted into the adventurers years ago, then was petrified by a basilisk while outside the walls. He'd been cured only recently, thanks to a gift from the elves.

Nirav glanced to Jayna from behind Frond, his expression confused. Jayna grimaced and shook her head.

"Surprise!" called Micah from the stairway. "Everything's bad again."

✷

Zed watched as Alabasel Frond lifted a piece of blissberry cake to her mouth and took a luxurious, spongy bite.

She was sitting in her quarters, silently eating her birthday cake while Hexam and Lotte argued in front of her desk. Behind her, the guild's flag—now sprinkled with six stars instead of five—hung like a window to another world.

"Our first step," said Hexam, "should be to find *where* the Danger actually came from. Mindteeth live in dark, subterranean caverns, especially ones with access to water. Send patrols to investigate all the caves within three miles. There could be more of those things out there. Champions forbid that a colony of them gets the chance to amass into a brain-jaw."

"Ooh, brain-jaws," said Foster. *"Nasty things, those. Zahira once told us of a little hamlet in the east whose town wizard accidentally summoned one straight from Astra. All the villagers became mindless slaves, of course, but* then *they began luring unsuspecting travelers to—"*

"Quiet," puffed Zed. *"I can't hear."* The two were eavesdropping from the windowsill, having followed the guildmistress and master adventurers up to their closed-door meeting. Despite the frustrations of being invisible, Zed had thrilled at the chance to listen in on a private conference of the guild's leaders. He felt like a daring spy in a story of courtly intrigue.

Brock would love this, Zed thought with a pang. His friend had always liked the spy stories best.

Lotte was shaking her head, her arms crossed. "We need to make inquiries *within* the city," she said. "That thing was already inside the wards. Despite my reservations, I think Ser Brent was right: This could be Mother Brenner all over again. Let's find out how it got here, and how many more might be inside. I say we begin with the Silverglows."

"Oh, for Fie's sake, we aren't knights," Hexam grumbled. "We can't just waltz into the hall of a High Guild and expect them to cooperate. Our purview is outside."

"Our *purview* is monsters," Lotte countered patiently. "Frond was the *only person* who saw something was going on with Brenner, and it was our guild who stopped the Lich and saved Llethanyl. We should be proactive. Go to the king and explain that we're the best equipped to handle an investigation. Plus, the victim, Phylo, was a magus in the—"

"Phylo?" Hexam's timorous voice brought Lotte up short. It was the soft trembling of a clothesline, just before a storm rolled in.

Frond swallowed a half-chewed bite of cake. Then she licked her dirty thumb, still smeared with blissberry drizzle. "You knew him?"

Hexam nodded slowly. "Phylo . . . was the mage I told you about. The one responsible for my expulsion from the Mages Guild. He discovered my books on the theory of fiendish magic and reported me to Archmagus Grima."

Lotte frowned from Hexam to Frond and back again. "Hold on a moment. I've never heard this. Hexam, you were expelled for *witchcraft*?"

"No," Frond said firmly, "he was not. He was expelled for reading."

"I was already considered an . . . eccentric within the guild," Hexam explained. "I argued that all magic was inherently dangerous, and all of it merited study. Without an understanding of the magic of Fie—along with the other lost arts, like necromancy, druidry, or psionics—how could we hope to combat them? Archmagus Dinesh, Grima's predecessor, tolerated my ideas. But then he died, and Grima was appointed on a platform of stamping out dark magic." The wizard sighed. "I made a perfect example.

All she needed was a reason. And Phylo, my rival since apprenticehood, was happy to give her one."

"Their loss was our gain," Frond said, surprisingly gently.

Hexam flashed her a grateful look, but then his worried gaze returned to Lotte.

"'The Sea of Stars exists to take on the risks that others can't or won't,'" he muttered. "That's what Frond told the king . . . as he considered whether to formally charge me as a warlock. In the end, he permitted me to join the Adventurers Guild, but instructed me to keep my studies well out of sight from then on. He said Frond wouldn't be able to save me a second time." Hexam grimaced at the memory. "I'd appreciate it if you kept this between us."

Lotte nodded, her skeptical gaze softening. "Of course," she said. "None of this leaves this room."

Foster snorted, glancing Zed's way. But Zed's eyes were wide as he watched the three master adventurers.

Hexam had nearly been tried as a warlock? The news sucked all the fun out of their snooping, bringing Zed back to his own crisis. Even if he managed to warn his friends about Makiva, what would they do when they realized he was possessed by a hostile witch? What would happen to him? Zed was beginning to feel like he shouldn't be here anymore. Fie knew what Makiva was doing with his body right this very moment.

Without a word, he floated up from his spot by the window, heading toward the door.

"Where are you going?" called Foster. *"This is just getting good!"*

But Zed was only inches away when three loud raps sounded against the other side. Hexam and Lotte snapped around, startled. Frond narrowed her eyes, her mouth still spotted with crumbs.

"This is a private meeting," she barked. "What is it?"

The door creaked open, and Zed found himself face-to-face with . . . himself. Though they were inches apart, Makiva ignored him completely, peering instead toward Frond with Zed's own big brown eyes.

"Sorry!" the imposter chirped. "I wouldn't have interrupted, but the castle seneschal just arrived with a summons. King Freestone wants us to meet him for a council—Frond and the rest of us who were at the market." The false Zed gulped, the very picture of anxiety. "He says we're to head to Silverglow Tower."

Chapter Four
Brock

The Adventurers Guild was known for its parties—rowdy, spirited affairs where veterans and apprentices all came together to enjoy absurd amounts of food, off-key sing-alongs, and mild to moderate property damage. Based on what Brock saw on his return to the guildhall, Alabasel Frond's birthday celebration did not appear to be one for the history books.

"Did I miss it?" Brock asked, taking in the unfinished decorations and sparse attendance. Aside from his fellow apprentices, there were only a few small clumps of adventurers scattered about the room. Brock noticed that Zed was absent, but that wasn't so unusual. Zed didn't socialize much these days. "The party's over already?"

"It is for us," Liza said glumly. She'd washed her face, and her olive skin glowed in the room's candlelight, but her leathers were still stained with a smattering of dried blood. "We've been summoned by the king."

"But there's still time for a game!" Fel said brightly. "Could I interest you in a lively round of 'Pin the Tentacle on the Grisly Gullet'?"

"Grisly what?" Brock asked.

Wielding a floppy paper tendril, Fel gestured toward an illustration, nailed to the wall, of a fleshy, toothy sack. It looked like a pink meatball with fangs.

"I tried to tell her," Micah groused. "It's not a real *game* if everyone wins."

"But there's no wrong way to do it!" Fel insisted. Then she leaned toward Brock to whisper, "Grisly gullets have tentacles *everywhere*."

Brock was interested in spite of himself. Fel had spent much more time in the wilds than any of the rest of them. As a result, she was a font of information on all sorts of horrid creatures. She knew what they ate, where to find them—and, often, how to kill them.

"Let me guess," Brock said, grinning. "They're vulnerable to arrows." It amused him how often Fel claimed that her weapon of choice was the absolute best weapon to use in any number of situations. Not that he liked getting within arm's reach of a monster, but with his aim, daggers were a much safer choice than a bow. Safer for his teammates, at any rate.

"It's difficult to get an arrow past the tentacles," Fel said. She twisted a braid with her finger. "Difficult for *some* people . . ."

"You know what game I miss?" said Fife. "The one where we'd throw dirty undergarments at the statue."

"What statue?" asked Nirav, but Brock could see the answer dawned quickly. "Oh," said Nirav. He crossed his arms. "Good one, Fife."

"He's teasing you, Nirav," said Jayna. "We didn't . . . Frond would never allow—"

"It's all right, Jayna," Nirav said, shrugging. "It's funny."

Brock hadn't spoken much to Nirav since watching him burst from his stony prison weeks before. Technically, Nirav was a few years older than Brock and the others. He was closer in age to Syd and Fife—or he should have been.

But Nirav hadn't aged in all the time he'd been encased in stone. His friends had grown older; they'd forged stronger bonds in the face of danger and graduated from their apprenticeships to journey rank.

Nirav had been left behind. He'd blinked, and suddenly found himself surrounded by strangers. Brock couldn't begin to imagine what that would be like—or how hard it would be to adjust.

"Mousebane, no!" Fel cried. Brock turned in time to see the cat retreating beneath a table, a paper tentacle clutched in her teeth. She proceeded to rip the paper to shreds. "We need that for the game!"

Brock sighed. "I have seen some sorry parties in my day," he said. "But this one takes the cake."

"Speaking of which, Frond took the cake," Jett said. "I mean the *whole* cake. She just picked it up and walked upstairs with it."

Brock rubbed his eyes. "It's just as well. I guess I need to get ready to see the king." He cast a lingering look at the two-dimensional fanged nightmare affixed to the wall. "Let's just hope he doesn't want to play another round of 'Pin the Blame on the Adventurers Guild.'"

*

Silverglow Tower stood at the precise center of Freestone. Brock knew there was a good reason for that. Directly beneath the tower, in a secure room underground, the mages kept the crystal focus that produced the city's protective wards—invisible shields that kept Freestone safe from Dangers.

That was the idea, anyway. Lately, those wards had proven less dependable than advertised.

Brock craned his neck to see the whole structure, and out of the corner of his eye, he saw Zed was doing the same thing.

"Well, pal, you finally made it here," Brock said. "You just took the long way, that's all."

"You have no idea," Zed replied absently.

Brock tried not to take offense at that. He knew very well what the Silverglows meant to Zed. Like the adventurers themselves, Freestone's magic users were set apart; unlike the adventurers, though, the mages enjoyed the admiration of the entire city. It was an exclusive club, one where being *different* meant being *special.* To Zed, who'd always stood out, a career of quiet study among the respected ranks of the Mages Guild had represented his best opportunity for a happy life.

He'd almost achieved it, too. But Frond had dashed those dreams upon the rocks, and she'd spoiled Brock's dreams, too, for good measure. They'd come to terms with it, even come to feel like the Adventurers Guild was where they belonged. But Brock knew the mages would always hold a fascination for his friend.

Frond made a rude noise, mucus vibrating in her throat. "If anyone needs to spit," she said, "do it now." And she followed her own advice with evident enthusiasm.

Brock glared at her. "We're good, thanks."

Lotte led the way around the base of the tower, the three apprentices and their guildmistress following behind. Brock shielded his eyes momentarily from the sun, until their path curved away from it.

"Have you been here before, Lotte?" Liza asked. Her sword was sheathed at her side, and though he had once teased her about taking it everywhere, he felt no small relief to see she had it now.

"Never," Lotte answered. "Other than Hexam and Jayna, I don't know anyone who's been inside the tower."

Within a few moments, the sun was in their eyes again. "Hold on," Liza said. "Are we . . . Did we circle the whole thing?"

Lotte stopped in her tracks. "There's going to be some Fey-jinxed trick to this, isn't there?"

Frond took the opportunity to spit once more.

As if Frond's vulgar sounds were some magic password, a crack appeared then in the surface of the tower. Perfect right angles of blackness formed between the individual stones, the grout holding them together replaced by empty space. Dozens of those stones swung outward to reveal a doorway—a jagged, irregular doorway that looked as if it should cause the entire tower to crumble.

"Well, come on," said a boy standing beyond the impossible threshold. "I'm missing class for this."

"You're welcome!" Brock said brightly.

"My name is Sulba," the young mage said. He wore neat blue robes and round spectacles. "I'm a Second Year. Can I ask you to take off your boots?"

"No," Frond said, and she pushed past him into the tower. The apprentices followed behind, Liza giving the boy an apologetic shrug.

"It's fine," Sulba muttered. "I'll just mop afterward, yeah?"

The adventurers trailed Sulba down a curved hallway lined with glowing crystals. The crystals gave off a warm, neutral light that felt closer to sunlight than the mage orbs used by Hexam. Outside it had been chilly, but the temperature within the tower was pleasantly mild, and the air smelled of flowers.

Frond sneezed, making no effort to cover her mouth.

Sulba paused at an imposing metal door marked with magical sigils of intricate design, circles and stars and looping letters all overlapping in a display of purposeful chaos. Those fanciful symbols aside, the door's iron rivets and heavy padlock made it appear like something out of a dungeon. "The vault," he said, producing an ancient key the size of his hand. "I'm afraid I *do* have to insist on taking your weapons."

He unlocked the door and dragged it open. Brock caught sight of shelves lined with objects—a helm of broken glass and razors, a gnarled wooden rod in the shape of a clawed hand clutching an orb, a kite shield with a design that looked almost like an anguished human face—and though he had no sensitivity to magic, he could swear the room radiated an unnatural energy. It felt every bit as haunted as the Lich's throne room back in Llethanyl.

Zed craned his head enthusiastically for a better view.

Brock surrendered his daggers, but Sulba barely noticed, captivated as he was by Liza's sword. "Interesting color," he murmured.

Frond handed over her curved sword, three daggers of varying lengths, a whip she'd somehow concealed in a pocket, a bag of razor-sharp caltrops, and a glass vial marked with a skull and crossbones. "Careful with that," she warned.

"It's her dinner," Brock put in.

"Uh, what about . . . ?" Sulba prompted, pointing to the throwing stars affixed to her belt.

"Forget it," Frond growled. "They're holding up my pants."

"Say no more!" Sulba said, heaving the door closed.

"The king is here already," the apprentice mage told them when they were on their way once more. "You're the last to arrive. But I suppose you had the farthest to walk. . . ."

"All the way from outtown," Brock said. "So how many flights of stairs do we have to look forward to?"

"Stairs?" Sulba echoed. He smiled, enjoying a private joke. "We don't *do* stairs here."

He ushered them inside a circular room, slightly cramped except for its enormously high ceiling. In fact, Brock couldn't see all the way up to the top; it was like being at the bottom of a well. The room was devoid of decoration other than a design painted directly upon the floor. Another sigil. Brock lifted his foot for a better look, but the design was all swooping lines and angles, utterly meaningless to him.

"Keep your arms at your sides," Sulba said, and then he performed a series of complicated gestures with his fingers. The design at their feet glowed with an inner light, and slowly, gently, it lifted from the floor, suddenly solid yet lighter than air.

A platform made of shimmering light raised the whole group upward.

"Wow," Liza said. She looked down through the translucent platform at the receding ground below them, and she giggled a little.

Brock smiled at her, then turned to share the moment with Zed. But Zed appeared lost in thought.

"Can you believe this?" Brock prompted.

Zed startled back to his senses, then grinned madly. "Coolest thing ever," he replied. They passed doors set into the curved wall at regular intervals, one after the other, and Brock knew they were ascending past the tower's many levels. Still he couldn't see the top.

"Quite impressive, right?" Sulba said. "I'll never understand how anyone managed to live in a tower before Krycek's Radiant Elevational Dais."

"Oh, gross," Brock said. "Is that really what you call this thing?"

"Mind your manners," Lotte warned.

"It's all right," Sulba said. "You see, it *elevates* a person or group from one floor to another, so—"

"No, I get it," Brock interrupted. "I just feel like there's a better option. I mean, who comes up with these names?"

"Well." Sulba sniffed. "In this case, it was Magus Krycek."

The dais came to a stop at the very last door, which opened

onto an antechamber. "The observatory room is just ahead," Sulba told them. "I'll be waiting to take you back down."

Assuming the king doesn't send us down the quick way, Brock thought. *Right out a window.*

✷

Tall, gray, and imposing: King Freestone had much in common with the mages' tower itself. In his case, however, there was no mystery about what was going on behind the façade. The king's displeasure and suspicion were etched upon his very features as if carved in stone.

"Frond," he said. "Adventurers. Thank you for coming."

Frond bowed slightly, and Brock's eyes swept over the entire chamber—three times. He'd been sure the Lady Gray would be here, skulking in the shadows and smiling her wolf's smile.

But the room held no shadows, its wide windows framing sun and sky and a staggering view of the green world beyond the walls. The glass of those windows was overlaid with handwriting and simple illustrations made with golden ink, mostly dots and lines that Brock recognized as well-known constellations. Seated with their backs to the view, on the far side of a table of silvery wood, were the king and the leaders of the four High Guilds: Ser Brent, Lord Quilby, Father Pollux, and their host, guildmistress of the mages, Archmagus Grima. There was one empty chair at the table.

"Frond, why don't you sit," the king said. Frond—apparently unused to having a seat at such a gathering—hesitated a moment before complying. Those assembled were silent as she edged around the table and sat, squirming loudly upon the padded chair in an effort to get comfortable. Brock could see the throwing stars at her belt cutting right through the chair's fabric, and he fought to keep his face neutral, hoping Grima wouldn't notice until after they'd left.

At length, the king cleared his throat. "I'd like to begin by hearing from those present at the incident."

"Yes, Your Majesty," Lotte said graciously, her noble rearing kicking in. As she launched into the tale of what had happened that morning, Brock considered the assembled guildmasters. Brent watched Lotte impassively, with no trace of the concern he'd shown for her earlier in the day. Quilby, too, was a portrait of detachment, his face neutral, though Brock was certain the merchant was fretting over the possibility that this mess could somehow land at his feet. They shared a moment of furtive eye contact, the only two people in the room who knew the dead magus had experimented with Dangers outside of the tower, both unable to reveal that information without exposing their own crimes. Pollux, the newest and youngest face on the council, looked as if he were adapting admirably to his role. His expression was at turns compassionate, troubled, and resolute. As far as Brock was concerned, the man had proven his worth when he'd opened his temple's doors to the elves during the refugee crisis.

And then there was Grima, who'd always struck Brock as a little . . . flighty. He'd seen her mind wander even in the middle of a Guildculling; she usually gave the impression of being only half present at even the most solemn of occasions.

Today, though, Grima's entire focus was on Lotte's story, and then on Liza's, when the girl spoke next.

"I heard my friends cheering me on," Liza said. "It gave me the strength I was looking for . . ."

Weird, Brock thought. He didn't remember anyone speaking in those awful moments. He certainly hadn't cheered anyone on. He'd been too busy bleeding from his face.

"I don't have anything to add," Brock said when it was his turn. "Except that I'm awfully glad Dame Liza was there." At the questioning faces, he said, "Oh, *dame* was the title for a female knight, back in the day. We figure she's earned it." He looked right at Ser Brent as he said it, daring him to object, but the guildmaster made no response.

"I agree with everything they said," Zed put in. "It was . . . it was *awful.* I've always respected the mages, and to think they'd allow something like that to happen . . ."

Grima bristled. "We're not sure what happened," she said. "That's what we're here to determine. However, I'm confident my people have followed every precaution and adhered, without exception, to the rules set forth for acceptable magical research." She turned toward the king. "It's not to say accidents are impossible, but they're unlikely."

"And what about sabotage?" Ser Brent asked the archmage.

"Sabotage?"

"Did this Phylo have any enemies? Anyone who would want him dead or discredited?"

"Absurd," Grima answered. "Phylo was among my most senior people. He was brilliant, and respected by all."

Brock found that exceptionally hard to believe, but he bit his tongue. You don't know him, he reminded himself. Never met him.

Pollux frowned. "It's a rare person who doesn't ruffle a few feathers in the course of a lifetime. The 'brilliant' ones seem even more prone to it, in my experience."

"Experience," Brent said, laughing. "You have so much of it, after all."

"But who *profits* by sowing such chaos?" Quilby asked. "There's no reason for anyone to do such a thing deliberately. It *must* have been an accident."

"That brings us back to forbidden research," Brent said.

Grima huffed. "Am I whispering into the wind? I've *told* you, you stone-brained tyrant—"

"That's *ENOUGH*!" The king's words cut sharply through the noise, and silence dropped like a curtain. Brock squirmed in his boots.

"I would like to hear from Frond," said the king.

Frond's eyebrows all but leaped from her scarred face. "Your Majesty?" she said.

"Your counsel, Frond. I would hear it."

Frond, who had been slumping in her chair, sat up straight and drummed her fingers upon the table. Grima clucked her tongue as Frond's movement exposed the ruined chair, its insides tufting free and drifting to the floor.

"I think we're getting ahead of ourselves," she said. "The *who* and the *why* are impossible to know without the *where*. We need to determine where the mindtooth came from. Was it somehow brought through the wards? Or was it summoned directly from Astra? Does anyone within Freestone have the ability to access the planes?"

"See? Mindtooth!" the king said. "Frond at least knows what the cursed thing was. Now we're getting somewhere."

"To answer her question," Grima said. "Summoning is among the *most* forbidden of the forbidden arts. As you all well know."

"Forbidden, but is it forgotten?" Brent asked. "We thought necromancy was a thing of the past as recently as three months ago."

"You're welcome to visit our library's forbidden section and see for yourself," Grima answered. "It's a bookshelf left completely empty except for a single urn. That urn is full of ash and cinder—all that remains of the evil books we put to the flame. *That's* how serious I am about dark magic." She turned back to Frond. "Ask your Hexam if you doubt my commitment."

Frond showed her teeth, looking ready to hiss.

"Right," said the king. "Hexam. We do have at least *one* wizard outside the purview of the Mages Guild, don't we?" He tapped his chin. "And you . . . Lotte, is it? You were a steward once, is that correct?"

Lotte bowed her head. "Yes, Your Majesty."

The king smiled. "And so a plan begins to take shape at last, despite the best efforts of this council to rob me of what remains of my hair, my humor, and my patience. Adventurers, please see yourselves out." At Frond's movement, he held out a hand. "Not you, Alabasel. I need you here for this. Your second may stay, too, if you like."

Frond eased back into her seat and nodded stiffly. "Yes, Lotte would be . . . I should much, uh, like to have her present at the . . . present discussion." She grimaced at her own awkwardness. Brock, however, was loving it. Frond was clearly much, *much* more comfortable in a hostile situation. Confronted with the king's deference, she was at a complete loss.

"Wait for us outside the tower, kids," Lotte said. "We should all walk back together."

"Grima," the king said. "Be a gracious host and give the woman your seat, would you?"

✷

"Woof, that was hard to watch," Brock said. "And yet I kind of hate to be missing the rest of it."

"They don't inspire much confidence, do they?" Zed asked.

They were descending upon the radiant platform, which

moved slowly enough to make the experience more novel than terrifying. Still, Brock opted not to look down.

"Didn't they solve anything?" Sulba asked.

"Not yet, but . . . I'm sure you don't have anything to worry about," Liza said.

"I just hope they don't suspend classes," he said.

"You *really* like school, don't you?" Brock asked.

"To be fair," Sulba said, "by 'classes' I mean 'learning to bend the fundamental laws of nature to suit my whims.' "

"Fair point," said Brock.

Sulba opened the vault's great iron door to retrieve their weapons. As he returned Liza's sword, he asked her, "Hey, I don't suppose you know Jayna?"

Liza smiled back. "Really well, actually. Are you friends?"

"More like rivals," Sulba answered. "We were apprentices together. It can get a little . . . *competitive* around here, but I respected her talent. Sort of figured she was meant for great things, before she got drafted."

Liza bristled. "She's done some pretty great things *since* getting drafted, actually. You might have heard about some of them."

Sulba waved her irritation away. "I didn't mean anything by it, I just– Hey, get out of there!"

Brock and Liza whirled around to see Zed stepping out from within the vault. "Sorry!" he said, flushing with embarrassment.

"What were you doing in there?" Sulba asked.

"I was just getting my scepter," Zed answered, holding it up with one hand and pointing at it with the other.

"You should have waited for me," Sulba said crossly.

"Hey, ease up," Brock said, matching the boy's sharp tone. "He didn't know any better. No harm done, right?"

"I guess." Sulba's eyes lingered over Zed for another moment. "Other than all the mud you've tracked in," he grumbled. "Let's get you out of here before you break any more rules."

✷

When Frond finally stormed out of the tower, she looked like she'd just swallowed a frog. "Come on," she growled. That was all the greeting she spared for them as she stomped past, counting on the apprentices and Lotte to hurry after her.

"What happened?" Zed asked Lotte. "Did they decide anything?"

"For better or worse, yes," Lotte answered. "We all need to be prepared for some changes in the days ahead." She frowned. "The mages most of all. They're all under suspicion. And the king wants Hexam and me to help sort it out."

"Hexam?" Brock echoed. "Isn't there bad blood between him and the archmagus?"

"Not the archmagus anymore," Lotte answered. "For the foreseeable future, Grima is suspended, Ser Brent and an elite group of knights are moving into the tower, and . . . Well, for all intents and purposes, the Mages Guild is answering to *us*."

Zed barked out a short laugh. "The irony is almost too rich."

"I don't like it," said Liza. "The guilds are supposed to be separate, for good reason."

"And it sounds like classes are canceled," added Brock. "Poor Sulba." Then a realization dawned on him, and he skidded to a stop.

"I've got it!" he cried. "Ugh. I *knew* something would occur to me as soon as it was too late."

The adventurers turned to look at him expectantly. Even Frond had stopped in her tracks.

"What is it?" Liza asked. "What did you figure out?"

Brock smiled. "They should totally call it a *spellevator*."

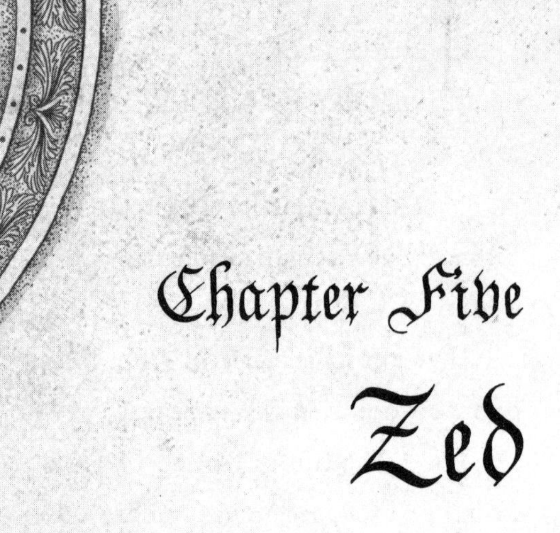

Chapter Five
Zed

"So," said Foster, rubbing his misty hands together until they'd formed a knot of smoke, "*whose innermost thoughts will we be invading first tonight?*"

"*I wish you wouldn't put it like that,*" muttered Zed.

"*Micah seems to have noticed something's amiss,*" Foster continued blithely. "*He might actually be a good bet. Though I'd avoid doing it within view of Makiva.*"

Zed frowned. "*Would she stop us?*" he asked. "*Could she, even?*"

Foster shrugged. "*That depends what you mean by* us. *We're tethered to the chain, but Makiva's never exhibited an ability to hurt or control me in this form. She does still possess your body, however.*"

The two phantoms were in the apprentice quarters hallway.

After the eventful day, most of Zed's friends had retired to bed early; Zed could hear Micah's spirited snoring even through the boy's thick wooden door. In recent weeks, with the elves gone and several journey-rank adventurers shifted to the upper floors, enough space had opened up that Lotte could furnish each apprentice with their own private quarters. If only Zed had been able to enjoy the luxury.

"We're starting with Brock," Zed said. *"If there's anyone who's likely to hear me, it's him."*

Foster shrugged again, but this time as he did, his shoulders folded forward like a wave of fabric. The smoke moiled downward, shrinking until a fox stood where the man had been. *"Lead the way."*

Zed wafted through Brock's door, passing bodiless through the knotted wood. The inside of the room was dark, but Zed could still make out his friend's form curled into his pallet, hugging his pillow. In sleep, Brock's casual swagger had fallen away. He looked more like the child he truly was.

"How do I do it?" Zed asked. *"Do I just . . . talk to him?"*

"I'm not an expert." The fox leaped through the door and up onto Brock's small trunk of personal effects. "You *were easy. Makiva's chain already connected us. And it's not exactly as if you're a locked chest. All those emotions are right out in the open."*

At Zed's look, the fox chuckled. *"See, I can practically read your mind already. And shame on you."*

The creature's shining eyes turned toward Brock. *"Oh, all*

right," he sighed. "*Remember, these aren't real bodies we're in. They're mana—magic. Without our true bodies, we can't shape it into spellwork, but by touching another person's mind, it's possible for us to perceive their thoughts. They just have to be open enough. Close your senses to everything else and speak to Brock. Not this boy in bed. The inner Brock. The idea of Brock.*"

Zed did as he was told, shutting his eyes. He thought of his best friend: the funny, whip-smart boy who'd been watching over Zed his whole life. He pictured their years together as children, and that day in the market months ago, when Brock had given Zed a silver piece to buy a lucky charm.

"*Brock . . .*" Zed quested in a small voice. "*Please. Help me.*"

Something changed.

The room drifted in a way Zed couldn't quite perceive, shadows grinding together like shifting stones in a secret passage.

Zed opened his eyes to find the small bedroom had disappeared. He stood now in a long, narrow corridor. The strange passage's walls were solid black, and a series of colorful masks hung at disparate heights, like eerie faces through which the darkness observed him.

Foster sat at Zed's feet, still in his fox form. He turned his head, gazing behind them toward the hall's obscured beginning. "*Interesting,*" the fox murmured. "*Well, we did it. We're in Brock's dream.*"

Zed peered cautiously at one of the masks, a glittering green domino. Then he yelped and took a sudden step back as two eyes darted open, staring at him with wide-eyed vigilance.

Though the corridor behind them seemed go on forever, the path ahead had a clear ending. At that end of the passage was a great obsidian doorway, in front of which stood Zed's best friend.

Brock was alone, his pale skin stark against the darkness. He looked up at the door with obvious trepidation. The portal was made of an odd black metal and fashioned in spiky angles. It almost looked like a mask itself, obscuring an enormous face.

Brock held a single tallow candle in a brass dish. The tiny flame danced, sending his shadow capering across the walls. Slowly, he placed his other shaking hand against the black door.

"*Brock!*" Zed shouted, bursting forward. "*Brock, wait!*" Foster hurried after him, billowing at his heels.

All around Zed, the masks came alive. Wild eyes rolled in colorful sockets, watching him as he ran. But Brock didn't seem to notice him. Before Zed could reach his friend, he'd slipped inside the door. Zed heard it close with a ponderous sound. The small bar of candlelight winked away.

As he finally reached the end of the hall, Zed discovered that all those angles in the metal added up to a larger shape. A great spiderweb stretched across the doorway, molded in ebony.

The door had no handles. Zed slammed his smoky fist into it and was surprised when it broke against the surface, the mist scattering.

"I can't get through," Zed rasped. *"Why?"*

Foster trotted up beside him. It was hard to read his expressions as a fox, but he almost seemed wary of the door. *"The boy's too closed off,"* he said. *"Too many secrets. They've become a barrier we won't be able to cross."*

"Secrets?" Zed whirled on the fox. *"What secrets?"*

Foster glanced away, toward the dark passage that watched them back. *"I haven't kept a close eye on your friend, so I can't really say. But I've seen this before. Dox was just as unreachable. I never did make it through to him."*

Zed's shoulders sagged. *"So what do we do?"* he said, turning back to the forbidding door.

Behind him, Foster's tail flicked. *"Shall we give Micah a go?"*

✷

They tried Liza next.

She'd already heard Zed once, and if being "closed off" was indeed a barrier to communication, then Zed suspected talking to Micah would be a little like banging his head against Freestone's wall in an attempt to get inside.

When Zed quested into the girl's dream, he found himself immediately awash in sunlight. After the dark guildhall and Brock's even darker dream corridor, the brightness was dazzling. Liza stood before him in a glittering breastplate. Her green sword, the Solution, was raised high in the air. Zed glanced around to find all his friends were there—or at least dream versions of them—and they were all gazing at Liza expectantly. By the look of the lush forest that surrounded them, it appeared they were beyond the walls.

"I know you're afraid," Liza said somberly. "Believe it or not, I'm afraid, too. But if we work together, we can take this thing down."

"What's going on?" Zed asked. *"Is this . . . ?"*

"But, Guildmistress!" Dream-Brock wailed pitifully. "Did you see the size of that thing? It'll massacre us for sure!" He threw himself at Liza's feet, cowering.

"Oh . . . oh, this is incredible," Foster said. *"Bra-vo, Liza. I hope they're all this fun."*

Liza lifted Dream-Brock to his feet with one hand. "You listen to me, Brock Dunderfel—*no one* is dying today." Brock sniffed, nodding slowly, and Liza's iron gaze swept out over the rest of the apprentices, her eyes settling on each of them in turn. "That goes for all of you. If we work together, there's nothing we can't accomplish. We're a team, right? The best protectors Freestone has seen since the Champions themselves."

Then her eyes stopped right on Zed.

She sees me!

Zed sprang forward. *"Liza!"* he shouted. *"Liza, you've got to help me! Makiva's taken over my body and she's planning something terrible and this fox is Foster Pendleton but he's not as bad as the stories say he's just a little depressing!"*

"Wow, thanks," Foster said, rolling his eyes.

"That's a good point, Zed," Liza said. "If we know how it hunts, it'll be that much easier to take it down. Fel? You're our expert tracker."

Zed howled in frustration as Liza turned toward the night elf. Dream-Fel nodded, her face growing thoughtful. "It's a lone hunter, which is good for us. No sneak attacks from behind. I could set a trap . . . but we'd need some kind of bait to lure it out." At her feet, Dream-Mousebane mewed in agreement.

"Liza, this is a dream!" Zed cried, waving his hands in front of her face. *"I'm speaking to you in your dreams! Can't you hear me?"*

Dream-Jayna snapped her fingers. "My shield spell! I could be the bait, then cast it as soon as the beast arrives, while the rest of you swoop in and set off the trap."

"It's dangerous," said Liza. "Are you sure, Jayna?"

The girl nodded, her expression resolute. "As long as you're leading us, I am. We all trust you, Guildmistress."

"Hear, hear!" shouted Dream-Jett.

Zed deflated, his smoky form settling beside Foster on the ground. *"She still can't hear me."*

The fox placed a paw on Zed's arm. *"Sorry, kid,"* he said. *"This is how it works most of the time. But we'll keep trying."*

"Three cheers for Dame Liza!" Dream-Micah called, rapping his sister on the shoulder.

Liza grinned at her friends, her blue cloak billowing gallantly behind her. "You can cheer me when we're all safe at the guildhall. For now, we've got a city to save."

*

Jett was having a nightmare. In his dreams he relived the night of the naga attack, over and over, as if searching for a way to stop what had happened to him. Each time, something small changed—Liza stepped in with her shield, or Brock parried the creature's bite with his dagger—but eventually the Danger's teeth always found Jett.

Through each loop, Zed tried to explain to his friend that it was just a dream, to draw him away from the horrible memory. But Jett couldn't hear him, and he couldn't break free.

Finally, the stress of the nightmare become too much; Jett awoke with a gasp. The cool evening beyond the wall dissolved like steam billowing from a kettle, and Zed found himself back in his friend's room.

He and Foster left without a word. The sounds of Jett's shuddering breaths quieted as they passed through the door.

*

Jayna, it turned out, was still awake. As Zed and Foster arrived at her door, they heard muffled voices from inside, low and urgent. She seemed to be having an intense conversation. Light flickered from the crack at the floor as feet passed back and forth.

"*Well,*" said Foster, placing his foxy ear to the wood. "*This is interesting. I didn't take the goody-goody wizard as one for late-night conferences. Maybe she's got more gumption than I realized.*"

"Let's leave her be," Zed muttered. *"We're here to find help, not to spy."* Jett's nightmare had shaken him. Zed still felt ashamed for intruding on something so private. He resolved to leave the dwarf's dreams alone from now on.

"Zed," Foster said exasperatedly. *"There is a very good chance you'll be trapped as a spirit for the rest of your existence. If you can't learn to enjoy the little dramas your friends provide, it's going to be very dull. For example, I've been rooting for Brock to finally tell Liza how he feels about her for weeks. Team Briza!"*

"Brock likes Liza*?!"* Zed blurted.

"Not that he's realized it yet." The fox whirled on Zed. *"Wait, don't tell me you're on Team Jeza. That ship sailed months ago."*

"What's a ship?"

"Fie, you Freestoners." Foster turned back to the door. *"We'll just take a little peek. For all we know, Jayna's confronting Makiva in your body right this very moment."*

Zed frowned, following the fox's gaze. If Jayna *was* speaking to Makiva, it was important that they know what about. She could even be in danger. *"Fine,"* he conceded. *"But if she's* kissing *anybody, I'm out of there."*

"Agreed," Foster enthusiastically concurred. Then he padded through the door.

Zed gave a misty sigh and followed the fox inside.

The feet moving behind the door were Nirav's. Zed yelped as the former squire stepped right through him, pacing the length of Jayna's room. He was waving his arms as he spoke.

"Just see it from my perspective!" Nirav fumed. "One day I'm with my buddies Syd and Fife, and you're this big-eyed, terrified little kid who looks *way* too young to be here. Then a monster attacks me, and when I come to there's half a dozen new apprentices running around. Plus, now Syd's a *teenager*, and you . . ." His arms fell. Nirav turned to Jayna, who was listening from her bed. "I don't know where I fit in anymore."

Jayna's eyes were on her hands. She sighed softly. "I'm sorry," she said. "I really am. I know this is all still a shock. But that instant for you was almost two years for the rest of us. The others *have* tried to include you."

Nirav took a deep breath. "Liza doesn't order me around," he said. "Not like the rest of you. I know it sounds stupid to complain about. Fie, if she *did* I'd probably tell her to go kiss a manticore. But I notice, you know? I'm different. I'm not one of you."

"But that's just the thing; we're *all* different!"

Nirav rolled his eyes. "That scrawny Zed kid sure is."

"*Ouch*," said Foster. "*I'd call you fine featured.*"

Jayna glared at the boy. "Have you ever considered that maybe your attitude is why you feel left out?" she said. "Ooh, you were always such a *Stone Son.* Even Micah's gotten past the chest-thumping. Mostly." Jayna shook her head, her red curls bouncing. "If you want to feel like part of the group, maybe *you* should make more of an effort."

Nirav seemed to shrink as she finished. His shoulders slumped and he kicked his foot against the floorboards. After a moment, he murmured, "I wish Frond had never saved me."

"Would you listen to yourself?" Jayna scoffed. "Boys! Honestly. You were *dead*. For *years*. And now you're back. You looked a basilisk in the face and lived. Not many people get that kind of a second chance."

Zed and Foster glanced at each other, their eyes both wide with surprise. Zed had never heard Jayna speak so passionately, even in her lectures about dark magic.

"I know things are different," she added, her tone softening. "And unfamiliar. And that isn't your fault. But change is always going to be beyond our control. It's all right to feel sad, even . . . even angry. But don't you ever give up on yourself, Nirav. Frond didn't."

Nirav wiped his eyes, turning away.

"Don't ever give up yourself," Zed whispered, his ghostly voice catching. Foster glanced up at him. The fox's slitted eyes were unreadable.

"You're not the same girl I remember." Nirav hesitated as he inched the door open on his way out. "When did you become so strong?"

Jayna's cheeks reddened slightly, and she looked back down at her lap. "A lot's happened these two years," she said. "I learned more magic. I've fought more Dangers." Then her gaze rose. "I also made a group of friends that I'd give my life for. And I know they'd do the same for me."

"Your friends are lucky to have you."

Then Nirav was gone, and the door creaked shut behind him.

✷

"*Well, I think we both know who's next,*" Foster said cheerfully when they were back in the hall.

"*Hopefully we'll have better luck with Fel,*" Zed agreed.

Foster chaffed. "*Hardly. It's Micah time!*"

Zed glanced down at the fox, quirking a brow. Micah's snoring still rattled softly through the hall. "*Why do you keep pushing me toward Micah?*"

"*Well, for one,*" Foster said, "*elves don't dream. Not the full-blooded ones, anyway. Their sleep is more like a trance. Much harder to break through. I keep forgetting you were separated from your elven parent, so you don't know all this. I was raised among my mother's people before I came to Freestone.*"

"*Your mother was elven?*" Zed asked. His smoky form dispersed a moment, re-forming on the floor, and he sat cross-legged in front of the fox. "*You visited the elven druids outside the city,*" he muttered. "*I forgot all about that.*"

Foster nodded warily. "*I went now and then. The druids gave me a sense of . . . familiarity. In return, I brought them sweets and bread from town. And they enjoyed Reyna's visits.*"

"*Reyna?*" It was the first time Zed had heard the name. Foster was usually so guarded about his past. He'd shared more today than he had in weeks. Zed wondered if the warlock was more hopeful than he let on.

"*My familiar.*" The fox blinked slowly. "*Sometimes witches and warlocks take them, to send as our agents in places we can't go. Though in truth, I'd say Reyna took* me. *She just appeared one day at the edge of the forest and followed me around from then on. She was my fox.*"

"*A fox!*" Zed gasped. "*That's why you take this form! You miss your familiar. Wait, what happened to her after . . . ?*"

Foster's teeth flashed, a glimmer of canine ferocity shining through. "*We're not here for a history lesson,*" he snapped. "*So how about we get on with your little quest, hmm?*"

"*Fine,*" Zed grunted, his feelings bruised. "*But you still haven't explained your obsession with Micah.*"

"*More like his obsession with you. Don't tell me you hadn't noticed.*"

In the silence that followed, it seemed like the hallway had contracted around Zed, closing in while he wasn't looking. If he had real ears right then, he suspected they'd be burning. "*I . . . what? That doesn't make sense.*"

"*Oh, I'm sure it doesn't,*" Foster drawled. The humor had returned to his voice, but Zed found he preferred it when the warlock was angry. "*In any case, I think he's good for you. He keeps you from getting too angsty.*"

The fox turned his head toward Micah's door, from which several high snorts sounded, like a clogged flute. "*Um, after you.*"

✷

The inside of Micah's room was just as Zed remembered from their time as roommates, except the former noble's mess had now expanded like liquid to fill every corner of the space. Had Zed been in his physical body, he would have stepped over several piles of soiled linens to reach Micah's bed, so it was a small blessing, at least, that he could float right through them. In his fox form, Foster moved lightly over the mounds, as if traversing a hilly countryside.

"*Let's get this over with*," Zed grumbled. He closed his eyes, trying to shut out the sounds of Micah's wheezing. "*Oh Micah, please help*," Zed said quickly and without much enthusiasm. "*Makiva's taken over my body, blah blah blah. Well, I guess it didn't—*"

Zed opened his eyes.

"*—work . . .*"

He stood in a grand dining room. The walls were all constructed of dark, lustrous wood, and decorated with paintings of imperious-looking men and women who stared right at Zed. Tapestries of maidens with unicorns and armored knights riding horseback trailed from the high, arched ceiling.

In the center of the room a banquet had been spread over a colossal oak table. Zed could practically taste the sweetmeats arrayed artfully across their silver serving platters.

At the end of the table was Micah. He was dressed as he would have been back when he was still officially a Guerra—before the Healers Guild insisted that he renounce his name and title. His shirt was crisp and white, and he wore a hunter-green coat that complemented his dark eyes and olive complexion. He looked dashing and handsome and utterly at ease.

Until his eyes found Zed. Then he coughed up a bit of soup.

"Zed?" Micah choked out. "What are you doing here? Is that a *dog*?"

Foster leaped onto the table in his fox form and began investigating the food there. *"I told you he was sharp,"* he called back as he peered into a large serving bowl of creamy yellow bisque.

"Fine, he can see us," Zed said. *"Liza saw me, too. But can he hear what I'm saying? Micah, listen . . . this is all a dream."*

"And a perfectly good one, until you showed up!" Micah complained. "Wait. Why are you made of smoke?"

Zed's mouth fell open. Even Foster's gaze shot up in surprise, staring right at the boy.

"He can hear us . . ." Zed whispered, hardly daring to believe it. *"You can actually hear me!"* He exploded forward as a bludgeon of mist, crashing into Micah and sending him sprawling from the table.

Zed re-formed beside the boy as Micah crawled backward across the room's beautifully woven carpet.

"Fie, you're a klutz even in my dreams," Micah muttered. The boy's cheeks were pink. "What . . . what is going on?"

"Micah, just shut up and listen while there's still time," Zed pressed. *"The Zed you know—the one who's walking around the guildhall right now—he's an imposter. Old Makiva possessed my body. She's forcing me to do something terrible. The attack yesterday was* her *fault."*

Even though Micah could hear him, Zed had still expected the boy to react with skepticism to his claim. Maybe he'd laugh it off, dismiss it as the perplexing development of a particularly strange dream.

So Zed was surprised when Micah's eyes suddenly brightened with clarity. "I *knew* it!" he crowed. "I knew something was off! Wow, I am good. And Brock's been all, 'Give him space. He's been through a lot.'" Micah's impression honestly wasn't bad.

"*Brock!*" Zed exclaimed. "*Yes! Tell Brock. Tell Frond. Tell anyone who will listen!*"

"You bet I will. How could all those fools not see you were different? It's like you suddenly grew a backbone."

"*That . . . may not be wise.*"

Zed and Micah both turned to the fox lying at the edge of the table. Foster's smoky tail hung from the side, batting languidly in the air.

"What *is* that thing?" Micah asked.

"*He's sort of a . . . spirit guide.*" Zed sighed. "*It's a long story.*"

"*Here's a short one,*" said Foster. "*Frond, or Lotte, or even Jayna learns that Zed is a warlock who made a pact with Makiva and has now been possessed. Their sense of duty to the city requires them to tell the king. What do you think will happen then? Will they lead Makiva to a comfortable padded room, while they figure out how to exorcise her from Zed's body? No. Freestone doesn't tolerate witchcraft. Zed would be executed by the next dawn . . . just to be safe.*"

"*You don't know that,*" Zed muttered. "*And even so, if it stops*

Makiva . . ." But he couldn't finish. The thought still summoned a pit of dread that threatened to pull Zed right in. It was despair, and Zed wasn't totally sure he'd be able to claw his way out if he let himself succumb to it.

Micah watched him for a long moment, his brown eyes wide. "You made a warlock's pact? Zed, what were you *thinking*?"

Before today, Zed had never cared much about Micah's opinion of him. But the expression on the boy's face in that moment twisted something inside Zed's ghostly core. A blossom of shame, sprouting for months, had finally bloomed.

"*It happened during Brenner's attack,*" Zed explained, his voice a rasp. "*When I nearly died. Makiva came to me in a dream and told me I could save my friends. Save the city. That's how I got the green fire. It's not my amazing magical potential. It's hers.*"

It was done. Zed had admitted it. He'd spoken the words aloud. He'd expected to feel lost right now—for that pit of despair to swallow him whole. Instead, Zed felt relieved. Whatever happened next, he was free from his awful secret. Someone else knew, someone solid and real.

But Micah didn't respond. He just watched Zed, his mouth curling into a frown.

"*At the time, it was the only way to protect you all,*" Zed continued. "*Brenner would have killed you for sure. But then I was too afraid to tell anyone. I wasn't even sure it was all real. Not until it was too late. I know this doesn't excuse what I've done. Go ahead and call me whatever you want: I'm stupid and gullible and selfish. There's nothing I haven't already said a thousand times to myself."*

"It's okay," Micah said softly.

Zed looked up in shock, both at the words and the gentleness with which Micah had spoken them. The healer's eyes were averted, but he was sitting up on the carpet, picking at its lush fibers.

Micah took a deep breath. "I'm not going to scold you, Zed. Me of all people. I practically shoved you out of Makiva's tent the morning of the Guildculling so I could get to her first. If she'd offered me a way out of the Healers Guild, I think we both know I'd have taken it without a second thought. I understand desperation." He grimaced. "And I knew something was wrong with you. I sensed it. On the trip to Leatherfall—"

"Llethanyl."

"—whatever—I *saw* that you were upset. Terrified, even. And what did I do? I laughed at you."

Zed's smoky form shivered strangely. The boundaries of his shape loosened, like fog warming in the morning sun. He concentrated a moment, pulling himself together.

"You also tried to comfort me that day," he said. *"In your own way."*

Micah sighed. "I could have handled that better."

"You didn't know what was going on," Zed muttered. *"But now that you do, it's time to end this. You've got to tell Frond about Makiva."*

"No!" Micah's wide eyes finally rose from the floor. "The

creepy ghost dog is right. The king would kill you for sure, Zed."

Zed waved his arms in exasperation. "*If we don't do something, Makiva will destroy the whole city!*"

"Then I'll find another way," Micah shot back. "*Someone's* got to have a dusty old book on how to deal with possession. The Mages Guild. Or Hexam, maybe."

Zed started to argue, but faltered. He frowned. "*That's not a terrible idea, actually. Hexam once gave me a book on dark magic, even though Grima said she'd destroyed them all. So clearly he's kept some forbidden knowledge. If anyone's likely to have information on exorcisms, it's him.*" He glanced from Micah to Foster, the fox watching silently from the table. "*We could snoop around his study, but we can't actually interact with anything physically.*"

"*I* can, though," Micah said. "Tomorrow I'll sneak in while Hexam's not there. See what he's got."

Zed nodded, his eyes brightening. "*It's a long shot, but it's something.*"

More than something. It was a plan! They had a *plan*! Weeks of screaming at his friends for help, and finally a real chance at stopping Makiva was within his smoky grasp!

And yet, one question still burned at the back of Zed's thoughts like a glowing ember. "*Micah . . . why do you care what the king does to me? I thought you—I don't know, I thought I annoyed you.*"

Micah bristled. "You *do*," he said. "Especially right now. But that doesn't mean I want you beheaded in front of the whole city.

You made your bad deal to save us. We're guildmates. We take care of each othe—oh, Fie, I sound like Liza."

"Well, thanks," Zed mumbled. He wasn't sure why, but suddenly he felt awkward sitting next to Micah, even as an incorporeal spirit. Both boys averted their eyes, Micah clearing his throat.

A dull knock sounded throughout the room, echoing dreamily in the grand dining space.

"What's that?" Zed asked, searching for the source of the noise.

"I think someone's at my door," Micah said. "My real door. It must be morning." He glanced back to Zed. "How do I contact you?"

"We'll be watching, even if you can't see us." Foster leaped from the table to Zed's side. *"Tomorrow night we'll visit you again. Zed, we should go now."*

Micah's eyes widened. He reached for Zed's arm, but his hand passed right through the smoke. "Wait, Zed, what about Bro—?"

The dining room cascaded away before he could finish. Paintings and tapestries and the table full of food all gushed to the floor as a flood of mist. In an instant, Zed and Foster were back in Micah's squalid quarters.

The door burst open just as Micah sat up in bed. With a gasp, Zed saw his body standing in the doorway with Liza. Both apprentices were backlit by a pane of sunlight.

Makiva's gaze slid over the room. Her eyes narrowed when she found Zed and Foster buried among Micah's dirty piles of laundry.

Micah still seemed dazed, as wakefulness slowly braced him. Then he noticed who was standing in his doorway. His expression tightened and he shifted on his pallet. "Oh, hey Zed. Hey Liza." He swallowed laboriously. "What's, uh, what's up?"

Makiva turned from Zed and Foster, her cold glare landing on Micah. "Time to get dressed, sleepyhead," Zed's voice said flatly. It dripped with suspicion. "Lotte's calling us to drills."

"Honestly, Micah, it's nearly second bell," Liza added as she tightened her baldric. "You need to be able to rouse yourself without Zed's assistance." She gazed across the room, her eyes passing obliviously over the two spirits. "And for the love of Lux, will you do some laundry?"

Chapter Six

Brock

It was Brock's turn to be the monster.

There was part of him that greeted the news with relief. He'd slept poorly after the traumatic events of the previous day; his dreams had been dark, full of watching eyes and leering grins. After that, Lotte's early-morning drills—a brutal series of exercises in the guildhall's training yard—were nearly enough to make him collapse. And that was just the warm-up.

The heart of the morning's training was what Lotte called an asymmetrical drill. *Asymmetrical* as in uneven, lopsided . . . unfair. It would be seven apprentices—Liza, Zed, Jayna, Jett, Micah, Fel, and Nirav—against one. And Brock was chosen to stand alone.

But in an asymmetrical drill, it was the solo agent who had most of the advantages.

"Brock has a deadly appendage," Lotte said, and she handed him a ten-foot pole. "Picture it as a clawed arm or a barbed tail—whatever motivates you to avoid it." As Brock tested the weight of the pole, she added, "If it touches you, even just a tap, you're out."

She distributed short wooden rods to Liza, Zed, and the rest. One end of each rod had been painted red. "Your weapons," she said. "Imagine the red end is the pointy end. The only way to win is to stab the monster's weak point right . . . here." Using two fingers, she dabbed a dot of red paint on Brock's training leathers, right beneath his heart.

"What about magic?" Zed asked.

"Pretend this Danger is impervious to fire," Lotte said. "The only way to win is to use your weapon."

"Yeah, thanks in advance for not setting me on fire!" Brock said. He shuffled alone toward the far end of the yard, dragging his staff behind him. "This might just be the worst game of tag ever."

Liza patted him on the shoulder as he passed. "Don't worry. It'll be over before you know it."

Brock got into position, planting his feet firmly in the dirt. With his back to the guildhall, the apprentices would have to come straight at him. He began moving the staff back and forth in a wide arc. If he could keep that up, he'd be difficult to reach.

"All right," Liza said, shifting into a fighting stance. She watched Brock from across the yard as she addressed her teammates. "Jayna, your shield could be the key to this, if we can get close enough. Let's you, me, and Jett move forward in tandem."

"I'm with you," said Nirav.

"No, hang back, Nirav," she said. "Jayna can only cover so many of us."

"So take me instead of the dwarfson! I've got better reach."

"My reach is perfectly adequate," Jett growled. "I could reach your scrawny neck from here *just fine*."

"Hello? My arms are getting tired," Brock said. "Is that your strategy?"

There was a dull thump against Brock's ribs, followed by a bloom of pain. "Ow!" he said, dropping his pole and cradling his side. It took him a moment to register what had happened. Someone had sent their rod soaring unerringly across the yard.

Brock looked up and saw all eyes were on Fel. Her hands were empty, and she smiled bashfully. "Sorry. Was that cheating?"

Lotte shrugged. "I'll admit I didn't think anyone would be able to make a shot like that. But I'll allow it."

"You'd better," Brock groused. "Because it's someone else's turn to be the target dummy."

Fel brightened. "Thank you for the distraction, Nirav," she said.

"Yeah, sure," Nirav said glumly. "Real team effort. Happy to help."

"This is pointless," Micah said. The healer had been uncharacteristically quiet all morning. But there was nothing more characteristic for him than a complaint aimed at Lotte.

She was unfazed. "Micah, I've told you, please commit all your complaints to paper. I can always use more kindling for the evening fire."

"Look, we *know* how to hit things with our weapons," Micah said. "And I can heal any idiot who wanders into a Danger's claws or teeth. But like Zed said: *What about magic?* How do we fight something that can set us on fire from ten paces?"

Zed gave Micah a dark look, apparently taking offense. But for once, Micah had a point.

"I don't disagree," Brock said. "Dangers that cast spells are supposedly rare, but we've had more than a few close calls out there."

Lotte pursed her lips, thinking. Her eyes lingered over Zed. Finally, she clucked her tongue. "All right," Lotte said. "New drill, same as the old drill. Any contact with the Danger's weapon, and you're out. But this time, I'll be the Danger, and my weapon will be . . ." She shoved her hands into a bucket, pulling up a wet clump of soil. "Fireballs."

"Ugh," said Nirav. "Is that compost?"

He was right. It wasn't just soil in Lotte's grip, but a loose-packed ball of muddy waste. Brock saw greasy skin hanging from a chicken bone, and he tried to remember how many days it had been since the guild had dined on chicken. More than a few.

Lotte wound up for her first toss. "Come and get me!" she called.

"Scatter!" cried Liza.

They did, all moving quickly in different directions. Brock looked for a hiding spot, but the best he could do was to get behind one of the hay-stuffed training dummies that dotted the yard. It provided scant cover, however.

After Fel's impressive display minutes earlier, Brock assumed she'd be Lotte's first target. Instead the quartermaster took aim at Jayna.

It was the smart move. If Jayna got her shield spell up, she and anyone standing next to her would be untouchable.

Jayna flexed her fingers. A faint blue bubble began to take shimmering form.

"Jayna, watch out!" Nirav cried. He lunged forward, shoving her out of the path of Lotte's projectile.

"Nirav, no!" Liza yelled.

Too late. The spell was interrupted before the shield took solid form. Nirav was pelted with the mudball meant for Jayna—and it spattered on impact, slapping slimy waste across Jayna, Jett, and Liza.

Half their team was down in a single shot.

"What's our plan?" Micah called from behind another dummy.

Brock looked instinctively to Liza, who sat heavily on the ground. She made a large shrugging gesture. *Don't look at me. I'm out.*

"Rush her!" Brock said. "She can't get us all. Now!"

Brock wheeled away from cover, ducking low as a mudball soared just overhead. "Ha!" he said, and he ran forward, trusting Zed, Micah, and Fel to be right behind him. Lotte returned to her bucket for more ammunition, but she'd be lucky to get off a single shot in the time it took them to reach her, let alone four. They had her!

But Lotte didn't rise from the bucket with a handful of muck. Instead she hefted the entire bucket.

"Wait—!" Brock cried, and he skidded to a stop, throwing up his arms.

It didn't help. Lotte swung the bucket in a wide arc, splashing them with refuse.

Brock gasped as it hit him. The smell was overwhelming. Micah to his left and Fel to his right stood as rigidly still as he did, dripping and horrified.

"As valuable a teaching moment as any I've seen," Lotte said smugly. "Anyone want to tell me where mistakes were made?"

"I will," said Zed. He appeared just behind her in a burst of silvery mist, and he held a red-tipped rod against her throat. "You took your eyes off the *real* mage."

Lotte gasped aloud. For just a moment, Brock recognized genuine fear in her eyes. She'd been thoroughly caught off guard.

But she came quickly back to herself, smirking. "There are far too many of you these days. Well done, Zed."

"Yeah, great job, Zed," Micah said, wiping muck from his face. "Way to have our backs."

"Lay off him," said Brock. "It was just a drill."

Micah looked like he wanted to argue, but Liza stepped between them. "It was a valuable reminder, is what it was. That we have work to do before we can start functioning like a team again."

"Is that directed at me?" Nirav asked.

"It's not any one person's fault," Liza said. "But if what you told Jayna is true . . . if you want to be part of this team—"

"You told her?" Nirav said, turning on Jayna. "I told you that in confidence!"

"Don't you yell at her," Jett warned him.

"Jett, it's fine," Jayna hissed. "Everyone needs to relax."

"And bathe, maybe," Brock put in, sniffing theatrically.

"Yes, I think that's enough for the morning," Lotte said. "We'll pick this up again next time."

Nirav stormed off immediately, heading inside. Jayna moved to follow after him, then stopped, uncertainty written on her face. "He's a good person," she said to no one in particular. "A good person in a difficult situation."

Brock rubbed his bruised ribs and pondered her words. Back when he'd been under the Lady Gray's thumb, he'd thought of himself in much the same terms. *A good person in a difficult situation.*

If the Lady were looking to exploit another adventurer,

someone with little reason to be loyal to the guild, she could do worse than Nirav.

"I'll talk to him," offered Liza. "After he's cooled off a bit."

Micah grunted. "As much as I'd love to all hold hands and talk about our feelings, that drill proved my point! We need better defenses against magic."

"We could talk to Hexam," Jayna said. "See if he has any ideas."

"Brock and I are due to see him shortly," Fel said. "We're to aid his examination of the Danger from the marketplace."

"Oh yeah?" Micah said, perking up. "How long will that take?"

Fel shrugged. "The Danger is small, but complex. And very damaged. It may take some time."

"And in the meantime, don't worry so much, Micah," Jett said. He reached up and slung his arm around Zed's shoulders. "The best way to fight magic is with magic. And between Jayna and this guy, we've got the two most brilliant spell-casters I've ever seen on our side."

Zed wrinkled his nose momentarily at the smell of compost, but then he smiled sweetly. "Jett's right. I've got your back, Micah."

"Yeah." Micah swallowed. "That's great, Zed. Thanks."

*

Brock's hair was still wet from bathing when he drifted down the stairs to the guildhall's expansive basement. Fel and Syd were there, standing before the grim wall of trophies.

"There *has* to be a story about that one," Fel said, pointing to a fearsome reptilian head with a colorful spiked crest and unnervingly human teeth in its elongated jaws. "You don't see a Kierannosaur every day!"

"If you do, you're doing something wrong," Syd deadpanned. The older boy radiated calmness to an extent otherwise unknown in the guild. Little wonder, thought Brock, that Hexam had chosen to take him under his wing when it came to the study of Dangers. Syd had a scholar's curiosity and an iron stomach, and his steady temperament was undoubtedly an asset during Danger dissections—and his steady hands even more so.

Brock's own interest in Dangers was more pragmatic. He had no great desire to look over Hexam's shoulder during another autopsy. But it was the best way to learn practical information about Dangers, such as their strengths and weaknesses.

All the better to survive them, he hoped.

And his interest had led to an unexpected benefit, as he and Fel had struck up an unusual sort of friendship in recent weeks. The girl's time with Llethanyl's rangers had exposed her to a large variety of Dangers, some of which even senior adventurers had yet to encounter. Brock figured that was an opportunity for knowledge they couldn't pass up, so he and Fel had been going through Hexam's manual of known monsters, expanding the existing entries and drafting new ones from scratch.

She greeted him now with a smile. "Hello, Brock. It's good to see you—"

"Good to see you, too, Fel," he said.

"—*particularly* after the sound thrashing I gave you during drills. I feared you might be confined to bed."

Syd's usually placid eyes sparkled with sudden interest. He gave Brock a pitying look.

"I think *sound thrashing* is overstating it a little," Brock said defensively.

"Possibly," Fel said. "The human language does have *so* many subtleties."

He gave her a sidelong look, uncertain whether she was teasing him. The more time they spent together, the more she seemed to be picking up his sarcastic sense of humor.

He didn't *love* being on the receiving end of it.

"Ah, good, you're all here," Hexam said, emerging from the hallway. "Come on. Everything's set up, and time's short today. I was supposed to be at the tower hours ago."

Brock and the others followed the archivist to his laboratory, a room warded with cold and lined with bottles. Those bottles contained a gruesome array of monster viscera: eyeballs and teeth and wet, pulpy organs of every color. While the trophy wall outside presented stuffed and sterile mementos of great battles, these trophies were more honest. An adventurer's work was bloody and violent, and every fallen Danger was a potential resource to be harvested.

In the center of the room, upon a gleaming table, was the mindtooth. Or rather, what was left of it.

Hexam clucked his tongue as if in disapproval. "Young Liza certainly did a number on this thing," he said.

"I'll be sure to pass on the compliment," Brock said.

Hexam cleared his throat. "In any event, the mindtooth is quite *malleable*, physically. Or squishy. No bones to break. The pieces we're interested in should be intact, or close enough." He tossed a pair of gloves at Syd, who caught them handily. "*Don't* touch it with your bare skin. Especially not the pink mucus."

"Words to live by," said Syd.

Brock drifted over to the podium that held Hexam's book. It was open to a labeled illustration of a mindtooth. "So they're mostly . . . goop. Are they related to that ooze that tried to eat Zed?"

"Or to grisly gullets?" asked Fel. "The tentacles are familiar."

"You'd be surprised how common tentacles are among Dangers," Hexam said. "They must be a *very* useful adaptation across several planes." He took a knife to the creature and made a careful incision. "The mindtooth is a native of Astra, just like the oozes and the slimes. And they all thrive in damp underground environments. But the mindtooth is a psychic parasite—quite unlike the slimes and oozes, whose appetites are of a more physical nature."

"Speaking of appetites," Brock said, "I think I'll be skipping lunch." But he craned his head around Fel for a better look. While Syd peeled back the top layer of the creature's gelatinous skin, Hexam was using the tip of his knife to root around its insides. "What are you looking for?"

"Well," said Hexam. "I just said that mindteeth are from Astra, but that's only half-true. The Day of Dangers was two hundred years ago—and mindteeth don't live nearly so long. That means that this specimen should have been born not in Astra but on Terryn."

"I follow you so far," Brock said.

"We actually know quite a bit about mindteeth," said Hexam. "Because the Champion Zahira encountered them before the Day of Dangers. She wrote about them. And I've read all her surviving works. Ah, here we are!"

Hexam made a deft movement with his blade, then used his fingers to remove a small pink sac from within the mindtooth.

"Is that its stomach?" Fife asked.

"Yes . . . no. Sort of." Hexam placed the sac upon the table. "A mindtooth doesn't eat in a traditional sense, but it has to . . . well, *gnaw* its way through its victim's cranium. It drills a small hole right through the skull. And this organ holds whatever pieces of bone, hair, or fabric it swallows in its effort to get at a brain."

Brock's mouth went dry. "So there's pieces of the dead magus in there?"

"Well, yes, but . . ." Hexam hesitated. "They're very *small* pieces."

Sensing his distress, Fel put a steadying hand on Brock's shoulder. "Let's just get this over with," she suggested.

"As you say." Hexam took his knife to the organ. He pulled out several fragments of bone, a clump of gray hair, and . . . fur.

"There you have it," Hexam said, rubbing the fur between his gloved fingers. "I'm *certain* that's animal fur. And based on everything we know of Astra, while it is a plane of innumerable, unfathomable horrors, one thing it does not have . . . is furry mammals."

"So this mindtooth has been feeding in the woods," said Fel. "It came from outside the wall."

"And Magus Phylo *didn't* summon it here directly from Astra," Brock added.

"So it appears." Hexam sighed. "I'm not sure what I hoped for. But this is troubling news. The wards should have made this impossible."

Brock said, "Hexam, that must mean—"

The archivist held out a slimy hand. "Let's save the conjecture. We can point fingers *after* we've made sure there aren't any more of these things out there." He pulled off his gloves. "Syd, can you handle the rest of the procedure? That mucus is a key ingredient in a cure for migraines."

"You can count on me," said Syd, and he set immediately to his task.

Brock whispered to Fel, "I would have said: *'s not* a problem."

"Brock, Fel," Hexam said. "Fetch some salt from the kitchen. It'll instantly dry up whatever's left of the carcass and make it safe to discard." The man paused halfway through the door. He rubbed something between his fingers. Brock realized it was one of the small fragments of bone—perhaps all that was left, at this point, of Master Curse.

"On second thought, let's just have Zed incinerate the thing," Hexam said darkly. "It killed thirteen people. Snuffed them out as if they were nothing." He frowned. "The least we can do is return the favor."

Chapter Seven

Zed

"Hey Zed, remember that time you dressed all in black to sneak out of the guildhall? After the king put us under house arrest? I always wondered . . . where did you even *get* an entirely black outfit?"

Micah gently shut the door to Hexam's office behind him, cutting the warm ribbon of sunlight away. The room fell into darkness. Hexam and the others would be down in the dissection chamber for a while yet, so even after bathing and dressing and scoping out the halls, Micah had plenty of time to snoop.

"*I got most of it from Brock.*" Zed smiled, remembering. "*But he banned me from touching his socks again after the alphabetizing incident, so I borrowed those from Jett.*"

"Why does no one remember?" Foster groused. *"Even if you respond, he won't hear it!"*

"I don't think that's the point." Zed billowed into the murky room, reconstituting beside an enormous stack of books. *"Micah's nervous. He's babbling. Me too, I guess."*

"Well, I wish you'd babble silently. Makiva knows something is wrong. We'll need absolute stealth and subtlety from here on out."

A flash of brilliance suddenly illuminated the office, waves of golden light spilling from Micah's raised palm.

"Oh, for—!" Foster sputtered a string of curses that would have normally set Zed's ears ablaze. Zed distracted himself by taking in the refurbished space.

After the locustrix attack the previous season, Hexam had rebuilt what he could of the office and classroom, but some of the destroyed items had been harder to replace. Thankfully, most of the wizard's books survived; almost all the lovely, magically glowing orbs had been shattered, however, and the Danger skulls were pulverized to flakes of bone.

What remained after the cleanup was a desk scattered with papers, three uncomfortable-looking chairs, and a row of simple storage chests.

That and books. A wall of them loomed just beyond the desk, stacked in chaotic rows that switched from vertical to horizontal without any system or pattern that Zed could suss out.

He frowned at the titles on the spines as Micah approached, bringing the light with him.

"If last night was just a crazy dream," Micah said, "I'm going to feel really dumb for every part of today." Then the healer snickered. "Though it *was* fun to see Liza get pelted with chicken skin."

Micah scanned the weighty-looking tomes. "*Math and Mana*—blugh; *Memoirs of a Magus: Zahira's Story*—pass; *Insidious Predators: Vampires, Werewolves, and Djinn, the Dangers Among*— Fie, this is the longest title ever."

The fox leaped onto Hexam's desk. Foster puffed a gout of smoke, then swallowed it back up. "*Can't he hurry this along?*"

Zed perked up. "*I think I see one!*" He waved his ghostly hand in front of a spine bound in black leather. "*Micah, look here! It's right over here!*"

"*No one ever listens to me,*" Foster muttered. "*Even the ones who* can *hear me. Zed, he won't*—"

"What's this?" Micah reached forward with his glowing hand. His light-etched fingers passed through Zed's to the black book.

Zed raised a brow at the fox, but Foster just rolled his slitted eyes. "*Coincidence.*"

Micah pulled the book free, frowning down at the title. "*Rituals of Banishment and Purification,*" he read. "Well, that sounds creepy but promising."

Micah carried the tome over to Hexam's desk and sat down, the two spirits crowding invisibly at his shoulders. He leafed through the table of contents, pointing a glowing finger to highlight the text as he read. "Possessions and exorcisms, page six sixty-six. A little on the nose, but fine."

Micah flipped through the pages, more roughly than Zed was comfortable with, until he found the passage. "Once a Danger is summoned to Terryn, banishment to its home plane is impossible . . . blah, blah, blah . . . something about the Veil between worlds . . . et cetera, et cetera. Here we go . . . fiends, fey, shadows, undead . . . possession by witches and warlocks!"

Micah's eyes grew wide. "Oh. Oh, wow. Zed, if you're really here, let me just say you are one lucky ghost. 'Exorcisms of this kind are best carried out by the hand of a skilled *healer*, rather than a mage. Being magically repellent, combining the mana of Fey and Fie is ineffective at best and potentially deadly for the host at worst. *Anima*, however, can safely purge a body of harmful magic, depending on the strength of the healer versus the strength of the spell.' "

Micah punched his glowing fist into his palm, cracking glittery knuckles. "So, all I have to do is fight fire with anima? I'm practically the best healer in Freestone! This'll be over before supper."

"*This sounds dangerous.*" Zed glanced at Foster. "*Isn't using too much anima . . . Can't it hurt the healer?*"

The fox's eyes moved rapidly across the page, gleaning what he could before Micah slammed the book shut and tossed it nonchalantly back to the pile.

"*Zed, this is more than dangerous,*" Foster warned. "*It's suicidal. Makiva is centuries old. Perhaps older. And she's consumed the magical potential of every one of her apprentices.*"

As Micah strutted across the room to the door, the fox's slitted eyes met Zed's, practically glowing with fear. *"She's going to destroy that boy."*

✷

"Zed! Oh, Zed-dy!" Micah made his way through the guildhall, shouting as he went.

Zed floated after him, trying in vain to warn the healer, but there was no way to break through until Micah fell asleep. He could only follow with growing dread as Micah rounded the corner from Hexam's office . . .

. . . to where the imposter stood alone in a dark, narrow hallway.

Zed and Foster both screeched at Makiva's sudden appearance, but Micah was unfazed. "Just the guy I was looking for," he announced cheerfully.

A smirk curled the corner of Zed's mouth. The imposter stood totally still on the other end of the hall, Zed's hands hanging limp at his sides. It was almost like Makiva had been waiting for them. Or searching.

"Hello, Micah."

For the first time since reading Hexam's book, Micah seemed to hesitate. He frowned suspiciously, then jutted out his chin. "I'm making the rounds today, healing the injured and tending to the clumsy. All that good stuff. Lotte mentioned you got hurt in the mindtooth attack. She told me to fix you up."

"Did she?" Zed's voice was empty of inflection or emotion. Makiva simply watched Micah, her gaze never straying to the spirits cowering nearby.

"Yup! Dolt's orders. So, get on over here." Micah held out his hand, which shimmered with amber light. Waves of liquid gold washed across the hall. "We'll get you sorted out in no time."

"Afraid I don't need sorting, Micah." Now the imposter narrowed his eyes. "Thanks, but no thanks."

"Afraid *I'm* going to have to insist, little guy." Micah took a step forward. The swells of light lapped toward Makiva like a grasping hand. "Gotta keep in practice, you know?"

Now Makiva's gaze finally shifted. She looked right at Zed, the imposter's expression curious. "Micah, just leave me a—"

Makiva didn't get a chance to finish. Micah surged forward, charging the imposter with all the strength and speed of a boy who'd once been a shoo-in for the Knights Guild. He grabbed Zed's body by the tunic, slamming him so hard against the wall that Zed heard the breath leaving his own lungs.

"*Oof.*" Foster flinched, the fox's tail batting to the side. "*Good thing you're not in there, huh?*"

"Sorry," Micah said. "But it's for your own good." Then he placed his glowing palm right on Zed's forehead.

Zed had seen Micah do some incredible things with the healing power of his anima. He'd illuminated pitch-black dungeons and stitched together adventurers who'd suffered grievous injuries. He'd punched through *ghosts*—the life-giving properties of anima dissolving their undead energies until there was nothing left.

This, by far, was the most powerful burst of anima Micah had ever produced. The light was overwhelming, filling the hallway like a newborn sun. It spilled through the guildhall windows, illuminating even the late-afternoon streets below. Zed and Foster both gasped as the anima passed through them. Though still in his smoky body, Zed could feel something like *warmth* rippling across his form.

Several moments of incandescent blindness passed, during which Zed could see neither Micah nor the imposter.

Then he heard a voice, low and strange.

How dare you?

The quality of the light shifted, yellow-gold curdling into eerie green. Micah gasped, and the radiance dimmed suddenly, like a snuffed candle. Peering forward, Zed saw his own face twisted in rage, his brown irises ringed in fiery emerald. Micah hissed in pain. He was covered in sweat and his eyes looked sunken, like he hadn't slept in days.

"How *dare* you!" Makiva shouted. She lifted Zed's hand, the air around it blistering with heat.

Then the look of fury faded, just as quickly as the light had dimmed, and in its place Zed saw his own eyes go wide with fear. They were pointed straight at him.

"Brock!" the imposter screamed. "Brock, help me!"

"What in Fie is going on here?" Brock's voice bellowed from behind Zed. Apparently, the dissection of the mindtooth had gone faster than anticipated. "Get *off* of him!"

Zed's smoky form shivered as his best friend barreled through him, knocking Micah away from the imposter. Having used so much anima, Micah simply fell back against the far wall, then crumpled to the floor. Dark circles ringed his eyes.

"He just attacked me!" the imposter cried as Brock helped steady him. "He kept rambling about healing me, though I told him I was fine, and then he pinned me to the wall!"

"Micah, what is *wrong* with you?" Now Liza had entered, too, blurring past Zed and Foster, then Brock and the imposter. She stood over her brother, hands on her hips. "You nearly killed yourself over a prank?"

"A *prank*?" Brock said hotly. "He just assaulted Zed! I'll tell you what's wrong with Micah: He's a bully! And he's done nothing but torment Zed since the first day they met. That ends *now*."

"No!" Micah protested, but his voice was weak. "You don't understand. I'm trying to *help* Zed."

"Help him how, Micah?" Liza asked. She shook her head, frowning at the imposter. "He's fine. He was probably the least hurt of us all yesterday. You needed to blind the whole guild just to heal a day-old nosebleed?"

Micah opened his mouth but faltered. He chewed on his lip.

"I'm not . . . I'm not a bully. Maybe I was. Maybe I . . . deserved . . . but Zed—!"

"Stay. Away. From Zed." Brock thrust his finger at the healer like a dagger. "Because if I hear one more time that you've so much as looked at him wrong, we're going to have big problems. Come on, buddy."

Brock took the imposter's hand, leading him out of the hall the way they'd come. As she passed, Makiva's gaze flicked briefly toward Zed. A look of cold amusement touched her expression.

Liza sighed at her brother. "You picked a really bad time to pull this stunt," she said. "We're going out beyond the wall tomorrow at first light, to search for more mindteeth." When she reached a hand down to him, Micah took it, rising shakily to his feet. But he still leaned against the wall.

"Liza, you've got to believe me. I wasn't trying to hurt Zed."

Liza shook her head a second time, puzzling over her brother as if he were a bad combat strategy she couldn't seem to solve. "Micah, if something's going on, you know you can tell me, right? I'm your sister, not your enemy. I still love you, despite sifting through years of your attitude."

"*Tell her,*" Zed urged.

And just as he said it, Micah's head lurched in his direction. The healer's eyes widened, darting back and forth between Zed and the fox at his side.

Beside Zed, Foster gasped. "*Wait. Did he hear you? Can he see us?*"

Slowly, Liza followed her brother's gaze, her eyes passing sightlessly over Zed. "What?" she asked. "What is it?"

"You don't—you really don't see—?" Micah laughed deliriously. "Of course not. Of course it's just me."

"Micah, you're scaring me."

The healer laughed a second time, but now he just sounded weary. "Sorry, sis. I'm a bit worn out is all. Brock was right. I was being a jerk. Again." Micah lurched forward, wobbling away from Liza's steady arm. "I know, I know. I shouldn't waste my anima."

This time, when he found Zed's eyes, some of the old bluster was back. "I'll be more careful from now on."

✷

"Why are you being so careful all of a sudden?!"

Zed paced back and forth in Micah's room while the healer pushed piles of laundry aside in his slow march toward bed. *"Now that you can actually see me, we should tell the others. Then we can all form a plan to stop Makiva* together*!"*

Though the exorcism had failed, it *had* resulted in this happy accident of magic and healing. At first, Zed had been elated. He'd followed Micah through the guildhall, dancing and singing as the boy trudged sluggishly toward the barracks, crooning such ballads as *"You can see me, you can see me"* and *"Not alone anymo-o-ore."*

On the way, Zed tried calling out to the other adventures they passed, just to see if anyone else had been affected, but no one responded to his hails.

Soon, however, elation gave way to distress, when Zed realized this hadn't actually changed anything for Micah.

"In case you've forgotten the extremely recent past," Micah said, "I just poured so much anima into your pointy-eared head that it nearly killed me, and all I got for it was a scolding. That, and perhaps the most musical poltergeist of all time." Micah collapsed into his bed. His skin was pale and drawn, and the dark circles under his eyes had only intensified. "Even if I told Brock now, he'd never listen to me."

"*Likely it would just result in a worse confrontation,*" Foster agreed. "*And alert Makiva to our one advantage.*" The fox watched from the room's far corner, giving Zed a wide berth as he paced.

Zed glowered at him. "*So we tell someone else. Start with Liza, or even Frond.*"

"*Liza's too responsible,*" the fox said. "*She'd definitely go to Frond with the news. And Frond would go to the king; even her protective impulses have limits.*" Foster shook his canine head. "*Micah's right. We need to be careful, now more than ever. If Makiva feels truly threatened, she'll bring the whole guild down around her before she relinquishes you. Whatever her game is, she's deadly serious about winning.*"

"*Well then, what are we* supposed *to do?*" Zed cried. "*Just let her kill more people?*"

He turned to Micah for help, only to find the boy was already asleep. Micah looked about as drained as Zed had ever seen him. His breath was weak and uneven, and his dark hair lay matted to his forehead.

"We regroup tomorrow," Foster said gently. *"Zed, I know it's frustrating. I* do. *But we've done something today that I thought was impossible. It gives us an edge while we seek out a weakness."*

Zed shook his head. He couldn't believe this! Two allies, and neither of them was willing to press their advantage. He billowed out of the room without another word, leaving Foster among the piles of dirty laundry.

He spent the rest of the night alone, calling to Frond and his friends as they slept. None responded.

Chapter Eight
Brock

Winter had been short but brutal, and Brock was glad to see color returning to the hills and forest outside the city. Gone was the grim, endless white of the previous season, replaced by a sweeping view of green in dozens of shades for as far as the eye could see. Patches of new grass, wet with dew or snow-melt, stretched to cover the expanse of dirt that lay between Freestone and the tree line; verdant blades stabbed right through the cracked cobbles of the Broken Roads. Leaves of emerald and olive had sprouted from all the trees of the forest, and new flowers grew at the base of Freestone's great wall, their buds still closed against the chill air even as their stalks strained for the sun.

It looked like spring was here to stay. It wasn't unheard of, however, for a late-season freeze to descend, forcing Freestoners to retrieve the winter cloaks they'd only just stashed away. A minor inconvenience for people; but if the snow returned now, the new plant life beyond the wall would wither and die, flowers wilting away before they'd even had a chance to bloom.

Brock thought his friends had too much in common with those vulnerable flowers, and he frowned at the morbid thought.

"Are you scowling at flowers now?" Liza asked. "Is anyone really that grumpy? Next you'll be kicking puppies."

His frown curled up at the corners. "I might. Anything on this side of the wall falls under my 'kick first, ask questions later' policy."

Liza grinned back at him. "Present company excluded, I hope."

"Nope!" he said brightly. "But I assumed that's why you wear the armor."

Liza really did look more like a proper knight all the time. Aside from occasional patrols outside the wall, an apprentice's main duty in the Sea of Stars was to train. Brock had never been so fit in his life, but even he cringed at the thought of wearing as much metal as Liza did. His own armor—a mismatched set of brown, black, red, and green leathers sourced from natural animals and Dangers alike—probably weighed a quarter of what Liza's chain-mail shirt, pauldrons, and steel greaves did. But then, Liza tended to confront monsters head-on. Brock preferred to sneak up unseen behind them.

The rest of the apprentices were stepping through the door set into the base of the wall, the one that allowed adventurers to come and go without having the Stone Sons raise Freestone's massive portcullis. Micah looked pointedly at Brock, clearly remembering yesterday's encounter. Good. Brock had meant what he said, and he had no desire to repeat himself.

Zed, meanwhile, didn't even seem to register Brock's presence. He walked alongside the others, but his eyes were unfocused, his mind gone to wherever it wandered these days. Beside him was Jett, his expression solemn and his hefty hammer already in his hands. They all took missions beyond the wall seriously, but none more than the dwarf, who had been gravely injured on their very first. Jayna was running through a series of finger stretches that Hexam had assigned her. They looked so ridiculous, Brock would be sure the assignment was some kind of practical joke, if not for the fact that Hexam had rarely exhibited anything like a sense of humor. Nirav watched her, trailing behind her like a lost puppy. Of all of them, only Fel was smiling, tilting her head back and grinning into the sunlight.

"*Astrella limae*," she spoke to the air. "It's so good to be outside once more!"

Mousebane, Fel's scraggly cat, peeked out from behind her legs and produced a strange and horrible mewling noise. It set Brock's teeth on edge.

Fel laughed. "And it's wonderful to see Mousebane so happy!"

Brock and Liza shared an amused look. That was the cat's *happy* sound?

"All right, eyes up here," Frond commanded, and the dozen conversations going on around her fell instantly silent. More than half the guild was present, and they made a sharp contrast with the Stone Sons watching from atop the wall. At this distance, the knights appeared identical in their regulation armor, swords sheathed at their hips. The adventurers, on the other hand, were an ill-matched jumble, each dressed in his or her own style and wielding swords, maces, bows, lances, and, in one case, a thorned whip.

"The plan for today is reconnaissance only," Frond said. "For the thickheaded among you, that means *look* but don't *touch*. Of course, like all plans, this one is likely to fall apart like a handful of week-old manticore dung."

Brock sighed loudly at her choice of imagery, and Liza elbowed him.

Frond rooted through a canvas sack hanging from her belt, producing a brilliant ruby. "Lucky us, babysitting the mages comes with some perks. Hexam sent these over from the tower. Distress gems. If you get into trouble, throw one on the ground and a flare will go up. If you see a flare, run toward it with your favorite weapon. Lotte?" She made a sucking sound with her teeth, then turned and spat into the dirt.

Lotte shuffled forward. Her outfit was like a blend of elements from Brock's and Liza's: full-body leathers accented with heavy steel gauntlets and pauldrons. "Hexam wants us checking every cave and hollow within a few miles of town," she said. "These are caves we clear out periodically, but anything might have moved in since our last visit. Today we're specifically looking for evidence of a mindtooth nest. It shouldn't be hard to identify. Mindteeth without a host need ample moisture to survive, so they produce a thick rose-hued mucus which doubles as a paralyzing agent." Her pauldrons clinked as she shrugged. "So we're looking for . . . caves dripping with poisonous pink slime, basically."

"Again," Frond said, "if at all possible, you are to avoid engagement. Look for the pretty snot, then retreat and report back. Do not *touch* or *eat* the snot. That should go without saying, but unfortunately some of you can't seem to help yourselves from licking monster goop."

"That was *one* time!" Fife protested. "And it was on a dare!"

"To be very clear," Syd added, "I dared him *not* to lick it."

Frond grunted, and Lotte stepped forward again. "If a mindtooth gets ahold of you, you'll have just moments before it penetrates your skull, at which point the damage is done." Her eyes cut to Syd and Fife. "Please, no jokes about thick skulls. Even steel helms don't offer much in the way of resistance against this thing's tongue. That means you need to be aware of your surroundings and ready to stab, slash, or smash it if it comes within reach of you or your teammate."

"But only if it comes within reach," Frond added. "Its psychic attack has a range of about ten longswords, so avoid getting any closer than that."

"A longsword is *not* a recognized unit of measurement," Brock said, and Liza shushed him instantly.

"We'll break up into teams," said Lotte. "I'll come by with your assignments . . . as well as an extra treat from the kitchens, courtesy of Brock and Fel."

Jett chuckled. "Baked us cookies, did you?" he asked.

"It's way better than that," Brock promised, and Fel bounced excitedly on her toes.

"Micah, are you sure you're up for this?" Liza asked. "You still don't look very good."

"I'm fine," Micah said. But Liza was right. Micah looked drawn and pale, as if he hadn't slept at all.

"Looks like a guilty conscience to me," Brock whispered to Zed. "But just steer clear of him as much as possible."

"I will." Zed smiled. "Thanks again for having my back, Brock."

"Always," Brock said. He saw Nirav standing off alone, hovering halfway between the apprentices and Syd and Fife. Brock felt a stab of gratitude to have such a steadfast friendship.

"I can't take the suspense, though," Zed said, turning to

include Fel in their conversation. "What's the surprise you two came up with?"

"Well," Fel began, "it has to do with what we learned about mindteeth yesterday." She took a step toward Zed.

Mousebane suddenly fluffed up and bared her teeth, hissing with startling intensity. The cat leaped from Fel's feet to lunge at Zed, who flinched back, but too slowly. Mousebane's outstretched claws raked across his forearm.

Fel shouted and reached for the cat. Brock nearly fell back in surprise. And Zed–

Zed snarled, his face twisting with fury. It was almost unrecognizable to Brock–in all their years of friendship, he'd never seen Zed so angry.

By now Fel had Mousebane in her arms, though the cat writhed against her fiercely before finally submitting. "I'm sorry, Zed," she said miserably. "I don't know what got into her."

"Are . . . are you all right, Zed?" Brock asked.

Zed seemed to come back to himself. He blinked hard a few times and gripped his forearm. "I'm okay," he said. "Man, that hurt!" He chuckled.

"What in the reeking realm of Fie is going on here?" Frond commanded, suddenly looming over them.

"Nothing," Brock answered.

"Then why is Zed bleeding?"

Brock took another look. Sure enough, where Zed gripped his injured forearm, blood was seeping between his fingers.

"It was an accident," said Liza. "Micah will have him fixed up in no time."

"Who, me?" Micah said. "Sorry, sis. I'm under strict orders to leave him alone." He looked pointedly at Brock. "I wouldn't want there to be *problems*."

Brock expected Frond to put Micah in his place, but she only narrowed her eyes and considered him in silence.

Fine. Brock would do it, then. "Seriously, Micah?" he said. "Maybe just *once* you could shut your mouth and try to make something better instead of making it worse?"

Micah snorted. "You don't know the first thing about me, you slippery little windbag."

"Ah, children," Frond mused. "So like Dangers, except I'm not allowed to stab you."

"Verbal abuse is generally frowned upon, too," Brock said.

"It builds character," countered the guildmaster. "So does breaking out of familiar routines. I want the lot of you to spread out among more experienced adventurers today."

"But–" Brock began.

"But, Guildmistress," Liza said, cutting Brock off and shooting him a look. *I'll handle this.* "We've been training as a team, and–"

"Your team is currently dysfunctional," Frond said flatly. "And we don't take chances out here. Tomorrow you will get your act together. Today you'll split up." Her eyes passed over the group. "Zed, you're with me. Maybe we'll get lucky and find something to set on fire."

Zed smirked, rubbing his fingertips together like kindling. "I live to serve."

*

After all this time as an adventurer, Brock still hated to be separated from Zed.

Not so long ago, that had mostly been out of an impulse to protect his friend. He'd been forced to accept, however, that Zed was in fact a formidable sorcerer. It was a complicated idea to wrap his head around. Zed was still the weakest member of their team in many respects. Yet from another perspective, he was the most powerful. There were very few Dangers that could withstand that green flame of his, and Brock liked to keep an advantage like that where it could do him the most good.

Frond had seen fit to separate them, however, so Brock now found himself stepping off the Broken Roads and into the thick of the forest alongside Jett and four journey-rank adventurers. They were led by a sour man who went by the nickname Clobbler. He almost made Frond seem pleasant by comparison, but in Brock's first few weeks with the guild, he had befriended the man by playing cards with him.

In truth, Clobbler was terrible at cards. In order to get on his good side, Brock had been obligated to lose several games on purpose, which had actually taken a good deal of cunning—it wasn't easy to throw a game without being obvious. He didn't mind. When forced to fight monsters, befriending the biggest, scariest human around felt like a smart move.

At that moment, the big, scary human in question twirled his index finger in the air, a gesture that meant he'd heard something up ahead. Then he waved Brock forward.

Brock looked over his shoulder. He pointed to himself. *Me?* he mouthed.

Clobbler's next gesture was impossible to misunderstand, and quite rude.

Brock crept reluctantly to the front of the column.

"You recognize that thing?" Clobbler whispered.

Brock peered through the branches. They were budding with small leaves, but still bare enough to allow him a good view across the forest. He knew that worked both ways, though, so he kept himself as still as possible.

There was a large creature directly ahead of them, many yards away but standing squarely between them and the cave they were meant to be exploring. It resembled, in most ways, a bear, with mangy brown fur and short, powerfully built limbs. But around its neck was a tufty mane of feathers, and its head had many bird-like features—not least of which was its razor-sharp, hooked bill.

"It's a beakbear," Brock whispered. "They're dangerous and tough, but slow."

"Dangerous how?"

"Sharp claws," Brock answered. "Sharper beak."

Clobbler inclined his chin at the woman beside him. "Eyva, get your crossbow ready," he said. "Sounds like we're better off attacking at range."

Eyva nodded, sheathing her shortsword and shrugging the crossbow off her back. "Do they travel in packs?" she asked.

Brock wracked his brain for more details from Hexam's book. "No. There could be a baby in the cave, but they're mostly solitary hunters. And nocturnal. They've got amazing vision, but bright light can easily daze them."

"What's *nocturnal* mean?" asked Clobbler.

"It means . . . huh. It means they only come out at night." Brock furrowed his brow. "That's weird . . ."

Brock considered the beakbear once more. Now that he thought of it, the creature didn't look particularly healthy. Its fur was patchy, revealing pale skin at the creature's joints and along its back. When it took a step forward, it stumbled, and it appeared to be drooling from its slack beak.

"I think it's sick," Brock whispered. "We shouldn't take anything for granted. Sick creatures can be more dangerous than usual."

"Or more vulnerable," Clobbler said. "We need to get in that cave, and the longer we wait here, the more likely something else with claws comes along and makes it a real party."

"Reinforcements?" Eyva suggested.

"I don't think we'll need 'em," Clobbler said. "But just in

case . . ." He pulled the ensorcelled ruby from his pocket and handed it to Brock. "Daggers won't be much good against that thing. I don't want you kids anywhere near it. But you call for help if things go poorly."

Eyva loaded a bolt in her bow. "Normally I'd suggest we could use the pelt," she said. "But not if it's diseased."

"Right," said Clobbler. "I'll get close and make some noise. With luck, it's skittish and it'll run off. If it comes at me, you put it down."

"Will do," Eyva said.

Brock was impressed. Clobbler's card skills didn't paint him as a strategist, but he supposed no adventurer made it far without learning their way around a battle plan. He rubbed his thumb over the ruby, feeling the weight of the responsibility Clobbler was giving to him. He looked to Eyva, who appeared apprehensive but nodded in agreement with the plan.

"Stay here and stay quiet," Clobbler ordered, and he crept through the undergrowth, moving around to the beakbear's far side before stepping into the clearing.

"Hey, you!" he said, waving his arms. "Know what you get when you cross an ugly animal with a *very* ugly animal?"

The beakbear turned toward him, cocking its head. Eyva held her crossbow up, locking the creature in her sights. Brock held his breath, waiting to see whether it would charge or flee. But the beakbear stayed where it was, the drool dripping from its beak looking thick and ruddy, almost like . . . like pink slime . . .

A series of ripples ran across the beakbear's body, like a nest of writhing snakes just beneath its skin. Then a fleshy tendril tore through its back, ripping a hole that widened as it lashed about in the air. More tendrils followed, and within seconds the beakbear's skin had sloughed off completely, falling to the ground in bloodless tatters of flesh, fur, and feather. The skeleton remained, held together not with muscle or sinew, but with a translucent, undulating mass of slime. Eyeballs floated atop the gelatinous mass, more than a dozen of them, no rhyme or reason to their placement, and a mass of pink tendrils whipped about it, groping and grasping at the empty air.

Clobbler went suddenly taut, and Brock thought the man was preparing to run. But instead his eyes rolled back, he foamed at the mouth, and then he collapsed to the ground.

"No!" Eyva screamed.

And then the thing's many eyeballs shifted onto them.

"Back!" Brock said. "Fall back! We're too close!"

"Move it, kid!" one of the adventurers cried, shoving Jett farther from harm.

Eyva didn't listen. She loaded her crossbow and sent a bolt soaring. It pierced an eyeball, then traveled through the slimy mass, between two ribs, and out the creature's back. Ooze rushed in to fill the hole as quickly as she'd made it.

Brock pulled at her arm. "It's a score of mindteeth all piled up on top of each other," he said. "You don't have enough bolts to hurt it."

"Watch me," she said, and she tore from his grip to load another bolt. Brock knew that she was lost; she would die here, fighting this Danger, before she would turn and retreat to safety.

But they had a secret weapon. The idea he and Fel had come up with.

He looked at the strips of beakbear flesh the mindteeth had left behind. The remains were leeched completely of any blood, any moisture at all.

"We have to dry it out," he said. He pulled a small sack from his belt, pouring its contents onto the ground. "We have to use the salt!"

He took a bolt from Eyva's quiver, doused it in oil, then rolled it around in the pile of small white crystals.

"Use this," he said, shoving it at Eyva. Her nose had begun to trickle blood. "Use it now!" he cried.

She loaded the bolt and sent it flying right into the creature's center. Where it impacted, the pink ooze turned brown and brittle, flaking away in solid clumps. Now she'd put a proper hole in it.

Brock prepared another bolt, and another. With the fourth hit, the creature doubled over so suddenly, Brock could see the spinal column break in two. Tendrils waving uselessly, bones pulling apart and twisting, the gelatinous mass lost its shape and slumped to the ground.

Brock pulled Eyva back, and this time she didn't resist. "It could still be dangerous," he said. "We don't know if some of them are still alive."

"You know what they say," drawled the adventurer who had shoved Jett to safety. He held up a lit torch. "When in doubt, burn it beyond recognition."

"Nobody says that," Brock said. "Do they?"

The man smirked. "They will now."

*

Brock felt the mindteeth die. As the fire engulfed them and those slashing, swaying tendrils fell still, the Dangers cried out with a sound beyond hearing, a cry he felt at the base of his skull and in his molars. It lasted only a moment and was gone.

He couldn't feel sorry for it. The creature had snuffed out a man's life with as little thought as it took Brock to blink, and twice as fast.

"Poor Clobbler," he said sadly.

"His name was Justyn," Eyva said, her voice thick with emotion. "He was a good man."

"We'll bring him home, Eyva," said another adventurer. "A hero's pyre for our Justyn."

Brock grabbed Jett by the elbow. "I need to talk to you," he whispered.

Jett nodded, and he followed Brock a short way back into the trees.

"Before Clobbler—*Justyn* put himself in harm's way, he gave me the distress gem," Brock said, keeping his voice low. "He told me to use it if I thought we needed help."

"Brock," Jett said. He shook his head. "You can't blame yourself for what happened."

"I'm not," Brock replied. He pointed at his feet, and the dwarf looked down into the dirt. It took him only a moment to spot the ruby.

"I called for help," Brock said. "Immediately. But it didn't work. The gem is a dud."

Jett's eyes went wide. He kicked at the jewel. Poked it with his hammer. Nothing happened.

"I'm not blaming myself, no," Brock said. "But someone *is* to blame. And I'm going to make them sorry."

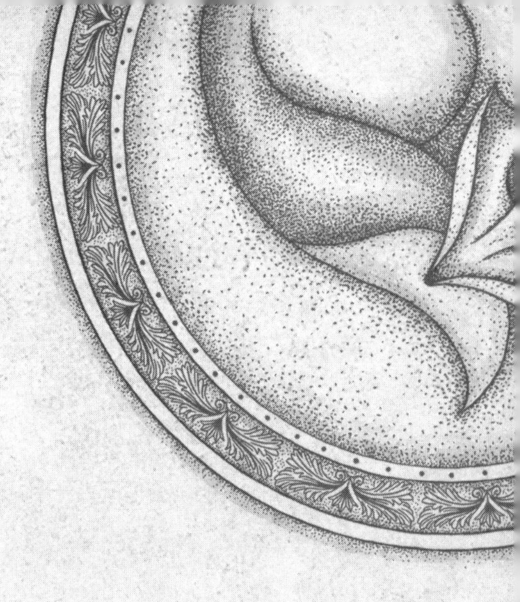

Chapter Nine
Zed

Zed trailed Makiva, watching as the imposter followed behind Frond.

The two adventurers were alone in the woods, far from the city and out of sight of their nearest guildmates. This section of the forest was crowded with caves, so Frond had broken the groups into smaller pairs, though they all clung within a relatively tight radius. Frond's eyes were narrowed on the trees, alert for any signs of approaching trouble. She had no sense of the trouble ambling yards behind her.

If there was ever a moment to strike against the guildmistress, this would be it. And Zed would be powerless to stop it.

Only Micah could see or hear him, and he *still* refused to alert the others to Zed's possession.

Zed had tried to give both Micah and Foster the silent treatment that morning, but having had no one else to talk to for weeks, he'd broken fairly quickly. Instead, he spent the early hours pestering Micah to alert the others. Micah pointedly ignored him.

Now there was nothing Zed could do but watch as the witch who'd ended the world sneered at Frond with *his* lips.

"*I don't like that look,*" Foster said gravely beside him. "*Makiva's up to something.*"

With Micah out of sight, the warlock had returned to his elf-blooded form. They'd decided to keep it quiet that Zed's ghostly conspirator was the Traitor of Freestone—at least for the moment. Foster passed himself off to Micah as Zed's "spirit guide." The idea sounded flimsy to Zed, but thankfully Micah was almost supernaturally uncurious about the supernatural.

Zed thought the edges of Foster's smoky body looked particularly unraveled this morning. Twice he noticed lines of mist sifting away from the spirit, like ribbons of smoke from an extinguished candle. He remembered the two witches before them who'd eventually dissipated to nothing, and felt a spark of fear.

"*Foster, maybe you should stay in your fox shape,*" he suggested in a whisper, "*if it's easier to hold together.*"

The warlock glanced down at his sleeve in time to see a small line billowing away. "*Fie,*" he breathed. "*You may be right. I haven't been this active in decades. I blame you, of course."* But Foster's expression was appreciative as he transformed, the mist curdling into a smaller canine shape. "*Thanks for the warning.*"

Zed nodded, and they hurried after Frond and Makiva.

The guildmistress held her sword loosely, tilted from her side at an almost casual angle. But there was nothing casual about her gaze as she scanned the forest for Dangers. She'd given Hexam's warning crystal to the imposter Zed, while she led the way to their assigned cavern.

"Stay close," Frond muttered. "And keep that green fire ready. If we spot a mindtooth, don't approach it. Engage only as a last resort. But if you do, then give it all you've got. No holding back."

The imposter's lips curled upward. "No holding back," Zed's voice echoed.

The hike was long and tense. Though Zed himself was in no peril from any Dangers, he still jumped and twitched at every sound that coughed out from the forest. Twice, Foster had to tell him to be calm. After a time, a cavern finally shouldered into view, crowding between the scant spring buds.

It was little more than a tumble of great stones, its mouth a toothy sneer. With the morning light still so thin, the entrance was cast in shadows too thick to see through.

Frond turned to the imposter skulking several yards behind her. She pressed a finger to her lips, then held out a flat hand. *Stay.* Zed watched himself nod in acknowledgment.

The guildmistress crept closer, as did two smoky shadows—Zed and Foster following behind.

"*Well,*" said Foster in an exaggeratedly loud whisper, "*this is all very exciting, isn't it? Gets the magical smoke pumping. Monstrous horrors ahead, possessed and traitorous apprentices behind—Frond's in quite a fix.*"

"*If you don't have any anything useful to say,*" Zed hissed back, "*then go keep an eye on Makiva.*"

"*Oh, so* now *nervous rambling is a problem,*" the fox muttered. "*You know, this reminds me of the time you went alone into the druids' shrine last summer. I was with you then, too. You couldn't see or hear me, of course, but I cheered you on the whole way. And I had some choice insults for that blob monster. Really devastating stuff.*"

Zed's gaze flicked over to Foster. "*You were there?*"

The fox nodded. "*Of course. No one deserves to die alone. I should know.*"

Frond stopped suddenly, her gray eyes alert. Zed and Foster both snapped their attention to the cave mouth, but Zed couldn't spot any creatures prowling within, or hear any psychic hums. He didn't see anything at all.

Until the shadow fell over Frond.

Frond leaped to the side, just as an enormous shape plummeted from the trees. She curled her shoulder forward, rolling along the forest floor and arriving back on her feet, her sword raised and ready to face—

Zed gasped as he finally got a look at the creature unfurling before them. It had the long, undulating body of a gigantic worm. Its skin was a colorless membrane, beneath which some kind of purple-red liquid churned, looking suspiciously like coagulated blood.

But the Danger's head was the true horror. There its worm-like body bloomed into a flower of violet tentacles, each as thick as a Stone Son's arm. They were all lined with rows of suckers and serrated barbs, and they reached hungrily in Frond's direction, hoping to pull her toward the nest of teeth that awaited within the writhing mass.

Zed knew this creature.

It was perhaps the most infamous breed of Danger in recent Adventurers Guild history, the one that had given Alabasel Frond her distinctive puckered scars. A tentacle just like the ones that now waved before him was mounted in the guildhall. Sometimes adventurers still whispered of the monster that had nearly taken down the great Alabasel Frond back in her prime, years before she became guildmistress.

"A lurker," Zed wheezed. *"Oh no . . ."*

What color had risen to Frond's cheeks immediately fled as she took in the creature before her. Her eyes, usually sharp as throwing knives, went wide and vague. Zed saw her loose grip on her sword clamp suddenly tight. The curved blade trembled in the air.

Frond took a step back. For the first time since Zed had known her, she looked utterly terrified.

And that moment of fear was all the lurker needed.

The Danger shot forward, slithering with shocking speed along the forest floor. Frond thrust her sword out just as a tentacle lashed toward her, the blade making a dull sound as it struck meat.

Frond pulled it free and hopped quickly backward, but the Danger was faster. A second tentacle snapped around her wrist like a bladed whip. The guildmistress screamed, hacking at the tendril just as a third snatched her other forearm. The lurker yanked her arms wide, sending the sword thudding to the ground.

Frond now faced the Danger's maw, surrounded by a halo of slithering tentacles. Her mouth slacked open. Her eyes were wild with panic. "No!" she howled. "No, no! Zed! HELP ME!"

"Help her!" Zed screamed, but Foster only shook his head sadly. His tail was tucked between his legs.

Zed scanned the forest, and soon his eyes landed upon himself. Makiva stood partially obscured behind a tree, smirking as Frond struggled for her life. The red summoning crystal was unbroken in the imposter's hand.

"This can't be happening!" Zed billowed to Frond's side, where the lurker's tentacles snatched at her shoulders and hair. One landed on the side of her face with an awful wet noise. Frond screamed as they began pulling her head toward its puckered mouth.

"Frond, fight it! Fight!"

But the creature was too strong. Though Frond was resisting with everything she had, her face still slid forward. Soon, it was inches away from the lurker's barbed teeth. Zed caught one last glimpse of his guildmistress's eyes—wide and white with animal fear—before the tentacles closed over her head like a grotesque mask.

Then they flew open again.

An arrow pierced the lurker's sinewy body, fired from an unseen assailant. Purple ichor began pouring from the wound, bubbling as it touched the air. A second arrow struck, and the creature's body writhed. Its tentacles released Frond so it could turn and face its attacker.

Zed turned, too, and saw Fel and Micah standing several yards away. Fel was already loosing another arrow, Mousebane hissing at her side.

This time the lurker was too quick. Having surrendered its prey, it contorted its body to dodge the missile with revolting agility. Then it lurched forward to attack.

It didn't make it very far. With a boiling scream, Frond recovered her sword and stabbed it down into the Danger's body, pinning it to the ground. The lurker gave a cry all its own—a high, chittering sound like insects shrieking at summer sunsets. It lashed out at Frond, but the guildmistress had already rolled clear of its reach. She stood hunched and panting, mere feet away from the beast. Her skin bled from a dozen new puckered wounds, and her eyes shone with hate.

Which was when Makiva arrived. Zed watched himself burst from the forest, huffing as if he'd just sprinted miles to get here. "What's going on!" the imposter shouted. "Fie, what *is* that thing?"

"It's firewood," Frond growled. "Light it up! *Now.*"

Makiva nodded obediently and held out Zed's scepter. Green fire poured from it, broiling the lurker alive. The Danger thrashed and made a terrible hissing noise as it was consumed. Then, when the flames finally died, the forest was silent again.

Fel and Micah approached from the trees as Frond caught her breath. Micah glared at Makiva, but then turned his attention to the guildmistress. He held up his hand, which began to glitter with warm yellow light.

"I can heal those," he said, indicating toward Frond's new wounds—younger, bloodier versions of her notorious scars.

"Leave them!" Frond snarled, pulling away.

"Guildmistress . . ." Micah said, slowly and calmly. His dark eyes bored into her. "I can heal them. If you let me."

A beat of quiet passed. Fel looked nervously from Micah to Frond and back again. Then Frond's shoulders slackened. "All right," she said. She took a deep breath. "Go ahead, Micah."

The apprentice held his hand inches over her skin and the honeyed light intensified. Slowly, Frond's wounds closed, the angry welts rendering back into smooth skin.

It was over in moments. But though the injuries had been erased, and the monster reduced to a dark smudge on the forest floor, Zed suspected this attack would stay with the guildmistress for a long time to come.

"What are you doing here?" Frond finally asked, when Micah had pulled away and extinguished his mending light. She yanked her sword from the earth, wiping away the few bits of charred crust which were all that remained of the lurker.

Fel shook her head, turning to the healer with wonder. "It's like Micah *knew*. He kept saying we had to find Zed. I tried to argue, but he was so insistent. He begged me to track you both here."

"Zed?" Frond asked. "What do you mean?"

Two dots of color touched Micah's cheeks. "I . . . well . . ." His eyes flashed in Zed's—the *real* Zed's—direction.

"Yes, Micah," Makiva said curiously. Her gaze flashed toward Zed as well. "What *does* that mean?"

"Don't react," Foster ordered in a whisper. *"Fie, he's going to give us all away."*

Now Micah's cheeks really burned. "You seemed out of sorts today." His gaze fell to the ground. "And I thought: There's a fool who's going to get Frond killed. Looks like I was right."

Frond frowned, suspicion crinkling her brow. Finally, she shook her head. "We'll talk about this later," she said. "For now, we need to find out who was protecting this cave. And why."

"Protecting it?" Fel asked.

Frond nodded. She pointed to the earth, then traced a line with her finger up into the trees. Zed finally saw what she meant. A thick rope ran along the cavern's entrance, leading up to a net set high in a tangle of branches. Frond must have activated the trap somehow, releasing the lurker right on top of her.

Fel knelt. Her cobalt eyes darted back and forth along the ground. "I don't see the trigger," she said. "There's no snare or trip wire."

Frond shook her head. "There wasn't one. The trap was activated by magic. When I approached the entrance, a circle of glyphs glowed beneath my feet, then disappeared. Whoever set this was a mage."

"A . . . mage?" the imposter asked. "But how? The mages never leave the city."

Frond spat onto the ground, then frowned at the bloody wad. "That's what we need to figure out. Stay close to me, Zed. We're going to find out what this . . . *thing* was protecting. If there are more magical traps, I'll need you to sniff them out."

The imposter nodded, looking every bit as nervous as Zed felt. Makiva walked to Frond's side, and the two edged carefully toward the cavern.

Suddenly Micah shifted, ambling so he stood just beside Zed.

"Sorry," he whispered. "Do you think she noticed when I looked at you?"

"Micah, who are you talking to?"

Zed, Micah, and Foster all screamed as Fel approached with a nervous smile. Mousebane trotted beside her, but the cat's eyes followed the imposter Zed as he approached the cavern.

Fel raised her hands in the air. "You've been acting strangely all morning. Perhaps you were enthralled by a psychic parasite after all?" Her smile tightened. "That was a joke."

Micah blew out a puff of air. "And yet you may just be right, Fel. It would certainly make more sense than the last few days I've had."

"Well, if you were, then I'm grateful it brought us to save Frond." The elf turned toward the cavern, where the guildmistress and the imposter had disappeared inside. "Shall we?"

Micah cast a quick glance at Zed. "Let's go."

*

Micah lit the cave with a flourish of his hand, sending gentle waves of light cascading along its walls. Ahead of them, Zed could see Frond and the imposter disappearing into a larger chamber.

"*You'd think she would be more careful,*" Zed muttered.

At his side, Foster turned his fox head quizzically. "*And yet I don't think we'll find any more traps.*"

"*What do you mean?*"

"*It's just a bit convenient that Frond was greeted by her worst nightmare, don't you think? Whether she lived or died in the attack, that's practically a banner saying:* Check here! *The adventurers were meant to find this cave.*"

Zed frowned, glancing toward Micah, who watched the smoky fox without a word.

They arrived at the main chamber—really, a small alcove that had been carved into the rock. The space was filled with books, candles, and a simple chair and table.

It was also filled with monsters.

Cages lined the cavern, from which glittering eyes watched the newcomers warily—some in pairs, some in clusters of as many as eight or more. The place was packed nearly full of Dangers. Most had been crammed into simple containers, but a rare few were sealed behind intricate magicked barriers formed from glittering sigils, just like the wards that kept these very creatures *out* of Freestone.

Zed saw a creature made of metal and bolts and covered in unfamiliar runes with two shimmering blue bird wings that exploded from its back. The wings were pressed against the wires of its cage. One particularly robust container—lined with many concentric rows of magic sigils—contained a floating orb of flesh with a toothy smile and a single menacing eye at its center. Stalks capped by smaller eyes extended from the top of the Danger, like a watchful head of hair.

Mousebane sniffed curiously about the space, her wide eyes watching a cage containing several chittering pixies. Their compound eyes followed the cat with insect-like vacuity.

She paused before a series of cages containing half a dozen variations of imp, sorted by color. All six scratched murderously at their prisons, trying to attack their neighbors.

One particularly unfortunate monster lay upon the chamber's central table, though Zed couldn't say what it was. Its stomach had been sliced open and its skin pinned to the wood with stiletto knives. Zed didn't really have a head—or stomach—for such things, but he got the impression that it wasn't carrying all the organs it had started with.

Fel's hand flew to her mouth. "How awful. What is this place?"

"Someone's been experimenting out here," said Frond. "Away from prying eyes. But how did they make it in and out? Even adventurers would be noticed carting this many cages through the guildhall."

"I think I may know," said the imposter. Everyone turned to find Makiva standing in front of an enormous pedestal, on which rested a small silvery orb. "This is mythril," the false Zed explained. "And right now it's practically overwhelming the room with the smell of brimstone—fiendish mana. I've sensed magic this powerful only twice before. One was the focus that powers Freestone's wards. The other was Elderon's Shade."

Fel gasped. "The spell that let us enter Llethanyl undetected . . ."

The imposter nodded, Zed's eyes sparkling with excitement. "I think this orb is the focus for a demiplane."

Then Makiva reached Zed's hand out to touch it.

"Zed, no!" Frond shouted.

But the imposter had disappeared before she finished. Zed's body curled away in a confounding blur of movement and color.

In that same instant, Zed and Foster both yelped, their smoky forms tugged by the chain that bound them to Makiva.

The world muddied. The dark tones of the cavern melted into bright panes of color, like the stained glass windows that decorated the Golden Way Temple.

As Zed came to, he discovered he'd arrived at some kind of long, expansive bridge made of glimmering bricks. The space was lit from afar by eerie windows. Each was a layer of pure, bright color, separated by a metallic membrane and lit from behind by some unseen light source. It felt to Zed like he'd stepped inside an enormous kaleidoscope.

At his feet, Foster shivered in his fox form. Both of their bodies were leaking away in alarming quantities, forming tiny streams of mist that trailed apart in the air. For the first time since he'd been trapped by Makiva, Zed felt something akin to real pain. It was like his body was being stretched and compressed at the same time.

Farther down the path, Makiva grinned. She tossed the red crystal off the edge of the mystical bridge. As it fell, the crystal stretched impossibly, twining into a ribbon of ruby that fed into one of the colored panes. "Whatever you think you're doing with Micah, Zed, it won't work." Zed's own smug voice echoed across the ensorcelled platform. "The pieces are already set."

"Please, Makiva, stop this!" Zed cried. *"I'm begging you. I'll do anything."*

The imposter shook Zed's head. "What I want is beyond your giving, but not beyond my taking. I'm going home, boy. Very soon."

Three loud pops were all that preceded the arrivals of Frond, Micah, and Fel. The young elf clung to Mousebane with one arm.

"Zed!" Frond's shout echoed, too, as she stalked toward Makiva. "Are you out of your Fey-addled mind? Do not *ever* touch an unknown magical item again without my say-so. Do I make myself clear?"

The imposter nodded, eyes wide in contrition. "Sorry, Guildmistress!"

Frond sighed, studying the strange bridge. "So it *was* a demiplane," she muttered. She glanced behind them, where a pedestal identical to the one in the cavern stood at the bridge's end, the mythril orb still resting upon its plinth. Was it the same orb on the same plinth, occupying two spaces at once? Zed's mind twisted at the thought. He set the question aside, lest he sprain something.

"We should go back," Micah suggested. "Call for the others."

"But look!" Fel pointed with her free hand.

The group turned as one toward the other end. A squat container of some kind sat waiting. Its details were too bleary to make out beneath the shifting colors.

"May as well see where it goes," Frond breathed. "Everyone, get behind me."

They formed a line behind the guildmistress and crept forward along the path. As they moved, the colorful blocks beneath them exploded with changing hues, each step sending variegated ripples over the surface.

About halfway across, Frond spit off the bridge's edge. The wad fell a short distance, then slowed. It began to sparkle iridescently, the edges pinching into several small points like a glittering star. Each point trailed away in a different color, until all were absorbed by the panes that surrounded them.

Frond rolled her eyes and continued.

"*Zed,*" Foster whispered. "*This place . . . it's tearing at me. I can feel it. The powerful magic here is pulling me apart.*"

Zed nodded to the fox. "*I feel it, too,*" he said. "*Just hold on a bit longer.*"

Finally, they arrived at the far end of the tunnel, where the squat shape came into focus. It was a simple wooden storage chest, banded in metal, like any outtowner in Freestone might have. Zed felt a lance of dread. The chest looked familiar. He'd seen one just like it recently. But where?

Frond touched the lid with her boot and it opened easily, revealing a second (third?) mythril orb tucked in a bed of cloth, identical to the first.

"Let's *not* touch that," Micah said. "Everyone agreed?"

"What are you talking about?" the imposter countered. "It'll lead us right to whoever's been experimenting with monsters!"

"Or it'll dump us off this rainbow bridge! Remember the time your *best friend* got stuck in a giant, endless shadow? It was only a few weeks ago."

"There *are* risks where demiplanes are involved," Fel agreed, glancing up at Frond. "Elderon's Shade proved that."

"Risks are what we do," Frond said resignedly. "It's probably safer to follow me than wait here. Have your weapons ready, apprentices. We don't know where—or what—we're walking into."

The apprentices all nodded, Micah glancing nervously toward the imposter. Frond unsheathed her sword, then touched a finger to the orb. Her body blurred and twisted out of existence. Makiva followed eagerly, reaching Zed's hand toward the sphere and dragging Zed and Foster along for the ride.

The colors around Zed coalesced, re-forming into shapes he recognized: a chair, a table, a row of simple chests. One of the chests was open, revealing the mythril orb. Two popping noises, and Micah and Fel appeared behind him, their weapons raised.

But no enemies greeted them. Just books—a wall of them that had been stacked into haphazard columns.

In front of Zed, Frond looked aghast. Her eyes were wide with shock as she took in their surroundings.

"This can't be," she rasped.

They'd arrived in Hexam's office.

Chapter Ten
Brock

Alabasel Frond was a fearsome woman at the best of times. Right now, she was like something out of Brock's nightmares. Her leathers were torn, stained dark with blood and a substance that reeked of vinegar and bile. Though he could see no injuries, there was new blood smeared across the old wounds on her face, and more blood drying black in her gray hair. Her eyes were dark pinpricks of fury, and she tapped the throwing stars along her belt as if daring their razor-sharp tips to pierce her.

Brock's every instinct rebelled at the thought of delivering bad news to her in this moment. Seeing his hesitation, Jett stepped forward.

"I'm sorry, Guildmistress," he said. "Justyn is dead."

The news was met not with more anger, but with a moment of such profound sadness that it quenched her fury in the space of a single breath. She stopped her pacing, closed her eyes tight, and winced as though he'd struck her.

But when she opened her eyes an instant later, the fury was back.

"Tell me," she growled.

It was only the second time Brock had set foot in the guildmistress's private quarters. He and Jett had been sent upstairs to debrief her while the rest of their party brought Justyn's body—which they'd all carried back together, atop a canvas sheet—to a basement room they called the morgue. The adventurers who'd greeted them on their return had looked on somberly, saluting their fallen comrade. Clobbler had been well-liked and a little feared; most adventurers had expected he would outlive them all.

They'd been the last group to return, and Brock had breathed a huge sigh of relief at that. He'd been on edge the entire walk back to Freestone, straining his ears for any sign that another party had run into trouble. If any had, and they'd tried to signal for help, none would be coming.

Whatever trouble Frond had found, Zed appeared unscathed. He leaned against a far wall, frowning. Micah was there, too, and Fel and Lotte, all of them standing well clear of Frond while Jett told her about their encounter with the brain-jaw.

"Any sign of magical traps in the area?" Frond asked. "Did you get a sense the Danger had been put there in your path?"

"Is this a 'Why did the brain-jaw cross the road' sort of thing?" Brock asked. "What do you mean *put there*? Weren't we *looking* for a brain-jaw?"

"Traps?" echoed Jett. "What happened out there, Guildmistress?"

Frond actually gritted her teeth and snarled.

"Kids, why don't you give us the room?" Lotte suggested.

"Wait," Frond said. "Zed. As a sorcerer, you can . . . smell magic, is that right?"

Zed perked up. He nodded cheerfully.

"So if there were any mages among us. Any adventurers hiding magical abilities. You'd know?"

Lotte sighed wearily. "Frond, you're grasping at straws."

"I'm considering all the possibilities." Her voice was low. "I won't condemn one of our own unless I'm absolutely sure."

"Wait, what?" Jett said. "Condemn who? What's going on?"

"Well, basically," Zed began, "Hexam created a demiplane that circumvents the wards and allows him to perform gruesome experiments on Dangers in secret." Frond gave Zed a murderous look. "*Allegedly*," he added, but he didn't shrink from her. "There's no one else, Guildmistress. If anyone in this guildhall were accessing mana, I'd have noticed."

Jett rubbed his face. "I didn't understand half of that, and even the part I understood doesn't make sense."

Brock thumbed the useless summoning crystal in his pocket. Hexam, a traitor? Was it possible?

"I'm with Frond on this one," Micah said. "We need to slow down here. There could be another explanation for all this."

"Oh yeah?" said Zed. "Like what?"

"Like all sorts of things!" Micah said. "Maybe there's a coven of criminal elves who never went back to their city. Maybe Fel's creepy cat is an evil spell-caster playing us all for fools. Maybe, I don't know, maybe one of us is possessed! That Jayna girl knows magic, doesn't she?"

"Mousebane is *not* creepy," Fel said, bristling with annoyance.

"*That Jayna girl?!*" Jett said hotly.

Micah put up his hands. "I'm just saying . . . there could be stuff happening here that we don't understand. Details we're missing . . ."

"You're right," Brock said.

Micah looked taken aback. "I am?" he said. "I mean . . . *I* know I am, but you agree with me?"

"Rarely," Brock said. "But there are some additional angles here we need to consider." He took a deep breath. Since his very first day as an apprentice, he'd been keeping secrets from his guildmates. Chief among them was the Lady Gray's insistence that there was a smuggler operating within the Sea of Stars. He'd kept that knowledge to himself because he was never sure whom to trust.

But whoever the smuggler was, they'd been at it longer than

any of the apprentices had been around. And Lotte had nearly gutted Brock when she'd caught him doing some smuggling of his own during their journey to Llethanyl. As for Frond . . . the guild was her whole life.

That meant everyone in this room could be trusted with what he knew.

"The penanggalan. The thing that grew inside Mother Brenner. It had to come from somewhere. It had to come from outside the wall." He leveled a look at Frond. "How would it get past the wards? We're the only people who go out there!"

Frond met his gaze. "We've always taken care not to bring anything dangerous back with us. And we have some theories about what went wrong in that case. The spore could have been brought in accidentally by the previous delegation from Llethanyl—lain dormant within the Luminous Mother for more than a decade."

"That was Hexam's theory," Lotte said softly.

Brock shook his head. "Other people have theories, too. The . . . well, some people in the Merchants Guild, they say sometimes things show up for sale. Things that could only come from beyond the wall. Weapons. Poisons . . ."

Frond started tapping her throwing stars again. "It's not possible," she said. "I would have known."

"Certainly it'd have to be someone clever," Brock said.

"Not so clever," Lotte said, a bitter edge to her voice. "If they accidentally killed the Luminous Mother—and almost brought down the wards."

"I'm not sure it *was* an accident," Brock said. "I thought so for a long time. A hapless smuggler, smuggling the wrong thing. But after what happened to that magus? Infected with a monster? Doesn't that sound a little too familiar?"

"Then it's definitely not Hexam," Frond said. "I could see him making a mistake—letting his passions carry him away without fully considering the consequences. But the man is no murderer."

"He had bad blood with the magus, though, didn't he?" Zed asked. "Wasn't Phylo the one who got Hexam expelled from the Silverglows?"

Frond narrowed her eyes. "Fie. And how do you know that?"

Zed shrugged meekly. "He would talk about it sometimes in lessons."

Micah made a sound like he wanted to object, but in the end he shook his head. He glared so intently into a far corner of the room that Brock turned to look, but nothing was there.

"I don't believe Hexam's capable of this," Fel said.

Jett grinned. "Yeah, but you *always* see the best in people, Fel."

"No, forgive me," she said. "I mean I do not think he is a capable enough spell-caster."

"Oh," Jett said. "Ouch."

Fel continued, "Elderon's Shade—the demiplane through which we entered Llethanyl—is very old magic, only vaguely understood by our finest scholars."

Zed scoffed. "Even elven humility sounds like bragging."

Fel flinched a little, and Brock gave Zed a dirty look. He wasn't the only one.

"What?" Zed said to the room. "I can say that. I'm elf-blooded."

Brock thought it was strange that Zed didn't blush in that moment. He always blushed when he was the center of attention. When had he stopped blushing?

"Anyway," Brock said. "There's also this." He took the broken crystal from his pocket, holding it up for everyone to see. "We tried to call for help against the brain-jaw. This thing—it's a dud. And it's the reason someone died out there today."

Frond went still, fury seeping back into her eyes. Lotte dropped her face into her hands. "Oh, no," she breathed.

"He gave us these, right?" Brock said. He tossed the crystal onto Frond's desk. "And where was he today? Where is he right now?"

"He's at Silverglow Tower," Frond answered. "He's cataloging their vault. Looking . . ." She cursed under her breath. "He's looking for anything *dangerous*."

*

The apprentices were kicked out of the room while Frond and Lotte discussed what to do next.

"I can't believe it," Jett said as they descended the staircase. "Hexam's trying to get us all killed?" His eyes widened with realization. "This is going to break Jayna's heart. She practically worships the guy—when she's not ready to strangle him."

"I should find Mousebane," Fel said. "She picks up on interpersonal conflict. It makes her very anxious!"

The way she wrung her hands, Brock suspected Fel was actually speaking about herself.

In fact, Jayna and Mousebane were both in the common room at the foot of the stairs, along with Liza and Nirav. Mousebane showed no signs of anxiety as she sniffed curiously at a bowl of two-day-old porridge.

"Where have you all been?" Liza asked. "Everyone's downstairs. Clobbler—"

"We know," Jett said. "Boy, do we know. Listen, Jayna, you might want to sit down. . . ."

They all sat around a table, and as Fel launched into the story of how she and Micah had saved Frond from a Danger, Brock made an excuse about needing to change his clothes and slunk away.

Zed's room was unlocked. Brock crept inside and shut the door softly behind him. The space barely looked lived in. Zed had no mementos on display. No dirty dishes cluttered the surfaces. The bed was neatly made.

Brock looked under the pillow, then slid his hand beneath the cot. Nothing.

He examined the dresser, pulling the drawers out one at a time. Zed's guild token, the one he'd dropped in the mud the day he'd been drafted, sat atop a carefully folded pile of laundry. Otherwise, it was nothing but clothes. Zed didn't own many; the bottom drawer was entirely empty.

In the end, what Brock was looking for was sitting out in plain view atop Zed's desk. His friend hadn't even thought it worth hiding his forbidden tome on fiendish magic.

Zed was a sorcerer, not a wizard—and as Brock understood the distinction, that meant Zed could sense and even access the forbidden mana of Fie. He'd done it during their initiation, unleashing the fiendish magic stored within a staff, and he'd flushed with panic when he finally confessed about it to his friends. Brock had told him it didn't matter—that magic was magic.

But people were put to death for using fiendish magic. And the man who had encouraged Zed—who had insisted the taboo was misguided, that people would look the other way for an adventurer—he had clearly been working in secret to destroy them all along.

And Brock knew he'd given Zed a dangerous book.

There were two books, though, on Zed's desk, and Brock wasn't sure which had come from Hexam. Maybe they both had. He picked up the first, *Bonds of Blood and Fire—that* didn't sound harmless. But when he turned to a random page, he couldn't make heads or tails of what he read.

The second book had no title that he could see, which was somehow more worrying. It was white and silver, with a sheet of folded vellum inside, used like a bookmark. Brock put the paper in his pocket and examined the page where it had been left. It was all about breathing and focus and self-control. It didn't sound especially fiendish. . . .

There was a shuffle of footsteps from outside, and a shadow broke the line of light beneath the door. The doorknob began to turn. Brock hurriedly placed the book back on the desk and swiveled toward the door as it swung inward.

Zed stood in the open doorway, his expression unreadable.

"Surprise!" Brock said weakly.

"Let me guess: You lost a bet with Micah, and now you have to do all of our laundry for a week." Zed grinned. "Although, having encountered Micah's dirty laundry before, I hope for your sake that I'm wrong."

Brock nodded playfully. "On the subject of Micah's dirty socks, I think magical fire is the only solution."

"Ha!" Zed barked. "Don't tempt me."

Brock smiled, but it was a tentative smile. He hated to spoil the moment, but this was too good a chance to pass up.

"Listen," he said. "These books of yours. Are they from Hexam?"

"One of them," Zed answered. He sat on his cot and pulled off a boot.

"I think maybe you should give it back," Brock said. "Let someone take a look and make sure it's not . . . bad."

Zed sat still, considering. "Let's make a game out of it," he said at last. "If you can pick out which book is from Hexam, you can have it."

Brock crossed his arms. "And what if I get it wrong?"

Zed smiled menacingly. "A small thing," he said, rising to his feet. "A trifle." He closed the space between them in a single step. "You must only give me . . . a piece of your soul!"

With that, Zed tickled him, worming his fingers beneath Brock's crossed arms. Brock laughed, squirming away. The small room offered no escape. "Stop it!" he cried when his laughter had left him short of breath.

Zed relented, smirking at him. With one boot off, he stood lopsided. His hair was a mess.

Brock's heart ached with happiness. These last few months, moments like these—silly moments with his best friend—had been hard to come by.

"Take the books," Zed said with a shrug. He walked back to his cot and plopped himself back down.

"Really?" Brock asked.

"Yeah, I don't need them. But for the record"—Zed pointed at the first book, the one with the sinister title—"that one is from Hexam. The other is from Selby."

Brock couldn't keep the shock from registering on his face. "Are you kidding me? Selby the lich lord of Llethanyl, that Selby?"

Zed pulled off his second boot. "I think technically it was from the queen."

"And *she* was such a gem." Brock huffed. "We've really got to find you a mentor who isn't a murderous megalomaniac."

Zed gave him an appraising look. "Why do you hate magic so much, Brock?"

"I don't," he said.

"You do, though," Zed said. "You always have."

Brock crossed his arms again. "Where is this coming from? I *always* encouraged you—"

"Is that it? Is it because it's the one thing I had that you didn't?"

"That's not fair," Brock said.

"I'm not trying to be mean, Brock," Zed said lightly. "But I think I get it now. You're right—you *don't* hate magic." He narrowed his eyes. "You're scared of it."

At that moment, Micah burst into the room. "There you are!" he said, red in the face and panting. "I . . . was just wondering where everyone had gotten to."

Brock felt redness in his own face, as well. He was hurt and embarrassed—and angry.

"Micah, give it a rest," he snapped. "Nobody likes a clingy friend."

Zed snickered at that.

He snickered in a way that said: *Look who's talking.*

"Actually, you know what? You two make each other miserable all you want." Brock stomped toward the doorway, pushing past Micah. "I'm going to find a solution to our problems that, for once, doesn't involve setting them on fire."

"So you won't be burning my books, then?" Zed teased.

"No promises," Brock said, and he slammed the door behind him.

*

Sounds of revelry floated upstairs from the basement, but the common room on the ground floor was still mostly empty. Liza, Jett, Fel, and Jayna sat huddled around a table, whispering furiously about Hexam, while Nirav leaned against the wall, somber and silent. Jayna's eyes were red.

"Everything okay?" Liza asked Brock.

"No," Brock said, sliding onto the bench. "What's going on in the basement?"

"A Sea of Stars wake looks a lot like a Sea of Stars party," Jett said, grinning. "Which looks a lot like a riot."

"At least they're consistent," Brock said, trying for humor but only sounding bitter.

"They say they're celebrating his life, not dwelling on his death," Liza explained.

"I'm afraid to ask what they did for me," said Nirav.

Brock chuckled darkly. Then the front door swung open. A cold wind blew in from outside, and Hexam stepped into the room.

"Ah, hello!" he said cheerfully. The apprentices shot to their feet as he removed his outer cloak. "Just the young adventurers I'd hoped to find."

Brock still had his daggers on his belt. He put his hands on them, trying to strike a casual pose, and he watched Liza for a signal. None of the others had weapons, though he saw Jayna flexing her fingers.

Hexam was oblivious. He hung his cloak on the rack by the door. "No evidence of anything untoward happening in the tower, so far, but I've already found some most remarkable artifacts. Their enchanting has come a long way in the last few years . . ."

"Fel," Liza said under her breath. "Get Frond."

Fel slipped away without a word, unseen by Hexam, who was rummaging through his cloak pocket. "Ah, here," he said at last, producing a wand. Even Brock could tell it was a special one, a gleaming length of obsidian set with a series of bright pink gems. "I brought you something, Jayna."

Tears leaked from Jayna's eyes, but she held firm. "How *could* you?" she asked, her voice thick.

Confusion crossed Hexam's face. He seemed to really look at the apprentices for the first time. "What's happened?" he asked, suddenly worried. "Where's Frond?"

"Frond is fine," Liza said, her voice hard. "Why do you ask?"

The furrow in Hexam's brow deepened. He paused, wand still in his hand, outstretched in offering.

"Put the wand down, Hexam," Frond said coldly as she emerged from her staircase. "Put it down and let's talk."

"Alabasel," he said. "Something's happened?"

"Something did," she said. "The wand, Hexam."

Flustered, Hexam looked from the wand to the guildmistress.

Brock could see the moment the mage realized there was blood smeared across her face. Hexam's gaze swept from her to the apprentices, where it was met with naked hostility. His eyes landed on Brock's daggers, halfway drawn.

Hexam tightened his grip on the wand.

"Let's talk first," said Hexam. "*Then* I'll put this down."

There was a chilling moment of silence, during which Hexam and Frond locked eyes. Brock hardly dared to breathe.

But Frond relented. "All right," she said, signaling for the apprentices to back down. "All right, let's talk this out."

The tension left Brock's shoulders. He breathed again.

"That smell–" said a quiet voice. Brock turned to see Zed had entered the room. His nose was wrinkled up as if he'd caught a whiff of something foul. Then his eyes went wide.

"Frond!" Zed cried. "Hexam's casting a spell!"

Frond reacted so quickly it was all but over by the time Brock whipped his head around. His mind raced to catch up with what his eyes were seeing. The wand clattered to the ground; it was bloody; bladed silver stars were embedded in Hexam's palms.

Someone was shouting. Someone was crying. Hexam did neither; he gazed at his hands in shock and horror in the instant before Frond slammed her sword's pommel against the side of his head.

The mage crumpled heavily to the ground. In the stillness that followed, Brock heard laughter filtering up from below. The celebration in the basement was in full swing.

Chapter Eleven

Zed

"How could this happen?"

King Freestone watched Frond with barely restrained fury. "How could this happen to Alabasel Frond, the paranoid? The unwavering. The *Basilisk*."

Spittle flew from the king's lips as he hissed out Frond's nickname, an unkind epithet that Zed was surprised the royal knew at all. "A warlock working right under your gaze! And one who I *expressly* warned you to watch!"

Frond's face was still as granite, but she lowered her eyes. Even she had better diplomatic sense than to challenge the king in this. As far as she knew, as far as anyone knew, Hexam was guilty of witchcraft. Even worse, Frond had allowed him to smuggle deadly creatures into the city while under her supervision.

But Zed knew better. Whatever was truly happening here, it was far more complicated—and more dangerous—than it seemed.

Zed drifted behind Frond, with Foster padding beside him in his fox form. They weaved invisibly among the apprentices who had accompanied Frond as witnesses to the master mage's alleged misdeeds. Brock, Liza, and the imposter.

Makiva stared forward, watching the king from behind Zed's eyes. *She* was responsible for this. For everything. Zed felt a flare of hate just looking at himself. It was a dismal feeling.

The pieces are already set.

Zed glanced across the king's council chamber, a grand but stark space in the heart of the castle. Seated around the king, the assembled guildmasters of Freestone's four High Guilds all frowned at Frond, their expressions grave.

All except for Dafonil Grima. The archmagus of the Mages Guild looked positively serene.

"Your Majesty," she said smoothly, "I move that the Silverglows be released from the . . . stewardship of the Sea of Stars immediately. Clearly Frond's time would be better spent tightening the reins on her own people, without the added burden of playing warden to mine. If Hexam had been dealt with as I originally proposed, we would not be in this mess."

The king tapped a finger against the heavy wooden table. His gaze circled toward Grima. "Do you *move* it, Archmagus?"

he asked slowly, pronouncing each syllable with the languorousness of a coiled snake. "I was not aware that the council had the power to compel *motions* from their king. Perhaps I am merely a puppet, here to dance this way and that as you tug my strings?"

Grima's eyes widened slightly. She swallowed. "I meant no offense, Majesty. But the fact remains that my mages are innocent in this debacle. I plead on their behalf. Humbly."

"The *fact* that remains," the king growled, "is that it was *your* mage who, through his own malfeasance and petty rivalry, made himself a target of this warlock. There are no innocents in this story." The monarch's eyes swept across the room. "Least of all around this table."

At this mysterious pronouncement, the various guildmasters glanced at one another.

"Majesty," Liza ventured bravely, "If I might speak in my guildmistress's defense?"

The king watched Liza for a beat, his gray eyes still as stone. "You're the apprentice who ended the market massacre. Your friend here called you *Dame* Liza?" King Freestone's lips pursed, testing out the word. "That's a title I hadn't heard in a long, long time. My mother once told me stories of Dame Rosa, a lady knight-errant who wandered the trade roads outside Freestone, protecting pilgrims. Not many know this, but the queen's famous rose garden was dedicated in her honor." The king smiled wistfully at the memory. "Speak, then, Dame Liza. It's the least of what Freestone owes you."

Zed didn't know who looked more stunned, Liza or Ser Brent. The guildmaster of the knights was practically choking on his indignation. He seemed ready to protest, but Liza found her voice first.

"You honor me, Your Majesty," she said. "More than . . . more than I think you realize. But Guildmistress Frond wasn't at fault here. Every day we adventurers put our lives in each other's hands. Without trust—without believing that we can rely on our guildmates to watch our backs—everything falls apart. Hexam's betrayal was wrong, and it's a wound that will take time to mend. But Frond wasn't wrong to trust him. Trust is *essential* to her mission."

Liza raised her arms, settling her gloved hands upon the shoulders of Brock and the imposter beside her. "Right now, Freestone needs to come *together*," she said. "We've suffered a horrible attack. It will be too easy to turn against each other—to cast blame and suspicion like we did with the elves."

The king quirked a brow at this provocative statement, but kept silent.

"Instead," Liza said, pulling Brock and the imposter closer, "let's work as one to rebuild. Let's prop each other up. Deceit got us into this mess, but *trust* will get us out."

"My, she's quite the little orator," Foster muttered. *"Madly naive, of course, but I like her spirit."*

Zed could hardly believe the king was listening to an apprentice with such rapt attention, but he wasn't the only one. Frond nodded appreciatively to Liza, and the Luminous Father Pollux looked ready to weep. Brock wore a grin so wide that Zed worried he'd injure his face.

After a moment, King Freestone let out a heavy sigh. His sturdy shoulders, usually square as bricks, sank. "Deceit," he rasped, "has nearly destroyed this city twice. And it has turned my guildmasters against each other. Whatever our reasons, we're all guilty of harboring secrets. Our enemies have used these secrets as a shroud, hiding within them. You've humbled me today, Dame Liza. More than *you* realize." The king nodded resolutely, raising his chin. "No more secrets."

"Majesty . . . ?" Lord Borace Quilby licked his lips nervously. Zed and Foster exchanged ghostly glances. Something was happening.

"Lady Gray," said the king. "If you would please join us."

And then, suddenly, she did. Zed wasn't sure when the serving woman in gray had arrived, seated separately from the table but with her gaze on the proceedings. He felt a brief flicker of recognition—had he seen her here once before?—but she was otherwise completely unremarkable. A plain woman whose skin was neither dark nor pale, her features neither comely nor homely. Only her eyes sparkled with any keenness. They darted from figure to figure, landing finally on the king.

"*That was odd,*" said Foster. "*I didn't see her at all before now. Did you?*"

"Majesty!" Now Quilby truly protested. "The apprentices!

Perhaps they should be excused before any dire decisions are made."

"On the contrary," the king said. "These three, especially, should hear what follows. Lady Gray, if you would grace our table with your presence. Bring your chair."

The servant–lady?–stood from her perch and approached the council table, settling beside Quilby. The guildmaster of the merchants looked about as uncomfortable as a fly seated beside a spider.

"Your Majesty," the woman said blandly.

"Those around this table know who you are," the king began. "At least in part. But for Frond's sake, may I introduce the sixth member of my council: the Lady Gray, guildmistress of the Shadows–Freestone's Thieves Guild."

Frond watched the woman with undisguised suspicion. "I'd heard rumors, but–" She faltered. "Pleased to–well . . . Hello, anyway."

"The Shadows are the hidden arm of the Merchants Guild," the king continued, "and like their sister guild, they were also formed by the Champion Dox Eural. Even once reformed of his more unsavory hobbies, Dox understood the necessity of secrets. There's the business that can be undertaken in the light of day, and then there's the business that cannot, though it's no less crucial. The Shadows' offices are these disagreeable obligations: spying, thievery, and even murder. It was with an act of murder, after all, that Dox finally saved us from Foster Pendleton's treachery."

"*Dox* . . ." Foster whispered. Beside Zed, the fox exploded into smoke, billowing up until it reconstituted into Foster's true, elf-blooded shape. "*No wonder I couldn't reach you. All those secrets. You'd closed your heart off completely.*"

"Though she and the merchants occupy the same administrative body," King Freestone said, "the Lady Gray reports directly to me. Not even Quilby was aware of this. Her black market exists because I allow it. She sends her little spiders out to snare a prize when I demand it. She is my spymaster, and she's been spying on all of you—every single one—for many, many years."

The room was utterly still as this news passed through it like a shadow, darkening every expression it touched. Grima frowned, her thin brows knotting together, while Quilby licked helplessly at his ever-dry lips. Father Pollux's eyes were wide. He glanced from Lady Gray to the king, and finally to Ser Brent.

For his part, the commander of the knights looked furious. In all the chronicles of Freestone, Zed had never heard of a knight turning against his king. Historically, the Stone Sons were the crown's *most* loyal subjects, being its last line of defense.

Today, Ser Brent appeared ready to revolt.

"After everything I've done for you," he grated. But a hard look from the king silenced further complaints.

"Your Majesty," Frond began guardedly. "I appreciate the

trust you're showing by revealing this information to me. To us." Frond's eyes flicked toward her apprentices, where all three stood watching the Lady with naked shock. Even Makiva seemed genuinely surprised by this revelation, and Brock had actually taken several steps backward—away from Liza's hand.

"But I have to ask," Frond continued. "Why tell us now?"

"Because secrets, while necessary, can occasionally grow too tangled. They choke out the light. Your gallant young apprentice here has reminded me that trust is paramount, not just among my council, but among the adventurers, as well."

The king's eyes flicked toward Lady Gray. "Tell her," he ordered.

"My king!" Quilby shrilled.

"Your Majesty, *please*," the Lady Gray muttered. "I beg you to reconsider."

"Either you tell her," the king said, "or *he* does."

Then those stony gray eyes landed right upon Brock.

"Brock?" Both Zed and Liza said the word at the same time, though only Liza's voice echoed uncertainly throughout the room. Her dark eyes were round with disbelief.

"Very well," the Lady Gray said. Whatever plea her voice had held was gone now. She spoke coolly. "For two months, Brock Dunderfel operated as my agent in the Adventurers Guild. He spied for me, stole from the elves of Duskhaven, and smuggled in useful tissues from Dangers outside the wall."

Frond's eyes were ablaze, though she never once looked at

Brock. She kept her gaze locked onto the Lady Gray, who seemed immune to the fire.

Liza, however, couldn't take her eyes *off* Brock. Her cheeks were flushed with emotion.

"In order to keep Brock's loyalty," the spymaster continued, "I blackmailed him with the threat of revealing Zed's aptitude for dark magic. The sorcerer had touched the mana of Fie and successfully turned it to his will. In truth, however, I'd already revealed this information to the king."

Zed gasped. He glanced to Makiva, who was looking similarly stunned. The imposter's eyes were narrowed. Whatever Makiva's unstoppable plan was, Zed suspected that *this* hadn't been a part of it.

"I nearly had the boy arrested right then," the king said. "But the Lady bade me wait. Apparently, the spell was an accident, and cast outside the city walls." His eyes landed upon the imposter. "That's what saved you."

"Eventually, my threat no longer swayed Brock," the Lady Gray continued. She spoke evenly, without a hint of guilt, or humor, or any other emotion. It was as if she were reading her shopping list for the market. "He left my service shortly after the elves returned to Llethanyl, despite the apparent risk to his friend. We haven't been in contact since."

A cry. A crash. The thunder of rapid footfalls as they fled the room.

Brock was gone.

The king sighed at the open doorway, slowly shaking his head. "Perhaps you think I'm punishing you by revealing this, Frond. I hope you'll come to see it as a gift. What I offer you today is trust. A guild free of tangled secrets. At least the secrets I have the power to cut away."

Frond glanced at the door. A strange, stormy emotion brewed behind her eyes, one that Zed couldn't quite read. Perhaps there was no adequate translation. She stayed silent.

King Freestone leaned back in his chair, looking suddenly very tired. "The adventurers are excused for today, though my council will remain. *We* have much left to discuss."

Liza nodded dumbly, her eyes red and wet. She and the imposter staggered breathlessly from the room, as if they'd just run laps around the city walls.

Frond lingered a moment, turning back to the king. "Hexam," she grated. "Where is he? What will become of him?"

The weariness melted from the king's face momentarily, but what replaced it was worse. "The warlock is being held in a magically warded chamber in Silverglow Tower," he said through bared teeth. "Tomorrow, the Lady Gray will extract what information she can from him. His plans. His methods. What he hoped to gain. She has a single day to make her inquiries."

The king turned his gaze dismissively from Frond. "Because at the dawn of the next day, Hexam will die."

✷

"You have to tell Frond!" Zed shouted at Micah. *"There's no more time to waste! Hexam will be executed!"*

Micah sat in his cluttered quarters, pulling at his hair, while Zed swirled around the room like a frenzied, smoky tornado.

After the king's pronouncement, he and Foster had rushed back to the guildhall. Where exactly Brock, Liza, or even the imposter had scattered to after the disastrous council were mysteries, but for the moment Zed had more pressing concerns.

He'd told Micah everything. Zed recounted Liza's speech and the king's revelation, his mind whirring with conflicting emotions as he spoke. Brock had betrayed the guild to protect *him.* No wonder Brock had been so distant in past months. Zed cursed his own selfishness. If only he'd gone to his friend before! If only he'd seen that Brock was struggling with a burden of his own.

"No," Micah answered simply. "There's still time to fix this."

"While that's technically true," Foster added from the corner, *"even I'm starting to get nervous."* The fox looked wispier than ever. As much as Foster liked to project an air of indifference, it couldn't have been easy to hear his best friend celebrated for murdering him. *"And every moment we dally is one that unnerving woman spends interrogating your mentor. I don't understand how she's escaped my or Makiva's attentions all these years, but it isn't natural."*

Micah rolled his eyes. "To be quite honest, I've forgotten what natural feels like."

"Micah, please," Zed pressed. *"The king already forgave me once. He might do it again!"*

The healer shook his head. "If anything, that makes it *more* unlikely, Zed. Don't you see? He forgave an accident, not a fiendish pact! Your spirit dog was right before. It's too risky." Micah stood with a groan. "Listen, if I head to Hexam's office now, maybe I can find something else about banishing Makiva before the king burns the whole library to ash."

He stepped with practiced ease over the many piles of laundry that blocked his way to the door, then threw it open.

Alabasel Frond waited directly outside.

"Gah!" Micah bellowed in surprise. "Ga-Guildmistress!"

Frond's eyes were hard as she took in Micah and his squalid living space. "My quarters," she growled. "Now." Then she stalked away.

"*Tell her!*" Zed floated beside Micah.

"As annoying as you were in your own body," the boy grumbled, "you are way worse as a spirit." Then he marched after Frond, into the guildhall.

✷

Micah and Frond sat in silence in the guildmistress's personal quarters, neither looking particularly comfortable with the arrangement. Zed wondered as he floated nearby whether the two had ever had a real conversation since Micah joined the guild.

At least Foster seemed entertained. The warlock was perched at Frond's bay window, watching the proceedings with the wide-eyed delight of a child at a puppeteer's stand.

"Micah," Frond began slowly. "You're going to hear some . . . alarming things in the coming days, if you haven't already."

"*Tell her!*" Zed urged, gusting beside Micah.

The boy ignored him, staring forward.

"I won't fairy-coat it," Frond said. "This mess with Hexam is a blow to the guild. Our most senior wizard is now a fourteen-year-old apprentice. I've never seen morale so low as when Lotte announced his arrest during Justyn's funeral. On top of that, it's been brought to my attention that some of your guildmates—your fellow apprentices—have been harboring secrets of their own." Frond paused, chewing on her next statement. Once sufficiently chewed, she spat into the half-full spittoon beside her desk.

She began again. "I've asked you here in case there's anything *you'd* like to share with me. Something you've been holding on to. I know that I'm not the most—" She hesitated.

"Warm?" Micah offered. "Approachable? Good-natured?"

"*Kindhearted? Friendly? Maternal?*" Foster echoed from the window.

"—*casual* figure in the guild," Frond ground out testily. "But right now, we're fighting for our very survival. Not against a werebeast or a clockwork menace or any other plane-cursed monster. We're fighting against secrets. The kinds of secrets that can eat us alive if we let them."

"*She knows.*" Zed gasped. "*She knows, Micah. Just tell her!*"

Micah frowned. "If you want secrets, you should drag Jett

and Jayna in here," he said. "You know those two are conducting experiments away from the guildhall, right?"

"We'll be speaking with everyone in turn over the next couple days," Frond said. "But this conversation isn't about Jett or Jayna. It's about you . . . and Zed."

The room became abruptly quiet. Micah's mouth stretched into a thin, flat line.

Frond exhaled. "Listen, if I could have assigned Lotte to have this talk, I would have. But in this particular case, I'm probably the best person to speak with you. Micah, you and I are . . . different. Aren't we?"

"Different?" Zed asked. *"Different how?"*

At the window, Foster squeaked in joy. *"Oh. My. Shambling. Blob. Is this really happening? I can't believe this is really happening!"*

"You've always been"—Frond cleared her throat—"a little preoccupied with Zed. Teasing him more than the others. Watching him when you thought the adults weren't looking. And then this morning in the woods . . . Well, you disobeyed a direct command so you could come find him."

"But that's because he's an imposter!" Zed shouted. *"Micah, tell her. Tell her this is all a mistake."*

Zed glanced from Frond to Micah, but the boy wouldn't meet his gaze. Instead, Micah was shaking his head, his eyes wide. "This is not happening," he mumbled. "Not right now. Not like this."

Frond's usually stony face flushed. "I . . . Oh, Fie, I don't mean to pry, Micah. I won't force you to confirm anything, one way or the other. And what's said in this room won't leave it. Certainly Zed will never hear of it. I just wanted to let you know that, if you ever *do* need to talk, I have some . . . personal experience with . . . romantic feelings toward persons of the same . . . Fie, is it hot in here?"

"*Yes!*" Foster said.

"Miserably," Micah groaned, his face in his hands.

Frond ran a hand through her cropped gray hair. "Should have sent Lotte," she muttered. "All right, here is what I'll say, since I'm making a grisly mess of Lotte's 'outreach' plan. When I was your age, I started developing feelings for the pretty lasses around me, instead of the handsome lads. For a time, I hoped those feelings would go away, but eventually. . . . Well, eventually I realized they were a part of who I was. You and I and everyone in this guild knows what it means to sacrifice. To accept that the lives we'd planned for ourselves don't always work out. You, especially, have given up a lot on your path here, down to your very name."

Zed watched Micah as the boy sat unmoving, his face still buried in his palms. Micah's shoulders were trembling.

"Sacrifice," Frond said, "is our duty to Freestone. We put our lives on the line every day. Like Justyn." Frond's voice constricted. She swallowed, then took a breath and continued. "For all that we give this city, I will never ask my guild members to live what short, precious lives we *have* in shame. Lotte and . . . and Hexam always agreed with me. Micah, as long as you're a member of *this* guild, you can be who you are. *Whoever* that is."

Zed expected Micah to protest. To burst out laughing or reply with a rude quip. Instead, the boy sucked in a hitched breath. "It's so hard," he said. Micah lowered his hands, and his eyes were red rimmed.

"I know it is," Frond said gently.

"I thought if I joined the Knights Guild, I could toughen up. *Bash* it out of me or something. But the morning of the Guildculling, I went to Makiva's tent and I saw this *boy* my age standing inside and I just . . . I knew. The way I felt when I looked at him—at his stupid, pointy, *adorable* ears—that wasn't going away."

Micah's gaze darkened. "Then I landed in the Healers Guild. I'd heard what the Golden Way thought of kids like me, of course. Brenner especially. I panicked."

"You aren't in the Healers Guild anymore," Frond assured him. "You found your way to *us*."

"I'm sorry, Zed," Micah mumbled. Fie, he was actually crying! Zed took a step back, shaking his head. Micah flicked his eyes in his direction.

"*No,*" Zed muttered. First Brock and now this. It was too much. He felt his body growing strangely loose the more upset he became. The mist that made up his form was harder to hold together. "*No, this doesn't make sense.*"

"Micah," Frond said soothingly, "it's all right. Zed doesn't need to know any of this if you don't want him to."

Micah barked out a despairing laugh.

"*Zed,*" said Foster, billowing to his side. "*Listen, it's okay. Just keep calm.*" The fox actually looked worried. The joke had been taken too far.

Zed whirled on him. "*No!*" he shouted. "*No, it's actually* not *okay! Nothing is okay right now, if we're being honest! But what do you care, right? As long as you can get some entertainment out of* our *lives, because you've given up on your own!*"

Foster billowed back, his canine expression pinched in either grief or guilt. The edges of his shape began to bleed slowly into the air. "*Zed . . .*"

"*Just leave me alone!*" Zed bellowed.

And the last thing he saw as he flowed from the room was Micah's face.

Those red-rimmed eyes stayed on him until he passed through the wall, into darkness.

✷

Makiva sat alone in Zed's room. No candle had been lit, and the door was wedged shut, blocking the warm glow from the guildhall.

She didn't mind the dark. Many, *many* of her long years in Terryn had been spent submerged in gloom and quiet. Darkness was an old friend now.

She sat with her eyes closed, a small smile playing across Zed's face. She didn't open them even when the door creaked quietly open.

A shadow stood in the pane of light that fell over her, a figure looming silently for a moment, before exhaling.

"I said wait for *me* to contact *you*," Makiva chided her visitor. "For all you know, Zed and Foster could be here right now, watching us this very moment."

"You also said they couldn't stop us. That no one would hear them."

"There are always surprises where magic is involved. Even for me, it seems."

"Was all this really necessary?" the figure asked. "Hexam? The market?"

"It was," Makiva answered plainly.

"But *why*?"

Now it was her turn to exhale, Zed's face twisting in annoyance. But Makiva kept her eyes closed. "I needed suspicion pointed elsewhere," she said. "On the wrong targets. Don't lose heart now. The plan is nearly ready. Zed's power has grown."

The figure shifted uncertainly. "And when this is over, things will be right again? You'll grant my wish?"

"Of course," Makiva said. Finally, she opened Zed's eyes and smiled at her visitor. "Together, you and I will save this world."

Chapter Twelve
Brock

Brock moved as fast as his legs would carry him. He didn't know where he was going; he didn't have a plan. He just knew that he had to get away.

He couldn't deal with their questions, their accusations—the shock and disappointment in their eyes. What could he say? It was all true. They'd trusted him, and he'd been lying the whole time.

Had he really thought he wouldn't get caught? That Zed, Frond . . . Liza . . . that they would never learn what he'd been up to behind their backs?

Brock punched a stone wall, and his knuckles came back

pink and raw. Not smart—he'd feel that later. Right now, though, all he could feel was fury.

"Stupid," he said, and he rubbed his burning eyes. He was used to being angry. People—adults, mostly—made him angry all the time. But this? This was different.

Brock wasn't used to being so angry at *himself*.

Her little spider . . .

He took a shaky breath to steady himself, then looked over his shoulder. He didn't think Frond would chase him down and murder him in the middle of intown, but it *was* possible.

He needed to get off the streets and get his head together. He needed to go home—not to the guildhall, but to his parents' house, the house where he'd grown up. Just thinking of it, he felt a sudden and overwhelming desire to sleep in his old bed and eat his mother's cooking.

Brock missed feeling like a kid.

He ran the rest of the way, approaching the house from the rear, where there was a trellis. Back when he would sneak out of the house, skipping out on studying or chores to meet up with Zed, he'd used that trellis to climb down from, and back up to, his second-story bedroom. And right now, sneaking into his bedroom sounded far preferable to explaining everything to his parents.

He put a foot on the trellis and tested it. He was heavier than he used to be—all the training and exercise and running for his life had built muscle—but it held his weight, and he scaled it effortlessly, his hands and feet moving over its surface in a familiar sequence. He slid the window open without making a sound.

The room was dark, and Brock was blind as his eyes adjusted. But he knew the room's layout even with his eyes closed, and as the adrenaline left his body he let a wave of weariness carry him straight to his bed.

He realized too late that the bed was occupied.

Some small animal shrilled, squirming out from beneath Brock and snapping its jaws at him. He flinched away, tumbling out of the bed; something gripped his ankles, keeping him from standing, and he heard the creature hit the ground nearby with a thump. It circled him in the dark, its talons clacking on the hardwood, yipping fiercely.

Kobold! his mind screamed.

Brock drew his daggers. He slashed blindly ahead of him in wide arcs. "Come on, then," he said. One of his daggers cut into something soft. "Come on!"

The door to the room slammed open, and a figure stood outlined in the lantern light that came flooding in from the hallway.

"Brock Lilyorchid Dunderfel!" his mother cried. "What in all of Terryn are you doing?"

Brock froze, taking in the chaotic scene. He had a blanket wrapped around his feet, and a dagger in each hand—one of them hilt-deep in a tasseled pink pillow. Feathers drifted all around him like snow. The creature, cowering in the corner, had fallen silent and looked anxiously from Brock to his mother. It was no kobold.

"You . . . got a dog?" he asked.

"And new bedding," she said. "Feel free to stab anything you don't like, though." She stepped over him to take the trembling fluffy white dog up in her arms. She cradled it like a baby.

Brock untangled himself and drew slowly to his feet. The room was unrecognizable. Lace doilies adorned every surface, and chewed-up rag dolls were strewn across the floor. There was pink everywhere—pink curtains, pink bedding, pink rug. A big pink ribbon sat atop the dog's head.

"Where's all my stuff?" he asked.

His mom hesitated. "Well . . . Princess Dandy Lion has a very small bladder. . . ."

"Did you give my room to a dog?" he asked, his voice breaking and his eyes welling with tears.

"Oh, darling, what's wrong?" His mom took a step toward him, and he leaned forward for a hug—but she pulled back when the dog emitted a low growl.

Brock burst into tears then. He just stood there in the middle of the pink room, covered in downy feathers, feeling small and alone, his breaths hitching and his shoulders shaking.

His mom put the dog down and wrapped her arms around him, and Brock let the tears flow while the dog yapped and growled and nipped at his ankles.

*

That night, Brock dreamed of a long hallway lined with doors.

Those doors were important, he knew. They held dark things

at bay. He could hear some of those things scratching, clawing, gnashing their teeth on the other side.

One of the doors flew open. Brock strained with all his might to close it again, but a howling gale blew in from the darkness beyond the doorway, pushing against Brock so that he made no progress. The wind smelled of rot. And while Brock fought against it, another door farther down the hall banged open. And a third . . .

Suddenly Zed was there, standing right beside him.

Brock felt a rush of hope. "Zed, help me close this door!"

Zed's face lit up. "*You can— You can see me?*" he asked.

"I'd love to see you *helping* me right now," Brock said, straining.

But his friend looked suddenly fearful. "*You have to wake up.*"

"What?" he said. "But these doors . . ."

"*Brock, you're in danger! Wake up! Wake up, Brock! Wake—*"

Brock sat bolt upright in bed. It was too dark to see, but he could feel someone else's presence in the room.

A small green flame lit in the darkness.

"Zed?" Brock said. "Am I still dreaming?"

"Aren't we all?" Zed sighed. "Isn't Freestone itself a dream, if you think about it? A shared delusion that the world never ended."

Brock rubbed his face groggily. "Okay, it's *way* too early for that kind of talk. Or too late. What are you even doing here?" The events of the previous day came back to him all at once. "I . . . guess I owe you an apology. . . ."

Zed scoffed. "An apology?" He used his flame to light Brock's bedside lantern, then closed his fist. Smoke seeped out from between his fingers. "For what? For protecting me against the ignorant and superstitious?" He shook his head. "You were a true friend to me. It's not your fault you were manipulated."

Something that had been coiled up tight in Brock's chest loosened on hearing that. Maybe he'd been right to keep Zed's secrets at any cost. Or to try to . . .

"Well, then I owe you an apology for not being secretive *enough*. The king apparently knew everything all along."

"Not everything," Zed said. "He seems to know only what this 'Lady Gray' tells him." His eyes glittered in the eerie green light. "So who is she?"

"You mean is it spelled *g-r-a-y* or *g-r-e-y*? I always wondered, too," Brock answered. "But I can tell you from experience that she also answers to 'Lady Beige,' 'Lady Nay-Say,' and 'Lady-You're-the-Worst.'" He smiled. "She really hates that last one."

"I mean who *is* she?" Zed said hotly. "How does she mask herself? It's not magic . . ."

Brock frowned. He shrugged.

"Where would you meet? In her home? Does she live in the palace?"

Brock was already shrugging, so he hitched his shoulders up even higher. "She had an office underground. There was a door to it in the merchants' guildhall, but they sealed it off."

Zed's frustration was evident, even in the low and flickering light.

"Why's it matter to you?" Brock asked. "Did Frond put you up to this?" King's orders or not, he could imagine the guildmistress would hold a grudge against the spymaster. The spymaster, *and* her spies.

Zed ignored the questions. "So if you wanted to meet with her, right now, you'd have no way to get in touch?"

"She contacted me, not the other way around. Listen, is Frond . . . very angry about all this?"

Zed smirked. "How could you even tell?" There was a scratching sound at the bedroom door: nails on wood.

"Weird," Brock said. "That's just like my dream. You and I were in a hallway . . ."

Zed's focus shifted to a corner of the room, like he was looking at something Brock couldn't see. "I was in your dream, was I?" He clucked his tongue.

The dog whined on the other side of the door.

"Did I say anything . . . interesting in this dream of yours?" Zed asked. In the green light cast by the lantern, he looked sickly—even menacing.

"I don't remember," Brock said hesitantly.

The dog started barking, so high-pitched that Brock winced.

Yap yap.

"I should go, then," Zed said. "Let you get some . . . undisturbed sleep."

Brock turned in bed; he could swear Zed was focused on the far wall, but there was nothing there. He heard his mother coming up the hallway, making shushing sounds, and that dog—

Yap yap yap.

"I'd keep your distance for a few days, Brock," Zed said.

"What, really? I thought maybe—"

Zed shook his head. "I'd just lie low if I were you, okay? Let me try to smooth things over with Frond."

"If you say so . . ."

Yap yap yap yap yap.

The door swung open, and the dog charged into the room. Brock turned to warn Zed—its little teeth were sharp—but his friend was already gone. If not for the wisp of silvery smoke, Brock might have thought he'd dreamed the entire thing.

His mom leaned in the doorway, half-asleep. "Sorry, Brock. I know it's your room, but maybe you two could share it for the night?"

"That's fine," Brock said, watching the dog turn in frantic circles before fixing her gaze on the far wall and cocking her head.

If his mom noticed the green fire in the lantern, she didn't mention it.

✱

Brock hardly slept the rest of the night. Zed's visit had unnerved him, and the dog, small as it was, somehow managed to claim a disproportionately large share of the bed.

He shuffled groggily downstairs. "So, fun fact: Princess Dandelion snores," he said, yawning.

"It's Princess *Dandy Lion*," his mother corrected.

"Yeah, that's what I said." He yawned again, scooping himself a bowl of oats. "Where's Father?"

"Left early for guild business. We're supposed to go in together, but lately Quilby always has some pressing business that just can't wait. . . ."

Brock swallowed a dry spoonful of oats, imagining today's "pressing business" had to do with yesterday's council meeting. Quilby hadn't been any happier than Frond with the king's revelations. He cleared his throat.

"That's funny, because things have been *super quiet* with the Sea of Stars lately. I keep asking, 'Where is all this *adventure* you guys promised?' Grr!" He shook his fists in mock frustration. "So I thought I might just hang out here for a day or two."

His mom's eyes lit up. She slid into the seat across from him. "Maybe I'll take the day off, too. You can help me with my project!"

"Sure," Brock said. "Is it finding a new home for the dog?"

Her smile didn't falter. "You are not as funny as you think you are," she sang. "But no. I thought it would be nice to do something for all those poor elven refugees."

Brock quirked an eyebrow. "You know they . . . went *home*, right? They're not refugees anymore. Or poor."

She waved his words away. "Yes, well, I had the idea months ago, but things were just so hectic."

"For some of us more than others," Brock said, remembering the endless parade of undead horrors. He shuddered, pushing the memories away. "All right, so it's a welcome-home present, then. A sign of continued friendship between the cities. I like it! What have you got?"

She raised her hands, spreading her fingers to let the anticipation build. Then: "Ear warmers," she said.

"I'm sorry, what?" Brock asked. "What are ear warmers?"

"They're like . . . well, imagine mittens. Same idea."

Brock frowned. "So why don't you just make mittens?"

"Oh, those are very complicated. All the . . ." She gestured at her fingers. "The shapes. Besides, it's too late to change course now."

"Why?"

Her eyes darted to a large wicker basket in the corner. And one on the counter.

And two under some chairs.

"Mom . . . how many ear warmers have you made so far?"

"I'm not sure, but . . . it's definitely an even number. That's very important. As you can imagine."

Brock grinned awkwardly. There was a long beat of silence.

"It's also not winter anymore," he said.

"Now you're just being contrary!" she said. "It's a fine idea. Don't you think they'll like it? Maybe you can give a few pairs to Zed. Do you know his top four favorite colors?"

There was a knock at the door. "I'll get it!" Brock said, happy for the interruption.

As Brock opened the front door, he was chuckling to himself. But his laughter stopped cold when he saw Lotte standing on the threshold. She looked ashen.

"What is it?" Brock asked. "Did something happen? Is Zed all right?"

Lotte rubbed her temple. "Honestly, Brock, I don't know if you're the most self-centered person I know or the least."

"Okay," Brock said. "Well, I guess *I* don't know whether to say thank you or slam the door in your face."

"I just mean you should worry more about yourself," she said, sad and sharp at the same time. She shook her head mournfully. "I warned you, Brock. When I caught you sneaking around, I told you that you had to stop."

"I did stop," Brock said, his heart speeding up. "I stopped as soon as . . . well, not long after that."

Lotte gave him a sad little smile. Then she blinked twice, dropping the emotion from her face. Now she was all business.

"Brock Dunderfel," she said coldly. "Per city statute five-E and the bylaws of our own organization, I regret to inform you that effective immediately, you are no longer a recognized apprentice of the Adventurers Guild."

The words were nonsense to Brock. His mind was reeling, struggling to make sense of it.

"What– What does that mean?"

"It means–I'm so sorry, Brock," she said, emotion flashing once more across her face before she squashed it down again. "It means you're guildless."

Chapter Thirteen
Zed

Makiva moved swiftly between the market stalls, clutching Zed's satchel to his chest. After the mindtooth attack, this section of the bazaar had been closed to the public for the adventurers' investigations. But between a rogue warlock in their leadership and a thieving rogue among their apprentices, the Sea of Stars had little time for scraping pink goo from the bricks. So the market remained eerily empty.

Just as she'd designed.

She was so close now. Worlds away from home, and yet tantalizingly near. Behind her, Zed floated forlornly in his etheric body—the technical name for his current intangible state, not that he knew it. His brooding eyes watched her intensely. Zed had been quiet all morning, but he was an especially sticky shadow today, never straying far from her side. As usual, Makiva ignored him.

It had been a mistake to speak to him in the demiplane, even for a brief moment. She'd managed to hide her secret ally from him these past weeks—and from Foster the previous *year*—only through extreme prudence, meeting exclusively in the rare moments they were away.

Now her little indulgence had added fire to Zed's determination to frustrate her plans. Somehow he'd made contact with the healer, she'd sensed that much. Makiva couldn't understand exactly *how* until Brock himself revealed that he'd dreamed of Zed.

So the boy could reach his friends while they slept? It must not be easy, or he'd have warned the whole guild by now. Still, this complicated things. It would only be a matter of time before Zed broke through and someone went to Frond. And beyond the fact that Zed's etheric body could stray only so far from the chain, Makiva had no power over where he went or what he did. Not even her green fire could touch him as he was. Not until the ritual.

Micah, however, was another story.

Why *hadn't* Micah given her away already? He'd attempted an exorcism, the fool. Whatever his reasons, Makiva would have to deal with the healer soon. She was *too close* to fail now. How many long centuries had she suffered here, enduring even the misstep with Foster? Her patience was vast, but it wasn't infinite.

"Hello there, goblin." A low growl crept from between the tents.

Behind Makiva, Zed let out a little gasp, just as a lumbering figure stepped into view. The man was thick with muscle, his wrists at least as large as Zed's neck. He grinned merrily at Makiva. His bright blue eyes shone with cheerful loathing.

"*Dimas Orlov . . .*" Zed breathed behind her.

Makiva studied this man, Dimas, as he watched her like a lion on the hunt. Some tormentor of Zed's, then? How small she must appear to him, alone in the empty market. Easy prey. Makiva's many apprentices had all been hunted by similar figures at one time or another. It was what brought them to her, what spurred them to accept the power she offered. They wished to drive away the prowling lions.

"Hello, Dimas." Makiva spoke with Zed's voice, clear and calm. "I don't think you're supposed to be here. This part of the market is for adventurers only." She tilted Zed's smile into a smirk. "It's not safe."

"Safe . . ." Dimas grated. "Seems nowhere's safe anymore. When I was your age, there were no monsters in Freestone. That all started with you, goblin. I wish you'd disappear from this city." The man took a step forward, his grin widening. "Maybe you will today."

Makiva could smell the mead on the man's breath, odiously sweet. She reached nonchalantly into her satchel, closing Zed's fingers over the cool stone handle inside.

"*Run,*" Zed pleaded, though to whom Makiva couldn't say. Her gaze stayed on the brute before her.

"I can promise you that the monsters didn't begin with Zed Kagari," she crooned with a smile of her own. "And they'll be here long after you and he are both gone."

"You talkin' down to me, goblin?" Dimas's accusation came out slurred, which only riled him further. He took another step. "You think you're better than me, you pointy-eared *pansy*?"

"Am *I*? Assuredly. But I'm going to let you in on a secret, Dimas." Makiva pulled the blade from her satchel. "I'm *not* Zed."

"What?" Dimas's eyes flicked down to the curved knife in Zed's hand.

Months ago, when she'd fled her tent, Makiva had been forced to leave the blade behind. Retrieving it from the Mages Guild storeroom had taken weeks of careful scheming, and not a small amount of luck—tempting Phylo with the mindtooth to implicate the mages, then framing Hexam to draw attention from her coconspirator.

But now that the ancient focus was back in her possession, she had nearly everything she needed to finish her plan.

No one—not Zed or Micah, not Brock or Frond; *certainly* not this ogre of a man—would be allowed to stand in her way.

"Don't get me wrong," Makiva muttered, lifting the blade

so it caught the morning light. The metal reflected with a green tinge. "Zed was better than you, too. At least as far as people go. He was a diligent boy with an innate gift for magic. Given time and proper training, he might have become a great sorcerer. But when I stole this body, Zed's grasp of his own gift was still unrefined."

Makiva turned her gaze back from the dagger to Dimas. The man watched her with equal parts shock and skepticism, his mouth curled into a sneer.

"Let's see what he can *really* do," she said. With that, Makiva disappeared in a silvery cloud of mist.

Behind her, Zed yelped as his etheric body was yanked into the world of gray. No doubt Foster—wherever he was hiding—had similarly found himself in this foggy domain. It wasn't the first time she'd pulled them here while elf-stepping, and Zed had pulled Foster many times more in the weeks preceding his possession. Small jaunts weren't too taxing on them, but what came next would be an ordeal for the two.

All the better.

In an instant she was back in the market, standing just behind the Orlov goon.

Makiva thrust the dagger forward, stabbing into his side.

Dimas screamed as the blade struck. He twisted around, swinging his meaty fist like a cudgel. Makiva ducked below it, then raised Zed's hand to clamp around Dimas's overextended wrist. She summoned a gout of green flame between her fingers.

The man's hand and forearm burned suddenly black, his veins shimmering prettily with green fire. They were incinerated into a puff of oily ash in all the time it took her to exhale.

That was when the screaming *really* began.

Makiva elf-stepped again, lest they draw unwanted attention. The market dissolved into mist, all the tents and stacked stalls melting into the strange silvery world that Zed traversed when he used his sorcery.

She'd carried Dimas with them, her blade still buried in his side. It was a feat Zed hadn't even realized he could accomplish, taking someone along during his elf-steps. If only he'd had a teacher who was more versed in sorcerous approaches to magic. Poor thing.

Now she'd show him another trick. Instead of appearing somewhere new, Makiva clamped down on Zed's mana, siphoning it gradually to suspend the spell. She could feel the silver mist that surrounded them protesting, trying to spit her back into Terryn. It roiled in displeasure at this trespass, these foreign bodies treading where mortals were not welcome.

"*What's happening?*" Zed cried out in a warped echo, after a long moment had passed without them phasing back into Freestone. "*Why haven't we reappeared?*"

The boy's etheric body was dissolving in the demiplane. Zed's form trailed away in lines of smoke, to merge with the mist. Best hurry, then. She still needed enough of Zed left to perform the ritual.

Makiva yanked her blade from Dimas Orlov's side, then took a step back and kicked him off his feet. His fall echoed strangely against the floor of this place. Now, as he lay prone in the fog, Dimas's screams abated, but the weeping was almost worse. Blood poured from the wound at his side, soaking through his sweat-stained tunic. He cradled his destroyed arm.

"This place once had many names, depending on who you asked." Makiva spoke mildly, squatting beside the man. "The In-Between. The Ether. The Veil. It's the membrane that separates Terryn and the other planes, at least when it's working correctly." She smiled at Dimas. "I've always found it eerily beautiful. The quiet is calming. Perhaps that will be a small comfort when the world has forgotten you." Makiva stood again. She hitched her shoulders in an apologetic shrug. "Because this place will be both your deathbed and your grave."

"*Makiva, no!*" Zed protested.

Dimas's eyes widened in horror. He reached toward her with his remaining hand. "Please, don—!"

Makiva released the spell. Instantly she was back, the silvery mist burning away to reveal the marketplace once again. Zed curled beside her, struggling to maintain his shape after their prolonged exposure to the Veil. Otherwise, the market was completely empty of people.

No one would ever see Dimas Orlov again.

Zed fled the market as fast as he was able. His smoky body still felt tenuous after all that time in what Makiva had called the Veil. It was an effort just to hold himself together, but he had to get back to the guildhall, to tell *someone* what had just happened.

Makiva had murdered a man. She'd left Dimas in some ethereal in-between place to die alone. And she'd used Zed's magic to do it.

But who *could* he tell? Zed had made fleeting contact with Brock—*Brock spoke to me!*—but the connection was severed too quickly to explain anything. Zed wouldn't be able to try again until Brock slept, and by then it might be too late. Too late for Freestone, too late for Hexam, and too late for anyone else unlucky enough to stand in Makiva's way.

It was still morning in Freestone. The sun hadn't yet breached the wall, but the colorful noise of its siege filled the sky with a riot of pinks, yellows, and pale blues. All around Zed, people were rousing. Sleepy-eyed men and women swept the footpaths in front of their homes. Neighbors called out greetings.

None noticed Zed, the invisible herald of doom.

Micah was his only option. Even as he tried to think of *anyone* else, the boy's face flashed through Zed's mind as he'd last seen it, those dark eyes hurt and vulnerable. The thought of facing Micah now filled Zed with a cavernous sense of uncertainty. All this time, the boy Zed had thought of as an unfeeling braggart had in fact been harboring a hidden . . .

What? A crush? It seemed ridiculous and presumptuous to

even think the word. Boys like Micah didn't get *crushes* on boys like Zed; not unless crushing them into the dirt counted. And yet Micah had admitted it to Frond with Zed standing right there. He'd *apologized*, even.

Zed could barely process the combination of *feelings* and *Micah*, much less understand his *own* feelings on the matter. Certainly there were more pressing issues at hand.

And yet, even as he billowed toward the guildhall—toward Micah—he thought of the boy sneaking into Hexam's office on his behalf. Of Micah challenging a centuries-old witch to a mystical battle of wills, and refusing to give up on Zed, long after Zed had given up on himself.

And as Zed thought of these things, something deep inside him—hidden within that dark, cavernous uncertainty—rang out. It was like the first warm note from a minstrel's harp.

It didn't take long after his arrival at the guildhall for any such music to be buried again. As Zed passed through the door, he found his friends and half a dozen journey-rank adventurers standing in the receiving room, all shouting at Frond. The guildmistress stood with her arms crossed, stoically accepting their anger, even as their voices drowned one another out.

Lotte stood to the side of the room, looking tired and sad.

Zed found Micah among the apprentices, shifting anxiously from foot to foot. He floated to the healer's side, just grateful that he didn't have ears to burn or a heartbeat to race.

"*Micah!*" Zed chirped. "*We've got to talk! Makiva just attacked*

Dimas Orlov in the market and she trapped him in the Veil, and I think she knows I can . . ." He trailed off as the boy's eyes widened with his arrival. "*What's going on? Is this about Hexam?*"

"No," Micah whispered. "It's Brock. Frond kicked him out of the guild. She sent the Dolt to do it this morning."

Zed's mouth fell open. A fresh storm of shock squalled through his cloudy body. He'd just seen Brock last night! He would have assumed this was Makiva's handiwork, except he'd been watching his body all morning.

Could *Frond* really have abandoned one of her own apprentices?

"Guildmistress!" Liza's voice cut through the shouts as cleanly as her blade through a carelessly stuffed practice dummy. The room quieted as she spoke, and Zed realized that he recognized many of the older adventurers in the room. Beyond Syd and Fife, there were Eyva, Preet, and Raif . . . and others whose names he didn't know. All were guildmembers whom Brock had taken the time to befriend since joining.

"Please don't do this," Liza continued. Her voice buckled beneath some heavy emotion. "I'm as angry as anyone, but we both heard the Lady Gray's testimony. Brock was blackmailed!"

"He's one of us!" Jett chimed in, Jayna nodding furiously beside him. "You told me once that the Sea of Stars doesn't abandon our own. That we guide the lost by working *together*!"

At that, Frond's face finally moved, tightening into a grimace.

"Frond," Lotte began cautiously, "maybe they're right. Brock is still young. Whatever bad habits he's developed, it might be possible to show him a better way. Perhaps we're being hasty."

"And he's been trying to atone!" Fel added. "He helped stop the brain-jaw before it killed more adventurers!"

"It's already done," the guildmistress grated. "Brock betrayed us. He betrayed all of *you*." She uncrossed her arms, her fingers hurriedly tapping the pointed stars on her belt. "I don't like it, either. Losing another guildmember so soon after Clobbler and Hexam . . . this has severely hurt our numbers. But it had to be done."

Liza's expression darkened, her shoulders stiffening. "Is that really all we mean to you?" she rasped. "Numbers? We just lost three of our own—one an apprentice who you discarded like a broken blade—and you're worried about the *roster*?"

Zed had never heard Liza sound so bitter—so heartbroken—and certainly never at Frond. All eyes fell to her.

Frond, too, narrowed her eyes on the girl. "Lest you forget," she said, "*our numbers* are the first and last defense that Freestone has against the things out *there*." She pointed sharply toward the back wall. Somewhere behind it, a thick metal door offered passage to the horrors beyond.

Liza shook her head, her lips pressed into a hard line. "I can't believe what I'm hearing. Even a *thousand* adventurers won't stand a chance against the Dangers without faith in their leader. Today, Guildmistress . . ." She paused, her eyes burning. Jayna placed her hand gently on Liza's arm, perhaps in an effort to keep her from stepping too far.

Liza stepped anyway. "Today you lost my faith," she murmured. With that, she stormed toward the front door, passing right through Zed on her way there. Liza paused for a moment, a look of confusion softening her expression. Her eyes searched the spot where Zed was standing.

"*Liza!*" Zed shouted. "*Liza, I'm here!*"

But she'd already turned away. The whole room shook as she slammed the door closed behind her.

Technically, Zed didn't need to breathe anymore, but it still felt as if all the air had departed the room with Liza. The remaining guildmembers watched the door in a daze. Frond in particular wore a miserable scowl, her fingers playing across her throwing stars in a frantic, soundless percussion. The room was utterly silent. Finally, Frond herself broke the spell.

"Fel," she grumbled. "Come to my quarters. I have a job for you."

The night elf still frowned after Liza. Her gaze was cold as she turned it from the door to the guildmistress, as if weighing who to follow.

"Fel," Frond said, her voice softer, "please."

The girl nodded, but the coldness never left her eyes. "Yes, Guildmistress." The two disappeared up the stairs.

As other adventurers began exiting the room, Zed turned

to Micah. "*I can't believe this is happening. Everyone's at each other's throats.*"

"Zed . . ." Micah whispered. "It gets worse. I need you to follow me right now."

Zed's smoky body churned apprehensively. "*Micah, I'm sorry I ran away. You don't have to explain anything. If I'm honest . . .*"

The boy's face pinched and he shook his head. Zed grew quiet at his serious expression. "It's not about that," Micah muttered with a sigh. "It's your friend. Your . . . spirit guide? I think he's sick."

Chapter Fourteen
Brock

Brock was walking his mother's dog and feeling thoroughly sorry for himself when he spotted a familiar face among the midmorning crowds.

Working for the Shadows, masks had been a requirement whenever he'd spent time at the Lady Gray's court. The masks were largely ornamental and symbolic, a reminder to keep the guild's business a secret. As a result, Brock had actually recognized a few of his guildmates—including the town's perfumer, who'd assisted Master Curse's experiments on Dangers.

Somehow, things always got complicated for Brock after that man crossed his path. And he was crossing it now, cutting toward outtown with steely purpose.

Brock thought to himself: *Who cares? It's none of my concern now.* But by the time he'd finished the thought, he was already unconsciously trailing the man, dragging the dog along behind him.

He couldn't help it. He was naturally curious. And the perfumer might have been there when Curse was infected, might know something more about what had happened. Furthermore, as a member of the Shadows, he could lead Brock to the Lady Gray's lair. Brock had half a mind to tell her off.

The other half of his mind was seriously considering begging her to take him back.

Guildlessness was no small thing; it was, in its own way, as sure a death sentence as being banished beyond the wall. It's just that it took longer, and stripped you of your dignity first. With no source of money and no way to contribute to Freestone, the guildless might survive for a time on charity. Brock's parents could take care of him for as long as they were around—but he was forbidden to inherit from them, and their status would diminish the longer he stayed with them.

He tried to pretend his father wouldn't care about losing status, but he knew better. In fact, it was his father's hunger for prestige that had gotten Brock recruited by the Shadows in the first place.

He felt the Lady Gray owed him—that she should fix this somehow. But as he continued following his best lead to the Shadows, he realized that she wouldn't see it like that. Certainly he had nothing to offer her now—no details about the adventurers, no maps of the wilds outside the wall, none of the trinkets and treasures she so coveted.

That was the whole idea behind guildlessness. Brock had nothing to offer anybody—nothing of value at all.

He stopped at the end of an alleyway and peered around a corner. The perfumer was pressing into the crowd around the marketplace, skirting around the barricaded area and heading for the open quad with the statues of the Champions. Brock knew the man's shop had not yet reopened since the elves left for Llethanyl. Maybe he was on an errand for his gray mistress—or maybe he was just shopping.

Should he turn back around? Was this pointless? Brock wasn't accustomed to indecision, but the path forward had never been so occluded before.

Then he heard a voice whisper at his shoulder: "Are you being incognito?"

Brock yelped and spun around. "Fel? What are you— Why— How do you even know what *incognito* means?"

Fel cocked her head, as if to say, *Oh really?* "I've been here for months, Brock. And the humans' trade tongue is actually quite simplistic."

"I think you mean 'simple.'"

"Do I?" Fel said. She tapped her chin. "And I just thought of something. You tease dwarves for having so many words for *rock*. But why do humans have so many words for *sneaky*?"

Brock sighed. "You may have a point. I take it you heard about my . . . change in status?"

Fel's mirth dropped away. She put a hand on his shoulder. "I did. I'm sorry. But I trust it will all work out."

Brock smiled sadly. "Of course you do. You're optimistic like that." He slapped his forehead. "Oh, I forgot!" He peeked around the corner again, but his quarry was gone. Brock had been sure the perfumer was heading for the statue of Dox, but the area all around the statue was empty. "I was following someone."

"I'm an excellent tracker," Fel offered. "Do you have a piece of him?"

"A . . . piece?"

"A lock of his hair. A toenail clipping."

"Uh, no," Brock said. "Thanks anyway. It's nothing."

Fel's cat, Mousebane, sniffed warily at Dandy Lion. Brock wrapped the leash around his wrist, keeping the dog just out of Mousebane's reach.

"You have a cute dog."

"Thanks, do you want her?"

"No, thank you," Fel said. "I already ate."

Brock's eyes went wide.

Fel's laughter tinkled. "I am making a joke, Brock."

"Oh." Brock bashfully scratched the back of his head. "That was wicked. I think I'm rubbing off on you, Fel."

"I'm glad we've learned from each other these past weeks.

It's given me a good sense of your capabilities, and I wonder if I could ask for your help with something."

"Sure." Brock shrugged. "I've got nothing but time. What do you need?"

Fel looked all around them. "It's a sensitive matter. Do you know of a private place we could speak?"

"Why? Fel, what's going on?"

Fel lowered her voice. "It's about Hexam. They intend to execute him."

Brock felt a contradictory swirl of emotions. Hexam had been a kind and patient mentor, and far more lenient than Frond or Lotte. Brock had genuinely liked the man. But when he tried to picture Hexam now, he saw Justyn dropping to the ground. He remembered Curse's eyes, cloudy with terror and confusion.

He fought to keep his emotions off his face, but Fel was hard to fool. Her eyes drifted over his tense shoulders and clenched fists. "I know you're hurt," she said. "Betrayal poisons us as surely as any Danger's venom. But we *must* speak of Hexam before it's too late."

"All right," Brock said. He rolled his shoulders back and puffed out his chest. "I know a place we can go." At his feet, the dog sniffed the ground and spun in a tight little circle. "Just as soon as the princess has had a tinkle."

Brock led Fel through the outskirts of intown, keenly aware of the stares, though the elf seemed used to them. The looks they drew were mostly looks of curiosity. Freestone was small enough that word of the elf who'd stayed behind had found every ear, and Fel seemed to benefit from the adventurers' newfound respectability. Many passersby gave small smiles or polite nods.

Brock remembered, though. He knew how many of these people had refused to help the elves in their hour of need, and it was a stain on the city he'd once loved without reservation.

His mother, for her part, lit with genuine joy at the sight of Fel. "You've brought a friend!" she crooned. "A little elf friend!"

"That's right, large human mother," Brock replied. "This is Fel."

His mother clucked her tongue at him. "I'm *medium* at most. Welcome, dear. Make yourself at home."

"Your house is so big," Fel said, cradling Mousebane to her chest and looking around with wide eyes, to the evident delight of Brock's mother. "And yet so lifeless," she said. "So much dead wood in this city."

Brock's mother drooped a little at that, but she quickly sprang back. "Actually, Fel, I'm glad you're here." She took a thin cloth ruler from her crafting table. "Would you mind terribly if I measured your ears?"

"We're going to my room!" Brock said, tugging on Fel's arm.

"Or, I guess, the dog's room. We're going to the pink monstrosity that used to be my only refuge!"

Brock pulled Fel up the stairs, Mousebane following at their heels. The cat slipped into the bedroom just before Brock slammed the door shut behind him.

"Sorry about that," he said. "She can be a bit intense at first, but when you get to know her, she's actually quite evil."

Fel smiled shyly. "You're lucky," she said, and Brock remembered that Fel's parents had been rangers. They'd died defending Llethanyl.

He cleared his throat. "You, uh, wanted to talk about Hexam?"

"Yes." Fel nodded. "I've been thinking about it. And I don't believe Hexam is guilty."

Brock sighed. "Fel, listen, I know it's hard to accept, but the evidence was clear. The magus who died in the marketplace was the same magus who got Hexam kicked out of the Mages Guild."

"That's true," Fel said.

"And when Hexam was given free run of Silverglow Tower, he provided us with potentially lifesaving magical devices—devices that didn't work."

"Also true," Fel said.

"And, oh yeah—we found a very magical, super-forbidden planar tunnel leading right through the wards and into Hexam's personal workspace!"

"So many true things," Fel said, scratching the fur under

Mousebane's chin. "Also true: Hexam is a very intelligent man. And while intelligent men make mistakes—"

"—those are three really big mistakes," Brock finished. "Almost like . . . like we were meant to catch him."

"You said it yourself: The evidence was clear. In truth it's *so* clear as to be unbelievable."

"Oh, man." Brock ran his fingers through his hair. "I think maybe you're right. How could he believe for a second he'd get away with those things?" He sat heavily in a chair. "Unless he was never meant to. It's a setup, and we all fell for it."

Fel grinned. "Most of us."

"But why? And how? The magic involved . . . the Dangers . . . Who in all of Freestone could pull it off?"

"That is an excellent question to ask Hexam. Preferably while his head is still attached."

There was a soft knock on the door.

"Brock? Are you in there?"

It was Liza's voice.

Brock snapped his head around to Fel. "Does she know you're here?"

"No!" Fel whispered. She bit her lip. "This is supposed to be a secret mission."

"Hide!" Brock said, shooing her and Mousebane toward the closet door. "Go!" As soon as they were out of sight, Brock struck a casual pose, leaning against a bookcase with one elbow. "Come in!" he said, and his voice cracked.

The door swung open. "I'm sorry to just drop in unannounced," Liza said immediately. "I had to— Why are you standing like that?"

"Like what?" Brock said. He leaned farther into the bookshelf.

Liza gave him a suspicious look, then her eyes drifted across the room. "I didn't know you were so into pink," she said.

"Oh, uh, long story—"

"I like it," Liza said. "I think it's silly that boys and girls are supposed to like or dislike certain things. It's so random." Her fingers trailed along the pink curtains. "I like that you don't buy into that."

"I . . . have always loved pink," Brock said. "And . . . doilies."

"Enh," Liza said, scrunching up her nose.

It was strange, having her here. Though Liza wore training leathers instead of her usual armor, she still carried herself with the unmistakable poise and power of a warrior. The Solution, as always, was sheathed at her hip. Brock could only hope she wasn't spoiling for a fight. But if she was, who could blame her?

"I can guess why you're here," he said. Heat rose to his face. "I wish I could explain it all in a way that makes sense, but . . . all I can really do is say I'm sorry. I never meant for things to go so far."

"Sorry?" Liza scoffed. "For what?"

"Uh," Brock said. "Did you miss the part about me being a spy for a shadowy organization answerable only to the king?"

She waved his words away.

"You're not angry?" Brock asked in disbelief. "Liza, I've been lying to you since the day we met. And I don't know if you remember, but you recently gave a very rousing speech about the importance of being able to trust your guildmates."

"I *do* trust you," she insisted. "I trust you to go to absurd lengths to protect your best friend. I trust you to assume it's up to you to solve everything despite being surrounded by some pretty amazing people. I trust you to do bad things for good reasons and to come at problems from . . . unusual angles . . . which sometimes causes more problems . . ."

"Is that good?" Brock asked. "I'm not sure if this is a lecture or what."

Liza huffed. "I also trust you to make every conversation somewhat exhausting. My point is that I know who you are, Brock. And you belong on our team, flaws and all. I'm going to fight Frond on this."

Brock's eyebrows quirked. "You? Disagree with Frond? About a thing?"

"It's a day of firsts. After all, you *did* apologize to me a minute ago, didn't you?" She put out her hand. "Can we agree to a fresh start? No more lies?"

"No more lies," Brock echoed, taking her hand and shaking it.

She didn't let go, and neither did he. The handshake ended, and they just stood there, hands clasped, for a long beat of silence.

Brock felt stupidly happy just to have her there. And to know she didn't hate him.

He was lost in her brown eyes. Could she feel his heartbeat thudding in his fingertips?

Could she hear the cat meowing in his closet?

Liza cocked her head to the side.

"Brock . . . do you have a cat in your closet?"

"Not that I'm aware of."

Liza dropped his hand, looking deeply suspicious once more, and Brock knew the moment had passed. He sighed loudly. "Fel, come on out here."

The door slid open, and Mousebane leaped into the room. Fel smiled brightly and gave Liza a wave.

But Liza turned to Brock. "Really?" she said. "You couldn't go two moments without lying to me?"

"I honestly forgot they were there!" Brock protested.

"I just want you to know that I was not listening," Fel said.

"Thanks," Brock said.

"However, I heard everything. Dead wood does very little to block sound."

Brock groaned. "And they said guildlessness would be so lonely."

"But why are you in his closet?" Liza asked.

Fel bit her lip.

"It's okay, Fel," Brock said. "Total honesty, right?" He looked at Liza. "She's got our backs."

Fel nodded. "All right. Liza, how did you put it? We are about to do a bad thing for a good reason. We will defy the rule of your king and act without our guildmistress's knowledge. We will do all this to save an innocent life."

"We're breaking Hexam out of Silverglow Tower," Brock said. "And we're doing it tonight."

Chapter Fifteen

Zed

Zed burst through the door to Micah's room before Micah could even open it, passing bodilessly through the wood. Inside, he found Foster curled in his fox form, shivering on the bed.

He looked horrible. Mist trailed away from his body in ribbons. Even in his smaller shape, Foster was clearly having a difficult time holding himself together. His body billowed and frothed, the foxy features contorting.

"*Zed.*" Foster's voice was alarmingly weak. An echo of an echo. "*I think it's time . . .*"

"*No.*" Zed crouched over him as Micah hovered at the open

door, watching from a distance. "*Foster, hold on. You're going to be all right.*"

"Foster?" Micah repeated. "That's *Foster Pendleton*?"

Foster gasped out a wry laugh. "*We both knew . . . this would happen eventually. Zed, I'm sorry I couldn't help you stop Makiva. Among so many other things.*"

"*Stop it,*" Zed whimpered, shaking his head. "*You can't give up now. Don't leave me alone.*"

"*That . . .*" he panted, "*I'm happy to say . . . I won't be doing. You have Micah. Do you know . . . why I think he could hear you, Zed? Why you reached him above the others? You were already in his thoughts. He was just waiting for you . . . to hear* him." The foxy grin widened, Foster's eyes twinkling. "*You're both good kids. Work together. . . . End Makiva's plan.*"

Zed nodded. His misty body shivered with emotion.

"*Zed, will you do me one favor . . . before . . . ?*" Though Foster's form was rapidly softening, those two slitted eyes grew sharp.

"*Of course,*" Zed breathed.

"*Enter my memories . . . like you did with your friends. It will be easier. . . . The chain connects us. I want someone to see . . . the truth of that day.*"

Zed hesitated. Foster was asking him to live through the Day of Dangers firsthand? To witness the end of the world? He glanced toward Micah, but the boy just stared at him, his face clouded with bewilderment.

"Please, Zed," Foster huffed. *"For two hundred years . . . I've been Terryn's greatest villain. If just one person could be with me . . . in my worst moment."*

Zed nodded, turning back to the fox. *"Of course,"* he rasped. *"You told me once that no one deserves to die alone."* He billowed closer to the bed. *"I'm here, Foster. Close your eyes."*

The fox did as he was told, a look of peace passing over his canine face.

Zed, too, closed his eyes, and quested for the man within the fox.

✷

The change happened immediately. Zed didn't need to speak a word before he felt the room shift around him. He opened his eyes to discover the piles of laundry had become tufts of fallen leaves. A copse of trees surrounded him, from which green flames flitted like fireflies within the branches. The woods were cool and quiet, and charged with the thrill of magic.

Zed knew this place. It was the will-o-wisp forest from his dreams. The very place where he'd made his pact with Makiva.

He scanned the circle, taking in the bent trees and the setting sun beyond. The sky was purple-turning-gray. Nightfall.

Then Zed glanced down at his hands. Instead of his own palms, these were larger and lined with age. The skin was much paler than Zed's own.

"Foster?" Zed muttered. Thin silvery chains encircled his

wrists, leading up to the same mythril necklace that Makiva had given Zed. He pulled against his bonds, but the delicate-looking links were surprisingly solid.

A figure emerged slowly from the trees. A woman wrapped in fine cloth appeared before him, with an easy, pleasant smile.

Makiva. She was as young and pretty as Zed remembered her from the market, though this version of her had existed more than two centuries ago. In her right hand, she clutched an elegantly curved dagger. In her left was the limp body of a fox.

Reyna! Foster thought, his memory completely subsuming Zed. The warlock's chest tightened with grief.

"Ah, you've finally awoken," Makiva said, dropping the lifeless animal to the ground. "I hope you're excited. You've been such a marvelous student, Foster. It's time you graduated to better things."

"Makiva, please!" Foster called in his low tenor. "Whatever this is, we can talk it through."

The woman shook her head, still smiling. "The time for talking is done. I've waited many years for this. Waited for the chain to harvest enough mana, for a pupil who could wield it. I appreciate your sacrifice, I really do. As I do your fellow students'."

The woman waved her hands, and with the gesture a series of ghostly figures appeared in a wide circle around Foster. They were men and women, young and old, humans and elves and dwarves, orcs and halflings and gnomes. All were made of smoke, and they were chained just as Foster was, with silver strings around their throats. The chains formed a barrier around him, the figures' heads hanging low in mute despair.

"What?" Foster gasped, taking in Makiva's assembled victims. "This isn't happening. My friends . . . my friends will come. They'll stop you before—"

"Before?" Makiva's voice was bright with humor. "Foster, *before* has come and gone. You've been unconscious for a whole day! Look up!"

With rising dread, Foster did as his was told, shifting his gaze skyward. Just above them was a . . . a *hole* in the air. That was the only way Foster could make sense of it. The edges of the strange breach were filmy with silver mist, like a gauze that had been torn through.

Beyond it was an utterly alien landscape.

It was a place of teeming liquid darkness, in which an enormous blue moon hung from the sky, dripping oil into the murk. Shapes scuttled across the surface of the mire, and then flew suddenly into the air, their forms changing before Foster's eyes.

One such figure emerged from the portal, into Terryn. A gigantic shadowy hand led to a gigantic shadowy body. The horrific titan squeezed through the break like its body was made of putty, then it disappeared into the forest before Foster could truly understand what he'd witnessed. The creature's gibbering laugh vibrated in his chest.

"Nox," Foster rasped. "You opened a gate to bleeding Nox!"

Makiva shook her head patiently. "You always thought too

small, Foster. Not just Nox. *All* the planes have been opened to Terryn, everywhere in the world. And they've been open for nearly a full day now. Your world's precious position in the cosmos makes passing into Terryn through the Veil a simple matter. But sadly, moving in the other direction isn't as easy. In fact, it's been nearly impossible. For that, I still need time. Time for the Veil to weaken further. Soon, though. We're almost there, my student. Then your world will fall away like a bad dream."

Foster screamed. He pulled at his chains, weeping and cursing and calling for help.

Makiva just watched him. As she did, her eyes began to burn green. Her grin tightened into something frightening and inhuman.

My friends, Foster thought desperately. *They'll come for me. Jerra and Zahira, Aedra and Dox. Yes, Dox! He'll track me. He'll find where Makiva brought me and end this madness.*

The snap of a twig behind Foster caught his attention. He glanced toward Makiva to find she'd disappeared, leaving no trace except for the bloody body of Reyna and the curved dagger.

The spirits of her other victims had also vanished. Foster was alone in the glade.

He tried to call out, but an unseen force held his tongue. Makiva must have jumped back inside, possessing him.

"Foster?" a low whisper sounded uncertainly. Dox's voice was a cool sip of hope down his parched throat. Foster struggled against Makiva's paralyzing control. If he could just get his lips to move . . .

His friend curved around the glade to where Foster could see him. Dox looked awful: bruised and bloody and splattered in a rainbow of monstrous fluids. If what Makiva said about opening the planes was true, then only shadowcraft could have gotten him this far. And Dox would have paid a dire cost for it.

The man's bangs hung over his eyes, long and lank. Foster had often told his friend he should cut his hair, but today his gratitude soared on seeing that artfully obscured face. Dox would right this. He would sniff out the hidden truth, as he always did.

"By the gods, Foster." Dox gaped as he came upon the body of the fox. "Is that Reyna? What . . . what have you done?"

A chill ran up Foster's spine. He tried to protest. *This isn't me! Help, Dox!* But his body stayed totally still, his eyes glazed, as if in a trance.

"How did he find us?" Makiva's voice hissed furiously across the surface of Foster's thoughts. *"How did he make it here without my knowing?"*

Dox picked up the blade Makiva had left behind. He held the dagger up, frowning at the gleaming metal. "You can't even hear me, can you?" he asked huskily. "You're still inside that fiend-cursed ritual." Dox's face twisted in anguish. A tear ran down his cheek. "You've destroyed the *bloody world*, Foster! And for *what*?"

Dox suddenly leaped toward his friend, his furious eyes staring right into Foster's from behind his cage of hair. "Huh?!" He shouted in Foster's face. "What was worth all this?!"

Destroyed the . . . world? How was that even possible? Foster tried desperately to speak. He fought against Makiva's control with everything he had. His lips trembled.

The chain! he thought. *The mythril shackles! Dox, don't you see! You see everything! It's not just a ritual; I'm a prisoner!*

Dox took a step back, the anger in his face melting into resignation. He shook his head. "Every moment I hesitate is another moment those things are allowed into Terryn."

Foster felt the blade, rather than saw it. Pain unlike anything he'd ever experienced shrieked from his side. "I'm sorry," Dox whispered, pulling the curved dagger free.

The world closed slowly around Foster then, darkness blanketing the edges of his vision. He realized belatedly that his body had fallen to the ground. So Dox had struck an artery. Even in killing his best friend, he was efficient.

Foster's last sight was of Dox Eural bending over him. The assassin's eyes were hard. He pulled the chain from Foster's throat, then held it to his face, squinting at the intricate, beautiful links.

"*Zed!*" A voice sounded within his fearful thoughts, weak but insistent. Foster's. With it, Zed felt his mind separating from the warlock's last memories. "*The chain! I can see her now! Find her inside the cha—*"

✷

Zed gasped as he reappeared in Micah's room, the vision of the forest liquefying like morning frost. The quarters were still dark, except for the light that bled through the open door. Zed wrapped his arms around himself, working desperately to keep his form together against the churning of his emotions. Micah still stood at the doorway. He looked worried.

"You're back?" he asked tentatively.

Zed nodded. He glanced toward Micah's bed, where the only signs that Foster had ever been there were a few thin wisps of vapor, quickly dissolving away. A chime of despair rang through Zed, wracking his ghostly body again.

"He's gone," Zed breathed. *"I never said I was sorry, and he's gone. I didn't believe it could really happen."*

Micah frowned, glancing down at his feet. "He said you both knew that it would. Zed . . . are you going to disappear like that, too?"

Zed curled his knees into himself. *"These bodies are made of magic, but without my real body to draw mana from, eventually we just sort of . . . fade away."* Zed glanced to the empty bed. *"There were others before Foster. They're all gone now, too."*

Micah shook his head. "I'll do it," he said, taking a step forward. "I'll tell Frond. Tell Brock. Tell Liza. Whoever you want. Fie, I'll even tell the Dolt."

"Micah . . ."

"Frond was right," Micah grated. "As much as I want to hate her for it, she saw what I couldn't admit to myself. You're . . . special to me." Micah swallowed hard. He shifted his weight from foot to foot. "I didn't want you to find out that way. And I sort of wish we'd never talk about it again. But I'm not going to let you just disappear. You heard what Foster said. We have to work together to stop Makiva. So come on and let's—"

Zed's eyes widened as he saw the figure, outlined by the light of the door.

"*Micah!*" he screamed.

Makiva plunged the blade in.

Micah's eyes widened. A red stain unfolded across his jerkin. First it was just a wrinkle. Then a handkerchief. As the imposter removed the dagger, Micah's life cloaked him in red. He gasped noiselessly and took a step toward Zed, his mouth opening and closing.

He fell to the floor.

"This reminds me of the morning we first met," Makiva drawled with Zed's voice. "The three of us, together before the Guildculling. Even then I knew this blade was for you, Micah Guerra. Just as much as the chain was for Zed. It was only a matter of time."

Her gaze flicked over to Zed. "I *did* warn you about interfering," his own voice chided him softly.

"*Micah!*" Zed flew to the boy's side, where Micah's eyes were fluttering. "*Micah, hold on! Oh, Fie. Oh, no. Please—HOLD ON!*"

"Now, for the evidence. Seems Dimas will have some company after all." Makiva sighed and reached down, ready to abduct Micah into the Veil.

Until another shadow appeared in the doorway.

"Hey Micah," Jett called. "Jayna and I are going looking for Liza. Do you want to—"

The dwarf froze. Before him stood Zed with a bloody dagger clasped in his hand. Micah's limp body lay at his feet. For a long, suspended moment, the room was motionless.

"What?" Jett rasped.

Makiva narrowed Zed's eyes on the dwarf. "Well," she said. "Fie."

Then she lifted his empty hand, around which a storm of green fire began to broil.

Before she could get off the spell, Jett stumbled backward with a yelp. He stamped his mythril leg twice, sending a sequence of glowing sigils cascading across the metal. A semitransparent barrier bloomed into the air—Jayna's signature Wizard's Shield—but instead of wrapping around Jett, this one encircled the imposter in a magical encasement.

"Jayna's Spectral Prison!" Jett bellowed.

Then he lifted the hammer from his side. It, too, hummed with arcane energy. Lights flared in intricately knotted symbols wrought into the steel. "Jett's . . . Bewildering . . . *BELL!*"

With the last word, Jett cracked the hammer against the orb, setting off a thunderous shock wave that quaked through the entire guildhall.

Voices cried out in alarm from the lower floors. Zed heard footsteps pounding against the wood above.

"We're under attack!" Raif shrilled from somewhere nearby.

Within the bubble, Makiva screamed and clasped Zed's hands to his head. She was still vibrating with the force of Jett's blow. Somehow the orb was extending the energy of the impact, rebounding it back onto its prisoner.

But Zed barely registered the arcane battle happening right in front of him. He was still crouched over Micah, his misty body heaving in invisible grief. For the first time since Zed had known him, Micah looked . . . small. Broken. The boy who'd been so obnoxiously full of life that it radiated out of him as healing energy was completely still.

Zed called to him, commanding Micah to *fight*. To *open your eyes and look at me!*

Through the punishing reverberations in the orb, Makiva turned her gaze on Jett. Her eyes—Zed's eyes—shone green with hate. Then, in a cloud of mist that quickly filled the sphere, she disappeared, dragging Zed into the Veil with her.

For a moment, Jett stood wide-eyed, his heart pounding in his chest, along with the vibrating orb. He readied his hammer, searching for the spot where Zed's magical leap would land. But after several nervous moments, the room remained empty.

He stayed there, guarding Micah, until a tide of adventurers finally flooded the hall.

Chapter Sixteen
Brock

Brock's family den looked suddenly small to him, crowded as it was with familiar faces. Fel and Nirav were there, sitting upon a small sofa, while Liza paced the room and Fife leaned against a bookshelf. His mother had initially asked that they leave their boots by the door, but when she'd seen the state of Fife's filthy feet, she'd changed her mind.

"Nice place," Fife said, taking a handful of small quiches from a tray Brock's mom had set out.

"Easy. They're called finger foods," Brock said. "Not palm meals."

"I've got five fingers, haven't I?" He shoved a few of the pastries into his mouth, then said, "Unflike fome adfenturersf."

"So, who's in charge?" Liza asked.

Brock smirked at her. "The fact that you even ask that question means it's you."

She gave a prim nod. "Let's get started, then. Welcome, everyone, to the first official meeting of the Adventurers Guild's shadow team."

"Ooh," Fel said, clapping.

"Our actions must not be traced back to Guildmistress Frond," continued Liza. "Given the severity of the crimes that Hexam is accused of and the absolute certainty the king has shown in his guilt, the consequences for her and for the whole guild could be disastrous. So if anyone asks—if we're caught—we're working on our own. Got it?"

"Now I get why I'm here," Fife said. "I'm very good at taking the credit."

"Let's hope it's credit and not blame," Brock said. "But you're here because, according to the Stewards Guild's records, you're not an adventurer."

Fife nearly choked on a sixth quiche. "I'm not?"

"I learned a lot of things while I was spying on you all. For instance, Frond actually recruited Syd, but you, Fife, sort of just . . . followed him into the guild. No one was going to turn you away, but apparently you never filed the paperwork to make it official."

Fife continued choking. “Paperwork?” he asked in horror.

“Paperwork,” Brock said. “The same paperwork that says Nirav is legally dead.”

“That’s how I like it.” Nirav flashed a smile. “Because dead men pay no taxes, baby.”

“As for me, I’m not a citizen of Freestone,” Fel said. “I haven’t been through a Guildculling. The Sea of Stars is my home, but I am not under Frond’s legal authority. I am a proud subject of Llethanyl’s queen.”

“We all know I’m no longer associated with the guild,” Brock said. “But what about you, Liza? Are you sure your involvement won’t get Frond in trouble?”

“If I have to, I can spin it,” Liza answered. “I stormed out earlier today after a public argument with Frond.”

“Oh yeah?” Brock waggled his eyebrows. “And what was that argument about?”

“Not everything is about you, Brock.”

“That was, though,” Fel put in. “I was there. The argument was about Brock.”

Brock grinned devilishly.

“Anyway,” Liza said. “Yes. I’m in.”

“Good. Because I have a feeling that sword of yours will come in handy.” He turned to address the others. “We’re attempting something no one has ever done before—breaking into Silverglow Tower, then making it out again without raising any alarms.”

"Didn't you two already do that?" Nirav asked. "When you defended the focus from Brenner?"

Liza shook her head. "The focus is technically beneath the tower, but we accessed it through a doorway hidden in a nearby shop. The cells aren't connected, and it's unlikely we could use that same route again anyway."

"And that time, our success hinged on brute force," Brock said. "I've got something a little more elegant in mind for tonight, but it'll take all six of us working together."

"Six?" Liza said. Fife started counting out on his fingers.

"Don't tell me you've forgotten our most valuable asset." Brock smiled, inclining his head toward Fel—and toward the cat sitting on her lap. "Mousebane is the key to everything."

As if she had some sense of what was coming, Mousebane mewled pitifully.

*

"Members of the Mages Guild use their tokens—the ones they receive at Guildculling—as all-access passes to the tower," Brock explained. They were huddled at the end of an alleyway with a clear view of the base of Silverglow Tower. Like everything else intown, the alley was immaculate. "Hexam was given a loaner, but it was confiscated, and Jayna had to turn hers over when Frond drafted her. It might be possible to replicate the spell they use, but we're lacking in magical talent at the moment. All of which means we need to get our hands on a current mage's token." The door to the tower opened, and a young man in robes stepped outside. "And there's our poor sucker Sulba now. Nirav, you're up."

Nirav sighed. "For the record, I don't feel great about this," he said. "But Sulba *was* always a bit of a louse."

"And we can apologize to him," Brock said. "*After* everyone is safe."

Nirav nodded, then stepped out of the alley and made for Sulba. Brock strained his ears to listen.

"I got your note," Sulba said. The boy was already irritated. "I'm happy you've returned to us, Nirav, but I don't think now's the best time for a mage and an adventurer to be seen together. This mess with Hexam . . ."

"But that's why I needed to see you tonight," Nirav said. "Without Hexam, there's no one in my whole guild who can help me with this." Nirav pulled back his sleeve to reveal a gray forearm covered in brittle stone flakes.

Sulba gasped.

"The cure is failing," Nirav said. "And it's failing fast. This started out as a spot the size of coin."

Sulba shook his head mournfully. "Nirav . . . we tried already. After Frond brought you back, the mages pored over every book we have, looking for a cure. There's nothing."

"But the elves worked it out," Nirav said. "They found a temporary cure, at least. I think the formula might be in one of the books they left behind with us, but I can't make sense of any of it. Even Jayna's stumped."

"Oh really?" Sulba smirked. "Wasn't she supposed to be the most magically gifted apprentice in our year?"

"This is no time for your little rivalry," said Nirav. "Although . . . if you *were* the one to figure it out, that would be pretty big for you, wouldn't it?"

Sulba's eyes went wide. He looked over his shoulder, biting his lip. Brock could swear the boy was practically bouncing on his toes at the thought of receiving credit for bringing a lost bit of elven magic to the Mages Guild.

They had him right where they wanted him, and all it had taken was a bit of old plaster.

"All right, but we can't do it here," Sulba said. "Take me to these books of yours. Careful not to touch me, though. You know, just in case."

"Thanks, Sulba," Nirav said flatly. "Your concern is quite moving."

Brock pulled back into the alley, staying out of view. He listened for their approaching footfalls, and when the sounds of boots on cobblestone were just around the corner, he stepped from the alley—and right into Sulba's path.

The boys collided, and Sulba cursed. "Watch where you're going, fey-brain!" he spat.

"Sorry!" Brock cried, but he kept moving and kept his hood up. If Sulba recognized him, it could complicate things.

But Nirav led Sulba onward, and they had soon disappeared in the direction of outtown.

"So?" Liza said, peeling away from the shadows.

Brock grinned. He opened his hand to reveal a Mages Guild token.

"Phase one is complete," he said. "As if there were ever any doubt."

"Don't get cocky," Liza warned. "That was the easy part."

"Nobody look," Fife said. "I'm changing clothes back here."

"Fife!" said Fel, averting her eyes. "You can wear the robe *over* your clothes!" She covered Mousebane's eyes for good measure.

"Say the words, Liza," Brock said. "Help us get into character."

Liza tossed a blue robe into Brock's waiting hands. "Brock Dunderfel," she said. "I hereby claim you for the Mages Guild."

*

The token got them into the tower without an issue; the hidden door opened for them as if they belonged there. Brock held his breath, and he didn't exhale until he saw that the entrance chamber was empty.

"Okay," he said. "We have to make some assumptions from here, but I think they're good ones. First is that the cells are underground. Second is that they wouldn't lock dark wizards up anywhere near the guild mages."

"Third," Fel said. "When a group of knights drags a prisoner inside, they don't leave their boots at the door like a proper apprentice." She held Mousebane to her chest and scanned the stone floor. "The dirt trail says we go that way."

"Fife, you stand guard at the juncture," Brock said. "If anyone heads our way . . ."

"I dissect them," he said. "I know. I got it."

"No, you—I said you need to *distract* them."

Fife shrugged. "You're telling me that wouldn't do the trick?"

Liza sighed. "Let's just hurry. These robes your mom stitched together from old curtains might fool people from a distance, but if a mage gets a good look at us, we're done."

Whereas the direction Sulba had led them days before had curved around the tower, this path ended quickly at a door.

"If this is the right place," Fel said, "then it'll be locked."

Brock produced his lockpicks with a flourish.

"I mean locked by *that*," she clarified, pointing at a circular, luminous sigil right where a doorknob should be.

"Oh," Brock said, deflating a little. "Okay, give me a minute."

But Liza simply pierced the sigil with her sword. It flashed and faded, and the door creaked open.

"Always with the brute force!" Brock complained. Liza primly shushed him.

"I'll wait here," Fel said. She handed Mousebane over to Brock. "Good luck. I know you'll do great."

"Thanks," Brock said, shifting Mousebane into the crook of his arm. "Oh, wait. You were talking to the cat, weren't you?"

Fel smiled in a patronizing way. "I'm sure you'll do great, too, Brock."

They descended a winding stairway dimly lit with magelight globes. Brock didn't know whether the globes were low on mana or if the mages kept this path gloomy for atmospheric reasons. It certainly gave him the creeps.

He counted 130 steps before they reached the bottom—where an armored Stone Son sat blocking their path.

This was the real reason for the disguises. While the mages were few enough in number that they would all know one another, Brock assumed a visiting guard wouldn't look past the blue robes. Everything depended on him being right about that.

He projected confidence. Confidence, and superiority.

"Wake up, man," he said. "Or do you want Brent to know you were sleeping on the job?"

"I'm not sleeping," the knight said crossly, but he stood quickly as if caught slacking.

"Here," Brock said, and he held Mousebane out in front of him. The Stone Son gave him a confused look, and Brock waved the cat around impatiently. "Come on. I haven't got all day."

"Yeah, but . . . why are you waving that cat at me?"

"Cat?" Brock echoed. "Have you been paying *any* attention?"

"I—I thought so, but—"

Brock had to suppress a grin. The Stone Son was completely off-balance, afraid he'd missed something . . . and ready to swallow any crazy story they gave him.

"That 'cat,' as you so naively called it," Liza said, her voice sharper than he'd ever heard it, "is a parasitic, poison-spewing monstrosity from the realm of Fie. It's also the traitorous warlock's familiar, as I'm sure was explained to you when you reported for duty. We're done examining it, and we'd like to deposit it back in its cage." She sucked her teeth. "*Immediately* would be good, if you're done gaping?"

Brock snuck her a look from beneath his hood. *Nice*, he mouthed.

Liza didn't break character to respond, but Brock thought he saw an appreciative twinkle in her eye.

"Uh, does it go in with the prisoner, or . . . ?"

"What do you think? Of course it does," Brock said. He watched carefully as the knight produced a single iron key from his belt. As soon as the man turned away to unlock the door at his back, Brock cried out in pain.

"Ow!" he said, dropping Mousebane to the ground.

Liza quickly stamped her foot, scaring the cat into fleeing up the stairs.

The Stone Son turned his bovine eyes back to them. "What happened?"

Brock gripped his hand as if wounded. "It's gotten loose! After it, after it! Up the stairs."

The knight, to his credit, leaped into action, not stopping to think what he'd do with a fiendish cat should he catch it.

But he wouldn't catch Mousebane. Fel was waiting right

upstairs to scoop up the cat and exit the tower. Fife would stay behind long enough to urge the knight deeper into the tower's winding hallway.

By the time the knight realized Brock had palmed his key, they'd all be a safe distance away.

"I had no idea you were such a good liar," he said as he turned the key. The door came open with a heavy thunk. "Tell me the truth. You've been waiting for your chance to get into some mischief, haven't you?"

Liza didn't go along with the joke. As her eyes fell upon the man within the cell, she uttered a single gasp. Her hands flew to her mouth, and she hesitated at the threshold.

Hexam was in bad shape. One of his eyes was swollen shut, and he had crusty blood in his beard, just beneath his nose. His hands were wrapped in bloody bandages. Brock took an involuntary step back as he caught the reek of sour sweat and urine coming from the cell.

"Oh Hexam," Liza said. "What did they do to you?"

Hexam squinted into the light. It took a long moment before recognition dawned on his features. "Liza? Brock? Why . . . why are you here?"

Brock had thought he'd be happier to see them. Then he remembered how their last meeting had ended. "We're here to rescue you," he said.

"I'm . . . I'm absolved, then?" Hexam asked.

Brock looked warily over his shoulder. "We'll, ah, figure that part out eventually. Right now we need to get you out of here *quietly*."

"Drink," Liza said, and she held a waterskin to his lips. As he drank, she took in the state of his hands, then gave Brock a worried look.

"Hexam, can you cast?" Brock asked. "I know it's asking a lot right now. But we need to get you out of here, and if anyone sees you . . ."

Hexam wiped his lips. He moved his fingers, wincing.

"It won't be easy," he said. "No more than a spell or two."

"Invisibility?" Liza asked.

He shook his head. "Not on all of us."

"Liza and I can manage," Brock said. "We've made it this far. Can you make *yourself* invisible?"

Hexam nodded. "Yes. But it's a fragile spell. I'll have to move very slowly."

"Great," Brock said. "Good thing we're not trespassing or committing treason or anything that would require speed."

Liza slapped him in the back of the head. "Do it, Hexam. We'll go slow."

The walk upstairs was excruciating. At every bend, Brock fought the urge to break out into a run. They were so close to making a clean escape. . . .

But at the top of the stairs, the way forward was blocked. The knight stood a few paces down the hallway, and he looked ready to run Fife through with his drawn sword.

Fife, however, appeared unconcerned. "How would you describe the sheen of its fur, though?"

"Oh, for– What does that matter?!" cried the guard. "Just tell me whether you've seen a blasted cat or not!"

"I thought you said it *wasn't* a cat," Fife countered.

The knight gurgled in frustration before he caught sight of Brock and Liza. "This one's no help," he said. "I need you two to go to the archmagus and–" The knight's eyes went wide. "What in Fie is that?"

Brock spun around and saw the air behind him was rippling, like the surface of a puddle in the wind. Only this puddle was in the shape of a man.

Hexam's spell was failing.

The knight advanced with his sword raised. "Get down!" he cried.

"Wait wait wait," Brock said, his palms up. He had to come up with a lie, something to buy them time. . . .

"Seraphina's Splendent Prism!" Hexam's voice was accompanied by a focused burst of light. It struck the knight full in the face with all the force of a physical thing. The man recoiled, nearly toppling backward in his desperation to escape the light. In the moments following the attack, as Brock blinked to clear his own vision, the knight stumbled in place, rubbing furiously at his eyes.

Before he could recover, Fife came up behind the man and put him in a headlock. "Fife's Coziest Hug!" he said, and though the knight was the larger of the two, Fife's grip held. In a matter of seconds, the man slumped unconscious to the floor.

Fel stepped from a shadowed alcove, Mousebane in her arms. "That was very exciting," Fel said, but her good humor fell away immediately as she registered Hexam's ragged appearance. "Oh, dear Hexam," she said. "What did they do to you?"

The invisibility spell had fallen away, and Hexam stood panting, physically exhausted by the spell-casting and the long, slow walk up the stairs.

"This is hopeless," he said. "They won't stop hunting me. Nowhere in Freestone is safe."

"We have no intention of hiding you in Freestone," Brock said. "We're taking you where no one will ever look—the nearest wayshelter. Halfling's Hollow."

Hexam shook his head. "I'll never make it that far."

Brock wanted to argue with the man. He looked to Liza, willing the girl to produce one of her vaguely fearsome motivational speeches. But the forlorn look in her eyes reflected his own fear back at him. This wasn't going to work.

"Unless . . ." Fel began. "Hexam. What if we could take a shortcut? The mages confiscated the mythril orb. . . ."

"The focus to the demiplane!" Hexam said. "Of course! If the mages took it, I know just where it will be." For the first time, the mage smiled. Brock couldn't help but wonder whether Hexam was more excited by the promise of escape . . . or the opportunity to use such powerful and ancient magic to do it.

They pulled the unconscious guard into the shadowy alcove, then hurried down the curving corridor to an imposing iron door. Brock had seen it once before. "This is the vault," he said.

"It's where Grima keeps dangerous artifacts that are too powerful to destroy," Hexam explained. "That focus fits the bill. They told me all about it when they . . . questioned me, and I'm certain Grima wouldn't allow it to be housed anywhere else."

Brock pulled his lockpick tools from his sleeve. "Then allow me."

Hexam gave him a pitying look. "That door is thick with enchantments, son. By all means, give it a go—if you don't mind electric shocks, boils on your tongue, or forgetting your own name."

Brock sighed, putting his tools away once more. "I guess I wouldn't mind forgetting my *middle* name," he grumbled. "Do *you* have a way to get in?"

Hexam put his hand against the stone wall beside the door. "Knock, knock," he said, and the wall exploded inward.

"Careful!" Brock cried. He waved his hand in front of his face as dust and pulverized stone rose up in a thick cloud.

"Not to worry," Hexam said. "We're leaving a mess behind, but as I told you—everything here is practically indestructible."

"I think he's more worried about the *noise*," Liza said, and she cast an anxious look over her shoulder. "Get what you need and let's go."

Hexam's eyes fell immediately on what he was looking for.

"The orb—it's in my chest. The one I bought to store my letters," he said sadly. "Who did this to me? Why?"

"We'll figure it out," Brock promised. "But right now, you have to go where they can't reach you."

"I'll go with you," Fel said, hoisting Mousebane onto her shoulder. "We'll have to travel through the night. But you'll be safe in the wayshelter for as long as it takes."

"Thank you," Hexam said, his voice husky. He turned from Fel to the others, holding their eyes, one after another. "Thank you, all. I . . . don't have the words."

Brock nodded somberly, and Liza pulled a satchel of food from beneath her cloak, handing it over. Fife's stomach grumbled at the sight. "Go easy on the quiches," he warned.

Then Hexam and Fel touched the orb in tandem, and they folded out of sight.

*

Brock strained his ears for signs of pursuit. They'd ditched their blue robes in an alleyway and split up, Fife heading north and Brock and Liza going south. They walked quickly along the streets of intown—but not so quickly as to arouse suspicion.

He didn't breathe easy until they'd made it to his parents' block. Even then, he buzzed with adrenaline. If he went home now, he'd be crawling the walls. "I'll walk you back to the guildhall," he offered.

"I'll walk *myself* back," Liza said. She took his hand and pulled him along the road. "But you may accompany me."

Brock grinned, basking in the pleasure of a job well done and the company of the girl he'd thought, earlier that very day, might never talk to him again. He wished the evening could last forever, that all the problems still ahead of them could be put off and forgotten.

But as soon as the Sea of Stars guildhall was in sight, Jett and Jayna came barreling toward them.

"Fie!" the dwarf cried. "Liza, where have you been? I've been all the way to intown and back looking for you."

"Liza," Jayna began, "there's been an accident—"

"It was no accident," Jett said crossly.

"Slow down," Liza said, her features clouding with worry. "What's happened?"

"It's Micah," Jayna said. "He's been hurt."

"He's been attacked." Jett seemed to register Brock's presence then, glancing over at him for a moment before saying, "Zed stabbed him."

Brock could scarcely process the words. He felt as if he were underwater; everything was gibberish, and his lungs burned, until he realized he'd stopped breathing.

"— doesn't make sense," he heard Liza say.

"It must—he must have been acting in self-defense," he said, and Liza immediately dropped his hand.

"Self-defense?" she said. Her eyes were furious. "What exactly are you accusing Micah of?"

"I—nothing, I'm just—"

Jett shook his head sadly. "Brock, I'm sorry. Zed . . . he came after me, too. If you'd seen what I saw. The . . . madness in his eyes. There was blood all over him, and he just . . . disappeared."

"Where is Micah?" Liza asked.

"They've taken him to the healers," Jayna said. "We should go right now. Liza, it . . . it looks bad."

Liza wiped at the corners of her eyes. "Let's go." She grabbed Brock's tunic and pulled.

"Liza, wait," Brock said. He refused to budge, and slipped from her grip.

She and Jayna were already moving in the direction of the temple. "I can't," she said. "You're not coming?"

Brock shook his head. "I have to look for him . . . for Zed. I'm sorry."

Liza was gone before the apology had left his lips.

Chapter Seventeen

Makiva emerged from a cloud of mist onto the roof of the adventurers' guildhall. Beneath her feet, the slate shingles creaked in revolt, but they held Zed's small frame. She touched the scepter at her side, confirming she still had it.

What a disaster. The sun hung just over Freestone's wall, the afternoon having toed into evening's cool waters. Makiva had waited until the evening bell—hiding within the Veil, then reappearing only in brief bursts to scout her escape. Departing hadn't been easy. Through her glimpses of the guildhall, she could tell the adventurers had spent the afternoon in a flurry of frantic activity.

Micah's body, she'd learned, had been hurriedly moved—to where, Makiva had no idea. The dwarf interrupted her before she could erase Micah permanently from Freestone, but she had little doubt the healer was dead. No one could lose that much blood and survive.

Then perhaps this was still salvageable. She could work with Zed's becoming a wanted criminal. *His* perceived innocence wasn't vital to the plan. But if anyone got wind that Zed was under the control of a greater power, they might start asking how that power had gotten its claws in and concoct a plan to free him.

Makiva fingered the chain around Zed's neck, frowning as his stomach quailed with hunger. She needed a place to rest, and food to replenish the boy's mana. She still had her agent in the Sea of Stars, but the guildhall was too risky at the moment. She could leave the walls and try to find a safe place beyond Freestone, but with the rainbow bridge demiplane confiscated by the mages, Makiva would have to chart her own escape. Doubtless that would require yet more magic.

There was only one solution. Zed still had one ally in the city, someone who would hide and protect him no matter what.

Makiva glanced at the shade that had been Zed's etheric body. Its murky shape was only vaguely humanoid now. Their prolonged time in the Veil had pulled the boy apart like a loose skein of yarn, but Makiva sensed he was still in there somewhere, drifting within the diffuse magic.

Foster had lasted for centuries by keeping sedentary, so Zed could survive a little longer, despite the week's traumas. Still, she would have to be gentler on him.

"Worry not, my brave little student," Makiva said to the forlorn-looking wisp. It floated silently, without even eyes to watch her. "I know just the thing to fix you up. You're going home."

Zed floated. He rode a tide of quiet oblivion, with no shore in sight.

Formlessness was peaceful. Zed felt no grief for Foster or Micah. He didn't worry for his friends or his city. The Veil had dispersed his thoughts like morning fog, and Zed had let it. He didn't mind.

He didn't mind anything.

Distantly he heard a voice, muffled and indistinct, but no words broke through the gauze.

The tide began to move and Zed floated with it, pulled gently by its tug. Colors and shapes shifted blearily, prettily.

Then, an itch.

A tugging at his thoughts.

Zed! The chain!

Zed ignored it. He was floating. He was free.

The tugging became more insistent. It was a memory. A half-finished plea.

I can see her now! Find her inside the cha—

Zed awakened. He was drifting behind Makiva above the outtown slums, watching the back of his body as it climbed carefully across the rooftops. He glanced down at his smoky hands, only to find they'd faded almost to nothing.

The last thing he remembered was being dragged into the Veil with Makiva. Zed had been so upset that it was difficult to hold himself together. When the silver tendrils of the misty in-between plane began pulling at him, he'd simply succumbed, falling into a sort of sleep.

A sleep he'd just been roused from. By a memory.

Zed searched his surroundings, finally focusing on the glittering streak of mythril that encircled his own throat just yards ahead.

The chain connects us, Foster had told him.

We're both trapped inside.

Find her.

Inside.

An idea was growing. A small, strange, impossible notion. Could the chain be *entered*, in the same way Zed had explored his friends' dreams? Foster had told him that technically all Makiva's victims were trapped *within* it, which was why the mindtooth attack hadn't affected them.

And in the vision of Foster's last moments, Makiva had disappeared inside to hide from Dox.

The chain. It was the means by which Makiva had ensnared him, along with every other witch and warlock who'd accepted her pact. Perhaps it was also the key to stopping her—or to discovering some weakness.

It was a wild, desperate hope, he knew. Little more than a hunch. But Zed was out of both allies and ideas. Foster had warned him there was always more to lose. That she would keep taking from him, long after he'd forgotten he had things to take. The warlock's solution was to give up. To stop *hoping*.

That wasn't Zed's solution. He'd spent his whole young life as an anxious kid, afraid of what was just around the corner: be it bullies, or failure, or deadly monsters.

Yet Zed had faced *all* of these and survived. He wouldn't give up. Even if Makiva destroyed his name—even if she turned every plan and wish against him—he would fight her until he faded to nothing. For Foster, and Terryn, and *every* life she'd destroyed.

For Micah.

Zed concentrated on the mythril chain. He quested toward it, willing it to let him in. He imagined the cool weight of the links against his skin. He remembered the way they'd sparkled in the tent on the morning of his Guildculling.

Makiva's back was turned. She didn't see the wisp behind her begin to moil and shrink. The wind picked Zed up and carried him away. Smoke on the breeze. Here, then gone.

*

Darkness.

That was all Zed saw, as silent and empty as a starless sky. Then, the trills of birds in a familiar, genial song.

Zed opened his eyes. He was standing within a small glade

of trees. Streams of light fell gently between the leaves, making a shimmery carpet of the forest floor.

He knew this place. It was Makiva's place, the same woods he'd visited several times now in his dealings with the witch. Always in dreams.

Zed stepped forward. As soon as he did, the woods responded, greeting him like a pet might welcome its master. The forest floor parted before Zed, leaves opening unnaturally to draw his path. It was just like the vision in which Makiva had lured him into her power.

Zed frowned at the enticing trail. He turned in a circle, taking in the rest of the trees.

"You want me to follow the path," he whispered.

The trees seemed to vibrate in affirmation. Beyond him, the narrow trail extended. Rustling leaves beckoned. What a helpful forest, carving this lane for him, like a groove in a wooden token.

"So what happens if I go in a different direction?" Zed asked. "What will you do if I choose my *own* path?"

And before he could second-guess his decision, Zed plunged into the woods.

Branches whipped by him, the birdsong going abruptly quiet. In an instant, all that friendly sunlight that had been spilling through the trees died out. This was *not* the friendly path, the forest seemed to say. But it didn't fight him. No witches or monsters came to snatch him back. Not yet, at least.

Zed continued. Soon his only illumination was from the

strange green wisps that occasionally flitted between the trees, warping Zed's shadow as they whispered by.

His . . . shadow. Zed ground to a halt. He looked down at himself. Long fingers, with fawn-colored skin. The sleeve of Zed's favorite doublet.

His hands. *His* hands!

Here, at least, Zed was back in his own body. The thought made him flush with happiness, heat prickling his ears. He laughed for the joy of feeling his ears burn, and the forest grew even quieter around him. Zed could practically feel the trees glaring at this noisy interloper. When he continued, he was still grinning like a fool.

There was no warning before the scenery changed. One moment Zed was alone in the woods. The next, the trees cascaded away in a blur of mist and a brilliant blue sky yawned open before him. Zed squinted, blinded by the sudden brightness. When his eyes adjusted, he discovered that the forest had disappeared.

It was replaced by four human figures.

Zed gasped aloud. He recognized them immediately. They were younger than the well-worn likenesses that stood vigil in Freestone's market square, but the Champions of Freestone were unmistakable.

Their clothes were humbler than Zed would have expected. Ser Jerra's armor was little more than a common iron breastplate belted over a leather jerkin. The metal was scratched and dented. Zahira Silverglow wore common traveling clothes instead of the intricate robes she was so famous for, and she carried a banded staff with a simple quartz crystal lashed hastily to the top. They looked like teenagers.

The four stood in the center of a wide highway paved with clean, sun-bleached stones. Behind them, the road stretched on for miles, and a whole caravan *filled* with horses, carts, and even ornate litters meandered lazily into the distance. None of the travelers seemed the least bit worried about monsters. Barely a third were armed! Zed realized with a thrill that he was standing on the Broken Roads, *before* they'd broken.

All four of the Champions were looking in the same direction, away from the retreating cavalcade. Ser Jerra scowled at something just behind Zed. Zahira sighed, shaking her head.

"You said he wouldn't be a burden," Jerra muttered, turning his glare onto Dox.

The young rogue still had his characteristic long bangs, but his face was smoother and his hair cleaner than the last time Zed had seen him, the day he took Foster's life. He wore his hood down around his neck.

"He's just a little green," Dox said patiently. "It's his first caravan. He'll figure it out. See, here he comes now."

A fifth figure jogged past Zed, his breath hitching as he ran. Foster Pendleton joined the four, his face red and his pointed ears dripping with sweat. He had a lute strapped to his back, the instrument at least half the size of the slim, young elf-blooded man.

As soon as he arrived, Foster promptly bent over and threw up on the side of the road.

Mother Aedra grimaced, but she tentatively patted Foster's back as he struggled between gagging and panting with exertion. Or was she a priestess yet at this point? Zed tried to remember the stories of the four. Before founding the Golden Way Temple and transcribing its sacred tenets, Aedra had been a wandering healer-for-hire. It was in saving Freestone that she'd found her divine charge.

Jerra smirked as Foster spat up the last of his sick. The young knight glanced at Dox. "You know, I think you're right, Dox. He *does* look pretty green."

Zahira giggled, locking her free arm inside the knight's. "Good one, Jerra," she crooned kittenishly.

"Honestly, Zah," said Dox, "I hope we don't have to listen to you two flirting the *whole* way there."

Zahira's dark face ruddied, her eyes narrowing. She pulled her arm from Jerra's and stalked up the path toward the convoy. Jerra frowned at Dox, his glare sharper than the pitted sword at his side.

"Better go after her, big guy. Don't waste that sparkling sense of humor on us. We'll catch up."

"Unlikely," Jerra said, his eyes flicking to Foster. He hustled after the wizard.

"Should I stay with you?" Aedra asked, dubiously eyeing the mess beside the road.

"Nah, go on." Dox sighed. "Being a little winded isn't exactly something you can heal."

"Don't fall too far behind." With that, Aedra turned and plodded serenely behind her friends.

"I'm sorry, Dox," Foster huffed once they'd gone.

"It's all right, kiddo. But I told you that thing was more trouble than it's worth." He flicked a thumb toward the instrument on Foster's back.

The elf-blooded boy nodded solemnly. "It didn't feel so heavy to start . . ." he admitted.

"Every pound multiplies by three before the day's over," Dox said with a smirk. "Why'd you bring it in the first place?"

Foster flushed, frowning at the cobbles beneath his feet. "I just wanted to be useful," he said. "I don't have any magic or combat training. I can't pick pockets. What good will I be when we get to Llethanyl? I thought maybe I could be the group's . . . chronicler."

Dox shook his head, a wide grin brightening his face. "You want to be our *bard*?"

Foster's face reddened further, but he didn't deny it. "All the best heroes have them. When you all find your fortune, you'll need someone there to sing the tale."

Dox raised his hands in friendly exasperation. "We're not *heroes*, mate. We're freelancers. Mercenaries. Sure, Jerra's got a fancy name, but sadly for him it doesn't come with a fancy inheritance. He's the *lowest* branch on the Freestone family tree. And

Zahira knows a flashy trick or two, but the girl's a magic-school dropout. Poor thing's got a fondness for bad boys—myself *not* included, sorry to say. Aedra's all right, but she's never really been all *there*. 'A sheep without a shepherd,' my mother would call her. And I'm the *worst* of 'em. A penniless clod of dirt whose best quality you could think of was 'picking pockets.'"

Dox shook his head, raising a finger to forestall Foster's apology. "The point is, Jerra and Zahira might turn up their noses, but none of us are any better than you. Certainly not when we started."

Foster smiled skeptically. "Did any of *them* throw up on their first day?"

"Worse. Jerra ate a bad mushroom on the trip to Everglen and twisted his bowels in a knot. We made him walk half a mile from camp to relieve himself, the stink was so bad."

Foster laughed, and Dox grinned again to see his friend relax. "You're one of us now," he said, twanging a string on the lute. "For as long as you want to be, anyway. You'll find your fit, just like we all did." Dox sighed, contemplating the instrument. "Even if it's as a bard."

As Foster reached out to take his friend's offered hand, Zed caught sight of something strange.

An animal observed him from the grass just beyond the road. Its vivid red fur shone like copper in the afternoon sun.

It was a fox. A real one. Or at least as real as this place got.

Though the Champions and Foster had all ignored Zed, the fox appeared to be looking *right at him*, panting lazily.

"Foster?" Zed whispered.

The fox cocked its head at him. The teasing gleam in its eyes seemed to say, *Try again.*

Foster's fox manifestation had only ever been smoky and ethereal, but this animal was all color. Zed had never even heard of the creatures before Makiva. He recalled his vision of the fox from Foster's last moments, its limp body falling to the forest floor.

"Reyna?" Zed asked, summoning up the name of Foster's familiar.

It didn't answer. The fox just continued to watch him, its orange eyes gleaming in the sunlight. They were gleaming still as the scene around them melted away, the bright sky and welcoming road eclipsed in near-total darkness.

Now Zed stood in a cavern. The only light arrived from a shaft in the cave ceiling, where dust and rubble were still falling from a collapse in the bedrock.

Foster lay groaning on the cave floor, encircled by the beam of daylight. He looked a bit fitter to Zed than in the last vision, his clothes a bit more worn.

Above them, Zahira's head appeared in the shaft, outlined by sunlight. "Are you all right, Foster?"

"No!" the young man called grumpily. "Wha–what happened?"

Zahira was joined by Dox, who grinned down at his friend. Their two heads bobbed in the watery radiance. "Looks like you discovered the tomb, lucky! Jerra's run to get the hook and rope. Just stay where you are, and try not to get cursed. The dwarf we bought the map from said the woman who's buried here was a w-i-i-i-i-tch!" Dox stretched the last word out in a spooky singsong, wiggling his fingers as he disappeared over the edge.

Zahira grimaced as she gazed into the cavern. "Honestly, though . . ." she said. "Be careful, Foster. We'll be back soon."

With her departure, the cave became intensely quiet.

Foster coughed, then stood with a groan, dusting himself off. After a quick search for injuries uncovered nothing dire, he turned in a circle, taking in his surroundings.

As his eyes fell upon Zed, they widened with shock. "What?" Foster said.

Zed gasped, stepping backward as Foster pressed in, but the young adventurer simply passed through him. Zed turned to find Foster examining two objects that were laid neatly across a stone slab.

Though everything else in the cavern was covered with layers of dust, the dagger and mythril chain sparkled in the scant light, completely unblemished.

"Hey, Dox? Are you sure we're the only ones who bought that map? There's something down here." When his friend didn't respond, Foster reached tentatively toward the chain. He hesitated, pulling his hand back.

"Hello, Foster," a voice called from deeper within the tomb.

Foster and Zed both shrieked in unison. Zed whipped around

to see a figure emerge from the shadows, her face young and pretty. She smiled a warm, not-at-all-frightening smile.

Makiva.

"Who—who are you?" Foster stammered. "Are you the . . . witch?"

Makiva rolled her eyes. "Do I look like a hundred-year-old witch?" she said, holding her arms out. "My name is Makiva. I'm an adventurer, like you. My crew bought a map to this tomb, but I got stuck in a cave-in. I've been looking for a way out for days."

"How do you know my name?" Foster asked suspiciously.

"I heard your friends calling to you." Makiva pointed up to the shaft. "Dox, was it?"

"Ah. Right." Foster's shoulders relaxed a bit, his posture slumping. "I think maybe we ought to have a talk with that map-monger. I sold my lute for the 'exclusive scavenging rights' to this tomb." Foster sighed and waved a hand over the chain and dagger. "Don't suppose I'll get lucky and you'll tell me these aren't yours."

Makiva nodded, taking a step forward. "They are, but I've little use for them anymore. How about you take them, as thanks for finding me?"

Foster frowned, glancing down at the items. "They look expensive," he said. "That chain's mythril, you know. Human wizards will pay five times its weight in gold. Mythril holds enchantments."

"Actually, it's priceless," Makiva said coyly. "It already holds some very *powerful* magic. If you want, I could show you how to use it, while we wait for your friends."

Foster's eyes lit up. His gaze rose from the chain. "You could teach me *magic?*" he breathed. "But I thought you needed mana to cast spells."

Makiva laughed. "Unlocking mana is the *easy* part. Wizards act like they're a special class, but unless you're born with innate magic, everyone gets theirs the same way."

"And what way is that?"

"Opening ourselves to the cosmos," Makiva said. She waved her palm upward. "Magic comes from the planes beyond ours. All people are vessels, capable of containing wonders. It's just a matter of making a small hole, to let the wonders in."

Her eyes flicked to the knife on the stone slab. Foster frowned down at the blade and chain, chewing on his cheek.

"If I could do magic," he thought aloud, "I'd be more useful to the team. I've always wished . . ." He trailed off, gazing hungrily at the items.

Slowly, he reached down and scooped them into his hands.

At the far end of the cave, Makiva's smile widened. Zed caught the unmistakable scent of brimstone drafting from within the tomb. "Foster," she said, "if you wish it, I can make you the most important mage of your time."

As the scene faded around Zed, the tomb's dark corners gradually curled back into the dim forest he'd started in. Zed realized the fox had reappeared. It was perched beside his feet, staring up at him.

"Poor Foster," he murmured. "But there's got to be more to this." Zed glanced down at the fox, pursing his lips thoughtfully. "Whatever you are, you aren't just another memory. Foster said I could find 'her' here. Did he mean you?"

The fox blinked at him, then glanced away. It stood and trotted into the trees. After several yards, it turned back toward him expectantly.

Zed frowned, but he stepped forward. He followed the animal into the dark.

✷

Makiva arrived at Zed's home just after the sun had set. She didn't know when she'd lost the boy—one minute he was behind her as an etheric wisp and next he was gone—but she wasn't overly concerned. Zed was still alive, she could sense that much. Perhaps he was off licking his wounds.

She touched the door's latch and found it opened without resistance, then quietly pushed her way inside the small home. A fire glowed warmly in the modest hearth, aided in lighting the space by two tallow candles. Makiva closed the door behind her, glancing around warily.

It was too quiet. There was no sign of Zed's mother.

Her suspicions were confirmed when Brock Dunderfel

emerged from the curtained threshold to the back room. He held both his hands in the air.

Makiva hissed at Brock, her eyes narrowing.

"Please, Zed," Brock rasped. "We just want to talk. To *help you.*"

"'We'?" Makiva said.

Jett emerged from behind Brock, his eyes wide. Unlike Brock, the dwarf gripped his weapon firmly. Behind him stood Zed's mother. Makiva found herself grateful that Zed hadn't followed her here. The crushed, pathetic look on the woman's face might have destroyed him outright, and Makiva still had need of him.

"Zed," she quavered. "What's going on? Please, baby, talk to us. Brock says you . . . you hurt a boy?"

"A lot's been going on these past months," Brock said gently. "Some bad, stressful, heartbreaking stuff. I know I . . . *we've* had our issues, too. In Duskhaven, you said you wanted to talk. I'm *here*, Zed. Let's talk. Tell us your side."

Makiva's mind raced. How to play this? She doubted Brock had called the knights, or they would have stormed the hovel already. He was hoping to get his friend to surrender peacefully, then.

Zed was almost ready, she could feel it. The chain was working its wonders, carving a deeper reservoir within the boy. Though his personal mana was nearly empty, the amount he *could* hold continued to expand, built upon by generations of witches and warlocks. First it had been enough to hold *her*. Now it was nearly vast enough to power the ritual. It was just a matter of filling the vessel.

She should burst out through the door right now without another word. Find a place to hide, while Zed's magic replenished.

But something in Brock's loyal, hopeful expression filled her with rage. Makiva simply couldn't help herself.

"You *fool*," she ground out slowly. "You brainless child. All this time, it's been staring you in the face." Makiva raised Zed's arms, wasting precious mana to set off two emerald gouts of flame. "*Fiendfire!*" she shouted. "There's not a sorcerer alive who was born with this gift. I'm a warlock, and I've been working for Makiva this *whole time*. Hexam was only a diversion. She's waiting just outside Freestone, with an *army* of Dangers ready to take this city!"

Makiva felt a surge of pleasure at Brock's stupefied expression. Behind him, Zed's mother burst into tears.

"I . . . I don't believe you," Brock muttered.

Makiva cackled. "And *that's* why you've lost," she said. "Even after everything this city has put me through because of my elven blood—all the degradations—you *still* thought I was too meek and incompetent to strike back." Makiva grinned from behind Zed's eyes, curling his innocent face into a sneer. "You'll never catch her in time!" she challenged.

With any luck, that would buy her precious hours. If the adventurers were busy searching for "Makiva" outside the wall, she would merely need to hide and wait.

She turned, Zed's scepter swinging loosely in his belt, and threw open the door behind her.

Liza Guerra stood just outside, her shield raised high. Her hand gripped the hilt of her elven blade. Behind the girl was the apprentice wizard—Jayna. By the hard and horrified looks on their faces, Makiva could tell they'd heard everything.

"Liza!" Brock yelped.

"J-Jayna!" cried Jett.

"Zed Kagari . . ." Liza's voice was low and measured, but it belied a fury that sent a shiver of alarm through even Makiva. "I'm arresting you for witchcraft, and for the attempted murder of my brother."

Chapter Eighteen
Brock

Brock felt like he was balancing on the edge of a knife. One misstep now, just one false move . . . He couldn't bear to think what he might lose.

"Let's all stay calm," he said, louder and more hotly than he'd intended.

Zed backed away as Liza moved fully into the room. Jayna followed, swiftly closing the door behind her. Firelight glinted off Liza's shield and off her eyes, her brown irises flaring orange like embers in the wind.

Brock stepped forward, putting himself between the girls and Zed. "Liza, calm down," he tried again.

"Get out of my way, Brock." She was all steel and flint. There was no hint of any doubt on her face—and none of the affection he'd seen there a short time ago. "And I'm *sure* I've asked you to stop telling me what to do."

Brock held out his hands in a steadying gesture. "I get that you're upset. *I'm* upset," he said. "But we have an opportunity here to figure things out, together."

"There's nothing to figure out," she said, her shield up and her voice flat. Her eyes moved from Brock to Zed and back again. Jayna stood a half step behind, flexing her fingers, her feet squarely on the ground—a spell-caster's fighting stance. The girls had come ready for a fight.

And they knew Zed couldn't elf-step away. With the door closed and the room's sole window reflecting the light of the fire, he had no clear view of the outside.

"We heard everything, Brock," Jayna said.

"Then you know there's still time to fix this."

Liza shook her head slowly. "It's too late."

"It's *not* too late," Brock insisted. "Zed knows Makiva's plan! We can stop her, with his help."

"Then we'll interrogate him when he's in custody."

"Like Hexam was interrogated? You saw what they did to him."

"That's . . . that's enough," Zed's mother said. "Girls, I don't know what you think gives you the right to barge in here, but . . . but this is a family matter, and—"

"A family matter," Liza echoed flatly. "My brother is . . . he's dying. They say he lost too much blood. There's a puddle of it back in our guildhall, so deep it could drown you." She turned toward Zed. "Was that the price Makiva demanded? Did you trade Micah's life for . . . for power?"

Out of the corner of his eye, Brock saw Zed shrug. "Honestly I did that for all of you. I got the impression nobody liked that kid. You seemed to hate him, Liza."

Liza seethed and took a step forward.

Brock drew his daggers.

"Jett!" he cried. "Get Zed out of here!"

"Don't you dare, Jett!" Liza commanded. "Hold him!"

"I . . ." Jett faltered. "Can I abstain?"

"No!" Brock and Liza cried in unison.

Brock slashed at Liza, blades shrieking against her shield, and she took a step back.

"Eldritch darts!" Jayna cried, and motes of azure light flew from her fingertips.

She's really got to stop announcing her attacks, Brock thought. The darts arced nearly to the ceiling, sailing cleanly over Liza and Brock before descending toward Zed.

Brock couldn't do anything about that. Liza bashed at his blades with her shield, nearly knocking them from his hands.

"I've got this!" Jett cried, and he stamped his mythril leg against the ground. Though Brock was otherwise occupied, he could tell by Jett's cursing that nothing happened—he'd already used his shield's charge.

Brock risked a glance over his shoulder to see Jett had put himself between Zed and the darts. It didn't matter; the magical attack found its target unerringly, veering around the dwarf and slamming into Zed with the force of three solid punches.

Zed was thrown to the ground, and his mother screamed.

"Jett, get them out of here, curse it!" Brock shouted.

Liza slammed him, but he held his ground.

"Liza, if you do this, you're killing him," he said. "They'll execute him; you know they will."

She advanced another step, parrying his slashes. "He'll have a fair trial. We'll make sure of that."

"He's *never* had it fair!" Brock batted at her shield, banging against it with the blunt pommels of his daggers. "This whole town has been against him since the day he was born."

"Try being a girl with a sword!" Liza said, and with a tremendous shove she knocked Brock clear off his feet.

Liza and Jayna advanced on Zed, who had propped himself up on one elbow and appeared dazed. His mother crouched over him protectively, while Jett stood nearby, wavering, wilting a bit beneath Jayna's glare.

"You big idiot," Jayna said. "Is jumping in front of an attack your only move?"

Jett blushed furiously.

"I'm sorry about all this," Liza said to Zed's mother. "We *will* make sure he's treated fairly."

"You don't have the authority to take him anywhere," she said. "You're not knights. You're supposed to be his friends!"

"It's better this way," Jayna said, "because we *are* his friends. Maybe his last friends in all of Terryn."

"Everyone in Terryn is dead," Zed said, and the sound of his voice, icy and cruel, pinned Brock to the floor. "Don't you know? The world ended two hundred years ago. And all of *this*," he shrilled through clenched teeth, "is just the rotting carcass the world left behind!"

Green light flared from between his fingers, which he'd splayed against the tenement's floor—its *wooden* floor. Slavering tongues of green flame lashed out, quick with hunger, spreading across the ground toward the furniture, the walls, the curtains.

Jett brought his hammer's pommel down hard against Zed's head, and the boy crumpled unconscious to the ground. Too late; the room was already ablaze.

Zed's mother acted quickly, slapping at the fire with a towel. Even at a good distance, Brock could feel the heat, far greater than that coming from the fireplace nearby.

"It's no use," Jayna said. "It's no ordinary fire."

Liza turned to Brock. "Can you stand?" she asked.

"You didn't hit me *that* hard," he groused.

"The other apartments," said Zed's mother. "This time of night, everyone is home—people will be trapped!"

Liza didn't hesitate. "We'll go door to door," she said. "Quick!

Jett, grab Zed and get him clear and *hold* him, okay?" She caught his eyes for a moment. "You have him?"

Jett nodded solemnly. "I have him."

"Jayna, go to the guildhall, quick as you can," Liza said. "Frond and the others need to find Makiva. She's out there somewhere beyond the wall, and the adventurers are the only ones who can stop her."

"Yes," Jayna said. "I'll tell her everything, but then I'm coming right back here."

"It's a plan," Liza said. "Move, move, move!" The flames had already claimed half the room. The bedroom beyond was cut off, whatever comforts and keepsakes it held lost forever—but Zed's mother didn't look back as she rushed outside and started pounding on doors, screaming the names of her neighbors.

Liza went off in another direction to do the same, shouting herself hoarse, and Brock knew she expected him to follow. Instead, he approached Jett, who had dragged Zed across the street and still held the unconscious boy's cloak tight in his fist.

"No, Brock," Jett said. His eyes were sad, and they flickered with reflected green light as the first of the flames groped around the doorframe of Zed's childhood home. "Don't ask this of me."

Brock gave a halfhearted grin. "I could knock you out and take him, if that's better."

"You really couldn't. Curse it, Brock, you heard him. You saw him. He just set his mother's thrice-hexed house on fire!"

"That's exactly my point. Jett, you know him! Better than

just about anybody. Zed's just not capable of *any* of this. He's sick, and he needs our help. . . ."

"He *needs* to tell us what the witch is planning," Jett said.

"That, too. And who's going to get that information out of him? Frond? Brent? Or me?"

Jett hesitated.

"Just give me until dawn. At sunup, one way or another, I'll turn us both in."

Jett cursed under his breath. "I knew I shouldn't have let you talk. When will I learn? You could smooth-talk half the fiends of Fie."

Brock flashed a smile, projecting a confidence he didn't feel. "Let's hope it doesn't come to that."

Jett cursed again. "Fine. Take the little prat. *Don't* tell me where you're going—I won't be able to resist telling Liza or Jayna."

"Good man, Jett." Brock hesitated as he felt the growing heat of the fire at his back. "It's going to be all right. You'll see. We can fix everything."

"Yeah, and I'd love to believe it." Jett released his grip on Zed's cloak and walked toward the blaze to aid Liza. "But I guess there's limits to what you can convince me of after all."

*

Brock knew he didn't have much of a head start. But he also knew that Liza was mostly unfamiliar with the streets of outtown. He weaved through the alleyways, resisting the temptation to make a direct line for his destination. The night shone with eerie green light, giving the town an aura of alien menace. The bells of the Healers Guild rang with emergency.

And Zed was not as light as he looked.

Brock huffed, hoping that his hunch proved correct. The area where the perfumer had disappeared that morning—it might be a coincidence, but then again . . .

The cramped alleyways of outtown ended at the market square. He'd have to leave his cover and hope that everyone was too busy with the fire to notice him as he lugged Zed across the open plaza.

No one raised the alarm, and he made it to the statues of the Champions. He set Zed down at the base of Dox's statue.

"The light offends my eyes," he tried. Nothing happened.

"*Lleth anyl*," he said. "Open sesame!"

He felt foolish, talking nonsense into the night. He paced around the plinth, then trailed his fingers along it.

He found a seam.

"Ha!" he said. "I've got you now."

He tried pushing. Then pulling. He tried prying his fingers into the narrow gap. The stone wouldn't give.

Finally he tried a dagger. He slipped the blade in and, using it as a fulcrum, pried the stone apart. The blade snapped, and Brock fell back, landing hard against the cobbles. But it had worked; there was a gap in the stone, big enough now for his fingers. He wedged them in, braced himself, and heaved.

He should have known from the start. The Lady Gray loved her theatrics. In all of Freestone, there was no more fitting spot for a hidden entrance to her lair than the base of the fabled assassin's statue.

He sheathed the shattered blade and, taking a deep breath, hefted Zed upon his shoulder. Then he stepped through the opening and into deepest shadow.

*

Members of the Shadow court milled about in the underground lair, oblivious to the chaos on the streets above. They sipped colorful cocktails and lounged on plush cushions, their fanciful masks glittering in the magelight. Soft music played from a small cherrywood box, an object enchanted to remember and play back music; it sounded as if the music were being performed in that very room. Even with as many treasures as she'd gathered, the Lady Gray clearly cherished it. The box was more than two hundred years old but was buffed and polished as if brand-new, and Brock had never heard it play the same tune twice.

He raised his voice to be heard above it now. "Everybody out," he said. "Out! I'm serious."

"Brock Dunderfel?" said a woman in a bejeweled emerald mask. "What is the meaning of this . . . impropriety?"

"Yeah, hello, Lady Crestwell. I recognize you, too. Nice mask, though. Form over function, right?"

The lady gasped, scandalized.

"Apprentice," the bartender warned in a gravelly voice. Gramit was generally affable—but he was also big, intimidatingly so, and he made no secret of his total devotion to the Lady and her rules. He rounded the bar now and crossed the room to Brock in a matter of moments.

Brock eased Zed down from his shoulder. "Oof," he said. "I'm not an apprentice anymore, Gramit. And I don't have time for games. The city is on fire right now, and that's just the start of our problems if we don't stop the witch prowling just outside the gates."

Gramit frowned, folding his arms across his chest. "Always did love your stories."

"I need to see her, Gramit. *Please.* There's literally nowhere else we can go."

Gramit's eyes softened. He looked at Zed, small and helpless and mercifully in no condition to brag about any deals with witches.

"Masters and mistresses," Gramit said, addressing the room. "I'm afraid we'll be closing down early tonight. Please remember your coats."

Tongues clucked at his back, but Brock breathed a genuine sigh of relief. "Thanks, Gramit."

Gramit walked away, giving him a look that said, very clearly, that Brock's thanks were insufficient.

"Well, this is a surprise," came a lilting, playful voice. "I was certain we'd parted ways for good." Brock turned to find the

Lady Gray watching from a doorway. He had no idea how long she'd been there, and he tried not to show his irritation at being caught off guard.

Then he decided he didn't care, and he gave her a sour look. "I definitely still hate you, if that's what you mean," Brock said.

She smiled, unfazed. "And yet here you are. With your little friend . . . who I believe stabbed a guildmate earlier this evening. About the time your Hexam disappeared from his cell. And based on the smell of smoke wafting off you and the peculiar shade of the flames, I'm going to guess you two had something to do with the fire overtaking half a block of outtown at the moment."

"Yeah, yeah, you're so well informed," Brock said, scowling. "But I know something you don't. I know where Makiva is." He scratched his chin. "Well, roughly."

"The trinket maker?" The Lady Gray was intrigued. "She disappeared off the face of Terryn some months ago. Just as that business with Brenner was coming to a head."

Brock winced at the pun. "Makiva didn't disappear from Terryn. But she *did* leave Freestone, and it's bad news for everybody." He frowned. "There's more. A lot more. I'll tell you everything I know. But . . . I need you to promise me something first."

She waited for him to continue. The music box filled the silence.

Brock sighed heavily. "I need a way out of Freestone. I need safe passage to Llethanyl for myself and for Zed."

"For that, you'd have to talk to Frond. Isn't she the one who makes unsanctioned journeys whenever Me'Shala bats her eyelashes?"

"Zed and I have *both* betrayed Frond now. We can't go to her. But Zed's not responsible for his actions. I'm sure of it. And if anyone can help him, it's the elves. Zed's uncle, Callum . . . or the queen. She's a mage, and she owes us."

She shook her head. "It's impossible. Llethanyl is too far."

"We don't have to make it the whole way alone. Duskhaven is much closer–from there, we'd have allies." Brock felt an unexpected flame of hope flare to life in his chest. This almost sounded like it could work. And if he could convince Fel to help, their odds would be even better. "I'll need equipment. I'll need someone to make sure Frond doesn't send her people after us. If we stick to the roads, and sleep in the wayshelters . . . It's possible. It's a chance, anyway."

"You think King Freestone will agree to this? Suppose the healer boy dies. . . . Suppose those flames consume all of outtown before they're contained?"

"I think the king will do what you say. I wouldn't be here otherwise. So you pull whatever strings you have to pull. Spin a story. But you get us out of here."

She narrowed her eyes, considering Brock like Mousebane did a rodent. "What's in it for me?" she asked.

"Information." He inclined his head toward Zed's limp form. "Zed says that Makiva is a witch, and that she's planning some sort of attack. We'll learn what we can from him, use it to save the town. That should make up for anything else he's done."

The Lady sauntered up to Zed and prodded him with her foot. "Well, let's get him off the floor, then. Why don't you move him to the cushions?"

"About that," Brock said, rubbing his head. "I was actually going to suggest we tie him to a chair. Securely. And let's confiscate that scepter of his for good measure."

She raised a curious eyebrow.

"How are you at tying knots?" he asked.

✷

Gramit brewed them tea while they waited for Zed to awaken. "The good stuff," the Lady had directed him—and it was quite good, fragrant with mint and other, less familiar spices.

"Some of the seeds you brought from beyond the wall," the Lady explained. "An intown herbalist has had great success cultivating them. We think the mature plant might be a new source of parchment."

"So it wasn't all for nothing," Brock said. "The smuggling. You know Lotte actually caught me once? She was furious. I thought I was finished."

"You were good at it," the Lady said. "We all get caught, at one point or another. Getting out of trouble? That's part of the skill set."

Brock looked at her sidelong. "I don't imagine you've ever

been caught at anything. I half forget you're there when I'm looking right at you." He considered her dull gray hair and plain gray robes; it was more than that. "How do you do it?" he asked. "Is it magic?"

She tapped her nose. "That is a secret passed down from Dox himself. One I will share only with my successor."

Zed wheezed; he seemed to be rousing at last. Brock's eyes drifted to his friend, bound to a chair, his head hanging limply. The sight made Brock feel sick and anxious. His stomach churned at the thought of what Zed might say or do next.

Makiva had twisted him somehow. Tricked him. Infected him with her darkness.

But even so—wouldn't Zed have had to let her in? Wasn't that how fiendish bargains worked?

"He was obviously running low on mana *before* he set a house on fire, so I don't think he'll be doing any spell-casting," Brock said. "But watch his hands just in case, and keep that scepter out of his reach. Don't give him anything to eat or drink but water."

Brock hoped he'd made the right call, coming to the Lady. He'd seen the state she'd left Hexam in. But this was different—Brock was here. And he wouldn't let Zed out of his sight for a moment.

Zed lifted his head, groaning. He blinked his eyes, trying to focus.

Brock's lips were numb with anxiety.

"Take a breath, Zed," Brock said. "You're sathe."

Brock shook his head to clear his muddy thoughts. Why was he slurring? Why did his mouth feel so funny?

"The tea . . ." he said, and he leaped from his chair. Too quickly–the room spun, and he had to grab at the table.

"Why don't you have a rest, Brock?" the Lady cooed. "I'll take things from here."

Brock fought with everything he had to stay standing. It was no use. The table slipped from his fingers. He fell to his knees.

"Just . . . hate you," he said. "So, so much."

As Brock slumped to the ground, he heard the Lady Gray slide her chair against that same stone floor, inching ever closer to Zed, who sat before her bound and helpless.

A fly in a spider's web.

"Now then, Zed," she said silkily. "It's time you and I finally have a talk."

Brock heard nothing more before unconsciousness took him.

Chapter Nineteen

"It's time you and I finally have a talk."

Makiva squinted. Her vision was blurry. Pain knocked at the door of her thoughts, its knuckles slow and heavy.

"A talk."

"It's time."

As Zed's eyes cleared, she discovered that she was in a dark space. Zed's body had been bound to a chair, his wrists pulled behind him. Off in the corner, Brock Dunderfel lay slumped on a supple daybed. The room was cool and lined in stone, the remnants of rusted metal bars striping the walls. A dungeon? But a homey one. Pillows had been laid beneath Brock, and the space was lined with a museum's worth of fascinating artifacts, including Zed's own scepter, all displayed artfully atop antique furniture.

Incense burned from a censer several feet away, its spicy smoke filling the room. And an ancient, obsolete map of the lands around Freestone covered the far wall, bristling with pins and tidy notes, like ants exploring the imaginary landscape it depicted.

Interesting.

Makiva summoned what dribbles were left of Zed's mana, hoping there was enough to elf-step. The world shivered, Terryn's membrane thinning around her. But it held. The spell had failed, and with it she felt the last of Zed's mana burn away.

Very interesting.

She glanced around the room. Something was wrong here. An itch tickled at the boundaries of her perception.

"How do you *do* that?" she asked curiously.

Suddenly, the woman was there. The spymaster from the king's council was seated *right in front of Makiva*, leaning casually in a wooden chair identical to the one Zed occupied. Beyond her humble clothes, she wore an amused smile that made Makiva want to kill her quite a lot.

"You'll have to clarify," the Lady Gray said. Her singsongy voice was smooth as silk. "Hiding in plain sight? Or keeping you from bamfing away with your magic?"

"I have to choose *one*?" Makiva asked.

The woman regarded her thoughtfully. She leaned forward. "I'd be happy to answer your questions," she said. "Provided you answer some of mine. Secrets for secrets."

"'If you have me, you want to share me,'" Makiva muttered, remembering the old riddle about secrets. "'But if you share me, you haven't got me. What am I?'"

"That," the Lady Gray purred, "is exactly the question I mean to answer."

A chill crept up Zed's spine, annoying Makiva. She kept his expression neutral. This woman was becoming a problem.

"As a show of good faith, I'll begin." The Lady reached her small, graceful hand into the pocket of her gray smock, removing a glass jar lined in delicate golden filigree. Makiva recognized it immediately.

Once, *many* years ago, the glass had been empty. Now the interior was darkened with smoky purple ichor, suspended eerily in the center. The air around the glass tensed, a muscle flexing. Makiva could feel its pressure even from here.

"This is a majiquary," the Lady said. "An old-world artifact capable of draining mana from the air and storing it within. Spells of all kinds fizzle in its presence, whether cast by wizards, warlocks, or sorcerers. Dox Eural stole it from a fugitive mage-hunter during his adventuring days, giving Zahira and Foster the opportunity to strike. It was a rare object then. Now it's one of a kind."

Makiva remembered. She'd watched the encounter from

behind Foster's eyes. The bounty collected for "Mage-Killer Matthue" had been a small fortune. Foster spent his share on a magical color-changing cloak, the fop.

"Now." The Lady Gray leaned back again, pocketing her relic. "Tell me about Makiva."

Makiva smiled Zed's most pleasant smile. "No."

The Lady sat silently, her face impassive. Her dark eyes looked bored. Uninterested. Hardly there at all.

Or was the woman there? The room contracted, the walls around Makiva breathing in time with Zed's lungs. Smoke billowed thickly from the censer nearby, pouring to the stone floor.

Focus, she told herself as she once again lost sight of the Lady Gray. Zed's mind was clouding. *It's her tricks*, Makiva thought. "She's trying to confuse you so you'll slip and reveal you're not—"

Almost too late, she realized she'd been speaking aloud.

The Lady Gray snapped back into view, her bored expression long gone. "Not what?" she asked gently. Smoke pooled at their feet, covering the woman's modest shoes.

"The incense . . ." Makiva coughed. She recognized the spicy smell now. It confounded her thoughts. Makiva had used the very same incense to confound the fools who visited her tent, masking her youth behind fragrant, bewildering clouds. The limitations of this body!

"A special concoction from a perfumer friend," the spymaster said casually. "He calls it dragon's tongue. It's relaxing, isn't it? Makes it easy to lose track of the conversation, though. You were saying you don't want to reveal something. I hope it isn't something bad?"

Makiva gritted Zed's teeth and tried to empty her mind. Around this woman, even her thoughts were dangerous.

The Lady Gray leaned forward. "Let me tell you what *I* think, Zed, and see if it helps jog anything for you. I think you've fallen prey to Makiva in the same ways Mother Brenner and Magus Phylo did. And I think a mole in the Adventurers Guild—one who does *not* report to me—helped her snag you. Has been helping her for months, in fact, to smuggle dangerous materials to vulnerable people. You haven't been in the guild long enough to be the smuggler, and after extensive questioning, I'm left doubting even Hexam's involvement. It's why I allowed Brock to take him. For now."

Makiva started as she felt the woman's breath in her ear. Somehow, the Lady Gray had gotten behind her, all without Makiva realizing she'd even moved.

"Lastly," the spymaster said. "I don't think you're *Zed* at all. Not anymore." The chill creeping up Zed's spine clenched into a cold fist now. The Lady curved around Makiva, gliding through smoke up to her knees. Was that possible? Or was Zed's addled mind simply hallucinating?

"So then the question remains," the Lady Gray said, sitting placidly back down in her chair. "Who or what are you?"

Makiva glared at the woman, indulging in her hatred for a long, languorous moment. Finally, she shook her head and sighed. "It seems you've got me," she said. "I'll tell you who I really am. But are you sure you truly wish to know?"

The spymaster narrowed her eyes curiously. Somehow, the smoke didn't seem to be affecting her the way it did Zed. Magic? Or an antidote, more likely. Finally, the Lady Gray nodded. "Of course I do."

"Very well. But first, a secret for a secret. How do you cloak yourself? Are you a mage of some kind?"

The Lady was silent a long beat. Eventually, she shook her head. "There are more ways to power than Mages Guilds," she said. "You, I suspect, know this well. As the leader of the Shadows, I possess the *final* secret of Dox Eural. It's a simple chant—almost a song. An appeal to the plane of Nox, made in a forgotten tongue. The first time you sing it, you lose something. Something terribly important. But the *thing* is different for everyone. The spymaster before me claimed that Dox lost his heart the first time *he* sang the Thieves' Carol. I have no idea if that's true; Cristo had a flair for the dramatic."

The Lady crossed her legs, watching Makiva with those dull, probing eyes. "I lost my identity. My name, my memories of my family and friends, along with their ties to me. All of it vanished. Anything that wasn't connected to the Shadows simply evaporated in a moment. I have no idea who I was before this guild."

Makiva stared at the woman, then she curled Zed's mouth into a grin. "And what happened the *second* time you sang it?"

Slowly, the Lady smiled back at her. "Luck," she said. "A bit of the plane of chaos in my pocket, ready to help when I needed it." Here she pulled a small, strange coin from a pouch at her side. The front was gold and gleaming, undecorated by any official heraldry. But Makiva could already see that the reverse was dark and deeply scored. The Lady turned the coin to reveal the spider that awaited on that side. "With this, eyes turn from me when I'm still. Old steps don't creak. When I die, the coin will crumble, its fortune spent. It's not a perfect tool, of course. Luck will get a foolish thief only so far. But when combined with skill, there are ways around everything."

"There certainly are," Makiva said. "Unfortunately for you, however, I think your luck has run out."

And with that, she lifted Zed's scrawny legs for all they were worth, heaving the crown of his already-battered head into the Lady's stomach. Makiva felt a dull crack as she struck, along with a nova of pain. She braced Zed's teeth against it, and heard the startled shout of the spymaster as she fell backward in her chair. The coin flew from her hand, disappearing beneath a carpet of smoke.

Makiva pitched over as well, into the fumes. She landed with a breathtaking jolt on Zed's side.

Still, it had worked. She could feel it now as the flexed-muscle sensation of the majiquary let go. She'd shattered the relic. Centuries of captured mana filled the air, the overwhelming scents of mint and brimstone mixing with the dragon's tongue incense. She might have gagged, if not for the dizzying rush of *power* as free mana washed over Zed, overfilling even his deep, empty reservoir. A simple wizard or warlock would have been scathed by the conflicting magics, perhaps destroyed. Not Zed, her precious sorcerer. Her final, perfect tool.

Makiva elf-stepped out of her bindings with a fine control that Zed could only ever have dreamed of. She appeared in a silvery puff at the far table where Zed's scepter lay. Zed's vision tilted dizzily from the incense, but she ignored the vertigo. Another cloud and she stood beside the Lady Gray, who was just rising to her feet. Makiva brought the scepter down, knocking the spymaster to the floor again.

In the far corner, Brock lay motionless on his pillows, undisturbed by the fracas. Drugged, then. That would make this much easier.

"A secret for a secret," Makiva said with a manic smile. "Let's grant your wish, spymaster. Your suspicions were correct, I'm afraid. I'm *not* Zed." She tightened her grip on the scepter, pouring mana into it freely. The crystal atop flared with green heat. She leaned down to the Lady Gray, savoring the sharp look of fear in the woman's usually dull eyes.

And as the flames began, Makiva exhaled, luxuriating in the defeat of a worthy foe. Slowly and clearly, she spoke her true name.

✷

The deeper Zed plunged into the forest, the less solid Foster's memories became. Scenes of adventure and camaraderie twinkled by in flashes, the words and colors melting like snow in the trees.

Zed's final vision of Foster was little more than a blue-and-pink horizon. It was a jaw-dropping image of what appeared to be a great turquoise pool of *water*, stretching as far as he could see. Zed gasped aloud at the memory, his body frozen by the vast beauty of it. Laid across a ribbon of clean white sand, Foster scratched Reyna behind her ear. The rest of the Champions reclined against a tumble of rocks, all calmly watching the sun rise over this improbable sight.

The ocean. Zed had heard of it, of course, but he hadn't truly believed . . . Off in the distance, a vessel with a huge white triangular wing glided across the water.

"We don't do this enough," Jerra said softly. The knight's armor was now glittering and fine. Zahira's hand was clasped in his own.

And then it was over. All that water faded, absorbed by the forest, and Zed was once again alone with the fox.

He immediately doubled back, hoping to find the memory of Foster at the ocean again. But whatever this place was, whatever revelations it forfeited to Zed, it offered them only fleetingly. Though he ran from spot to spot, the vision never reappeared.

Eventually, Zed gave up, leaning back against a tree. He turned to the red fox, which lay watching him with its curious canine stare.

"I never wanted a pet," Zed muttered.

The fox flicked its tail.

Zed turned his gaze to the woods around him.

It was cold in this part of the forest. And dark. The wisps had been left behind long ago, forcing Zed to light his own way. He took up a large stick now, igniting the end with green flame. In the shadows of the eerie light, the trees looked like the bars of an enormous cage.

"There's something here," he said. "I can feel it. The deeper I go into the chain, the more it pushes back. Do *you* know what it is?"

But when Zed turned back to the fox, he discovered it was gone. He was alone again in the forest.

He pushed off from the tree with a sigh, then continued into the dark.

Eventually, more memories enveloped Zed, each as brief and delicate as Foster's vision of the ocean. But *Foster* wasn't in these. Zed caught glimpses of other witches and warlocks—women and men and some who didn't appear to be either—all of them wearing the same glittering mythril chain.

It always began with a wish. Zed watched many as they made their pacts, holding their hands out to a smiling Makiva. And he witnessed Makiva as she reaped her students. Some she killed outright, draining their power into the chain. They were the lucky ones.

Most she forced to turn against the people and places they loved first.

As Zed traveled, misty figures began filling the woods, more with every new vision. Their bodies were cloudy and indistinct. They never approached, but they watched him as he walked, with eyes like burning green candles.

Slowly, Zed realized there was another constant to the visions.

Someone besides Makiva appeared in the memories, standing at the sides of the witches and warlocks she entrapped.

A red fox.

They all called it by different names. Foster had named his familiar Reyna. Tala, the dwarven witch whose tomb he and the Champions had scavenged, called hers Eztli.

The fox always came back, appearing to every witch and warlock who'd worn the chain.

All except one.

"Who *are* you?" Zed wondered aloud again as another vision faded, this one of an elven warlock who'd met Makiva in some kind of traveling performers guild called a *circus*.

Zed turned to find the fox had returned, sitting placidly in the now-murky woods. It didn't offer any response beyond blinking at him.

"So Makiva has been playing this game for centuries," he muttered. Zed began pacing, his feet kicking up the layer of smoke that had built along the forest floor. "How could she possibly be that old? How could *you*? It's not necromancy, or you'd be rotting liches by now."

The ghostly figures that surrounded him began to churn, their cloudy bodies shifting in a manner that felt nervous to Zed.

The fox stood. Its posture, too, was strangely anxious. The fur along its tail puffed out in alarm. Zed paused, gazing down at the smoke at his feet. "What is this?" he asked. "Is it . . . is it getting hot?"

Then, suddenly, Zed wasn't in the woods anymore. The forest ignited with green flames, the landscape burning away like a cloth backdrop set afire. Zed stood in a stone room, back in his wispy body.

Though the walls and floor of this strange space were made of carved stone blocks, it was filled with wooden furniture and odd materials, nearly all of which were ablaze with green fire. Zed caught a glimpse of himself—*Makiva!*—exiting through a nearby door. The imposter wore an excited, terrible grin.

Zed whirled around to find Brock unconscious on a daybed. Thankfully, the fire hadn't reached him yet, but it was only a matter of time.

"*Brock!*" Zed surged to the boy, shouting in his ear. But Brock still couldn't hear him.

There was no more time to waste. Zed closed his eyes without a second thought, clearing his mind of anything but Brock. As the world burned around him, he plunged into the mind of his best friend.

Chapter Twenty

Brock

Brock's entire hand fit into his mother's palm. He liked the feeling it gave him, a reminder that though *he* might be small, the adults who loved him were big enough to keep him safe. Even so, sometimes he wanted nothing more than to slip from his mother's grip and run free.

He was seven years old, and the sun was shining above Freestone.

During visits to the market, his mom let him loose. Sometimes she was there for shopping, and sometimes in some official capacity for the Merchants Guild. Brock wasn't even sure which it was today; he only knew how excited he was to dart among the colored tents in whatever direction his feet took him. Most of the merchants knew him, knew his parents, and so Brock could count on free candy and cookies and sometimes even a toy whittled down from wood scraps too small to be used in construction.

Today's bounty was mostly candy. In a matter of minutes, Brock's pockets were full of sweets. He put a few in his socks, too, in case his mom decided he had too many. (Brock was good at math and knew the *exact right* amount of candy, thank you very much.)

Someone tapped him on the shoulder. Brock turned to see his friend Shef standing there with a grin. "Hey, Brock. Wanna see something weird?"

Brock nodded enthusiastically, and Shef ran off. Brock followed him to the far end of the market–to the outtown side, where a boy he didn't recognize sat reading a book. The boy's ears were strange. Pointy.

"What a freak," Shef said. "See his ears?"

And Brock, without really thinking about it, nodded. "Freaky," he agreed.

"Hey freak!" Shef called.

Brock ducked behind the nearest stall, pulling Shef after him. "What'd you do *that* for?" he hissed, embarrassed.

"Relax," Shef said. He chuckled, giddy with transgression. "I mean, he *is* a freak, so what does it matter?"

Brock peered around the corner. The boy was still there,

scanning the crowd with wide eyes. He'd heard the slur; he'd *known* it was addressed at him. He hadn't seen Brock, though, which was a relief, if a sour one. Shame pooled heavy and cold in his stomach as he watched the boy put away his book with awkward, self-conscious movements.

"I bet he lives in a goblin nest. I bet he lives outside the wall!" Shef said excitedly. "We should follow him."

The boy wiped furtively at his eyes as he hitched up his satchel and turned toward outtown.

"Come on, or we'll lose him!" Shef said.

Brock acted without thinking, sticking his foot out–and sending his friend sprawling against the cobbles. Shef's knees were skinned, bleeding freely, and the boy grimaced against the pain. "You did that on purpose," he grunted.

"No, I–" Brock froze, fearful and guilty and confused. Had he done the right thing, or the wrong thing?

"You're a bad kid," Shef said. "You're a *terrible* friend, Brock, and this is *all your fault*!"

Then Shef burst into flame. The boy screamed and writhed there on the ground, in pain and in fear. He was reduced to ash in moments.

And the fire burned green.

"Brock, what did you do?" his mother cried.

"I'd say I'm disappointed," said his father, "but to be disappointed, I'd have to expect more from you to begin with."

Some part of Brock knew that this was wrong. *This isn't how it happened*. But that small voice of reason was drowned out by the horror of the moment.

"Run!" he told his parents. Too late. They were already ablaze. The whole marketplace was burning.

And Zed was right in the middle of it. The flames didn't touch him.

"Zed, stop it! *Please!*"

Zed looked surprised. "*You can see me?*" he asked. But the surprise gave way to alarm as he took in his fiery surroundings. "*Is this . . . is this how you see me now?*" he said sadly.

Brock braved the flames, reaching out to grab Zed by the shoulders—to shake sense into him. But his friend was insubstantial. Brock passed right through him.

"What—?" he said, turning back to see Zed's misty form cohere again. Mostly; he was hazy around the edges, like a drawing left out in the sun. "Zed?"

Zed nodded, his eyes wide. "*You're dreaming, Brock. But* I'm *real. I've been trying to reach you for—for weeks.*"

"I don't understand," Brock said.

"*Makiva stole my body,*" Zed said. As sensational a statement as it was, Zed delivered the news without any emotion. "*She took control of me after the battle for Llethanyl.*"

Brock wanted to argue, to say that was impossible. But on hearing those words, he knew immediately that they were true. "Of course," he said. "I mean, don't get me wrong, that is just totally bananas and I'm horrified to a live in a world where 'she stole my body' is a thing, but—it makes sense." Brock smiled. "I *knew* there was no way you were responsible for . . . for Micah, or the fire. . . ."

"*Micah,*" Zed whispered, and he clenched his eyes closed in unmistakable sorrow. Brock reached for his hand; he passed right through. "*I didn't do any of it, Brock,*" Zed said miserably. "*But I* am *responsible. I made a deal with Makiva. For the power to save us . . . or maybe just the power to be somebody. I don't know anymore.*"

"A deal?" Brock echoed. "What kind of deal?"

"*I tried to tell you. I wrote you a letter—a* confession. *But I was never able to get it to you.*" His misty shoulders hitched. "*It's probably still in the codex. The one Selby gave me.*"

"Selby's codex?" Brock said. Hadn't he found a piece of parchment in that very book?

"*We're out of time. You have to wake up.*" Zed swallowed hard. "*And when you do . . . You have to stop Makiva, Brock. Stop me. Whatever it takes.*" He looked Brock square in the eyes with unusual resolve. "*Whatever it takes. Promise me.*"

Brock frowned. "I can fix this."

"*You always say that.*" Zed smiled sadly. "*But this time is different, Brock.*" He cleared his throat and said more firmly, "*Promise me.*"

"I'm not going to kill you, if that's what you're getting at."

Zed sniffed. "*I don't* want *to die,*" he said. "*Brock, I—I think—*" His voice cracked and wavered. "*I think I'm already dead.*"

A sob erupted from Zed's small frame, and though his ethereal body produced no tears, his chest and shoulders heaved as he wept.

Brock felt a different kind of fire then—one that burned from the inside out, scorching away all his doubt and fear and resentment. All that was left was love for his friend, and pity, and the utter determination that Zed would not be alone—not now, not with this.

Brock wrapped his arms around him, and this time, Zed was solid to the touch.

Zed slowly calmed. He hugged Brock back, and his shaking stilled. "*How?*" he asked, sniffing.

"It's my dream, isn't it?" Brock answered, not letting go.

"*Thank you,*" Zed whispered. "*But you really have to wake up.*"

"Just one more minute, Mom."

"*You're the best friend anybody ever had,*" Zed said. "*And I'm truly sorry about this.*" And with that, he pinched Brock savagely on the arm.

✷

"OW!" Brock shouted, startling awake.

It was just like his dream of the market. Fire was everywhere, and the room was filling with smoke. Brock coughed viciously as the lingering sense of Zed's skin against his vanished.

He stayed low, rolling off the pillows and squinting against the firelight. Zed—*Makiva* was gone, and the Lady Gray . . .

He caught just a glimpse of her lying on the ground. A glimpse was enough to know she'd died badly.

Had she died knowing the truth? Or did she curse Zed's name in her final moments?

Brock pushed the questions away and began crawling toward the exit. The stone floor hurt his knees, but he was happy for it. All that stone meant the fire would burn itself out eventually—once it had eaten through the tapestries and the pillows, the map and the music box.

The map. Brock had spent weeks updating it with all the adventurers had found beyond the walls. But having been drafted before the Day of Dangers, the map showed dozens of sites the adventurers hadn't yet visited. There were roadside taverns and temples that no longer stood, but which might have had basements. With luck, those basements could yet be full of salvageable goods. The map also showed an old path to the dwarven city, partially subterranean, which no one had walked for two hundred years. It might be too far to ever venture, but what might they find along that ancient thoroughfare?

The map was on the far side of the room, though, beyond the burning bar. Brock knew he couldn't make it there and back.

But he could save the music box. It was just as old as the map, and as far as he knew, unique in all the world. He had to salvage *something* from all this.

Brock palmed the music box and kept going. By his estimate, he was halfway to outtown before the underground tunnel cleared of smoke enough that he felt it was safe to stand. Still, he was woozy and his lungs felt raw, and he didn't breathe easily until he forced the heavy stone door open and spilled out into the shadows beneath the statues of the Champions.

But Brock's nightmare continued unabated. Outtown was still ablaze with that evil green fire.

How would Freestone ever recover from this?

Brock slid to the ground, leaning against the base of Dox's statue. Parchment crinkled in his pocket, and he remembered what Zed had said about a letter. His confession, he'd called it. And Brock had been carrying it with him for days.

He removed the letter from his pocket, unfolding it with shaking hands. There was Zed's handwriting. And there was Brock's name, at the very top. *Dear Brock*, the letter began. *I'm scared.*

It had started with a dream—a strange dream of a forest. It was within that dreamscape that Zed had accepted Makiva's bargain.

The pact I made that night was for you all, to stop Brenner before she hurt you. But keeping the secret was selfish. I see that now. You've always been brave, Brock. You've defended me practically our whole lives. For once, I was able to protect you, and I was proud of that. Too proud.

Brock squeezed his eyes shut. He'd always liked that Zed thought he was brave. But he rarely *felt* brave. What looked like courage to his friend was usually just Brock being too foolish or angry or scared to quit.

And he knew he'd have taken that bargain. He'd have made a pact in a heartbeat, if it meant saving his friends.

In a way, he had. Hadn't he made the same choice as Zed when he'd gone along with the Lady Gray's demands? Hadn't he, too, kept his choices a secret?

So I'm coming to you again, the letter continued, *like I always do, to ask for your help. I'm sorry, Brock. I know I rely on you too much.*

But when we work together, it just feels like we can do anything.

Brock sniffled. He wiped his running nose with one hand and pocketed the letter with the other. "I should have seen it," he said, his voice quavering. "I should have *realized*."

A mote of emerald light hovered nearby—he'd missed it, at first, in the green light from the great fire. It was no ember, no insect—it was a shimmering particle of pure light, bobbing softly at his side. Something about it seemed almost . . . protective.

"Zed . . . ?" he asked tentatively. "Zed, is that you?"

The light bobbed, flaring more brightly for a moment. It might have been a *yes* . . . or a *no*. Or it might have meant nothing at all.

But Brock knew the truth. A tear rolled down his cheek, and he let it. "It's your spirit, isn't it? It's beautiful."

He sat there in silence, turning from the mote to the fire raging in the middle distance. "Your mom's safe, by the way," Brock said. "Everyone's safe. Liza will see to it. So you don't have that on your conscience. Okay?"

He took a moment just to sit there and catch his breath, eyes closed against the sight of Freestone burning. He felt Zed's presence beside him, and he basked in the feeling, allowing a fleeting sense of peace to wash over him.

When we work together . . . we can do anything.

Zed and Brock, together against the world. He could work with this.

✷

Brock only allowed himself a moment's rest before he found his feet and made his way out of the plaza. His mind raced with everything he'd learned, teasing out the implications.

The adventurers were all outside the wall by now, thinking Old Makiva was out there somewhere. But it was a wild cockatrice chase; Makiva was right here in Freestone, causing chaos while wearing Zed's face. He glanced over his shoulder to make sure Zed was still there. "Stay close," he said. "Just stay with me, if you can."

Hexam might have some idea how to help Zed, but he would be halfway to the wayshelter by now, along with Fel. Brock couldn't go to the mages; their solution would surely not account for Zed's welfare. The Stone Sons would be even worse.

It had to be Brock. He had to find a way to stop Makiva *and* save Zed at the same time. But he couldn't do it alone.

"Liza!" he called, running toward the fire. "Jett!"

The closer to the blaze, the more chaotic the scene became. All of outtown had spilled out onto the streets, families clutching one another tightly as they watched their homes sag and collapse before the destructive power of the flames. Each ruined building sent sparks flying into the air, spreading the fire farther. Scores of people, outtowner and intowner alike by the looks of them, formed snaking lines to transport buckets of water from the nearest wells, but whether due to magic or magnitude, the fire showed no signs of diminishing.

"Buildings can be rebuilt," he said, to himself and to Zed. "If Makiva is allowed to run free, this might be the least of our problems." He cast a guilty look at those gathered to help, including a large group of mages who appeared to be preparing an elaborate spell. The archmagus stood among them, and the rest of the king's council looked on from nearby. "We have to keep moving."

He didn't see Liza or any of the others among the crowds, so he turned toward the Golden Way Temple. Soot-stained townsfolk were congregating upon the steps, and the healers moved among them, administering healing wherever it was needed. The rich, honeyed glow of their anima warred with the night's otherworldly green gauze, casting strange shadows in every direction. Brock pressed on, stopping a nun as he entered the temple.

"The boy who was stabbed tonight," he said. "The adventurer. Is he here?"

The nun smiled softly. "Oh, we all know Micah by name here. You'll find him in the first room upstairs." She put a hand on his shoulder. "Brace yourself. We've done all we can, but it's up to him now. He's a fighter, though."

"Don't I know it," Brock said. "Does he have any visitors?"

"Just one," the nun confirmed, and Brock nodded gratefully.

As he took the interior staircase, he tried to decide what he'd say to Liza. No doubt she was furious with him. He owed her another apology, and he knew how she liked those. Although on second thought . . . he had been right. Right about Zed, anyway. Even if it was technically his fault that Makiva was loose in Freestone at the moment.

"Just let me do the talking," he said jokingly to Zed. He figured he'd start with an apology, just to be safe.

Brock was surprised, however, on opening the door at the top of the stairs. Micah's visitor wasn't Liza, but Lotte.

"Oh, thank Fey," Brock said. "Lotte, I'm so glad to see you."

Lotte turned, startled at the sound of his voice. She'd been crying as she stood vigil over Micah, but Brock's eyes quickly slid from her to his fellow apprentice. Micah lay shirtless upon a cot, pale and still. His wounds were bandaged and . . . glowing. As if Micah hid a burning furnace within his chest, and its light was leaking through, daylight through flimsy curtains.

"Is that normal?" he asked.

"Brock, what are you doing here?" Lotte demanded. She wiped her sleeve across her cheeks, her pauldrons clanking and the dagger in her hand catching the amber light.

"It's a long story," he said. "But the gist is that Zed isn't Zed right now. His body's been stolen by a witch, and we have to stop her before she hurts anyone else—and before the knights or the mages bring her down and hurt Zed in the bargain."

"That . . . is a lot to process," Lotte said. "How exactly did you learn all this?"

"Zed came to me in a dream," Brock answered. "And now that I say that out loud, I know what it sounds like, but it's true."

Lotte gave him a pitying look. "Brock, I understand how hard it is to accept this. But Zed flirted with dark magic, and it changed him. It's as simple as that."

"It *is* simple," Brock said. He gestured madly at the green mote at his side. "Zed needs our help. He's right here! This is all that's left of him!"

Lotte's eyes passed right over Zed's spectral form, unseeing. "Brock, I'm telling you," she said stonily. "You need to let this go. Leave it to the authorities."

Brock scoffed. "The authorities? Me? Have we met?"

The quartermaster looked at him sadly. "Of course. I know you. You're like a manticore with a bone. You're never going to let it go, no matter what. Are you?"

"We need Frond and the others back in Freestone. With all of the adventurers looking, we'll find Zed in no time, and . . . Wait. Why aren't you out with the rest of them?"

Lotte didn't answer. She had an unnerving look in her eyes.

"Lotte? What were you doing in here alone?" Brock took a hesitant step back. "Why are you holding a dagger?"

"You should have left it alone, Brock," Lotte said. And in a single fluid motion, she reared back and flung her dagger at Brock's chest.

Brock's training saved him. All those grueling, miserable

hours spent sparring in the training yard—exercises led by Lotte herself.

He'd seen her shoulder tense before the throw. Just the slightest sign, same as a gambler's tell at the card table. He saw her intention, and he rolled, and the dagger missed its mark.

But he was only so fast. The blade slashed across his arm, cutting deep.

Brock gasped in pain, and he lost control of his dodge, tumbling to the floor.

She was on him before he could regain his feet, gripping him by the tunic and slamming him back against the floorboards. "Curse you, Brock. Curse your incessant meddling."

"It . . . it was you," Brock said, gasping for air. "You all along. The smuggler—the traitor."

Lotte snarled. "Shut up."

"You—you killed Mother Brenner."

She looked pained. "Not on purpose. Never on purpose . . ."

Brock gripped her wrists, trying to pry her off of him, but she held him tight. "What do you *mean*, not on purpose?"

"Makiva told me . . . she *promised* me that she could fix the world. That she could make things better. I only had to . . . had to slip something into Brenner's drink. Had to get Frond to recruit Zed . . . and keep him safe . . ."

"Are you kidding me?" Brock seethed. "Lotte, Makiva *possessed* Zed. You served him up to her on a platter!"

"I know," Lotte said, her face lined with sorrow. "I know that now. And so . . . so do you and Micah." Something in her eyes went hard, and Brock felt a cold rush of fear.

"It's not too late, Lotte," Brock pleaded. "We can work together. Save Zed. Stop her . . ."

For a moment, Brock thought he'd gotten through to her. She released her grip on his tunic. She closed her eyes and steadied herself.

Then she shook her head sadly. "All you do is talk, Brock. And I . . . I can't let you talk."

She locked her cold fingers around his neck. *Stop*, he tried to say, but his throat was completely closed. She knew what she was doing, and she was far stronger than him.

He pulled at her fingers, desperate to pry them away. But his arms felt weak; his fingers tingled. His vision was going blurry, but he could see that she was crying. Her lips moved, and he thought she might be apologizing, but he couldn't hear anything over his pounding heart.

His vision went white, then yellow. The amber tones of dawn filled his view. Death had come for him, and it was golden. Brock felt his fear slip away.

Then he felt Lotte's grip slip away, too. She slumped to the side, falling off him, and Micah stood there in her place. The amber light was no vision of the afterlife, but the boy's anima seeping through his bandages.

Brock gulped greedily for air, taking it in so quickly that he felt his chest might burst.

"Before you thank me," Micah said, "you should know I've been wanting to do that since I met her." He was brandishing a candelabra, which he'd apparently slammed against Lotte's head. The amber light dimmed to nothing, and Brock could see how pale the boy was. With a deflated "woo," Micah slumped back against his cot.

Brock rubbed his neck. He felt like he'd swallowed broken glass. "Nice choice on the candlestick," he said, his voice raw. "Light as a weapon. Very on theme."

If it was possible, Micah seemed to go even paler. "Fie," he said. "Is that–is that you, Zed?" He was looking directly at the mote of light.

"You can see him?" Brock asked.

Micah nodded. "I could hear him, too, before. We talked. He looked . . . He looked like Zed before, but misty." He shook his head. "We're running out of time."

As if proving Micah's point, the green light dimmed right before their eyes.

Chapter Twenty-One

Zed was being pulled away. He could feel it.

It was like a part of him was still back in the forest, his stretched essence occupying two places at once. As he trailed Brock through the temple, the columns whizzing by transformed momentarily into twisted tree trunks. The white cloth partitions became walls of shadow, hemming Zed in darkness. Then he was back, floating behind his friend as a bodiless wisp.

Brock hurried to find Liza—or Jayna or Jett, any adventurers who weren't searching for Makiva outside the walls. Micah was too weak to follow, so he'd stayed behind to keep an eye on Lotte. Last Zed saw her, the quartermaster had been trussed up in a supply closet, her eyes wild and hair tousled as they locked her inside. Brock and Micah had bound and gagged her with the closest materials at hand—bandages and the silky cords the temple used as ornamentation.

Now, as Brock emerged onto the street, Zed could see that the sky was dark with churning clouds, lit green by the otherworldly fires still blazing outtown. But these were no natural rain clouds. Sometimes, in the event of an out-of-control fire, the Mages Guild would be called upon to work weather magic, summoning storms to douse the flames.

It was a measure of last resort, as the conjured rains were unpredictable. Six years ago, Zed had witnessed a spell-storm that was called to end a particularly dangerous blaze in the market. Three neighborhoods were engulfed in the floods, and it destroyed a season's worth of crops.

A high bell began ringing now from the temple behind them, warning Freestoners of the coming deluge. Stone Sons hustled through the streets in their clanking armor, shouting at passersby to find high ground.

Just as the first fat drops of rain began to fall, Zed caught sight of something shocking. A fox watched from across the cobbles. Under the green-gray sky, its vivid orange fur was loud as a scream. Still, no one else seemed to see the wild creature sitting calmly on the stone path. Not even Brock.

The fox's orange eyes widened as they found his wispy form; Zed felt the pull of the dream forest growing more intense.

"*We're not done, are we?*" he asked. "*I still haven't found what's inside the chain.*" In this wispy shape, his voice was almost too weak for even him to hear.

Zed wanted more than anything to stay with Brock. He wanted to find his friends and stop Makiva and save Freestone. He wanted to make up for everything that had brought them to this point.

But Zed couldn't help his friends. Not like this. Not yet.

"*All right,*" he said. His voice was less than a whisper, but it carried a grave weight. "*Can you take me back there? Back where we left?*"

The fox inclined its head, the gesture eerily human. Slowly, shadows began leaking up from between the stones like floodwater. The market tents billowed away, revealing still, dark woods just behind them.

Zed had one last glimpse of Brock before Freestone faded like a dream. His friend glanced back at him, his eyes wide with concern.

"Zed?" Brock asked. "Are you okay? You look—"

Zed was gone before Brock could finish.

The market disappeared and Zed stood once more in the mysterious woods, wearing his own body. The fox panted at him, tilting its head.

"I hope this is worth it." Zed frowned, balling his hands into fists. "Let's go."

The fox hopped up and turned to face the woods, glancing

behind it with an expectant grin. This time they continued together.

The visions came in dribs and drabs as they moved. The lingering ghosts of Makiva's victims faded into view, then disappeared just as quickly. They were people of all sorts—humans and elves and folk he had no names for. They wore clothes in styles Zed could never have imagined, cried out in unfamiliar tongues.

But for all their differences, Zed knew they were the same as him. Isolated, anxious souls caught up in a game they hardly understood. A coven of fools.

The forest thinned with every yard they walked. Zed felt an odd prickling sensation in his chest, more intense than before.

"There's something ahead," he muttered, wondering just how he knew. "Something is . . . buried back here?"

The fox turned to Zed, its eyes glimmering excitedly.

Then, a light. A green glare shone through the darkness, climbing the horizon like an eldritch sun. Zed shielded his eyes as he drew nearer. He and the fox stepped from the tree line to the wall of an overgrown cliff. Light spilled out from a crumbling passage into the stone.

They had reached the end of the forest. Here, hidden deep away, was the truth.

✷

Long ago, it began with darkness. Then, small dots of light—candles placed around a circle and carefully ignited.

The circle had been carved into the earth, its every curve precise. Sigils surrounded it, impeccably drawn, and a mythril chain lay at its center, set just so. No one wore the chain. This memory was its alone.

Seven hooded figures stood around the ring, their heads bowed. They had congregated in this wooded glade for an important task, but a desperate one. If they succeeded, then prosperity beyond imagining would be theirs. Their dying, once-great kingdom—now besieged by rivals and stricken with drought—would flourish again. But if they failed . . .

Well, it was best to do this far from the kingdom's walls.

The leader of the seven spoke the words, reading from a tattered scroll in a language that was ancient even before these ancient days. In his right hand, he held a beautiful curved dagger. As he spoke, his mages began curling their hands into frightening shapes, pouring their mana into the spell.

Suddenly, the flames in the candles flared green. All around the mages, will-o-wisps appeared in the forest, flitting eerily between the trees. A howl rose through the woods, ringing in each of their ears. It was a terrible cry of fear and fury.

It was a cry of resistance.

The leader kept reading, his hood falling away to reveal a regal golden crown. The mage-king raised his voice to shout over the din. Now that the ritual was under way, any hesitation would mean disaster. He couldn't fail his people.

Finally, he came to the end of the spell, and the mage-king

slammed the book shut. "I name you now, djinn!" he shouted in his own tongue, holding the dagger out. "And so summon you! Come to me—*Vetala!*"

There was an explosion of silvery mist that swallowed the mages, the remnants of the great tear they'd just made in the Veil. And there, floating at the circle's center, was a creature of pure fire.

Through the shroud of dissipating fog, the djinn at first appeared human. It had the lithe shape of a dancer, with two legs that skated over the ground as if it were walking on ice. But instead of flesh, the fiend's body was a burning furnace of green fire, shaped only by a strange, dark frame like charred iron. Its face was a twisted mask, through which two bright green motes like eyes turned toward the mage-king.

How dare you?

Its voice was not a voice, but a pressure that popped the mages' ears, raking at their resolve.

The mage-king took a step forward. "You are bound, djinn, by the mythril chain around your neck."

The djinn slowly inclined its head, registering the glittering line that encircled its fiery throat.

"And you are *commanded*," the king boomed, summoning his courage, "by the dagger I now bear, to grant my every wish. From this day forward you may never harm a mortal, unless it is the work of such a wish. Speak, fiend, for you've revealed you can! Acknowledge my authority."

The djinn regarded him in silence for a long, breathless stroke. The mages all trembled nervously within their cloaks.

Yes . . . master.

And so it was that the kingdom was brought back from the verge of collapse. The djinn resentfully served its master for many years, using its powerful magic to usher in a new age of prosperity.

And before the mage-king died, he passed the dagger down to his son, along with a dire warning. The djinn would grant its master's wishes to the letter, but its heart was full of hatred for its imprisonment. Every wish must be carefully worded; the fiend would use any opportunity it could to turn a wish against the wisher.

The prince hastily took the dagger, his eyes bright with possibility. But he promised his father that he would be careful.

The djinn was patient. It bided its time.

*

Hundreds of years later, a young adventurer stumbled upon the ruins of a long-forgotten city.

She'd taken a wrong turn somehow and was lost in the forest. Perhaps she should have listened when the locals warned her this was a cursed place, but no one would tell her more than that the woods sometimes sparkled with odd green lights.

"Oh Makiva," the adventurer muttered. "What have you gotten yourself into?"

Makiva wasn't usually the nervous type. She was a talented sorceress, after all, and a prudent explorer. She'd sailed oceans and fended off bandits in her journeys across Terryn. But something about this place set her teeth to grinding.

She pulled a small compass from her trousers, a helpful trinket she'd purchased after crossing the sea into this wooded country. The lodestone inside always pointed her north, not through any wizard's enchantment, but a force the merchant had called magnetism. Flicking the lid open, Makiva frowned at the pane of glass beneath.

The lodestone was spinning wildly in circles.

Makiva resolved to be less trusting of strange merchants. She snapped the lid shut, pocketing the compass again.

It was nearly dark when she finally decided to rest. Evening was approaching, and the wind had picked up, bringing with it dark clouds that roiled like a nest of snakes through the leafy canopy. Makiva arrived at the base of a stark cliff, covered with layers of vines. Perhaps the scarp would provide some shelter from the rain.

She sighed, shucking off her pack and leaning against the vegetation. To her surprise, the vines gave way behind her, revealing a wide-open archway—straight into the cliff.

No, not a cliff or a mountain. Makiva gasped as she pulled away layers of vegetation, uncovering heavy stones and carved figures beneath, the engraved faces now unrecognizable in their abandonment. She stood at the base of a great gray pyramid.

Makiva glanced behind her to the darkening forest. The townspeople had been right. Uncanny green lights were meandering between the trees. Thunder grumbled in the sky. Suddenly, Makiva found she did not want to spend the night in these strange woods.

She closed her eyes and took a deep breath, summoning her mana. Her body began to shrink, her clothes and gear melting into ruddy fur along with her skin. Makiva's ears exploded outward and her hands fell to the ground, transforming into two small paws. In moments, where before had stood a bright young woman, there was now a fox with curious orange eyes.

Makiva was a natural shapeshifter and metamorph, the first her humble village had seen in a generation. On the night she was officially named the village's mystic—tasked with exploring the world and bringing back stories of its wisdom and follies—her people had given her the title of Smiling Fox.

She grinned now as she shook out her fur, padding inside the crumbling doorway and into the ruins of the forgotten kingdom.

It didn't take her long to find the structure's center. After just a few turns through the cavernous halls, Makiva caught sight of a lambent green light, almost like a flickering torch. Was there another explorer here? Perhaps, like her, they'd stumbled onto this place. If there *was* a stranger within, best to scout first as a harmless fox.

But as she rounded the corner into the pyramid's main

chamber, the glare reflecting against her vulpine eyes, she found no torches inside.

Makiva was a worldly woman. She knew that mages of all kinds sometimes summoned beasts from the planes beyond Terryn, to serve as pets or bodyguards. She'd even seen such an unfortunate creature in her last major city. A great clockwork golem had wandered into the market in the early morning, its brilliant white wings stretching yards into the sky. Its wizard handler had called it a seraphex, and he'd laughed when Makiva asked if the chains which shackled its wings were uncomfortable for the creature.

Makiva thought it was an abominable sort of magic, pulling such beings from their homes and forcing them into servitude.

Just such a creature greeted her now. It drifted inches above the stone—a dancer's body formed of twisted metal and billowing green flames.

The fiery creature within didn't appear to be chained as the seraphex had been, except for a glittering necklace around its throat. But it *was* caged within a large iron cell. Or had been, once. Makiva noted that the cage's bars were long eroded by age. Why didn't it simply leave?

Because, Makiva, I am chained all the same.

Makiva yipped, her tail shooting out. As a voice raked heavily against her thoughts, her hackles stood on end.

The creature turned its masked face to her.

Please, sorceress. I beg you for mercy. I am the forgotten slave of a forgotten kingdom, left here after my masters have all died and rotted.

Somehow it knew she was no natural fox. Makiva shook off her fur, unfolding from her transformation. She stood tall as a human, squaring her shoulders and slowly approaching the creature.

"What are you?" she said. "How did you end up this way?"

I am djinn. I was dragged here from Fie—kidnapped from the burning blue mountains that were my home and heart—and shackled to the will of a madman. He used my power to make himself great, until it overtook him and he led his people to ruin. And yet I envy my mortal captor, for I remain here still. Abandoned.

"How awful . . ." Makiva's heart hurt for the djinn. It had been alone here all this time? It might have been centuries! "Is there a way to send you back to your home?"

The creature considered the question.

If there is, it's beyond even my power. Perhaps we could find a way together.

Makiva frowned, glancing around the enormous moldering chamber. Whatever grand embellishments had once decorated this place, they were all gone now. Rotted to dust. The palace had become a grave and a prison. "How can I help you?" she asked.

A dagger, at the throne. Only the dagger can cut my chain, unbinding me from this place.

Makiva climbed the steps leading up to a gray slab of a throne. Within the seat the desiccated remains of what must have been the djinn's cruel master reclined almost lazily. The skeleton looked so small. She saw an elegantly curved blade clutched in its palm. Besides the creature itself, it was perhaps the only item in this place not eroded by years of neglect. Makiva swallowed, then slowly pried the blade from the corpse's grip.

I would reward you for your help, the djinn intoned as she returned with the knife. **My kind are most powerful in the granting of wishes. Tell me yours. Whatever you desire.**

Makiva smirked at the djinn's expressionless mask. "I don't need any reward for freeing a creature in trouble. That is basic human decency."

The djinn's flames flickered pleasantly as it contemplated this.

The humans I've known have not been as decent.

Makiva sighed, nodding her head. "They . . . *we* aren't always as good as we could be. This world can be a cruel and heartless place, and I'm sorry that's all you've seen of it. But it can also be kind and beautiful. I've met so many people in my journeys, of both sorts. Surely your home had both as well?"

Fie is . . . untamed. For a moment, the booming, scraping voice of the djinn softened. It sounded almost like a faraway bell, tolling mournfully. **There are horrors there, things which would frighten you. But it's also a place of stark beauty, and raw elemental forces cascading freely.** The mask dipped briefly toward the floor. **I miss it very much.**

"I'm so sorry," Makiva said, her voice a whisper. Then she slowly reached forward with the dagger and brought its edge—still strangely sharp after all this time—against the mythril. The djinn was hushed as she cut the chain. It fell away as easily as a thread.

Freedom . . . the djinn said ponderously. **By a mortal's hand. Please, sorceress. I must reward you. You have given me my life. Let me give you yours.**

"My life?" Makiva laughed. "I still have it!"

Life unending. Eternal and ageless. I offer you time. Time to explore this world you love, and see what the future holds for it.

"You can do that?" Makiva couldn't keep the skepticism from her voice.

You need merely wish it.

Makiva contemplated the djinn's offer. She'd heard stories of the elves' supposed immortality, and of vampires and liches who were corrupted by Mort to live forever as undead monsters. There were any number of tales of adventurers and wizards who had earned the privilege of long life through their heroic deeds, blessed by rare and wonderful magic.

Was this such a tale?

Makiva smiled nervously at the djinn. "Very well, my friend," she said, her voice suddenly shy. "I accept your generous gift."

This is your wish?

"Yes."

The djinn killed Makiva quickly, in recognition of her kindness. With a breath she was gone, more dust for the ruins. The ancient dagger and chain she'd held both clattered noisily to the stone, still smoking from the heat.

Then, in a twisted fulfillment of its promise, the djinn took what was left of her.

Makiva opened her eyes again, green light flaring behind irises like clouded lanterns. She wondered at her new, mortal hands. Touched her fingers to her soft, fleshy face. She laughed at the strangeness of it all.

Then she scooped up the dagger and chain.

"Bother," she muttered, frowning down at the ancient tools of her imprisonment. Though she was no longer bound to this dead kingdom, she found that her *power* was still bound to the focuses. But even if all her magic *had* been at her disposal, it was a nearly impossible task to pass from Terryn back to Fie.

Nearly. She would need to figure out a plan.

But Makiva was patient. And now she was clever in the ways of this world. She would bide her time.

She took a step forward, her first in many, many years. And the first of many to come.

Zed watched as she left the pyramid, standing beside the eroded throne. He wiped a tear away, sniffing.

"It was never her," he ground out. "Never—never *you*." He glanced down at the fox at his side. Its black ears lay somberly against its head.

"You're just like the rest of us. It hid behind your face, like it's hid behind all of ours."

Slowly, the fox began to unravel and expand. Fur became a set of traveler's clothes, and the white paws transformed into smooth, dark skin.

Makiva stood before Zed, as young and bright as he'd ever seen her.

"You're the first to find me here," she said with a sad smile. "Some part of me lived on, just like the rest of you. But I think I took its place here when the djinn granted my wish. Just as it took mine."

Her eyes turned to the empty doorway. "I tried to call out to the others, but I was buried too deep to hear. The best I could do was change. I sent a small part of myself out. Sent it again and again."

"You were the foxes from the visions," Zed muttered in awe. "You were Reyna, Foster's familiar. You were all of them!"

Makiva nodded. "I watched out for the others as best I could. I delighted in their triumphs and mourned their defeats. If the djinn knew it was me, it didn't interfere. Not until Foster. That . . . took me longer to recover from. I didn't find you until it was almost too late. I'm sorry."

Zed shook his head, his chest tightening with emotion. "How did you go so long without losing hope?" he asked hoarsely.

The woman wiped a small tear of her own, laughing. "I *did* lose hope! Lost it so many times. Every defeat hurt, Zed, because every defeat was one of *you*. Hope isn't a sure thing. It's a candle that we must work to keep lit. *You* light the candle that lights your way."

Zed glanced to the dais that had once held the djinn. "How do we stop it?"

"The dagger," Makiva said, her eyes glittering with foxy mischief. "The djinn grants wishes, but turns them against the wishers. If you want to stop it, you'll need to do the sa—"

The world cracked. Dust and stone rained from the ceiling, the chamber crumbling all around them. Zed felt a tug in his abdomen, similar to the pull that had dragged him back here.

Except this was much stronger. He looked down at his hands, which were softening into smoke, the color draining away.

He cried out, "What's happening?!"

Makiva took his hazy hands in her own. "It's time," she said. "The djinn has everything it needs. Be strong, Zed. But better yet, be clever. Grant its wish!"

The chamber began to fall away. Collapsing rocks exploded into fog, the walls melting before Zed's eyes. The forgotten kingdom dissolved into a misty imitation, like the game Zed and Brock used to play, pointing to the sky beyond the walls and describing what they saw in the cloudplay above.

As the vision dissipated, Makiva's warm, hopeful expression split in two.

Zed stood face-to-face with her monstrous imposter.

✷

He was back in his body. His *real* body, which ached with the strains and injuries of the last several days. Zed lifted his hand in surprise, only to find his wrist was encircled by silvery links, leading up to the mythril chain around his neck. He'd been shackled.

Just like Foster, on the Day of Dangers . . .

"Welcome back, Zed," the creature before him crooned. It smiled Makiva's pleasant, companionable smile. "It must be nice to be back in your own body, after all this time."

The mages' storm had begun in earnest. Rain lashed his shoulders and face, falling from clouds so low they obscured the tops of the city walls. Zed had an errant worry for the adventurers still outside Freestone in this weather, searching in vain for a threat that was hiding within the city's heart.

They were in the empty market square. Zed had been positioned in the center of a dark smudge of a circle, at the crossing of a painted red X. This was where Makiva's tent had once stood, before it burned down during Zed's first days as an adventurer.

Zed glared at the imposter through the rain.

"I know the truth," he growled. "You're *not* Makiva. She was just another one of your victims. You used her like you used all of us—*Vetala*."

And with the name so uttered, the djinn was there.

It burned through the illusion in a moment, the false Makiva igniting and floating away on ribbons of ash. Here, flickering before Zed, was a being of metal and fire. It was beautiful, in a brutally elegant way. Its two feet hovered just above the ground, gliding upon but never quite touching the stones. Though rain pelted at them both, the fiend seemed unbothered by it. The furnace which stoked its flames was more than a match for the storm.

Well done. But it won't help you. All eyes are away from here.

The djinn's voice was a dreadful pressure. Zed glanced toward the curved dagger now clutched within its fiery claw and silently called upon his mana, clumsy from weeks of disuse. The world shivered with silver mist as he elf-stepped toward his captor, the metal links around his wrist and throat tightening and stretching.

Then it all snapped back with a force that knocked the wind from Zed's lungs.

The spell had failed.

The chain binds you, the fiend told him evenly. **Just as it once bound me. Your spells can't break it.**

"And you destroyed the one person who helped you!" Zed roared at the djinn. "You *stole* her life and her face. You turned her against the world she loved!"

The djinn rotated its head curiously. **Your world was already doomed, Zed. Your kind were too small to see it. Your lives are too brief.**

It floated closer, until its face was just inches from his. Zed could feel the blistering heat of the flames even through the rain. The scent of brimstone nearly choked him. **I've only ever given**

people what they ask for. Brenner wanted family, and Phylo a keen mind. Do you know what Lotte wished for? A better world. She'll have one. When the Veil is torn open this final time, I will cross back into Fie. Then, my power restored to me, I'll drag your wasted continent through behind me. Terryn will be welcomed as the newest layer of Fie.

Zed spat at the djinn's masked face. The spittle sizzled against the metallic frame, evaporating before he'd even taken a breath.

The creature floated slowly backward. **I appreciate your sacrifice, Zed. As I do your fellow students'.**

They appeared then, the others, as they had in Foster's ritual. At first they were just will-o-wisps, glimmering lights that floated in a gentle, twirling ring. Then languorous shapes enveloped the motes, smoky bodies that were stooped in quiet misery. Chained figures encircled Zed, the mythril links binding them all together. Zed recognized them as the figures who'd been watching him from the forest.

Last to appear was Foster. He billowed into being across from Zed, a gibbous shadow of smoke and embers. His burning green eyes stared emptily at the ground.

"Foster!" Zed screamed, struggling against his chains.

The warlock didn't respond. Like all the others, he'd been emptied out. A man-shaped imprint in the air.

It's time.

Suddenly, a bright light illuminated the circle. A core of brilliance ignited inside the first of the spirits like a flare, the floodlight beaming up into the clouds. Then a second spirit brightened, and a third. They moved in a line, each of the djinn's victims burning one after another.

With each explosion, Zed could feel his mana boiling inside him. He gasped, trying to clamp down on the magic, but the reservoir had become too deep. He couldn't control his own power. Green light began bleeding from his fingertips. The air around him rippled with heat.

Beyond the circle, the rainy market tensed peculiarly. Zed heard a loud, awful sound like ripping fabric. Then he watched as a tear opened in the very air, silvery threads of mist fraying and dissolving in the storm.

Within the tear was another world.

The landscape was more bizarre than any Danger Zed had ever seen. A city made of golden clockwork whirred and clicked with uncanny precision, the whole thing resting atop an enormous white cloud. Bright light poured from its blue sky, shining grandly. But no people walked the streets of this angelic metropolis. Instead, winged clockwork golems covered in glowing runes scurried and flew across the boulevards.

Lux, Zed realized with awe. He was actually peering into the plane of order firsthand.

As the djinn's victims ignited, more tears began to form, windows into worlds both wondrous and horrifying.

No, not windows. Doors.

He watched as a creature emerged from one of the tears—a

glittering, alien forest filled with enormous blue toadstools and flowering pink trees. *Fey.* The Danger was itself some kind of living tree. Its wooden face blinked slowly and curiously at the waterlogged world it had stumbled upon. Then it lurched into the city, its every step a quake across the cobbles.

Zed screamed, feeling his mana seethe with every new tear in the Veil, powering the ritual.

Then the line reached Foster. The shade's head ripped back and the core of green light within him flared, exploding so brightly it illuminated the whole square. A beam of radiance blasted into the air, completing a circle that stretched up into the clouds.

Only once he saw them all together, the lights shivering in the storm, did Zed realize what the djinn had made of its former students. He clenched his eyes shut, coughing out a ragged sob.

They were a ring of candles, with Zed at the center.

Just like the circle that had called it to this world.

Chapter Twenty-Two

Brock

The first Danger nearly took Brock's head off.

He was running blindly through the streets of Freestone, his vision all but useless in the vicious, pounding rain. The fires that had lit the night were mostly extinguished, reduced now to dark ashes and green embers, and the lanterns lit along Freestone's thoroughfares appeared dim and murky through the storm.

Zed's light had vanished, too, and he feared what that might mean. He refused to believe it was too late to save his friend, but he knew time was running out.

Against the darkness, a blacker shape swept toward him through the driving rain. He saw red eyes and outstretched wings, and that was all he needed to see for his training to kick in. Brock dropped to one knee, sliding across the cobbles as the creature soared just above his head. It shrieked in agitation as its claws raked empty air.

Then it wheeled around to come at him again.

This time he couldn't get out of the way, and the creature barreled right into him. It was half his size but built sturdy, and it knocked the breath out of his lungs as it slammed him to the ground. Now he got a good look at it—its marbled gray skin and savage red eyes and a hundred small pointed teeth aligned in eerily perfect rows. He got a good look at it all, and he wished he hadn't.

It snapped at his face, nearly taking his nose, but he shoved it back, and it took flight once more. Its bat-like wings, each as long as the creature was tall, lifted it effortlessly into the air. Brock had to squint into the rain to keep his eyes on it as it circled him, readying to strike again.

The wings gave it a huge advantage. But they were thin, with gray skin pulled taut as kites.

He timed his next move carefully, waiting until the last possible moment to pivot out of the way of its dive. But instead of ducking beyond its reach, he whirled right back around and slashed at the nearest wing with his unbroken dagger.

The creature shrieked again, slashing right back at him with its razor-sharp claws. It batted its wings to gain height, but one of them was soundly torn, and it pinwheeled out of control to slam and slide against the wet cobblestone streets.

Brock breathed heavily, wincing against the pain in his shoulder where the thing's claws had found purchase. He couldn't let the pain get to him, not yet; the monster was grounded now, but no less dangerous, and it watched him with murderous eyes from where it crouched, well out of reach of Brock's daggers.

It pounced, faster than Brock could blink. He stepped back, but too late. He wouldn't make it out of the way in time.

But the Danger flinched midleap. It pitched to the side, sailing harmlessly past Brock and screeching again as its body was suddenly riddled with a half-dozen gleaming throwing stars.

And Alabasel Frond stepped through the curtain of pouring rain.

"That thing doesn't belong here," she said, stalking toward the fallen form.

"N-no. No, it doesn't," he agreed. "It's a gargoyle—a type of imp from Fie." He fumbled with the pouches of his belt. "They're vulnerable to certain powdered poisons. If you can get them to breathe them in, they get vertigo and—"

Frond swung her sword in a single powerful arc, cleaving the Danger in two.

"Or that works," Brock said. "That works, too."

Frond turned on him. Her sword dripped with black ichor. "Where did that thing come from?"

Brock pushed his wet hair off his face. "I don't know."

"Where is Zed?"

"I don't know that, either."

"Brock." Frond bared her teeth. "I've just spent the last hour trying to explain a *raging green fire* to the king and his insufferable pet mage. The hour before that, I was promising answers to Micah's parents, who don't understand how he came to harm in *my* guildhall. Now isn't the time to defy me."

"Ha!" Brock barked. "That's rich. But I don't answer to you anymore, Frond. Remember? You kicked me out!"

Frond grinned humorlessly. "You didn't fall for that. Brock, that was just for show. So the guild couldn't be punished for Hexam's escape."

"Wait," Brock said. "That was *your* idea all along?"

"Don't be so surprised. Even I know when to use a sword and when to employ . . . finer instruments. Fel was under my orders the whole time, although I swore her to secrecy."

"So I'm . . . *not* guildless?"

She shook her head. "You're too valuable an asset to simply cut loose."

Brock scoffed. "I think that might be the nicest thing you've ever said to me. But I still don't know where Zed is. I'm looking for him, too."

"You. Me," Frond said. "And every Stone Son in the city."

Brock shuddered in the rain. "We have to find him before *they* do. Zed isn't responsible for any of this! He's been possessed by Makiva."

"Possessed?" Frond stared at him with undisguised alarm.

"There's no time to explain! We have to find him—her—before she does any more damage. Fie knows what she's up to."

"*Fie* is right," Frond said, and she took a shuffling step backward, her gaze scanning the sky.

Brock followed her gaze, looking up at the rooftops and chimneys of Freestone.

Dozens of red eyes glared back.

"They—they're *everywhere*," he said.

"Fall back," she said. "We need to get to the temple. Go!"

Frond shoved Brock to get him moving. The last thing he saw before turning toward the temple was the bobbing and weaving of red lights in the distance, gargoyles spreading their wings and taking flight.

Brock didn't look back. He ran as fast as he'd ever run before, heedless of the rain-slick ground. Frond stayed one pace behind him, slashing her sword overhead to keep the creatures at bay. Brock's blood ran cold at the noises they made, but they stayed clear of the sword, and soon he was back in the temple's receiving hall, Frond slamming the door behind them.

King Freestone himself startled at the noise.

The king was there with his council, taking refuge from the storm they'd called down a short time before. They stood amid a crowd of mages, knights, healers, and smoke-stained outtowners. All in all, the space was even more crowded than it had been when packed with elven refugees.

Brock realized with a pang that hundreds of Freestone's poorest citizens had lost their homes tonight.

"Frond?" said the king. "What's going on?"

"There are Dangers within the city," she answered.

A thread of anxiety and confusion spread through the room, starting with those in earshot and rippling outward.

"Keep your voice down!" the king hissed. "Would you start a panic?"

Frond stood her ground. "The best way to avoid a panic is to arm these people. Right now. They need to be prepared."

Outtowners were creeping forward to listen in on the conversation.

"Brent," said the king. "Get us some space."

At a gesture from Ser Brent, the knights put themselves between the council and the citizens, forming an unbroken ring of flesh and steel.

"A Danger did this?" Pollux asked as he tended to Brock's wounds. The pain was instantly replaced with a warm, pleasant prickling.

"Most of it," Brock said. Now wasn't the time to mention Lotte; they needed to focus. "There are at least a half-dozen gargoyles right outside. Flying creatures. They could fly over the city's wall, but . . ."

"The wards," Quilby said. He licked his lips nervously. "Grima, have the wards been compromised?"

The archmagus was already pulling a necklace out from beneath her robes. The gemstone upon it glowed faintly blue. "The wards are undisturbed." At Frond's questioning look, Grima explained, "We took certain precautions after Brenner's sabotage. If anything were wrong with the wards, I would know."

"Makiva did this," Brock said. "She's a witch, and she's been plotting something for months. Maybe much longer. What if she's opened a door between the planes?"

"Is that possible?" Pollux said.

Grima tapped her necklace. "Even if it is, the wards would still keep the Dangers at bay."

"You don't understand." Brock shook his head. "Makiva is *here*. She's inside Freestone. If she's opened a door . . . it's on *this side* of the wards."

The king paled. He took a long, shuddering breath. "That's it, then. The doomsday scenario." He turned to Brent. "Call your men in. Give the order," he said.

Brent nodded. "There's an entrance in Pollux's office, if I'm not mistaken."

"A what?" said Pollux. Brent ignored him and began whispering to his knights.

"What order?" Brock asked. "What's going on?"

"I have to get back out there," Frond said. She stepped to the ring of knights. "Let me pass."

"No," said the king.

Frond turned slowly to face him. "No?"

"Frond, if what this boy said is true . . . then we have already lost. But we don't have to lose everything."

"We've planned for this," said Quilby. "There is room for us in the warrens beneath Freestone. It's a defensible position with a dozen hidden exits and enough food and water stored away to keep us alive, if not entirely comfortable. For years, if it comes to it. Until such a time as we are able to retake the city."

"There's a place for *you*, Frond," said the king. "You've proven your worth ten times over these past months. Your resourcefulness, your grit . . . We will need those qualities, when the time comes to rebuild."

"How many?" Frond asked. "How many can we save?"

The king cut his eyes over to Quilby.

"Ah," the merchant said. "We have the resources for one hundred and twenty. Perhaps another ten, if we're cautious."

Frond showed no emotion. "One hundred and thirty," she said placidly. "There are *thousands* of people in Freestone."

"I know what you're thinking, Frond," said the king. "And this is not a decision I make lightly. Nor is it a decision without precedent. You don't know the *true* story of the Day of Dangers—the bloody version, passed down in whispers from royal to royal."

"Your Majesty," said Ser Brent, "we're ready to move when you are."

The king held up a hand for silence. "We celebrate and honor the Day of Dangers as the moment our heroes and our city came together to save humanity. But they couldn't save everyone. My own great-great-grandfather gave the order: All those left outside the walls once the wards were activated? Any man, woman, or child who fought their way to our gates in search of sanctuary? We turned them away, Frond. We told them *no*."

Brock's head felt light. "But that's horrible," he said.

"It's pragmatic," the king said. "It was the hard, right choice. Who knew what might follow them inside? Who knew how many we could feed or clothe? No. Though they clawed at our great and storied wall until their fingers bled; though they climbed atop one another, crushing one another in their desperate attempt for safety—the answer was no. And because of it, Freestone survived."

Silence descended on the group. Judging by their faces, even the king's inner circle had been unaware of this.

"People will forget the ugly choices we make tonight," the king said. "Those who survive."

"And if only cowards survive?" Frond asked sharply. "Cowards and murderers. What is Freestone worth if it's rebuilt by the very worst of us?"

"Alabasel," the king said darkly, and a shadow fell over the group.

Brock was slow to realize it was an actual shadow. Dark shapes moved just beyond the stained glass windows overhead.

"Look out!" he cried, a moment before one of those windows

shattered into a hundred glittering pieces. The glass rained down upon the crowd—and following it was a Danger.

At first, it appeared a featureless mass of tentacles. Brock could see no face or body, only the sinuous, writhing limbs. But as it scurried along the wall with alarming speed, using the puckers running along its limbs for purchase, Brock caught glimpses of the hideous maw at its center—a hooked beak already dripping blood—and a singular malevolent eye.

The room erupted into chaos. The townsfolk scattered, desperate for distance from the creature, but its haphazard movements made it impossible to know which direction was best. People slammed into one another; several pressed against the line of Stone Sons, making for the door, but the knights pushed back lest their king and commander be trampled.

"What do we do?" Brock asked, but Frond was already on the move. She pushed past the knights and hoisted herself onto an altar, scattering its candles as she took one running step and leaped onto a hanging curtain. Gripping it one-handed, she soared over the heads of the panicking crowd, and at the pinnacle of her arc, she let loose three bladed stars in a single overhead throw.

Each found its mark, and the Danger recoiled, lashing out blindly with its tentacles and losing its grip upon the wall. It crashed onto the ground, where it flailed violently. The crowd, screaming and pushing, managing to stay just out of its reach as it rolled.

Frond let go of the curtain and landed on her feet, but the

crowd was thick between her and her target. Even at a distance, Brock saw the worry on her face. In the long moments it would take her to reach the beast, any number of people could fall to it.

But a figure stepped from the crowd and slashed at the Danger, cleanly removing one tentacle, and then another, until he was close enough to put a Stone Son's sword through the monster's center.

Brock goggled at the sight of Father Pollux huffing triumphantly over his kill. He wasn't alone in his surprise; aside from a few crying children, the crowd had gone utterly silent and still.

Brock pressed through it, closing in on the Luminous Father just as Frond did. "Nicely done," she said. "I didn't realize you knew your way around a sword."

Pollux grinned bashfully. "I suppose anyone can handle a sword if the need is dire enough."

Frond blinked at him. "I suppose you're right," she said. And then she swept her arm out, gracelessly knocking the candles from a second altar and clambering on top of it, sodden muddy boots on clean white marble.

"Sorry," Brock told Pollux. "She's like this sometimes."

"Listen up, people!" she cried. She needn't have bothered; all eyes in the hall were already upon her. But now that she realized it, she hesitated. She tapped nervously at the remaining throwing stars upon her belt.

Brock had rarely seen his guildmistress pause to choose her words. But she considered them carefully now.

"That was a Danger," she said at last. "As you've probably guessed. And where there's one Danger, there's . . . more."

Murmurs rippled through the crowd; Frond silenced them with a look, like a stern schoolteacher.

"You're scared. I get it," she said. "Fie knows, the things are fearsome. We've all lost something to them. . . ." She shook her head. "But I love this city. It's a tragic mess and it infuriates me regularly, but I love it. And if you love it . . . well, it needs you now. And you can't let the fear stop you from acting."

"But what can *we* do?" cried a woman, her brow bloody from fallen glass.

"Help us, Frond!" yelled a man who clutched a crying child to his side.

"Save us!" cried another.

Frond appeared momentarily stricken. The naked desperation in those voices—the anguished appeal for her help. It was written all over her face: She felt the weight of every one of those lives, and the gravity of her responsibility to these people.

Brock wondered if perhaps she felt it every day, and had simply excelled at hiding it.

Frond's brow furrowed, and her eyes sharpened. "I can't save you all," she said. "But I can save some of you. And they can save others. And so that's what we're going to do. One life at a time, curse it. We're all going to save *each other*." She drew her sword, and began pointing at people in the crowd as she spoke.

"You," she said fiercely. "And you. You in the back with the stupid hat! I want every single one of you to find someone who is weaker than you. Someone who is more vulnerable, more afraid—and I want you to stand between that person and a Danger and then swear to *die* before you will see any harm come to them."

Some people nodded. Brock saw several in the crowd reach out to link hands. Knowing looks passed between parents: They would fight any odds, face any Danger, for the safety of their children.

"Protect your neighbor!" Frond commanded, spittle flying as she spoke. "Protect whoever needs protecting! Do that, every one of you, and you all might live to see tomorrow. Do that, and you prove that you are *worthy* of tomorrow. That *Freestone* is worthy. Freestone will endure!"

"Freestone endures!" echoed Pollux, and when he said it a second time, and a third, the crowd joined in.

Frond smiled—the fiercest, most fearsome smile Brock had ever seen on a human being. She let them chant for a moment, and then she shouted: "Hear me, Freestone! I am invoking the draft. As of this moment, you are *all* members of the Adventurers Guild!"

Cheers went up all around them. Men and women and children, the tears still wet on their cheeks from the terror of a moment before, now pumped their fists and roared their approval.

The king watched it all in stony silence. But in the end, when Brent tried to usher him toward Pollux's office and its secret door to the underground, the king shook his head and stood firm.

Whether because she had shamed him or inspired him, Frond had convinced the king to stand his ground. And that meant they could count on the knights, the mages . . .

Even Brock felt a little flare of hope. Maybe Freestone *would* endure this.

But would Zed?

He slipped away, weaving through the buzzing crowd. But just before he made it to the door, Quilby stood before him.

"A rousing speech," the merchant said. "But I, for one, remain content to wait this out underground." His shrewd eyes softened. "You could come, too, Brock. You don't owe her anything. And you've done enough for this town."

Brock was more tempted than he'd ever admit. "Zed is out there," he said. "I can't just hide away and hope for the best. But, Quilby . . . my parents. Can you get to them?"

Quilby nodded without hesitating. "Of course. Your father has been a friend to me. I will do everything I can to ensure their safety."

Brock exhaled in relief. "Thanks, Quilby."

"A merchant always pays his debts," Quilby said. "But tell me—the Lady Gray . . ."

"She's dead. Makiva killed her."

"Yes, her right-hand man, Gramit, told the king as much. But he also mentioned the loss of a cherrywood box. A trinket that held some meaning to her. . . ."

"I know it," Brock said, and he pivoted into a lie as smoothly as he'd dodged the gargoyle. "It must have gone up in the fire. Everything was burning—I barely got out of there."

Quilby considered him suspiciously, and Brock cast a suspicious glare right back at him. "What's it matter?" he asked. "It only ever played music."

"It bore a mimicry enchantment, which you might imagine would be of some use to a spymaster," Quilby answered. "It might have held any number of secrets. But there was one in particular that the king seemed to think her successor would need, in order to . . . inherit her gifts. A spell of some kind, a sort of otherworldly song that Dox Eural called the Thieves' Carol."

"Well, too bad for her successor, I guess."

"Perhaps." Quilby continued to watch him closely. "Or perhaps they're better off. From what I gathered, using the Thieves' Carol was costly indeed."

"Costly how?"

Quilby shrugged. "What's it matter? It's gone now, after all. Right?"

"Right," Brock echoed, and Quilby inclined his head in farewell as he stepped out of Brock's path. No one else seemed to notice when Brock slipped out the door.

✸

There were screams in the night—human screams and other, stranger noises. Brock kept to the shadows, hoping the rain would mask his scent as well as it hid his movements. He kept his daggers drawn, one whole and one broken, but both deadly sharp.

A hulking figure lumbered into view, and Brock pressed himself against the nearest wall. He held his breath, scarcely daring to look at the huge form as it crossed the road scant paces ahead of him. He caught a glimpse of branches and bark, and the sound of wind in leaves. The creature moved slowly but surely, and it showed no sign of seeing him as it continued on its way.

He pulled the cherrywood box from his pocket. There was a small button, and when he pressed it, a soft series of chimes emanated from within. He slid a toggle, and it played bagpipes. He winced at the sound, sliding the toggle again. This time, he heard a bard's voice singing a familiar, and very bawdy, song about an elf cursed with a luminous rear end. "Lovers in the Moon's Light" was a tavern favorite.

The next setting was strange. The Lady Gray's voice spoke through the device—it was unmistakably her—but she spoke words Brock didn't recognize, words whose consonants crashed together. It wasn't elvish, or dwarven, or any other language he'd heard before.

"Nezputh. Uth'rga. Mni fth'rai."

Something in her tone of voice or the words themselves chilled him. He listened to it a few more times, committing it to memory. But something kept him from repeating it. He couldn't shake the chill in his bones—or the memory of Quilby's voice, warning him of some hidden cost.

He wasn't desperate enough to toy with forces he didn't understand. Not yet.

He heard a great ruckus at his back as the Golden Way Temple emptied, its throngs spilling out into the streets. The clanging of armor told him that the Stone Sons were among them, likely leading the way to one of the knights' many armories. Frond would want her conscripts armed as well as possible.

So mighty was the noise at his back that Brock didn't hear his guildmates until he'd rounded a corner and walked right into a battle.

They'd been overrun by hobgoblins—tiny, vicious fey beings with barbed tails and sad little vestigial wings. They weren't deadly on their own, but they hunted in packs, and enough stings from their poisonous tails could send a full-grown adventurer into toxic shock.

There were at least ten of the things swarming Liza, Jayna, and Jett.

Brock rushed to his friends' aid. He crossed the space in a matter of seconds—and got there just as the last of the hobgoblins fell beneath Jett's hammer.

"Brock!" the dwarf said. "There are Dangers everywhere!"

"We're headed to the tower," Jayna said. "To the focus. The wards—"

"It's not the wards," Brock said. "Makiva's doing it. She's possessed Zed—forced him out of his own body."

Jayna gasped. Jett's jaw hung open. And Liza . . .

Liza glared at him.

Brock tried to ignore her. "He came to me in a dream and explained it," he said. "I've been trying to track him down and—okay, *why are you looking at me like that?*"

He turned to face Liza's glare. "So I was right," she said.

"No," Brock said. "*I* was right. I knew Zed wasn't responsible."

"And *I* said we should take him into custody anyway. Which would have avoided all of this."

"Or gotten a lot of people incinerated!" Brock cleared his throat. "My way, only one person got incinerated . . ."

They all gave him a horrified look.

"It's been a long night." He rubbed his face. "But there's good news, too. Micah woke up, Liza. He healed himself, somehow."

Liza brightened. "He's okay?"

"Yeah." Brock paused. "Well, I mean he's in a town that's overrun with monsters at the moment, so not really."

A great roar shook the night, and the rain stopped momentarily as a massive shape flew overhead.

"What in Fie was that?" Jett asked.

"Dire roc," Jayna said.

They all stared at her.

"Big . . . *big* bird," she clarified.

"Do you suppose the wards prevent it from leaving?" Jett asked.

"We need to find Zed *now*," Brock said.

"How do we do that?" Liza asked.

"Simple," Brock said. "Wherever the Dangers are coming from? Wherever they're thickest? We go there."

Jett chortled. "Simple, he says!"

*

They cut a path through streets that had erupted in chaos.

Everywhere they turned, there were monsters. In the alleyway where Brock and Zed had played jacks as children, Jett smashed a huge millipede with unnervingly human eyes and teeth. On the bench where Brock had pickpocketed his very first mark, Liza ran her sword through a huge jet-black cat with flailing tentacles growing from its back.

They encountered people, too. As Frond's militia spread throughout the town, more and more citizens rose to the challenge of fighting for their neighbors. They were armed with everything from morning stars and lances to pitchforks, kitchen knives, and old shoes. People were getting hurt—in particular the knights, who were learning how little protection their armor afforded them against caustic spit and serrated tails. But healers moved among them, some of whom were armed themselves, and they were pulling the most grievously injured out of harm's way.

They had moved past the fire-damaged area, and now the buildings of outtown were pressing in on them. Brock knew his way through the alleys well enough, but there was less room to maneuver, and that made him nervous. As he slashed a floating, twinkling gelatinous globe out of the air, Jayna blasted a rat off a pile of trash. "Oops," she said. "I think that was just a normal rat."

"They're on our side!" Brock quipped. "I'll bet Frond gave them a big motivational speech and everything."

"Get back," warned Jett, and the fear in his voice brought Brock up short. The way forward was blocked by a naga, larger even than the one that had nearly killed Jett months before. Its eerie masklike face watched them coldly, while its snakelike trunk coiled slowly around itself.

"We'll have to go another way," Liza said.

"There's no *time* for that," Brock argued.

The naga moved slowly forward—and an arrow sprouted from its side, then another, and three more. Its eyes went wide with surprise, and it listed to one side.

As the naga wavered and then collapsed, Fel let out a cry of triumph from a nearby roof.

"Nice one, Fel!" Jett called.

"Thank you," she said demurely. "But the lurker venom on my arrows did most of the work."

Brock grinned. "You can take some credit for it, Fel."

"*You* sure did, Naga Slayer," Liza said to him. "Fel, what are you doing here?"

Fel clambered down the side of the outtown tenement with

the surefootedness of a lifelong climber, using the irregular bricks and recessed windows for footholds. "We were halfway to the wayshelter when we saw the green glow of the fire. We decided you probably needed our help."

"'We'?" echoed Liza.

Hexam and Nirav rounded the corner. The wizard was out of breath, his eye still swollen, and he leaned on Nirav for support. "Sorry," said Hexam. "We had to take the long way."

"*Around* the building," Nirav added. "Not that I'm complaining. These two emerged from the guildhall just in time to save me from a *very* irate fire-breathing pig."

"Master Hexam!" Jayna cried. "You look terrible."

Hexam grumbled darkly, and Mousebane plopped half a rat at Brock's feet.

"The rats are having a bad night," Jett said.

"Let's keep moving," said Brock.

With Hexam and the others joining them, the group picked up speed. Fel's arrows took down Dangers before they could get anywhere close to the group, faster even than Jayna's eldritch darts. Those the girls missed fell readily to the long reach of Nirav's quarterstaff. Hexam called forth fire, frost, and lightning; he took out an entire swarm of vampire beetles with a simple flick of his wrist.

They made it to the edge of outtown, the maze of alleyways exiting out onto a broad, open space that led directly to the public square and the marketplace. Winged creatures took flight from the market's heart, and when Brock squinted, he could just make out–

"Green light," he said. "Something's happening in the market. I think that's where we need to be."

But there were monsters pouring from the edge of the market, crossing the open space in droves. Some of them clawed at one another, natural enemies; he saw a wolf made of pure shadow tearing apart a doe made of golden pistons and gears, chewing on the metal as if it were flesh. Most shuffled ever forward, seeking human prey.

"It's impossible," Jayna said. "There's no way we can get through all that."

"I can clear the way," Hexam said. "But it will take every bit of mana I have. You'll be on your own from there."

Liza nodded. "Do it, Hexam."

Hexam grinned. "Lisbeth's Infernal Regret. I've been saving this one for a special occasion."

The magus stepped from the alleyway, reciting a long string of elvish words. He gestured not just with his fingers but with his arms, moving them about him like an elaborate dance. The air around him grew hot.

Dangers began to take notice. A jackal standing on two legs turned his way and drooled, yipping for its brethren. A quivering ooze with a huge skull at its center began moving, slowly, in his direction.

Hexam shouted the final words of the incantation, and he lifted his hands to the sky.

Freestone shook. It shook, and then it splintered, the ground at Hexam's feet cracking apart like eggshell. The cracks traveled outward in a cone, away from Brock and toward the Dangers; and wherever Dangers stood, great gouts of lava spewed forth, or explosions of jagged rock and noxious gases. By the time the ground had stopped shaking, three dozen monsters had fallen.

And then Hexam fell, too.

"Master Hexam!" Jayna cried, and they all left their hiding place to run to him.

"Call me—call me *Magus*, Jayna," Hexam said as she and Fel helped him to his feet. "I've decided I quite like the title after all."

"Can you get to shelter?" Liza asked.

Hexam frowned. "I'm not done yet. That was only half of what I have planned."

"I thought you were out of mana," Jett said.

"Out of mana, yes," Hexam said. "But I never claimed to be powerless. Step back."

They did, and Hexam began another incantation. This one was low and rasping, and Brock felt the temperature plummet. Mist swirled upon the ground at Hexam's feet, and his eyes—

His eyes glowed purple.

"Hexam!" Brock cried. "Tell me that's not necromancy!"

Hexam ignored him. He continued his low chant, and the dead Dangers nearby . . . stirred.

Liza turned to Jayna. "Should we . . . Should we stop him?"

Jayna's eyes were glassy with tears, and she brought her hands up to her mouth. Brock knew the girl was unrelentingly suspicious and judgmental of dark magic. And necromancy was something altogether different—darker than dark, pulling its power from a plane of pure death.

"We . . . We have to trust him," she said.

Hexam's incantation ended, and he spoke without looking at them. "Necromancy is just another tool in our arsenal—rediscovered by an evil man, but not evil in itself."

"With respect," said Jett, "that's debatable."

"So we'll debate it," Hexam said. "In times of peace. Tonight, we can't afford to ignore any advantage."

"But there's a cost," Brock said. He saw the fingernails of Hexam's right hand had blackened and peeled away; his arm was puffy and lined with dark veins.

Hexam smiled sadly. "There is always a cost. I'll gladly pay it, if it means you don't have to." He winced, clutching his arm to his chest. "Go. I'll use my puppets to clear the way as much as I can, for as long as I dare."

Jayna's eyes lingered on Hexam's blighted hand. "We can't just leave you here," she insisted. "You can barely stand!"

"I'll stay," said Nirav. When Jayna seemed ready to argue, he added, "You know it has to be me, Jayna. I'm a good fighter, but you five are a team. You can handle whatever you find in there, if you stick together. Hexam can buy you time, and I can keep him safe."

Liza considered Nirav in silence for a moment, then nodded. "You're a part of the team, too, Nirav. You just proved that beyond any doubt."

Nirav twirled his staff with a flourish. "I'll see you at drills in the morning, then."

Jayna touched his arm, and Brock nodded solemnly at Hexam. Then Liza led them onward. Brock held his breath as he stepped past the undead Dangers with gleaming purple eyes who stood waiting for Hexam's instruction.

They stopped at the statues of the Champions of Freestone, right at the edge of the market.

"We need to decide what to do," Liza said. "When we find him."

"We all know the story," Brock said. "The Day of Dangers. How they stopped Foster."

Liza shook her head sternly. "This isn't the same thing."

"What if it is?" Brock asked. He looked up at the statue of Dox. "What if it's exactly the same?"

Jett put a hand on Brock's shoulder. "It's Zed in there, Brock. And he needs us to *save* him."

But saving him wasn't what Zed had asked Brock to do.

Stop me. Whatever it takes.

Brock frowned into the night. He looked back at his city,

where hundreds were homeless and dozens were dying. He knew more monsters would appear with every moment they hesitated—with every moment Zed's magic held open the door.

I think I'm already dead.

"I'll go alone from here," Brock said. "That way, whatever happens . . . it's on my conscience."

"Absolutely not," Liza said. "Brock, didn't you hear Nirav? We're a team."

He shook his head. "I can do this, Liza. But it has to be me. I have a . . . spell. I think it's the same one Dox used two hundred years ago. It'll let me get close to her. To him. They won't even see me coming."

"A spell?" Jayna said. "What kind of spell?"

"I don't like this, Brock," Jett said.

Fel narrowed her eyes. "What does it cost?"

Brock faltered. "I—I don't . . ."

"Hexam said it," Fel continued. "'There is always a cost.' So what would this magic cost you?"

Brock sighed. "I don't know," he admitted. "But I think . . . I think maybe it would be something precious to me." He snuck a furtive glance at Liza, who watched him carefully.

There was a moment of silence in which Brock nearly spoke the Lady's strange words. Because what price wouldn't he pay to stop this nightmare? All the same, he hesitated, staring hard into the ground.

"You have a choice to make, Brock," Liza said at last. "You

can take this all on yourself. You can wrap yourself in secrets, strike out on your own, fix everything with your own two hands." She stepped forward and brushed her fingers on his arm. He lifted his gaze and met her eyes. "Or you can trust us. Work with us. Openly, honestly. As a team."

"As friends," added Jett.

Brock held Liza's gaze for a long moment. Finally, he nodded. "All right," he said. "We're in this together. But if things go badly in there—"

"Then we pay the cost," Liza said. "Together."

Chapter Twenty-Three

In the faraway city of Llethanyl, Callum studied the horizon.

A great green light clawed at the sky, with beams like burning fingers that reached into dark, swirling clouds.

The light was coming from Freestone.

Alarm bells rang across the city, echoing from the great tree. Callum had been off duty, but with the appearance of this spectacle, he would be needed at Me'Shala's side. The rangers must have their orders.

"Zed . . ." he whispered. He hoped his nephew was safe. Despite the painful terms of their parting—or maybe because of them—Callum found the boy was in his thoughts almost daily. The suddenness with which Zed closed himself off had taken him by surprise, but it shouldn't have. The High Ranger had failed his nephew too many times. Perhaps he'd failed him again, not staying behind in Freestone as Fel had.

He hoped this unsettling view had nothing to do with Zed. He hoped Zed was surrounded by adventurers, safely nestled with Fel and his other friends in the guildhall.

But something like cold dread touched the back of Callum's neck, an icy finger that traced up his spine.

The light . . . the eerie emerald color of it.

It looked just like Zed's fire.

✷

Zed's eyes reflected the flames. He'd sunk to his knees, his chained wrists hanging at his sides.

All around him were gates that opened into other worlds.

The tears were spreading throughout the city, releasing monsters right onto the streets. Those that Zed couldn't see he could *feel*, his mana cresting painfully with each new crack in the air.

Yards away, the djinn floated before a tear no larger or more spectacular than any of the others, and yet its attention was completely focused on it. *This* had been the opening it was waiting for.

A gate into Fie.

Within it, an emerald star hung suspended in a bloodred sky. Blue mountains veined with molten streams loomed in the distance, cradling a black tower. The ground in this place was a charred wasteland, pocked by red pustules of flame. Winged fiends flitted through the air, only to be swallowed by larger, more monstrous shadows moments later.

The djinn watched it all covetously, reaching toward the view with its burning hand. But the portals only worked one way. Due to Terryn's strange place in the cosmos, the creatures which crossed through couldn't pass back home—including the djinn.

It raked its curved dagger against the tear, and silver fog billowed up to catch the blade. The Veil held it out, even as another Danger—its fleshy body screaming with no fewer than six enormous mouths—slithered from a nearby breach to starry Astra. Zed lost sight of the monstrosity as it fled into the city, but its wails lasted longer.

We're close now, Zed. The djinn spoke without turning to face him. **Fear not for your people. Once in Fie, I'll help them to change. To survive. After they've shed their mortal meat, the creatures wandering your city will be little more than prey to them. Brenner was just a taste of what you could become.**

"As I recall, that particular appetizer ended up a little burned."

Zed's eyes goggled as a familiar voice whispered in his ear. Brock—Brock!—BROCK!—was standing beside him, a finger already pressed to his lips. Zed hadn't heard his friend approaching. He looked to the djinn, but the fiend was still gazing through its private window into the infernal plane.

Brock looked over Zed's predicament, his eyes following the mythril restraints.

"Quietly," he warned. "In as few words as possible: How do I free you?"

Zed nodded toward his captor. "The dagger it's holding is the only thing that can cut the chain. Brock, that thing is a djinn. This whole time, it *wasn't* Makiva. She was a victim, just li—"

Brock put his hand over Zed's mouth. "And Liza says *I* can't help myself."

Then he pulled his hand away, frowning at it. Zed could see sweat beading across the boy's forehead. "You're burning up," Brock whispered.

Zed nodded, tears welling in his eyes. The air around him still rippled with heat. His fingertips were red and blistered. "It's using *my* magic to do this. I'm fighting it as hard as I can, but . . . Brock, you'll never get close enough to steal the dagger. If you . . . if you kill me, though . . ."

"Then the ritual ends," Brock muttered. "Like Dox." He looked briefly down at his own blade, then back up at Zed.

Zed nodded once, holding his gaze. "Like Dox."

A moment of silent understanding passed between them. They'd been friends for long enough that they didn't have to say it. In Brock's eyes, Zed saw acknowledgment for what he must do. Freeing Zed would be too risky. If the djinn caught them, it would destroy Brock, along with any hope they had of saving Terryn. But right now, with the fiend's attention turned elsewhere, there was still an opportunity to end this. They could stop this catastrophe before it became another Day of Dangers. Before it became something even worse.

It was the best way—the only way—and they both knew it.

"Brock, tell my mom . . . Tell her I love—"

"Jayna!" Brock turned before Zed could finish, his eyes landing on the djinn.

"What?" Zed cried. "No, I love my *mom*!"

"Jayna, aim for the green thing *now*!"

The djinn turned just as the orb appeared—a spectral circle of shimmering magic. It enveloped the fiend in a magical encasement, just like the one that had trapped Zed's body in the guildhall.

Jayna emerged from the market, her hands held in front of her. She pressed her palms together as if trapping a bug inside. Jett stood at her side with his hammer ready, glowing sigils sliding across the metal.

"Oh!" Jayna said, looking down at her hands with alarm. "Oh, wow! It's hot. Liza, hurry!"

"Already on it!"

Zed turned to find Liza racing toward him, a look of fury in her eyes. Liza raised her sword and let out a murderous bellow, bringing the blade down two-handed.

Zed flinched from the strike, until he heard the sound of grinding metal. He peeked his eyes open to find the Solution's blade pressed against his mythril bindings. Zed had seen Liza's sword cut through magic itself, but though she pressed with all her might, even the legendary sword was no match for the focus.

"Liza!" Zed cried, gratitude ballooning in his chest. "Jett! Jayna!"

"The dagger!" Brock said, pointing to the imprisoned fiend. "We need the dagger!"

"Why didn't you say that *before* you had Jayna cast her spell!" Liza hissed.

"I was trying to buy us time to think!"

"Umm, everyone?" Jayna called. "We have a big problem!"

Jayna's magical prison was filled with a torrent of green. Flames swirled inside in a miniature cyclone, pressing against the glowing walls. Small cracks began spidering along the orb, splintering it apart.

"Hot!" Jayna cried. "It's too hot! I can't hold it!"

"Scatter!" Liza shouted.

Liza and Brock broke away from Zed just as the barrier exploded, the spectral walls burning like kindling. The djinn emerged from the conflagration, visible at first only by its twisted metal frame.

Children . . . The djinn's voice raked against the cobbles like a crackling fire. **Grasping, greedy children. You came to "Old Makiva" with your wishes, begging for magic tokens.**

It turned its gaze toward Jayna, who was cradling her scalded hands against her chest.

The djinn raised its arm and the flames moved with it, flooding toward the girl in an emerald wave.

"Not today!" Jett stepped in front of her, stamping his mythril prosthetic. Sigils flared across the metal, and a semitransparent barrier erupted in front of him in a glittering arc. As the djinn's flames struck the barrier, they spilled harmlessly over it.

But the two weren't done. Jett nodded to Jayna, who raised her fingers, contorting them expertly even through the burns. "The sacred hollow," she muttered. "The impenetrable wheel." As she spoke, her voice began to echo strangely, the words crackling with accumulated power. "Two sentries in a vigilant parallax."

Jayna's irises brightened with blue light. She twisted her hands, and the barrier ripped, the softly gleaming material splitting into ribbons of magical matter. The strips reconfigured into a sphere of concentric rings, entrapping the green flames within.

"Jayna and Jett's Centrifugal Sphere!" Jett bellowed. The dwarf lifted his hammer, still shimmering with magic of its own, and struck the outermost ring of the sphere, thrusting the whole arrangement into motion.

The sound of the rings moving was ear-poppingly strange. They picked up speed as they went, faster and faster, warping the air around them.

The djinn's flames roiled within, compressing into a blindingly bright orb. Then Jayna closed her hands and the wheel abruptly stopped, blasting a wave of concentrated fire back at the fiend.

But the djinn just drank the flames into its body, absorbing them as easily as a rag wiping up a spill.

I remember you, dwarfson. Your mother came to my tent many times, once with a wish just for you. She wanted you to know the world beyond this humble human city. Did you enjoy your first trip beyond the wall?

Jett's face paled, and the djinn let out a laugh like water striking molten metal. A wall of green fire erupted from the ground, cutting Jett and Jayna off from the fight.

Liza screamed, sprinting toward the Danger with her sword raised. It dodged her blow with a dancer's grace, then parried the second with a lash of flame.

The Solution cut through the fire as if it were flimsy cloth.

Liza lunged again, the sword piercing the djinn's twisted carapace.

AhhhhhhhhHHHH! The Danger's cry was head-splitting. Zed grabbed his ears against the noise, but Liza simply smiled, raising her blade again. In that grin, Zed caught more than a passing resemblance to Alabasel Frond.

Enough!

A gout of fire slammed forward just as Liza raised her shield, knocking the buffer away. With the girl momentarily stunned, another fiery lash whipped out, snatching the Solution from her grasp.

The djinn raised a second wall of flame, and this time Liza disappeared behind the curtain.

You're too late! The doors are already opening. The djinn's voice echoed triumphantly, now alone with Zed in a tunnel of green. The others were all separated by the flames.

They'd lost. Their one chance, and they'd hesitated, just to save him. Zed had always thought of despair as a cold thing, a wintry chill that slowed his steps and stooped his back. But Zed's anguish was hot. It was a ravenous, blistering flame.

"Not . . . too . . . late."

A new voice echoed through the market.

Zed restrained a gasp as Lotte entered the square, hefting a maul that was dripping with monstrous ichor. She looked badly injured. Blood ran down her face from the wallop Micah had given her, and her left leg dragged in a limp. Her lips were pulled into a snarl. "You lied to me. *This* was never what I wanted. I wished to *save* Terryn!"

The djinn regarded her impassively. **I *am* saving your pitiful world.**

Lotte shook her head, her blue eyes shining with frantic energy. "All this time, and you were a *fiend*," she said. "All the sacrifices. All the death. They were all *lies*. I thought it would be worth it if I could just make the world whole again. Even Zed . . ." Lotte's eye's flicked toward him. "Oh, forgive me. I'm so sorry. I never wished for any of this."

Zed didn't respond. What could he say to the woman who'd betrayed them? Who'd helped orchestrate his own possession? He watched her silently, their eyes locked.

People . . .

The djinn floated away from the tear into Fie, toward the quartermaster. **People and your *wishes*.** The flames that made up the djinn's body intensified, billowing like an overfed furnace. **You wish, and you wish, *and you wish*, never caring for how the wish is granted. *Magic!* you think.**

The djinn swept its dagger out, as if pulling away a curtain. **But magic is just a cloak for *convenience*. It's the servant who cleans before her household awakens, so no one must witness her labor. It's the merchant who grows rich on the toil of his hirelings, men and women who cannot afford even to mend the spines he's broken.**

The djinn leaned forward, its blazing face just inches from Lotte's.

It's a world full of *people*—people who demand more, and more, and *more* convenience, until their demands have torn the very air apart. Do not come to me with your shame *now*, mortal. You are a *thousand* years too late.

Lotte laughed—a sad, frenzied sound. "Do you know what I think?" she said. "I don't think you can do *anything* unless you're twisting a wish around. Beneath your lies and your manipulations—beneath the stolen faces—all you really are is anger. Anger so shapeless, it needs others to give it form. That's why you had me do your dirty work. You asked me to hope for a better world, so you could forge that hope into a weapon."

The weapon is no longer in your hand. So what will you do now, Lotte? Try to stop me?

Lotte shook her head, a single tear trailing down her cheek. "I don't have to. I just had to keep you occupied." She closed her eyes. "I wish to be with Jak."

What? The djinn pirouetted just as an arrow flew from the top of one of the merchant stalls, knocking the knife from its grip. Zed glimpsed Fel before she leaped from the stall, taking cover with Mousebane a moment behind her.

In the span of a breath, Brock emerged from behind the tear into Fie. He snagged the knife and sprinted back toward Zed, his legs pumping wildly.

NO! The djinn reached out and grabbed Lotte's throat. It destroyed the quartermaster in one graceful movement. She was gone in a burning green heartbeat.

Brock leaped for Zed, the curved dagger raised, and Zed jumped forward to meet him.

Which was when everything exploded.

Something inside Zed had finally ignited. The deep reservoir of his mana, bubbling and boiling with every new tear in the Veil, caught fire.

Zed screamed, light pouring from his eyes and mouth.

Flames coursed from his fingers. His spine arched backward as he was drawn into the air, his feet floating just over the stones.

"Zed!" Brock called from beside him. "Zed, fight it!"

He tried. He tamped down on his magic with everything in him, trying desperately to cut it off. He calmed the fires radiating from his body, but he couldn't stop what he knew was happening all around the city. Zed's power was a well, and the ritual was drawing the mana out like a pump.

Across the square, the djinn turned its attention back toward the portal to Fie. It glided close, reached out tentatively with its burning hand. The Veil gave a wheeze of resistance, but then the mist broke away like gauze beneath its push.

Finally.

The djinn began ripping at the edges of the window, tearing the Veil apart to create a larger opening.

FINALLY! Its voice boomed in the night.

Brock drew close, squinting against the intense heat that rippled off Zed. He pushed the dagger to the mythril chain. "Hold still!" he cried.

A flash of red fur.

"Be strong, Zed. But better yet, be clever. Grant its wish!" Makiva's voice rang in his ears, as loudly as if she were right beside him.

"Wait!" Zed cried.

"Why?!" Brock shrieked.

Grant its wish.

If Brock cut the chain now, the djinn would still be trapped in Terryn. Even if Zed managed to escape it, this would all begin again. Maybe not for hundreds of years, but the djinn was patient. It would find another victim to exploit.

"Brock, do you trust me?"

Brock frowned, glancing toward the creature that was tearing open a gate to another world. A gate it intended to drag them all through with it.

"Yeah, buddy," he sighed. "I trust you."

"In as few words as possible: I'm going to give the djinn what it wants. Don't cut the chain until I tell you, okay?"

Doubt touched his friend's eyes. But a moment later, Brock nodded.

Zed took a deep breath. He'd been spending so long fighting against his own power, trying to keep a last desperate grip on his mana. But Zed's magic *wanted* to burn. It had ever since that morning in the forest, when he and Brock and Liza and Jett had faced off against a group of kobolds.

For the first time since that day, Zed stopped trying to control himself.

He let go.

Magic poured from him, filling the square. The city. The tears in the market grew suddenly wider, and fire flooded from Zed's hands in waves. The lights surrounding them—Makiva's previous victims—flared to incandescence, illuminating the entire sky.

Zed watched as the djinn floated forward, into the wide, welcoming portal.

"Now!" he screamed.

Brock yanked back with the blade, severing the chain.

All at once, Freestone was bathed in darkness.

The portals snapped shut, the air closing in with the speed of a guillotine. The fire pouring out from Zed died, too, green flames guttering quickly to nothing. Zed kept his eyes trained forward, but in the sudden darkness it was impossible to see if his plan had worked.

As his eyes adjusted, the chains encircling his wrists fell away. They dissolved into smoke, along with the barrier that had encircled him. Only the length of chain in Brock's hand remained, the mythril still glittering prettily.

Zed took a staggering step forward. Then another. Brock stood at his side, helping him along. One by one their friends joined them—Jett and Jayna, Fel and Liza, each looking as dazed as Zed felt.

Finally, they found the body. The djinn had been cut cleanly in half, its strange metallic frame smoking in what drizzles were left of the storm. Its mask lay in a puddle a few feet away, severed by a molten line that was still red-hot.

"Is it over?" Jett asked weakly. "I mean, besides all the monsters still roaming the streets."

Off in the distance, Zed caught sight of a creature not native to Freestone. A small red fox with enormous ears watched him with a vulpine grin. It disappeared into the market tents.

"It's over," he said.

"Let's go find Frond," said Liza. "Then we'll do what we do best."

"Protect our city," Zed agreed with a grin.

"Bicker endlessly," Brock said at the same time, only louder.

Chapter Twenty-Four

Brock

It took more than a day to track down every Danger in Freestone. Even then, Brock worried they might have missed something—that one day he'd find a shockroach in his boot or a decicentipede under his bed.

But he didn't sweat it too much. He certainly had experience, now, dealing with Dangers of all sorts. And he wasn't alone in that.

Frond's militia had grown throughout the night and over the long day of fighting. When joined by the experienced adventurers who had been outside the wall, the crowd became an unstoppable wave, scouring the city streets clean of every beast from Fey, Fie, and the farther planes.

Now it was night once more, and the day's bloody work filled the streets of Freestone. "Which guild has to clean up this mess?" Brock asked.

"I think we're still in an 'all in this together' moment," Jett said. "So grab a mop, buddy."

Brock sighed. "I like teamwork better when it's helping me with *my* stuff."

Despite his grousing and profound exhaustion, Brock was happy. He gripped Zed by the shoulder. "Good to have you back, friend."

Zed patted Brock's back, then grimaced, finding his hand covered in viscous green slime. He wiped the slime on his own tunic. "Believe it or not, I missed this."

Brock felt a pang of guilt. "I'm sorry, Zed. Sorry it took so long to see what was happening."

Liza edged in. "We should have had more faith in you, Zed."

He shook his head. "You shouldn't have had any faith in me at all," he said sadly. "This was all my fault. If I hadn't made that deal–"

"We'd all be dead," said Jett. "Brenner would have demolished us." He turned to Jayna. "Isn't that right?" he prompted.

Jayna looked unsure. She crossed her arms over her chest. "I suppose it's impossible to know what any of the rest of us would have done. If roles were reversed. Let's just . . . let's just not make a habit of this sort of thing?"

"No more secrets," Liza said in agreement. She looked from Zed to Brock and back again. "From either of you. Deal?"

"Deal," they said together.

But Brock caught Fel winking at him over Liza's shoulder. He had a feeling the Adventurers Guild's shadow team might not be totally done—not if Fel had anything to say about it.

And maybe he'd hold on to that music box. Just in case.

*

Frond took the news about Lotte poorly, but not in the way Brock had expected. Bracing himself for her fury, he hid partially behind Liza while he filled her in on what he knew. But the guildmistress reacted not with anger, but with sadness.

"Too much," she said softly. "Sometimes this job takes too much."

The apprentices had taken her aside while the townsfolk continued dragging Danger corpses into the central square. Brock thought it was sometime before midnight, but he had no way to know for sure. The temple's bells had not tolled all day, and they were all bleary with exhaustion.

"She saved us," said Jett. "In the end."

Frond tried to spit, but her mouth was dry.

"Maybe no one has to know," Fel suggested. "Freestone can remember her as a hero."

"We can't let that happen," Brock said. "I'm sorry, but . . . the king is going to demand answers. Someone is going to take the blame for this mess. And too much of the evidence points to Zed."

Frond turned her gray eyes onto Zed. To his credit, though he trembled, he held her gaze.

"Zed made mistakes," Brock said. "So did I. But only because Lotte backed us into impossible corners. People need to know what she did. She *has* to take the blame for this." After a beat of silence, he added, "She's dead, Frond. The truth can't hurt her."

"It will hurt her parents," Frond said gruffly. "Her friends." She closed her eyes. "But you're right. We must ask one last sacrifice of her. We must reveal her sins and let Freestone revile her for them."

"If it turns the king's wrath away from Zed," said Jett, "I think it's what she'd have wanted."

Frond opened her eyes and looked angrily at the dwarf. "Is it? Turns out we didn't know her so well. And to be clear, I don't care what her intentions were. Not if they led here." With a sweep of her arm, Frond indicated the blood-slicked cobbles and smoldering rubble. "So don't follow her down that road. Don't imagine that this fallen world can be saved. We fight monsters. That's the whole job, and that's as good as it will ever get."

Silence hung over the group, and Brock wiped Frond's spittle from his face. The euphoria of surviving, of reuniting with Zed, left him in a rush. Now he felt defeated and small. Because Frond was right. It was Lotte's hope that had left her vulnerable. Hope for a better world, a healed world. It had been a false hope, and it had cost them all dearly.

All they could do was push back against the endless dark. But the dark would keep coming. The dark would never go away.

Brock was so lost in hopeless thoughts that he nearly missed the sound of Zed's name being called in the distance. But Zed's pointy ears perked right up.

"Mom?" he said. Then he shouted it. "Mom!"

Brock and the others watched as Zed tore away from the group, racing across the slick cobblestones toward his mother. He slipped, and almost fell, but she was there to catch him, pulling him into a fierce embrace.

Brock remembered Frond's impassioned speech in the temple. He remembered her words to him when Nirav had been freed from his prison of stone. About saving the world in small ways. A little bit every day.

He looked up at her. "Freestone endures," he said.

The anger fell from her face. She looked tired, and sad . . . but also hopeful. "Freestone endures," she echoed.

"Frond?" Brock said tentatively. He opened his arms toward her. "Are . . . are we going to hug now?"

Frond shoved him away, but she barked out a laugh as she did it.

And in the distance, the first of the pyres was lit, as Freestoners set fire to the remains of the Dangers they had vanquished. Tentacles and teeth, carapaces and claws—it all went up in flames.

And the fire burned a mundane, everyday shade of yellow.

Epilogue
Zed

Zed inspected himself in the guildhall's common mirror: dark eyes and tawny skin; long fingers and pointed ears. All of them under his absolute control. Or at least as absolute as anyone could boast. He smiled into the dirty looking glass, but instead of feeling happy at the expression, Zed experienced a jolt of fear. His smile tightened into a grimace before sinking completely.

Even after all these months, sometimes the sight of his own face still scared him. Zed wondered if he'd ever get over the feeling; he wondered how his friends had.

A throat cleared nearby. Zed flicked his eyes to the mirror's edge, to find Callum standing in the doorway behind him. Zed's new dress jerkin hung from the elf's forearm, clean and bright.

"You left it in the main hall," his uncle said. "Considering how much ambrosia Nirav and Fife were spilling on the floor, I decided it was safest just to bring it to you."

"Sorry!" Zed chirped, summoning the grin again. "That was silly of me, huh?"

Callum drifted in, opening the jerkin for Zed to slide his arms through the sleeves. As Zed worked it over his doublet, the elf smiled down at him—a bit sadly, it seemed to Zed. "It's not your fault," he said. "I imagine there's a lot on your mind today."

Zed nodded, fussing over the jerkin's dainty little buttons. A life in outtown hadn't prepared him for the demands of fancy clothing, but in recent months his wardrobe had expanded with the adventurers' reputation. Still, this jerkin was particularly special. It was an elven design, made of a shimmering cloth that the wood elves harvested from fey silkworms.

Once, it had belonged to Zed's father.

Callum brought it with him when he returned to Freestone, accompanied by a small party of elves sent to check on the human city. Though the strange green lights that erupted from Freestone were visible even from Llethanyl, the worst of the Night of Dangers—as it was now being called—had been contained by the city wards. The very thing meant to keep monsters *out* of Freestone had instead trapped them within the city, like hornets in a jar.

Zed sometimes wondered if that was why the djinn had

performed its ritual in the market, instead of retreating to the forest. What were the wards, really, but a wish for seclusion? For safety from the things out *there*. One final wish to twist against its makers.

"It's not your fault," Callum said again, softly, drawing Zed from his thoughts. Zed caught a glimpse of his own bleak expression in the mirror and sighed.

"I know," he said.

"Even when we know a thing, sometimes it's important to hear it. Sometimes it's important to hear it again and again." Callum put his hand on Zed's shoulder, smiling at him in the mirror. "You and your friends defeated a great evil, Zed. The Danger that ended the world. That djinn destroyed countless lives, all without anyone knowing it existed. You accomplished what even your human Champions couldn't."

Zed giggled. "So you think *elven* ones would have done better?"

Callum shrugged, but his usually stoic expression brightened into a grin. "Who can say for sure? It *is* interesting, though, that there were two elves among the apprentices who finally stopped the djinn."

"Two?" Zed asked. "Fel and . . . ?"

Callum laughed, his palm squeezing Zed's shoulder. "And you, Zed. *Two* very good elves."

Zed's ears began to burn, and for once, when he gazed at his reflection, he felt completely safe.

"Zerend would have been so proud of you," Callum said. "Your mother is. *I* am. And though Frond may not say it, I know she is t—"

"CALLUM!"

As if on cue, the guildmistress's voice boomed through the hall. Both Zed and his uncle flinched, then laughed together.

"Duty calls," Callum said. And with one last squeeze of his nephew's shoulder, he headed toward the door. "I think Brock was looking for you," he added, before disappearing from the room.

Though most of the elves had returned to Llethanyl bearing news of Freestone's ordeal—and its survival—a select few remained in the human city, including the queen's *former* High Ranger. Callum now lived among the adventurers in the guildhall, taking up a small portion of the duties that had once been Lotte's, mostly combat drills and hunting patrols.

The rest—the much larger portion—had fallen to Liza. Or rather she'd taken them up herself, with a zeal matched only by her competence.

Of all Zed's friends, Liza had been the last to warm to him, avoiding contact even longer than Jayna in the days following his possession. Though she knew intellectually that Zed hadn't been in control of his own body, and even understood why he'd succumbed to Makiva in the first place, that didn't seem to bring her much comfort. Eventually, Zed wondered if she'd ever truly forgive him for nearly killing her brother.

Then, without warning, she'd arrived at his room early one morning, hammering against the door with a gauntleted fist.

"Get dressed," she'd shouted through the wood. "And meet me in the training yard."

Zed had been terrified, especially when he found Liza in full sparring gear, her metal shield and wooden training sword ready.

They fought all morning, without a word between them. Liza's hits were nonlethal, but they were still plenty painful. Zed spent most of his energy just trying to elf-step out of her range, but Liza always seemed to be there when he reappeared, as if she could sense where he was jumping.

They finished just as the midday bell rang, both panting and exhausted. Zed had collapsed into the dirt. When Liza offered him her hand with a big smile, cheers broke out from all around them. Half the guild had come to watch.

"Good fight, Magus Zed." The sun glinted off Liza's armor as she grinned down at him. She looked like a knight from the stories.

Zed couldn't help but grin back. "Good fight, Dame Liza."

*

Zed peeked into Hexam's office, where the archivist and Jayna were finally organizing his library.

"It's almost time!" Zed called inside. "A few of us are heading to the square, to snag good spots. Has either of you seen Brock?"

"He left early," Jayna answered. "He said you should save

him a seat." She squinted down at the book in her hand. "*The Book of* . . . oh, it's so dark."

Zed snapped his fingers, and a glowing mote of fire—beautiful, natural, *orange* fire—appeared over Jayna's head. With the death of the djinn, Zed had lost the ability to conjure the green-hued flames, but apparently the fiend had only altered what was already inside him. He was a natural fire mage, Hexam said, and in the last few months Zed had gained a fine control over his powers that amazed even himself. The orange flames were never as strong as the fiendfire had been—never as hungry.

But Zed was grateful for that.

"Thanks," Jayna called. "Let's see. *The Book of* . . . *Cruelest Curses*. Ah. Lovely."

"Add it to the pile," Hexam said from his desk.

Jayna rolled her eyes, then set the book atop the rather *large* stack reserved for Hexam's less savory grimoires. "We'll just . . . deal with these later," she said doubtfully.

The workroom was looking more like its old self every day. The beautiful color-changing orbs had been replaced, and a selection of new monster skulls even decorated the tables. Hexam had survived the Night of Dangers thanks to necromancy, but his right arm was never quite the same. It was now small and withered, and his hand sometimes trembled violently when he attempted to lift heavy books.

But in a surprising act of magnanimity, the Silverglows had

gifted the adventurers with a manual for one-handed spell-casting. Now, with daily exercises, Hexam was nearly as potent a mage as ever, though he still acquiesced to letting Jayna help him organize the office.

What took longer to rebuild was the archivist's relationship with Frond. Hexam was never outwardly angry with the guild-mistress, but he always seemed to have a pressing task when she called him to meetings.

Finally, after nearly a month of awkwardness between the guild's two surviving leaders, Frond stormed into the guild mess one evening and slammed her fist against the table. In the silence that followed, her eyes found the wizard.

"Hexam," she said thickly. "I'm . . . I'm sorry. It's not enough, I know. For weeks, I've been trying to find the words that *would* be, but I don't think they exist. We betrayed you. *I* betrayed you. . . ." The guildmistress took a deep breath. "And we were betrayed in turn. For now, this is all I can do. I want everyone in the guild to know: I made a mistake. A bad one. And I'll spend the rest of my life trying to make up for it."

The room was utterly quiet when Frond finished. Slowly, she turned to leave.

"I miss her, too," Hexam said.

Frond turned, her gray eyes downcast.

"And I miss you," he added.

Frond's expression pinched, her eyes squeezing shut. For a

moment, Zed had thought the fearsome Alabasel Frond—the Basilisk, guildmistress of the Adventurers—might *actually* cry.

Instead, she turned and spat on the floor.

"I'm holding a meeting tomorrow at second bell," she barked. "Master-rank adventurers only." Then she hurried from the room.

✷

Micah was waiting for him at the guild's front door.

"Brock was looking for you earlier," the boy said with an exasperated expression. "He wants you to—"

"Save him a seat, I know." Zed skipped up to the healer and smiled.

Two dots of color touched Micah's cheeks as he gazed down at Zed, then he quickly turned away. "You look . . . uh . . . nice. Very . . . elven? In a good way."

"Thanks. You do, too. Human, I mean. In a good way."

Micah took a deep breath and squared his feet, as if bracing himself to fight a particularly nasty Danger. "I got you something." Then, before Zed could respond, he pulled a small handful of flowers from his satchel. "They're elfgrass blossoms, from outside. Hexam looked over them. No parasites or body-stealing spirits that he could find."

Zed gazed down at the small, colorful flowers. Based on their current temperature, he could only imagine how red his ears were right now.

Flowers. From a boy. To a boy. It felt utterly strange and wonderful. Zed gently took the bouquet, cradling it against his chest. The red-orange petals of the elfgrass reminded him of a fox's fur.

On the day after the djinn's defeat, Zed had one last dream of the animal, as clear and vivid as a memory. He dreamed he was in the forest outside Freestone, exploring with his friends, when they came upon a wide, treeless hill. The fox waited atop, its fur bright as copper under the sun.

And the fox was something else. A young woman in the dashing clothes of an adventurer grinned warmly at him. Many figures surrounded her, but they weren't stooped and ghostly like the last time Zed had seen them. In the dream they were all real: men and women and others; humans, elves, and dwarves—and some peoples Zed had no names for. They were smiling at Zed and his friends. They were waving.

And Foster Pendleton waved the most energetically of all, practically leaping into the air. For the first time in his life, Zed awoke laughing.

"You two tomatoes ready for the Guildculling?" Jett said, arriving with a wink. He leaned on the cane Liza had made for him nearly a year ago. "My, it's gotten very red in here."

"Ready!" Zed blurted, more loudly than he meant to.

"Let's get this over with," muttered Micah.

"Liza's already at the stage preparing," said Jett. "And Fel's on an errand. Jayna said she'd catch up. For now it's just us chickens."

Jett passed through the door with a chuckle. "Adorably bright-red chickens."

"I hate having friends," Micah said, following him out.

Zed didn't move. He tried to follow the others, but found himself unable to take a single step. He was awash in gratitude, a whole reservoir of it, as wide and impossible as an ocean. Zed floated in the feeling for a moment, knowing that it couldn't last forever.

Monsters still roamed the world. There would always be darkness, and creeping claws which scratched their way through even the toughest wards.

But here, now, Zed was safe.

And happy.

And loved.

And as he took that first step into the daylight, Zed finally let himself believe that he deserved it.

Epilogue

Brock

Zed had saved him a seat, just as he'd asked.

"Where have you been?" Zed whispered. "You almost missed it!"

"Nonsense," Brock said, and he winked. "I'm right on time, as always." He nodded greetings to the other apprentices, all of whom sat together in a tight group. Despite the crowd, they had a good view of the stage at the heart of Freestone's public square.

And the Guildculling was about to begin.

The amphitheater thrummed with nervous energy. Brock could almost taste it in the air. This year's hopefuls, along with their family and friends—all their anxiety was on full display, whether that meant bouncing feet or clasped hands, tense chatter or silent prayers.

But Zed and Brock were calm. They knew they were already right where they belonged.

Everyone tried to look their best for the Guildculling, and Zed had never looked finer. He wore the immaculate shimmering jerkin Callum had gifted him, and though Brock knew Zed cherished it, he'd resisted wearing it before today. He had even slicked his hair back for the occasion, and he held a clutch of colorful flowers close to his chest.

"They're from Micah," Zed explained at Brock's questioning look. He grew suddenly bashful, his eyes lowering. "We met a year ago today. I think he wanted to mark the occasion."

"Right," Brock said. "As I recall, he called me an idiot and made fun of your ears."

"And I have no regrets," Micah put in.

"Interesting," Brock said. "But didn't you also insult a powerful and vindictive extraplanar being that morning?"

"I have one small regret," Micah amended. He cleared his throat and leaned in toward Zed. "And for the record, I've always liked your ears."

Brock smiled. Zed had learned a lot in recent months—spells, and a smattering of elvish, and a fair bit of his own family history. He'd even learned to forgive himself, mostly, for his dealings with the djinn—or at least, he'd learned to stop apologizing for the creature's actions while it was wearing his skin.

Zed had learned all that and more. But he had never quite learned how to take a compliment.

And he wasn't the only one. "You look nice today, Liza," Brock tried, smiling pleasantly at her.

She looked at him with deep suspicion on her features. "Why are you telling me that? What are you up to?" she demanded.

A few weeks after the Night of Dangers, Brock had gathered the courage, finally, to ask her out. His timing could have been better; they had been hip deep in the mire of Bonerot Swamp, surrounded by venomous bipedal amphibians with prehensile tongues. (In his defense, it had seemed like a now-or-never sort of moment.)

She had calmly informed him, as she skewered no fewer than three of their assailants with a single thrust of her sword, that she was not ready to date but would keep him apprised on the matter.

He hadn't brought it up again after that.

"I'm not up to anything," Brock said, attempting to sweeten his smile by batting his eyelashes at her.

Liza glared at him from behind her open scroll. "I'd much rather look well prepared than pretty. 'You look like a person who really knows what she's doing.' Why don't people say things like that?"

Brock couldn't blame her for being stressed. She had hardly slept all week, helping Frond prepare for the Guildculling by pulling together a list of potential recruits and ranking them by a complicated matrix of virtues. In the course of her research, Liza had learned something startling. This year, for the first time in the guild's two-hundred-year history, the Stone Sons intended to recruit two girls into their ranks.

Liza had smiled when she'd told him that, and Brock thought her expression had been a little wistful. It had been Liza's dream to be a knight, and though it had been an impossible dream, her actions had made it possible for others to live the life that she had so wanted for herself.

The expression had passed quickly. Liza wasn't the type to indulge in what-ifs and could-have-beens. Brock only hoped she felt some pride for her role in changing minds that had seemed, not so long ago, to be as immutable as stone.

Researching recruits was one of many tasks formerly performed by Lotte that Liza had taken on, without even being asked. In the quartermaster's absence, the guild quickly realized that she had done more to keep things functioning than even Frond fully understood.

The guildmistress had been a terror in the days following Lotte's death. Frond had barely eaten for a week, hardly stopped to rest as she led the guild on hunt after hunt for any Dangers still lurking within Freestone. When it became clear that none remained, she pursued whatever quarry she could find outside the walls, falling upon the monsters with a viciousness that Brock quailed to see.

He had long thought of Frond as heartless, but he knew now

that couldn't be so. For the woman's heart had clearly been broken those long, dark weeks following the Night of Dangers.

"Oyez, oyez," called the town crier, Forta, her voice amplified with magic. "Today, you sons and daughters of Freestone will become sovereign citizens of our city—one of the few lights that still dot the darkness." Brock's attention focused on the stage then, and on the banners of the various guilds who would soon be claiming new apprentices.

But first, Forta launched into a retelling of the Day of Dangers. "Two hundred and twenty-four years ago, Freestone awoke to a new world." It was a story Brock had heard countless times before—but he still hadn't decided what kind of story it was. A triumph, for the lives saved against impossible odds? A tragedy, for all that was lost? A story of heroism, or apocalypse?

He was beginning to think of it as the story of a friendship. A friendship that was almost strong enough to overcome great evil . . . almost.

He leaned in and whispered to Zed, "You know, if you and Micah . . . and me and Liza . . . Well, that would kind of make us brothers, wouldn't it?"

Zed pressed his shoulder into Brock's. "We're *already* brothers," he said happily.

Jayna shushed them, and then for good measure Jett did, too.

"Monsters destroyed our world," Forta said, and in the deliberate silence that followed, Fel oohed. The elven girl had never attended a Guildculling before, and she was rapt. Forta continued, "All in a span of a single day. It is thanks to the Champions of Freestone that we survive to this day, despite the machinations of a malevolent being of fire and spite."

That was new. Normally the storyteller would have laid blame for the Day of Dangers at Foster's feet. But in light of all they'd learned, Freestone was beginning to accept that the long-reviled "traitor" had been more victim than villain.

"A djinn," Forta continued, "who was able to bring ruin to Terryn by manipulating Foster the Warlock's weakness of spirit and lust for power."

Well. Brock doubted they'd erect a statue of Foster to stand alongside the other Champions anytime soon, but it was a start.

"Let us now begin," Forta said, "with the claims of a guild that has done much for our city since their founding more than two hundred years ago—but never so much, perhaps, as it has done this past year." She gestured to a deep blue banner sprinkled with white stars. "Alabasel Frond, the four High Guilds would be honored to cede right of first claims to the Adventurers Guild."

As Frond clomped gracelessly to the front of the stage, a raucous cheer went up—chaotic at first, but then coalescing into a rhythmic chant.

"Frond!" cried the crowd. "Frond! Frond! Frond!"

"Stop that," Frond said crossly. "Cut it out."

The crowd fell silent, save for a few chuckles, and Frond's

scarred face screwed up in disapproval. The guildmistress had not taken to her newfound popularity, and seemed perpetually annoyed that this was not a problem she could punch, stab, or incinerate away. (Surely, she was tempted to try.)

"No new recruits this year," she said abruptly.

Liza dropped the scroll of thoroughly researched recruits onto the ground. "I give up," she said.

Frond cleared her throat. "You all rose to the occasion, when Freestone needed it," she said. "I think you've earned whatever cushy little apprenticeships you've been coveting. But it's a *one-year* reprieve," she added fiercely.

It was a magnanimous gesture, Brock knew, and entirely her own idea, yet somehow she made it sound like she was furious about the whole thing.

Frond swaggered a bit, putting her hands on her hips. "Unless anyone wants to volunteer?" she asked with a sneer. "No?"

But before Frond could stomp back to her banner, a hand went up in the very front row.

And another in the next row.

And a third hand. And a fourth.

Brock whistled. "Will you look at that."

All told, there were more than twenty children—girls and boys, highborn and low—some of whom Brock knew were shoo-ins for the knights or the mages, with all the prestige that would have come with it. Yet here they were, volunteering for the most dangerous and most maligned guild in Freestone's history.

Frond appeared shocked into silence. She spit right there on the stage, took another look at all those raised hands, and then spit again.

"I . . . did not bring enough tokens with me," she said at last.

"Ach," Jett said. "They're so *little.* Were we ever so little?"

"You know they're all taller than you?" Zed said. "Every one of them."

"We'll have our work cut out for us," Liza said. "They'll need training . . . equipment . . ."

"You've got this, Liza," Brock said. "You look *stunningly* well prepared."

"You're shameless, Brock Dunderfel," she said, but she was smiling as she said it.

"Brock, I think I see some candidates for our little side project," Fel said, and she tapped her nose. She was right—the Adventurers Guild's Shadow could use some new blood, and kids made the best spies.

"Do you think any of them are mages?" Zed asked.

"They must be," Jayna said. "Maybe enough for proper classes." She clasped her hands in excitement. "With quizzes! And *grades*!"

"Quizzes?" Zed said, drooping.

"Don't worry," Micah said. "Hexam might meddle in the dark arts or whatever, but he's not *evil.*"

Brock's friends laughed, and he basked in the sound of their happiness—and in the hard-won approval of the city they'd all bled for.

People said the world had ended long before he'd been born; that the story of the Day of Dangers was the story of how it had ended. But that wasn't true. Not really.

The world had changed, and no amount of wishing could restore it to the way it was before. But there was laughter, still. And magic of all sorts. There was friendship, and love.

All of these things were proof of life, and of the value of life. They were little points of light in the dark. Alone, set against all the world's darkness, they didn't amount to much.

But put them all together, and you had a tapestry of blazing light.

A sea of stars.

Each one of them an adventure, just waiting to be undertaken.

Acknowledgments

Writing these books together has been, in all honesty, among the greatest and most rewarding adventures of our lives. While it's difficult to say good-bye to Zed, Brock, Liza, and all the rest, we are immensely grateful to have had the opportunity to spend so much time with them. Over the course of three books, these characters grew and changed in ways that surprised and delighted us. We hope they live on in your hearts (and perhaps a tabletop RPG session or two).

We remain so appreciative of the family, friends, and publishing professionals who have lent us their guidance, expertise, and encouragement along the way. But we want to save our final thank-you for our readers—especially those readers who have reached out to ask us questions about our world, share their fan art, or tell us they've been inspired to write stories with their friends. There is no greater joy for us than to know that our geeky obsessions are *shared* geeky obsessions.

We're nerds, and proud of it. Many of the kids we've met at school visits have proudly identified as nerds, too. There's magic—*real* magic—in taking pride in who you are. And the world needs more magic in it.

There were times when we weren't so proud. When it honestly felt like our communities, schools, even our country hated us. What we needed most desperately in those moments was to know that there were places we'd be welcome. (There were, and there are for you, too.)

So this is for the outcasts and the misfits. For those who find solace in books. For those who believe in magic. For those who are *different.*

We see you. We're with you.

Welcome to the guild.

ASTRA
LUX
SLIMES & PSYCHICS
LOTS OF TENTACLES
CELESTIALS, AUTOMATONS
FEY
FAIRIES AND THE LIKE
THE VEIL
GOLDEN WAY
SILVERGLOWS